PENGUIN BOOKS

A SENSE OF GUILT

Andrea Newman was born in Dover in 1938 and brought up in Shropshire and Cheshire. In 1960 she graduated from London University, where she married while still a student, and then worked as a civil servant and a teacher before becoming a full-time writer.

Her publications include *A Share of the World*, *Mirage*, *The Cage*, *Three Into Two Won't Go*, which was made into a film with Rod Steiger and Claire Bloom, *Alexa* and *A Bouquet of Barbed Wire*, which she dramatized for London Weekend Television to huge success. This was followed by *Another Bouquet*, *An Evil Streak*, and *Mackenzie*, which became a BBC television series. She has also contributed to many other television series such as *Tales of Unease*, *The Frighteners*, *Love Story*, *Seven Faces of Woman*, *Intimate Strangers* and *Helen, a Woman of Today*.

Andrea Newman is divorced and lives in London.

A Sense of Guilt

ANDREA NEWMAN

Penguin Books

PENGUIN BOOKS

Published by the Penguin Group
27 Wrights Lane, London W8 5TZ, England
Viking Penguin Inc., 40 West 23rd Street, New York, New York 10010, USA
Penguin Books Australia Ltd, Ringwood, Victoria, Australia
Penguin Books Canada Ltd, 2801 John Street, Markham, Ontario, Canada L3R 1B4
Penguin Books (NZ) Ltd, 182–190 Wairau Road, Auckland 10, New Zealand

Penguin Books Ltd, Registered Offices: Harmondsworth, Middlesex, England

First published by Michael Joseph 1988
Published in Penguin Books 1989
5 7 9 10 8 6

Printed and bound in Great Britain by
Richard Clay Ltd, Bungay, Suffolk
Filmset in Sabon

SPRING 1985

It had all started so innocently, as these things do.

'Felix is coming back,' said Richard, looking up from his letter. 'He says what's the point of paying no income tax if the climate gives you writer's block.'

'Elizabeth says it's because he can't find enough women to screw,' said Helen, putting down her letter. 'The Irish must be more discriminating than the English after all. Good for them.'

'Oh, never mind the reasons,' said Richard. 'They're coming back, that's the main thing.'

'There's no need to sound so jubilant,' said Helen. 'People would still like you even without your dreadful friend. You don't need the contrast.'

Richard looked at her seriously. 'D'you really dislike him?'

'I despise him,' said Helen. 'That's much worse. He's like a greedy child grabbing all the cakes on the plate. I think it's nauseating behaviour at his age.'

'Does that mean we can't have them to dinner?'

'Not until the end of term. Unless you do the cooking.'

'Of course I'll do the cooking. Don't want strychnine in the stew, do I? Anyway, Elizabeth would be very upset if you poisoned him. She loves him, you know.'

'Poor cow,' said Helen.

Sally put her head round the door. 'What's all the excitement?'

'Felix and Elizabeth are coming back, that's all.'

'Oh, good,' said Sally, disappearing. 'They're nice.'

People on the whole did not like Helen, which suited her quite well because it meant they left her alone. They sensed her impatience with them, her air of having better things to do with her time. Her painter's eyes looked them over and

3

assessed them and they felt themselves discarded. Helen moved on: tall and rangy, lean but large-boned, built like a cowboy, clad in denim, busy and preoccupied. Her hair was plaited or wrapped round her head; her tough square hands had short nails stained with paint. She had not worn make-up for ten years.

People who did like her, the few, liked her very much indeed. They valued her honesty, her loyalty, her integrity and her silence, which allowed them to talk.

'You look wonderful,' Elizabeth told her once. 'Rather like a Valkyrie.'

Helen, who thought this was rubbish, laughed rudely. But she knew what Elizabeth meant. She did have a faintly Nordic air, with her blonde hair streaked with grey and her cold green eyes that frightened people away. When she laughed it was a surprise, gutsy and raunchy, displaying enviable teeth.

Now she sat in the smoky room with her colleagues while students brought samples of their work and the tutors commented. They were also supposed to check on the progress of theses and post-graduate plans, but the atmosphere was casual and relaxed. Tutors and students looked equally scruffy, and everyone smoked except Helen, who had given it up painfully five years ago and was still waiting to feel the benefit.

The first student brought in a triptych of blue, mauve, rust, gold and purple in big vague shapes as if hanging in space. Mike and Andy went to help him arrange them. The paintings were taller than all of them and filled a wall of the room. Helen liked them very much.

'They look like a backdrop for Wagner,' she said. 'I think you could be a stage designer.'

The student looked pleased.

'I quite like the idea of a narrative,' said Mike. 'You've achieved an effect of illusionary space. Those bands belong to either side of the line. And those edges are real.'

Andy lit a cigarette. 'I can't say I enjoy them,' he said. 'They're very awkward. But that's a good quality. Intriguing.'

'The light catches them differently as you move them round,' the student said. He struggled to prove his point and

4

Mike went back to help him. They all studied the paintings in silence, then argued gently about which arrangement they preferred. Mike lit a cigarette.

'What's your thesis about?' Helen asked.

'Rothko,' said the student, lighting a cigarette. 'The interaction between his life and his work.'

Helen looked at the student, small and dark and thin, so talented but so young. How could he hope to understand depression and despair, whatever drove you to open an artery, so that when you were found, soaked in red, you resembled one of your own paintings. Sally had been three when Rothko died, drenched in his own blood, and Helen had just ended her marriage. Losing Carey, who seemed to her then the only man she would ever love, she felt that she and her daughter were emotionally huddled together in the draughty studio. It was a long time before she could forgive Rothko for deserting her when she needed him most, but she was grateful, too: the tears she shed for him released an avalanche of tears for herself.

Well, perhaps she had misjudged the student; perhaps he did understand. After all, when she had been his age, she had considered herself extremely grown-up. Aborting Carey's baby had been the only choice open to her, left alone with Sally. It was barely possible to support one child, never mind two, and Carey was obviously going to be no help at all. But she had cried all the same for the child that would have been Sally's brother or sister, and thought of her own blood and Rothko's quietly flowing together, as if into the same river.

'I didn't think I'd get probation for this,' said Richard's new client, chain-smoking. 'I thought I'd go to jail.' She sounded almost disappointed.

Richard said, 'Would you like to tell me about it?'

'You know, don't you? They've told you all about me.'

She was a small girl, hardly older than Sally, but without her robust strength. She had a mean, undernourished look about her, and an air of suspicion, like an animal that has

5

learned to be wary of man. She was watchful as she smoked her cigarette, glancing sideways as if anticipating sudden attack from some unknown agent, who might leap through the door if she were not vigilant.

'They don't know all about you,' Richard said. 'Nobody does, except you. I'd like you to tell me a bit, if you want to.'

She frowned, stubbed out her cigarette and lit a fresh one. 'Well, I took him, didn't I? He was there in his pram outside the launderette and I just took him. I knew it was wrong. I didn't even think about his mum.'

'Were you thinking about your own baby?'

'Oh, yeah. Course I was. That's what they said in court. Supposed to get me off, that was.' She smiled faintly at such a ridiculous hope.

'Wasn't it true?'

'Yeah. Didn't make no difference though, did it? It's still wrong, what I done. I know that.'

Richard said gently, 'Sometimes it helps to talk about how you feel.'

'But you can't do nothing, can you? I mean, I've had him adopted and that's it. You can't get him back, can you? So what's the point of talking about it?'

Her name was Tracey and she was eighteen. Her parents had persuaded her to have her baby adopted and now she blamed them. She reminded him of girls he had taught, growing up too soon, wanting something of their own to love. He longed to help her and he felt inadequate.

At the end of the long day, he went back in the office for a cup of tea.

'Your wife rang,' they told him.

'Which one?' Inge wouldn't give her first name and just called herself Mrs Morgan. It had become a standing joke in the office: Richard and his two wives.

'The German one.'

Richard went back into his room and dialled. He wasn't surprised; Helen hardly ever rang the office.

'Inge?'

'Oh, thank God. There's something wrong with the stove. I can smell gas. Can you come?'

'Ring the gas board,' he said, 'Inge, please.'

'I have rung them, of course. But they won't come till tomorrow. We could all be blown up tonight.'

'Tell them you can smell gas,' he said, 'and they'll come. They have an emergency service.'

'They don't believe me,' she said tragically.

Richard was reminded of Matilda, who told such dreadful lies. 'And every time she shouted "Fire," They only answered "Little liar." ' Something like that. His mother had read it to him. He had read it to his children. Perhaps that was where Inge had got the idea. The gas board were probably wise to her by now. If, in fact, she had ever rung them. If, that is, she could smell gas at all. But how could he take the risk? There was just a chance in a million that there was a gas leak and Inge and his children could all be blown up in the night. And the night he called her bluff would of course be the night it happened.

An endless chain of visits, false alarms, tears and recriminations stretched behind him like the apparitions in *Macbeth*, to the crack of doom, or so it seemed, and ahead as well, for the rest of his life. This must be what I think I deserve, he told himself, at some level anyway, or I would have learned to refuse by now. I deserted her, therefore I owe her a visit, unlimited visits. She was a good wife, she devoured me with her love, gave me children, cooked meals, cleaned the house, offered and demanded sex like the *Kama Sutra*, and I left her for Helen, because Helen didn't need me so much, because Helen could manage without me and had proved it by doing so for many years. I ran away from Inge because I was exhausted and ashamed that I didn't have enough left over to satisfy her at the end of the day.

'Please, Richard,' she said now, and he felt she had been saying it for ever. He glanced at his watch. A quarter to six. A journey from Stockwell to Camden Town in the rush hour, the time spent on talk, on tears, or just possibly on gas, even perhaps all three, then the journey back again – there was no way he could get home before eight. Helen would kill him. Today of all days.

'I'll be there as soon as I can,' he said sharply, and rang off before she could thank him.

'Oh, Richard,' Sally said. 'Not tonight. Not on Mum's birthday.' Her voice was always uncannily like Helen's on the phone.

'I know,' he said. 'It's a bugger but it can't be helped, it's an emergency. Tell her how sorry I am and explain about the gas.' He was full of ignoble relief that Helen wasn't home yet to receive this message in person.

Sally sighed. 'She'll never believe it.'

'I know. I'm not sure I do either.'

'Then why are you going?'

'Because. In case.'

'Honestly,' Sally said. 'You two.'

'I know. I hope you're learning from all this, what not to do. Have my flowers arrived?'

'Yes, they're lovely. But they won't do the trick.'

'They're a start,' he said. 'Tell her I sent my love as well.'

He hated visiting the house, so he tried to avoid it, so Inge had to demand his presence. He understood this dreary cycle of events very well but was powerless to change it. Guilt made him a soft touch. He would have advised one of his clients to take a firmer line.

Everything about the house was unchanged, and visiting it made him feel that he was in a time warp, still married to Inge and having an affair with Helen. He felt alienated and yet it was also completely natural: that was what alarmed him. Because he had been making the same journey, under duress, for eight years, he could almost believe, when he was very tired, that nothing had changed and the trauma of divorce and remarriage still lay ahead.

Inge preserved the house and garden in a state of ritual disorder that began the day he left her. Prior to that, she had been everyone's idea of a model hausfrau. He knew that the change was intended to shock but he still found it shocking. Clothes lay where they fell. There was grime in the bath and sink. The boys wrote messages in the dust on the furniture. The grass grew waist-high unless he cut it himself, although he had bought a motor-mower to make it easier for Inge, and the boys were big enough now to help. But they colluded with her. They liked the messy house and the unkempt garden; they felt comfortable not having any appearances to keep up. When they had nothing left to wear they went to the launderette with all their clothes stuffed into black dustbin liners; sometimes they took the sheets and towels as well. Inge cooked, and that was all. He never found out what she did with the rest of her time. The boys said she stayed in bed a lot, reading library books, drinking wine and taking pills her doctor had given her for depression, but how could they know when they were at school? Perhaps she only did that when they were there to see, so they could tell him about it.

He knew she was unhappy, even desperate, but he also knew she was doing it to punish him. He marvelled that she could be so persevering in self-destruction, that it could be rewarding enough, that she could find the energy to keep all this pain alive. On particularly crowded days when he was trying to fit in one more client, one more report, one more phone call, he even found himself envying Inge her free time. Miserable she might be, but at least she was miserable at her leisure.

In the early days of their separation he had implored her to get a job, but she told him she had no skills. Useless to point out that she could cook, drive, type and speak three languages: she countered with the indisputable fact that she was liable to burst into tears at any time and this made her unfit for employment. Now, of course, she could blame the recession and did not have to cry so often.

When he first moved out he had to visit her in order to see the boys, since she would not allow them under Helen's roof. Now they were big enough to meet him at the office or a cinema or McDonald's, but they still would not visit the house. He respected their loyalty to Inge but found it irksome and vaguely insulting. He took it to mean that they had not forgiven him for leaving them when they were little, but they denied this. 'We sort of promised Mum,' Karl said, 'and you know what she's like.'

Sometimes he thought the arrangement suited Helen very well. She resented his visits to Inge but she did not have to accommodate his sons, although she had always declared herself willing to do so. Her life was unchanged by their marriage: she lived in the same house with her daughter, taught at the same college, painted in the same studio. Richard was an addition to all this activity: from being a visitor, he had become a resident. Whereas he had to relate to two wives, support two homes, consider the needs of three children, as well as doing the same very demanding job. His life was transformed. Yet how could he complain about this when it was what he wanted, what he had chosen? He complained.

'You don't support two homes,' Helen said calmly. 'You support yourself and Inge and the boys. I support myself and Sally. That's perfectly fair and reasonable. Of course it would be nice if Carey supported Sally too, but he doesn't, what with Marsha and their brood, so there we are. You're a luxury, my love. An optional extra.' She kissed him, to take the sting out of the words. Teasing him was, he knew, her way of defusing her resentment of Inge's demands.

'I don't think you'd like Carey to support Sally,' he said. 'You prefer to have her all to yourself.'

'But I share her with you,' Helen said. 'You're more of a father to her than Carey ever was. What does it matter who pays the bills?'

But it did matter and they both knew it. Money was power: the hand that held the cheque book ruled the world. Helen earned less than he did, roughly half his salary, in fact, plus occasional sales of paintings, but it was enough for herself and Sally, just about, whereas he was trying to do right by six people, which was impossible.

*

Sally stayed in his mind as he drove through the heavy traffic. He had always thought of her as an anxious child, watchful and eager to please. When they first met her eyes darted from him to Helen and back again, gauging their moods; a smile seemed to hover near her mouth ready to be switched on or suppressed, whichever the situation might require. It did not make her false: he never thought of her as less than genuine. But it meant that she had a curious lack of self and he found himself wondering who she was inside. It seemed unnatural for a child to think so much of others and modify her behaviour to suit them.

'Sally's too good to be true,' he said to Helen one day on one of his visits.

'Yes, I know. Aren't I lucky?' She smiled. 'I expect she'll rebel in her teens like everyone else.'

In a way he would have liked her to be more perturbed by her good fortune. One day he arrived early at the studio and called her name as he mounted the stairs, only to be met by Sally at the door with her fingers on her lips.

'Ssh,' she said, managing to sound both friendly and disapproving. 'Mummy's working.'

He sensed an alliance between them from which he might be excluded or in which he might be invited to participate. Sally, having observed the chaos of her mother's life with her father, had appointed herself as Helen's guardian or minder, even a sort of juvenile business manager, whose primary function was to smooth Helen's path. They were two against the world, and in that sense he found the alliance very touching. But he also felt it was dangerous. He was conscious of desperately wanting Sally's approval, yet he knew that she would feel for him whatever Helen wanted her to feel and it would be real. He saw an adult beauty and gravity in her face, but there were also glimpses of the child Helen had been before experience marked her. Helen, he felt, relaxed only when making love: lost in an orgasm, she let him into her private world, even opening her eyes at the last moment to admit him so that he could drown. Sally, he discovered, was delightfully ticklish and would giggle and shriek to the point of hysteria. She also liked to be picked up and carried high on

11

his shoulders, trusting he would not drop her; then he felt she was able to shed her responsibilities. These were exhilarating times for both of them.

One day there was a moment of breakthrough when she said to him, 'Mummy was very sad when Daddy went away.'

'Yes,' he said, 'I expect she was.'

There was a pause while Sally looked at him very seriously before asking, 'Are you going to be my new Daddy?'

He said, 'I do hope so.'

That night he said to Helen, knowing it was the right moment, 'I want to marry you.'

'But you're married already,' she said, unsurprised.

'You know it was all wrong with Inge long before we met. I love you. I love Sally. I want us to be a family.'

'What about the boys?'

'I know. It's a mess. But so is this. How can we live like this for ever, with me coming and going and telling lies at home? Inge must know something is happening, we have terrible rows. I'd like to be straight with her.'

'I can't handle the guilt,' Helen said. 'If you come to me, you've got to feel all right about it, or I'd rather go on as we are, or even break up.'

The words gave him a chill of pure horror and he realised she had become indispensable, more than a romantic dream.

'Christ knows,' she said violently, 'I've been the deceived wife and I never fancied myself as the other woman. I don't know how I allowed this to happen. And you're too bloody nice to be in this situation.'

In those days they both still smoked and seemed to spend a lot of time lighting each other's cigarettes and pacing up and down.

'The thing is,' Helen said, 'I don't ever want to live in a mess again. I want to love someone who loves me and I want to know the bills are paid and the house is clean and there isn't going to be any drama. I want to get on with my work and come home to someone who's really there, not drunk or stoned or in bed with another woman. All that sixties rubbish, I don't ever want to live through that again.'

She had never spoken so openly about Carey before.

12

'I want to leave Inge and live with you,' Richard said. 'And I want to leave teaching and get into the probation service. I really want to change my life. Will you help me?'

'No,' Helen said. 'I don't want to be blamed if it goes wrong.'

'Then I'll have to do it all by myself.'

She took his hand. 'I'm sorry. I know it's lonely. But I couldn't leave Sally for you. How can I expect you to leave the boys for me?'

'Will you think less of me if I do it?' Her hand was rough and paint-stained; it felt very strong. Tough and square with short nails. He hung on to it as to a life-raft.

'No,' she said. 'I'll just think I'm very lucky.'

He kissed her hand and found that it was wet with his own tears.

'I do love you, Richard,' she said. 'You're a good man and there aren't very many around.'

She had not said that before, either, and he found it almost unbearably moving.

'I'll visit the boys a lot,' he said, 'and Inge as well, if she wants me to. You must be prepared for that. I want to make it as easy for them all as I can. I'll never abandon them.'

'I know,' Helen said. 'You'll do your best to make it all right. But I think you'll find it can't be done nicely.'

When he told Inge he was leaving her, she let out a great primitive scream that went on and on like an animal howling in some death agony. It was a while before he realised that she was actually screaming *nein* over and over again. The boys woke up and stumbled out of bed in their pyjamas to watch the scene with disbelief. Richard tried to pack but Inge clung to his legs, impeding every movement, and still the terrible screaming went on. He had never before heard such a sound come out of anyone's throat. The boys started to cry and he tried to comfort them and take them back to bed. Then there was sudden silence. When he returned to Inge, he found she had cut her wrists and was making a bizarre and terrifying

13

pattern of blood all over the sheets. He was totally horrified and unable to tell how serious it was, so panicked and called an ambulance. It was only while dialling 999 that it suddenly occurred to him that the German for no, if repeated three times, was also the emergency code, and that Inge had in fact been demanding the help he was now getting her, as if on some cosmic telephone.

'Shit,' Helen said. 'Happy birthday. Great timing she's got.'

'He said he was sorry,' Sally said.

'I bet.'

'He did. He was very upset about it. And she can't know it's your birthday.'

'God, you're naive. Of course she knows it's my fucking birthday. She's had eight years to find out.'

'Mum. Now you're being paranoid.'

'And I don't want any clever stuff from you. I'm not in the mood for jargon or compassion or any of that rubbish.'

'I know,' Sally said. 'I'm sorry. Have my present. Have a hug as well.' She laid a parcel on the table and put her arms round Helen.

'God, I'm a monster,' Helen said presently. 'Of course he has to go. They could all be blown up. The fact that I wish they would be is neither here nor there. You and I know she's lying and he knows she's lying but he still has to go. I'm just tired. I'm sorry.'

'Have a drink,' Sally said. 'Let me pour you a big birthday drink.'

Inge watched him coming at last up the path. She had been waiting at the window like an impatient child, willing him to appear, weaving spells, making bargains with God. None of it had worked. But now, in his own time, he was here.

She was reassured to feel her heart give its customary lurch, for if that did not happen, on what could she depend? Safe,

14

like a seraglio wife, behind her veil of net curtain, she gazed at him greedily as he stood under the porch light. Because she saw him seldom, he looked strange but familiar in the way that film stars do, and weary, with smudges round the eyes like make-up. It was a look she treasured. But if she told him that, he would be amused, embarrassed.

He rang the bell, glancing at his watch. She waited for the boys to open the door; she was no longer in a hurry. The sooner he came in, the sooner he would leave. She looked down at his short curly hair, shiny with rain, at the damp collar and shoulders of his mackintosh. She felt such piercing love that she ached. At the same time she could not remember if it had always been so, or if she had gradually tuned her feelings to a higher pitch since he left her.

One of the boys went to the door. She heard Richard say hullo and the child's casual voice answering.

'Oh, hullo, Dad. Mum's upstairs.' Then a shout to her. 'Mum? Dad's here.'

Other women did not go on loving like this. Not for eight years. Oh, she had read about people who never got over things but she had not met any of them. Not someone like herself. Old people, bereaved and heartbroken perhaps, waiting to die, but never anyone of her age, nourishing a passion, lying in wait for one false move, so that she could pounce like a spider, regain her territory and smother her prey with love.

In the fantasy he would have climbed the stairs, found her in the darkened room, been overcome by lust for her body and flung her on to the bed to make love until they were both exhausted. Then he would have admitted he could not leave her again.

'Inge?' A faint edge to his voice. 'Are you up there?'

She walked reluctantly, urgently, to the top of the stairs and looked down at him.

'I haven't got all night,' he said, the tone gentler than the words. 'Why are you upstairs?'

'I was lying down,' she said. 'The gas gave me a headache.' She thought how beautiful he looked, so tired and so concerned for her safety that he had come all this way when

15

he could have refused. He looked up at her, his eyes that curiously light brown, almost yellow, a colour she imagined belonged to wolves, a colour the boys had luckily both inherited instead of her own boring blue. She gazed longingly at the corners of his mouth where she had often placed her tongue in happier days to tease him. It didn't seem possible that all that passion could have disappeared for ever.

'Well, I'll go in the kitchen and have a look,' he said. 'Don't come down if you're not feeling well.'

There was a sink full of dirty dishes in the kitchen and a strong smell of gas. He checked all the connections as a formality but could nót find anything loose; Karl came in while he was doing it and stood watching him with idle, detached curiosity, as one might observe a man digging a hole in the road. Richard felt the reproach of years (you deserted me, why should I care about you?) and wondered if this was merely in his own head.

'Find anything?' Tone of polite interest.

'Not so far.' Richard looked up, but his son's face was without expression.

'Why not strike a match?' Karl suggested. 'That might do it.'

Peter followed him into the kitchen. He too gave the impression of having nothing better to do with his time. 'Mum's been fiddling with the taps,' he said helpfully. Karl glanced at him. 'Well, she has,' Peter added.

'I'd better go and talk to her,' Richard said, abandoning the search for the leak he had never really expected to find.

'She gets awfully low,' Karl said, 'and we can't cheer her up. Couldn't you come round more often?'

'She gets drunk,' Peter said flatly, though the row of empty bottles was there by the bin for Richard to see.

'I'm sorry,' Richard said. 'I know it's difficult for you.'

'Oh, we're OK,' Karl said. 'It's just her. She can't sort of, you know, get it sorted.'

They were taller than Richard already. They had shaved parts of their heads and dyed the remainder orange and pink and made it stand up in spikes. They were a team. He felt the force of their unity as he looked at their blank childish faces.

We are survivors, that was the message he picked up, and no thanks to you, so don't get sentimental with us, because we're giving it to you straight.

'If I came round every day,' he said, feeling ill at the thought, 'it still wouldn't be enough. She wants me here all the time and I can't do that.'

'No, well,' said Karl, shrugging. 'That's it. Cheers, Dad.' He drifted out of the kitchen and Peter followed him; Richard thought they were oddly like liberal parents creeping tactfully away to leave the young lovers together. He was reminded of the countless evenings he had spent with Inge when they were both nineteen and she was babysitting for his tutor. Then they could hardly wait for the sound of the car driving away before tearing their clothes off; now, as the front door slammed behind his children, he felt a profound apprehensive chill at the knowledge that he and Inge were once more alone in the house.

He went back into the hall and shouted up the stairs, 'Inge? I think it's all right. But I'll have to go in a minute.'

The hall was full of bicycles and dust and old newspapers; there was even, now he came to look more closely, the remains of a bread roll, green with mould, behind the umbrella stand. He marvelled yet again at her talent for creating such chaos: it seemed deliberate, subtly designed, like a film set. He could remember a time when this house, his house then, had been clean and tidy. He had helped; he had pulled his weight. But in those days Inge had cared.

Now she came down the stairs in a dressing-gown, which alarmed him. In the early days after their separation, she had often removed her clothes when he visited her, in order to tempt or reproach him, and the desolation of all that thin sagging stretch-marked flesh that he had once desired so strenuously made him feel unbearably sad for both of them.

'I was going to take a bath,' she said as she reached the foot of the stairs, 'but then I remembered there is no hot water.' She had washed off her make-up; she looked and sounded like a child. He felt he should have scooped her up in his arms and carried her back to bed, which was no doubt what she was hoping for, only he would have done it with promises of

17

a drink of water and a story. He would have sat by the bed until she fell asleep and then he would have gone home with a lighter heart. Sometimes he felt that he truly might do any of these things, perhaps on his next visit, so potent was the spell she cast on him, which made him afraid to visit her at all.

'You can turn it on again,' he said. 'It's quite safe.'

She shivered; her dressing-gown was of light material. 'I'm so cold,' she said. 'Come and have a drink with me.'

He followed her into the living-room where they had spent so many evenings together, not wanting to have a drink, not wanting to stay, but somehow swept along by the poignancy of their situation and the knowledge that it was all his fault. Inge poured whisky; he declined.

'You make me feel guilty,' she said, and he almost laughed. 'You've come all this way and you look so tired. I'm wasting your time, I've given you this awful journey for nothing.'

'It's all right, Inge,' he said. 'There's no point in both of us feeling guilty.'

To his horror she began to cry: large effortless tears welling up and spilling over, like a child being sick, without trauma or deliberation. 'Oh, Richard,' she said, 'I can't bear it. I love you so much. I miss you all the time. I know you think I do these things on purpose and you don't trust me any more, but I'm so lonely, if I can't see you I feel I'm going mad and I really don't want to live.'

'Yes, I know,' he said. 'And I'm sorry. If there was anything I could do, I'd do it.' It was a conversation they had had many times.

'You could leave her,' Inge said. 'She could manage without you. I can't.'

He mopped up her tears and she clung to him savagely. He held her for a while until she was calmer, and warm again; he poured her more whisky.

'It's impossible,' he said. 'You know it is. I care about you and the boys but I want to live with Helen. I love her. Forgive me if you can. I can't change. I don't want to hurt you but that's how it is. It's not your fault, it's mine.'

'I can't bear the pain,' she said.

He disentangled himself gently and got up. She followed

him into the hall, clinging and embracing him all the way to the door. He was appalled by the nakedness of her emotion and yet it aroused his admiration and respect. He kissed the top of her head and promised to see her soon. Eventually he was able to escape into the rainy night.

On the night of the dinner party Sally watched from the window to see Felix and Elizabeth arrive. She was almost afraid to look but it was all right, he was every bit as wonderful as she remembered. She felt a shiver of delight at the sight of him, his face, his smile, his casual elegant clothes, the way he moved. Even watching him park the car was a thrill. How lucky Elizabeth was to be married to him: did she appreciate her good fortune?

She was watching from Helen's room and had to go back to her own room to finish doing her face. She could hear the excited greetings downstairs, the raised voices, Richard's warm welcome, Helen going down after they'd arrived and being cool and polite. Then they moved into the living-room and the sounds became fainter while she went on painting her eyes. Waiting for her heart to calm down.

'It's not that I love England,' said Felix. 'It's just that I hate abroad.'

In fact he did love England, and he was not ashamed of his love, but he thought it unwise to admit it, since that would mean sharing it. So he pretended he had come back because he hated foreign food and foreign weather and foreign language, pretended that all this antipathy had finally forced him to tolerate the shortcomings of his native land. In truth England was a beloved mistress, whom he had betrayed with foreign whores, but it was safer to pretend that she was a boring wife. Only Elizabeth knew that Elgar and Noël Coward and even (God help him) Winston Churchill brought tears to his eyes; and Elizabeth would never tell. He was assured of her smiling complicity whenever he told the familiar tale of tax exile, and eventual disenchantment with the expatriate life, and returning to take his medicine like a man. Patriotism and sentiment were not part of his image.

'Well, it's good to have you back,' said Richard, pouring the drinks.

'I think I missed Radio Three most,' said Elizabeth. 'The World Service didn't make up for it at all. And you always get caught up with the other Brits, even though you swear you won't. It's really a very provincial way of life, with everyone gossiping madly about their neighbours.'

That must mean, Helen thought, that Felix's affairs had been common knowledge, whereas in London Elizabeth had at least a chance of not finding out. 'You both look very well on it,' she said.

They had tried just about everywhere. The Channel Islands and the Isle of Man, seeming to promise the best of both worlds, had turned out like most compromises to be neither one thing nor the other, so near and yet so far. Turks and Caicos offered the perfect climate, but it went with a shortage of culture and a multitude of insects that ignored Elizabeth and bit Felix so savagely that he spent most of his time not on the beach but at the local clinic, having humiliating injections in the bum. Ireland had provided whisky, scenery and conversation, but so many soft days that Felix began to fear he might drown while walking down the street.

'What about Andorra?' Helen asked. 'That might suit you.'

'Come on, Helen, give them a chance,' Richard said. 'They've only just got back.'

'Only trying to be helpful.' Helen smiled at Elizabeth to show she did not include her in the helpfulness. Long ago the animosity between herself and Felix had resolved itself into a form of regular teasing such as siblings might enjoy. It was a way of pretending she did not really dislike him, a way of tolerating Richard's oldest friend without embarrassing his wife.

'You both look pretty good too,' Felix said. 'Crime and art must be flourishing. I may have to touch you for a loan if I don't write something soon. I seem to have spent most of the money I went abroad not to pay tax on. God, what a sentence.'

'I thought Tony Blythe was meant to keep you in idleness for the rest of your life,' Helen said.

'That was the plan, yes. But it's come unstuck somehow. I think I'm bored with him, silly little sod. I might even kill him off, how about that? *Inn at the Death* I shall call it, about these two gays who run a hotel. Then he can go out with a bang and a whimper and I'll have to write the great English novel. I've had enough of crime and Tony Blythe.'

'Don't be too hasty,' Richard said. 'He's been good to you.'

'How's Sally?' Elizabeth asked Helen, as if anxious to change the subject.

'Fine. She'll be down in a minute but she's not eating with us, she's going to a disco.'

'She's got into Sussex,' Richard said, 'so we're rather proud of her.'

'I'm actually quite frightened,' Felix said. 'If I don't get another TV series pretty soon, I'm a ruined man.'

'You always say that,' said Richard, 'but you keep going. I think you need the fright to make you work.'

'Bloody masochism,' said Felix. 'What a ridiculous business.'

Sally came pounding down the stairs, wearing jeans and a shirt and silly shoes, with kohl round her eyes. She had never learned to walk lightly and Helen had given up trying to make her.

'Hullo,' she said, 'nice to see you. How long are you back for?'

'For ever, I think,' said Felix. 'We're too old and decrepit to run away again.'

'You speak for yourself,' said Elizabeth, and everyone laughed.

Sally came round the sofa to greet them and they both kissed her on the cheek.

'Well done about Sussex,' said Felix.

'Thank you.' She blushed. 'It's only if my grades are OK, so fingers crossed. Well. See you all later.'

'I'll fetch you at one o'clock,' said Richard.

She made a face. 'I'm going with Maria and Jackie. They'll walk me home.'

'And I'll wait round the corner so as not to embarrass you.'

'Honestly. I'll be OK.'

'Don't keep on,' said Richard, 'or I'll fetch you at midnight.'

Sally laughed. 'You *are* silly,' she said fondly.

The front door slammed behind her. She had never learned about shutting doors, either, Helen thought, or tidying her room, but apart from that she was pretty near perfect. Helen hoped the great warm gush of soppy love she felt for Sally was not too obvious to everyone in the room.

'My God,' Elizabeth said. 'What a beauty. Hasn't she grown up.'

'Well,' Helen said, 'you have been away three years.'

'Time to eat,' said Richard. 'I can smell burning stew.'

Over dinner the conversation drifted to Inge, as Helen had known it would. She heard herself becoming strident.

'In theory it ought to be better now the boys are older,' she said, 'but in practice it's worse. Now Richard doesn't have to visit her to see them, she has to keep thinking of other ways to get him to go round there. D'you know, one time she actually pretended there was a gas leak.'

She knew she shouldn't have said it but she couldn't stop herself. She didn't look at Richard but she could feel his tension.

'Don't they have an emergency service?' Elizabeth enquired mildly.

'Of course they do but she said they wouldn't come.' Helen was surprised at the anger in her own voice about things she thought she'd got over.

'I thought they had to come if you say you can smell gas,' Elizabeth persisted, as if this were an ordinary conversation, entirely missing the point.

22

'Maybe she'd pulled the same trick once too often.' Felix looked up, ever alert at the prospect of a row. 'What did you do, Richard? You didn't go, did you?'

'Of course he did,' Helen said. 'Inge snapped her fingers and off he went. On my fucking birthday, too.'

Richard said pleasantly, 'With two kids in the house I didn't have much choice.'

'And was there a gas leak?'

'No, of course not,' said Helen. 'Don't be silly, Felix.'

'I knew there wouldn't be,' said Richard, ominously calm. 'But it's not a risk you can take.'

'So she's got you over the proverbial barrel,' said Felix with interest.

Richard said, 'Well, she can't do it every week.'

'It must be quite flattering though,' Elizabeth said.

'She's amazingly persistent, isn't she?' Felix said. 'Eight years of unrequited passion.'

'Is this a record?' said Helen bitterly.

'It's not flattering,' said Richard, with the air of a man at the end of his patience. 'It's embarrassing and inconvenient and rather sad.'

Felix went on looking impressed. 'Nobody's ever loved me that much.'

Elizabeth said sharply, 'Unless you count me, of course.'

Oh God, Helen thought, now what have I started?

Felix smiled. 'But I haven't left you for another woman, have I, darling?'

Inge sat alone in a corner of the wine bar, drinking red wine and smoking a Gauloise. She had dressed herself up in some of her more exotic clothes from the second-hand shop: a mixture of velvet, satin, fur, chiffon and crochet in various shades of pink, purple, orange and brown, with beads and diamante. It gave her pleasure to make herself look as eccentric as possible, to attract maximum attention. She could feel people staring at her, but when she stared back rudely, challenging them, they looked away, embarrassed.

Smug little couples, most of them, out for the evening, flaunting their togetherness. She hated them all.

But there was a man sitting near the door, another failure like herself, alone on a Saturday night, and hoping to drown the shame of it in alcohol and the chance of being picked up. She stared at him. He was nothing special, but there was something, the short curly hair perhaps, or the shadows under the eyes, that reminded her, ever so slightly, of Richard. It was enough. It would have to be enough. She went on staring until he felt the strength of her stare and looked up. She smiled, despising him for being alone like her, and he smiled back.

She relaxed and finished her drink. It was only a matter of time, she knew from experience, before he got up and came over to her table. He would buy a bottle of wine and they would make small talk until they were drunk enough to desire each other instead of the people they had lost. Then she would take him home.

Sally needed the music. She needed the noise and the lights and the other people dancing. She needed to blot out Shakespeare and Chaucer and Browning and Thackeray and iambic pentameter and objective correlatives and dramatic irony. Sometimes she felt as if her head would explode with it all, but the music could wipe it away, could create a cool white space where nothing else was. It made her laugh that Helen and Richard probably imagined she was there just to dance and pick up boys. Helen had been right about her shoes, though; she had already had to take them off.

She thought how lucky Maria and Jackie were, not to have any of this pressure put upon them. In spite of all the talk about unemployment, Maria was going to work in a bank and Jackie was going to train as a hairdresser. They would soon be earning money and they would not have to study in the evenings. They did not feel their heads were being crammed to bursting point with useless knowledge like a force-fed goose.

24

If only I was a bit more academic, she thought, I'd find it easy; and if only I was a bit less academic, I wouldn't have to do it at all. Not good enough for Oxford and Cambridge but not bad enough to be turned down by everyone. A solid Beta plus. It made her want to scream. Then she felt guilty because she was supposed to be grateful for opportunities that were denied to other people.

She noticed Chris standing by himself in a corner and watching her while she danced. He had on his wistful, hang-dog look. It annoyed her, making her feel that she was meant to pity him. Why didn't he understand that if he looked cheerful and sort of OK, maybe even ignored her a bit, she might fancy him again?

Eventually she had to sit down, get her breath back, have a Coke. Out of the corner of her eye, she could see him coming towards her; not looking up, she saw his shoes arriving before she saw his face. She was intensely embarrassed. She felt everyone was watching her, feeling sorry for Chris, thinking she was a cow.

'Can I take you home?' he asked, but oh God, so humbly, adding, 'I've got the bike fixed.'

'My step-father's coming for me.' He had even cleaned his wretched shoes.

There was a pause. Surely he would go away now?

He said rapidly, 'Why don't I see you any more?'

'You see me every day at school.'

'You know that's not what I mean.'

She looked up then, reluctantly, and saw naked pain in his face. She felt terrible: guilty but angry too. She felt she had meant to make a quick, clean, merciful kill but had only succeeded in inflicting a messy injury which she would now have to deal with. The *coup de grâce*, to put him out of his misery.

She said, 'I'm sorry, Chris. I can't.' And shut her eyes while he walked away.

Jackie and Maria came over to her as soon as he had gone.

'Why don't you give him a break? He looks really miserable.'

Sally shrugged. She was afraid the shrug would make her

25

look heartless, but she couldn't explain. Had Felix noticed her blushing when he kissed her? Did he think she looked grown up now? Would he still be there when she got home? She had dreamed of him for so long, with nothing to nourish the dream, that it was hard to believe he was finally back in her life.

When the man tried to kiss her, Inge froze, turning her head away. 'No, don't kiss me,' she said urgently, for it was vital that he should not ruin everything, just when it was going so well. He hesitated, and she used the moment to slide her legs on to his shoulders, to make the kiss more difficult and sharpen the angle of penetration to give herself more pleasure. He fucked her harder then until she came, screaming, and saw him smile.

'Suck me,' she said. 'Go down on me, please.' She was afraid that because she had come, he would think it was all right for him to come and it would all be over too soon.

She saw a look of slight irritation cross his face, as if she had asked him to do something onerous, a burdensome chore such as emptying the dustbins when he was happily watching television.

'I did it for you,' she reminded him, for that was how they had begun.

He did it, making her feel he was doing her a favour, but she didn't care, she wasn't going to let him spoil her evening. She tried thinking about Richard, but it seemed like blasphemy, so she ran an old reliable blue movie instead and came quickly, sensing that the man was reluctant enough not to persevere for long. He surfaced with relief, breathing hard, as if he had been drowning, and fucked her again until they both came, one after the other.

Almost immediately, as if by mutual consent, they separated and lay apart in exhausted silence.

Inge dozed; she felt relaxed, almost happy, peaceful anyway, and tired enough, she thought, to sleep without pills for once. Presently she peered at the bedside clock; it said half

26

past midnight. She couldn't remember what time they had started but she knew they had left the wine bar at eleven.

Suddenly she was exhausted and wanting to be alone. She yawned ostentatiously but he didn't take the hint. 'It's late,' she said. 'You'd better be going.'

He made a strange noise, somewhere between a moan and a grunt. 'What? I was nearly asleep.'

'Only my husband stays the night,' said Inge, her favourite fantasy.

'I thought you said you're divorced.'

He had an unpleasant accent; all resemblance to Richard had vanished as soon as she heard his voice.

'I don't want you here,' she said, lacking the energy to be polite. 'I can't sleep with you here.'

He looked at his watch. 'Christ, is that the time? I've missed the last train.'

'There are night buses. Or you take a cab.' She was desperate now to be alone, to be asleep.

'Can't afford a bleeding cab, can I?' He sounded like a grumpy child deprived of pocket money. 'You've cleaned me out.'

'Come on,' she said, shaking him. 'You've got to go before my husband comes home.' They usually went pretty fast when she said that.

The man got up, but he moved slowly, annoyed and suspicious. Inge longed for him to go while she could still remember the pleasure, before irritation took over. She watched him dress, tried to concentrate on the good part of the experience, when suddenly to her astonishment she saw him go to her handbag and take a fiver from her purse.

'What are you doing?' she said, shocked.

'I reckon that's the least you can do for me, after all I've done for you.'

She leapt out of bed. 'No. That's all the money I've got.' It was not quite true but no matter. 'I have two children to feed.'

'Better ask your old man then,' he said with a kind of sneer. 'If he ever turns up.'

They struggled over the money, Inge trying to snatch it

27

from his hand while he held it just out of reach. They were like children in the playground. Then he got bored with the game, when Inge tried to bite him and kick him and knee him in the groin to make him give back her money. He hit her, not very hard, but enough to knock her off balance, enough to make her fall, so that he could run downstairs and out of the house. She heard him slam the front door. Lying on the floor with her face on the dusty carpet, she started to cry, more from outrage than pain. Then she reached for the phone. While she was dialling, she noticed the smell of herself and the man, a smell she no longer liked, and decided to take a bath as soon as her call was over.

'No, I'll be having a show in the autumn,' said Helen, grateful to Elizabeth for asking, 'but I can't think about that now. Some bloody fool wants me to do the *Seven Deadly Sins* for him first. As quickly as possible. Can you imagine?'

It was after midnight but they were still drinking coffee and brandy.

'Abstract?' said Elizabeth doubtfully. 'Won't that be a bit tricky?'

'It's what they call a challenge,' said Helen. 'He's a mad American called Jerome Ellis and he's going to live in an oast house. He seems to want paintings by the yard. Magdalen introduced him to me and I loathed him on sight. He hasn't a clue what my work is about but he says he likes my style, whatever that means. I think he imagines I'm a kind of interior decorator, only cheaper, of course.'

Elizabeth clucked sympathetically. 'Can't you turn it down?'

'Not really. The van failed its MOT.'

The phone rang and Richard answered it. Helen knew there was only one person who would ring at a quarter to one.

'Shame he doesn't want the *Stations of the Cross*,' said Felix.

Richard was saying, 'Calm down, I can't hear you. Now tell me again.'

'Inge,' Helen said, trying to convert fury into resignation before it choked her.

'Are you all right?' Richard was saying. 'Ring the local nick. You've got to report it.'

'Or a client,' said Elizabeth.

Helen shook her head.

'All right, I'm on my way.' Richard hung up and turned to her. The look on his face begged her to understand. 'Sorry, love, I'll have to go. She's hysterical. Some man's beaten her up.' His expression hardened as hers failed to soften. 'I'm sorry. Can you fetch Sally?'

Helen heard herself saying, 'Of course. She's my responsibility, isn't she? Just as Inge is yours.'

He turned away. 'Sorry, Felix, Elizabeth. See you soon.'

'Let's have a drink one evening,' said Felix, supportive, man to man. 'I'll ring you at the office.'

'Hope she's OK,' said Elizabeth.

Helen could feel them both scoring the points she had thrown away. Richard went out and there was an uncomfortable silence. She felt herself branded as a bitch. Not for the first time, but it still hurt. If only Richard would get angry with Inge. All this saintly patience was very hard to bear.

'Pity she didn't get herself killed,' she said, and meant it. What blissful relief it would be if Richard never had to go round there again. She didn't stop to think who would look after the boys.

'Oh dear,' Elizabeth said. 'Poor you.'

Now was the time, Helen thought, to be tactful, to play it down, to call it just one of those things and change the subject. Instead she chose to go into overdrive, just as one might choose to get drunk, a conscious decision, unwise but deliberate. She wanted to be sick, to make a scene, to spew out all the venom. Especially in Richard's absence.

'It's typical, isn't it?' she said. 'Bloody typical. And he always falls for it. First she cut her wrists when he left her. Then she took an overdose when we got married. Then we had the gas board routine. Now she's managed to get herself mugged. And round he goes each time.' She was shaking; she poured herself another drink. The silence in the room alarmed her: they were waiting for her to go on. 'Christ. After eight years, any other woman, any normal woman, would have found herself another man. And a job.' All the years of Inge's excesses spun in her head; she felt sick with rage.

Felix said mildly, 'Shall I go and collect Sally?'

Reality, sanity, made a dim reappearance. 'Oh, Felix, would you? I'm in no state to drive.'

'I didn't mean that, but you might like some time on your own with Lizzie.'

'Thanks. I would.' It was a new sensation, not pleasant, to feel gratitude towards Felix.

'You'd better give him the address,' Elizabeth said.

'Oh – yes. It's in the High Street. The Sick Parrot, it's called. You can't miss it. There's a bloody great drooping bird in neon lights outside.'

'Just like Inge really,' said Felix, and she almost liked him. They all laughed and he left the house. Helen was shocked that she had forgotten about Sally until he reminded her.

As Richard was parking the car the front door opened; Inge had obviously been watching for his arrival. She ran down the garden path and flung herself into his arms, starting at once to cry. He led her back into the house and poured whisky for her; he did not want a drink himself. She was wearing a dressing-gown, which he hoped she would not remove, and she smelt unusually clean. He felt he had been comforting her for most of his adult life and yet he knew that was unfair: when he had loved her, she had been cheerful. He remembered that clearly. There was an open and shut case against him: his departure had destroyed her happiness. He was responsible for the wreck she was now. If Helen chose to condemn her for being feeble, that was simply a moral judgment and had nothing to do with the facts.

'You should report him, you know,' he said, thinking of this unknown stranger who had injured his ex-wife but far less severely than he himself had done.

She shrugged. 'What for? I ask him in, I make use of him,

30

then I throw him out, so he robs me and hits me. It's fair. We both got what we wanted.'

'Inge, this is crazy.' There were no visible marks on her to indicate a struggle, but even if the attack had not taken place at all, the effect was the same.

'I upset him,' she said, almost with pride. 'I talked about you. I always talk about you, I can't help it, but they never like it. If they talk about their wives I listen and I don't mind, but it doesn't work both ways. It's funny, how can they be jealous when they don't even know me? It must be their pride. D'you think that's it?'

'I think you should stop picking up strangers who treat you badly.'

'How can I, if you won't come back to me? I must have someone, I can't lie here masturbating for the rest of my life. Is that what you want me to do?'

'Oh, Inge,' he said helplessly.

'Am I embarrassing you? Why don't you like me to speak frankly, Richard? You know I love you. I'll always love you.' She got up and poured herself more whisky; he was alarmed at the speed with which she drank. 'But I must have a man while I'm waiting for you to come back. If they treat me badly, it really doesn't matter. They can't hurt me the way you hurt me when you left. Not even if they kill me.'

He said, as if she didn't know it already, just to be clear that they both acknowledged reality, 'You're just trying to make me feel guilty.'

'Doesn't it work?' she asked in a curiously innocent, practical, almost child-like way.

'Oh yes,' he said bitterly. 'It works.'

Helen said, 'I think we made a mistake getting married, actually.'

Elizabeth was startled. She and Felix had left England shortly after the wedding, having taken credit for introducing them and seen them through all the mess of the separation and divorce. It was one thing for her to speculate in private as to whether they were happy; another thing to hear from Helen that they were not. She saw Helen noticing her shocked face.

'Oh, not like that,' said Helen, smiling. 'I mean from Inge's point of view. I think we should have just gone on living together.'

'Why didn't you?' Elizabeth felt a fool, caught out, wrong-footed. She tried to rearrange her expression, remembering that Helen had always had a knack of making her feel uncomfortable.

'I wanted to,' Helen said carelessly, 'but Richard said getting married would make it more final and she'd give up. I think it was the last straw. She's been much more difficult over the last three years.'

Elizabeth thought Helen sounded smug. Was the success of the marriage measured by Inge's distress? 'I suppose she's very lonely,' she said. She didn't like to think about Inge too much, feeling she had ratted on her, following Felix so blindly as he endorsed everything Richard did.

'Yes, of course she is, but we've all been lonely.' Helen somehow made it sound like having a cold. 'When Carey and I split up, I thought it was the end of the world. But you come to your senses eventually.'

Elizabeth hesitated, torn between honesty and tact. 'I've always been afraid I might behave like Inge if Felix left me.' She felt better once it was said. Like standing up to be counted. Like rows of extras calling out, 'I am Spartacus'. Why should Inge be crucified all by herself?

'Oh God, surely not,' said Helen, looking shocked at this unliberated attitude. 'Anyway, he never would. He knows when he's well off.'

'I hope so,' Elizabeth said, meaning it. She could feel herself and Helen moving further and further apart from their original meeting point, like scissors opening.

'If she'd only make an effort,' Helen said, 'try to get a job, even part-time, then she might meet someone else and she wouldn't be lonely and she wouldn't be such a bloody financial burden.'

But I could never meet anyone else like Felix, Elizabeth

thought, no matter how many jobs I took. And if I met them, I couldn't love them. Loving Felix is a life sentence. Maybe Inge feels the same about Richard. 'I do see it must be very difficult for you,' she said.

Helen poured herself another drink without offering Elizabeth one. 'Well, I support Sally and myself and Richard supports Inge and the boys. There's no shared money – in that sense we might as well not be married at all.'

'I suppose it's quite hard for her to find a job. I don't think she's worked since she was an au pair.' Elizabeth was beginning to wonder how she had ever got into all this. She hadn't even particularly liked Inge when she knew her and yet eight years later here she was defending her and upsetting a friend. It would be so much simpler just to agree. She wasn't sure why she couldn't do it.

'God, she can cook, type and drive, and she speaks three languages. She's more qualified than I am. Why does she imagine that having two children entitles her to sit on her arse for the rest of her life?'

It must be like stealing, or borrowing money, Elizabeth thought. You grow to hate the person you have injured, or the person who has done you a favour. It's simply too much to go on feeling guilty or grateful. She poured herself another glass of wine and Helen said absently, 'Oh – sorry.'

Felix would have to drive tonight, Elizabeth decided. She needed to drink if Helen was going to make her feel uncomfortable. She stared round the room, as the silence went on: it had hardly changed in the time they had been away. Helen had knocked down walls long ago, when she first bought the house, merging the hall with the living-room and creating an L-shaped space leading into the kitchen which Richard seemed to use more than she did, but it was still undecorated. The sofas and rugs were shabby from ten years' wear and the few paintings of her own that Helen had hung seemed incongruous, too stark and professional for such an unfinished room. It looked as though Helen had just moved in and did not intend to stay. Elizabeth marvelled that someone so visual could care so little about her own home. Clearly all Helen's energy went into her work.

*

33

They came out of the disco into the street and the comparative silence revived Felix as much as the fresh air. All the same, he regretted complaining about the noise: he was sure it would brand him as boringly middle-aged.

He said, 'Richard's gone to see her. Apparently some man beat her up.'

'How awful. Poor Inge.' Sally sounded genuinely concerned.

Under the street lamp, getting into his car, he noticed the purity of her profile, the healthy gleam of her uncreased skin beneath all the absurd paint. The cheap silly clothes could not disguise how lovely she was, but he caught himself thinking that dressed by him she would be really beautiful. He liked to take women over and change their image; he envied their potential. It would be fun to play Pygmalion to Sally's Galatea.

'Is Mum furious?' she asked as they drove off.

'You could say that, yes.' He had found it exciting to witness Helen's agitation; short of going to bed with her, which he knew, regretfully, would never happen, there was no other way he would ever see her lose control.

Sally said, 'She thinks Inge does it all on purpose to get Richard to go round there. And she is awfully accident prone. But I don't see how she could get someone to beat her up on purpose.'

Felix glanced at her swiftly, but she looked quite serious. Were the young really so naive? he wondered.

'It must be awful for Richard,' Sally went on. 'I'm sure he feels guilty.'

It occurred to Felix that she was talking a lot, as if she were nervous. 'D'you think he was wrong to leave her?' he asked. It would be interesting to get a teenage view of the subject.

'Well, he couldn't stay with her, could he? Not once he'd fallen in love with Mum.' She made it all sound very simple: obviously the young were still very romantic. 'You knew Inge, didn't you?' she added after a pause.

'Yes. Long ago. When they were first married.'

'What's she like?'

Felix thought about it: how to sum up all the hours, amounting to days, weeks, maybe even months of his life that

34

he had spent with Richard and Inge, talking, laughing and getting drunk; loving Richard, lusting after Inge, then tolerating Elizabeth as an intruder, a passenger and, later, an umpire in the rows before the whole thing split apart. 'Very intense,' he said carefully. 'Small and dark and thin and slightly mad, I think.'

Sally didn't appear to notice the emotion in the pause. 'I always imagine her like the Lady of Shalott,' she said, 'sitting there weaving and watching for Richard in the mirror.'

Felix liked the image and admired Sally for coming up with something so appropriate. He felt at once very tired and very randy, two states that for him often went together, and he wanted to prolong the evening, although he knew that nothing could come of it. He suggested they should stop at a nearby coffee bar and Sally agreed at once, sounding pleased and surprised. When he added, to cover himself, that he thought Helen wanted to talk to Elizabeth for a while, Sally said, 'Of course,' with a noticeable chill of disappointment in her voice that made him long to kiss her.

But the coffee bar proved only marginally better than the disco. A steady thumping beat with no discernible tune blasted out of the speakers and assaulted him; young people who looked as though they should have been in bed hours ago were sprawled at nasty formica tables in pairs and groups, smoking and attempting to talk to each other; a curious red glow from the lighting made everyone look as if they had spent too long on the beach. It was, Felix thought, the sort of place that would have made even Dante revise his ideas about hell.

'Whatever happened to Mozart?' he said. There seemed no point in trying to appear trendy or whatever the current word might be: his appeal lay in other areas.

'I think he died,' Sally said innocently, straight-faced.

'Coffee?'

'Yes, please.'

They sank down at one of the nearby tables into seats that

35

Felix knew would give him backache if he remained too long.

'Anything to eat?'

She looked shocked at the very idea. 'No, I'm much too fat.'

'God, you women and your weight,' he said without thinking (Elizabeth was always attempting to diet). He caught her looking pleased to be called a woman and then trying to conceal her pleasure in case it made her seem gauche.

'Don't you like this sort of music?' she said, meeting the problem head-on. 'It's number one.'

'Is it really?' said Felix.

'I like Mozart as well,' Sally said.

A waitress arrived, a badge pinned on her left breast announcing that her name was Shirley.

'Two coffees, please,' Felix said, deciding to be bold. 'And could you possibly turn down the music?' He achieved a fractional hesitation before the word music to register his distaste, but he thought the subtlety was probably lost on Shirley, who merely looked amazed and went away.

'Well, it was worth a try,' he said to Sally, adding, 'Oh dear, my age is showing,' because he knew it did not matter.

'Mum plays the Rolling Stones sometimes,' Sally said, placing him firmly in her parents' generation and gently sending him up. They both laughed and something eased in their conversation: it shifted into another gear.

'You must be very pleased about Sussex,' he said, feeling at once more comfortable with her.

'Yes.' She traced a pattern on the formica with her finger nail and he studied her profile: she had a straight, blunt nose and a short upper lip. 'Well . . . Mum and Richard are.'

Here was his chance to be understanding, a different sort of adult. 'I see. Like that, is it?'

'I am pleased, of course.'

'But?'

'Oh . . .' A long sigh. 'Feeling I didn't really have a choice. Everyone expected me to go, so I'm going, and I know I'm lucky, and I'm grateful not to be looking for a job that isn't there.' She looked up at him, her eyes pure and child-like behind the ridiculous orange make-up. 'Did you feel like that about Cambridge?'

'Not really,' Felix said. 'I was excited.' But not half as excited, he thought, as he now was about Sally's mouth. It was a rather large, firm mouth that looked somehow also delicate, as if it had hardly been used, the lips unpainted and sprinkled with freckles. It was the same shape as Helen's mouth, which he had always found extremely erotic. He imagined exploring it with his tongue, imagined it opening up to him, letting him in, then imagined it wrapped round his cock.

Their coffees arrived. Shirley put them down rather heavily, slopping them into their saucers, and went away. She had done nothing to moderate the music and Felix lacked the courage to ask her again. Once showed spirit, he thought, but twice was pernickety.

'Well, it's a bit special, isn't it, Cambridge? I know Sussex is supposed to be very good but . . . the way you wrote about it, Cambridge sounded so wonderful.' She stirred her coffee, rearranging the froth on top but making no attempt to drink it. 'I've read all your books, you know. Not just the Tony Blythe ones, the early ones as well. I liked *The Heartbreak Merchant* best. Especially the part about him and his mother. It made me cry.'

She was behaving like a groupie and he was flattered. 'Yes, I don't think I've done anything better than that,' he said, remembering. 'But it was a long time ago.'

'D'you prefer writing thrillers?'

Now she was interviewing him and the novelty of it reminded him how long it was since he had been interviewed. 'No. But it's a different sort of challenge. And it pays the bills. Not as satisfying as a straight novel though.'

'Can't you do both?' Sally asked, elbows on the table now as she gazed at him as if he were the most fascinating man in the world. Felix felt himself warmed by her attention; he had not realised how deprived he was of adulation, much as a hungry man might not realise the extent of his hunger until he began to eat.

'I've lost my nerve,' he said truthfully, something he had previously admitted only to Elizabeth and Natasha.

37

Sally said, 'Oh, Felix,' in a tone of such amazed tenderness that it was all he could do not to kiss her. Then he realised it was the first time she had used his name as one adult to another. He saw from her face that she was aware of this too and a little silence fell between them as the music blasted out.

Driving her back to the house, he was aware what a short journey it was, how little time he had to consolidate or make a move, how they might never be alone together again. It seemed like fate – Richard summoned by Inge, Elizabeth and Helen having a drunken chat: he had a strong sense of urgency and predestination mixed with ordinary sexual excitement. But he was also aware of the ridiculous aspect of the whole thing, that he should be allowing himself to get into such a state about someone he had vaguely watched growing up for the last eight years. The bit of his brain that monitored his behaviour nearly all the time these days made a note of the fact that he had not lusted after someone this young since he was young himself. But it was not simple lust: there was a lot of romance and yearning and fantasy wrapped up in it. That probably makes it a male menopausal crisis, said this part of his brain severely. What, already? said Felix, pushing it away. But I'm only forty, for God's sake. Elizabeth's fifty-one. We can't both be having the menopause at the same time, surely.

There was silence in the car after the easy conversation in the coffee bar. It reminded him of dinner parties where moving from the table to the sofa could ruin the whole thing. He had to be brave, summon up all his resources of age and experience, to plunge into a silence like this.

'We should really celebrate your getting into Sussex,' he said, before he lost his nerve. 'Even though it's not Cambridge.'

'I'm not there yet,' Sally said, sounding remote.

Neither am I, Felix thought, plunging. The cold-water swimmer risking a heart attack. 'Would you like to have lunch with me one day?' There was no time to be subtle: they were already at the house and he was parking.

38

'Yes, I'd love to.'

He could hear her surprise and pleasure, and the effort she put into trying to sound casual. It made him smile, made him want to put his arm round her, but he thought it was too soon for that. He scribbled his number on a piece of paper and gave it to her.

'Good, that's settled then. Just give me a ring any time and I'll take you out, OK?'

Now he was worried that he had made it sound too innocuous and she wouldn't want to come, or worse, she would announce their plans as soon as they went in, because they were so innocent.

'Won't I be disturbing you?' she said.

'I hope so,' he said, trying to sound as suggestive as possible, and then adding, to cover himself: 'I'll be only too relieved to get away from the blank sheet of paper.'

When Richard finally got up to go, Inge put her arms round him as she always did. 'Richard, can't you stay? Please. I don't want to be alone.'

'You know I can't.' It was awful to be asked, over and over again. 'And the boys will be home soon, surely.'

She shook her head. 'They won't. They've gone to an all-night party.'

Defeated at every turn. 'Oh Inge, they're a bit young for that, aren't they?'

'I think so, but how can I stop them? They are big boys now, I can't lock them up. If you were here, they would listen to you.'

He said, 'Inge, this simply isn't fair,' and she took her arms away.

'I know, but it's true. They don't want to stay in on a Saturday night and look at their mother crying. It's a bore. They want to go out and have fun. I don't blame them.'

'I'll talk to them,' he said briskly, making for the door. 'But now I do have to go.'

She followed him into the hall. 'Couldn't you ring her up

and say you're taking me to hospital? Or tell her the car has broken down?'

'Don't be silly.' His shoulders and the back of his neck ached with tension.

'It's not so silly. Think of all the lies you told me when you were seeing her. All the times you pretended you had to work late. Can't you tell her one lie for me?'

Rage mounted inside him with alarming force. He found he wanted to hit her as the unknown man had hit her, only harder and more often. He wanted in that moment to batter her swiftly to death and be done with all the suffering, hers and his. That must be how some of his clients often felt, though they could not always express it.

'I wish you wouldn't behave like this,' he said. 'It makes me feel very guilty and very angry. Is that what you want?'

'I just want you.' She seemed to be much calmer than he was. 'But I'll settle for making you guilty and angry if that's all I can have right now.'

'I'm going home,' he said, opening the front door. 'I'll ring you tomorrow.'

'Promise?'

The urge to kill her now was almost irresistible. Terrifying. Although he knew he would resist it.

'God, Inge, I've had enough for one night. Why do you always have to say things other people wouldn't say?'

'I'm honest,' she said. 'Don't you tell your clients to be honest?'

He started to walk down the path to the car. 'Take one of your pills now and go to sleep, OK?'

She called after him, in a conversational tone – as one might say, 'Drive carefully' or 'See you soon' – 'I'm going to wait for you, Richard. No matter how long it takes.'

Helen saw them out. She was tired now and angry at being an object of pity because Richard wasn't home yet. When she went back into the living-room, Sally was clearing the table.

'Poor Mum,' she said. 'What a rotten shame.'

'Yes,' Helen said briskly, 'I could have done without it.'

They worked in silence, side by side, piling the dirty dishes on to trays. Helen thought how sordid it all looked, now the fun was over and only the debris was left.

Sally said, 'I wonder what would happen if Richard just said no to her.'

A wonderful, farcical thought. Pure fantasy. But it was strange to hear it from Sally and not inside her own head. It was an old thought for Sally to have.

'With any luck she might try to kill herself again. And if she has enough practice she may just get it right.'

Sally hugged her, but Helen could see the shock on her face, quickly converted into amusement. They carried their full trays into the kitchen and Helen began loading the dishwasher. She remembered that she hadn't asked about Sally's evening.

'Did you have a good time?'

Sally looked evasive. 'It was all right.'

'Was Chris there?'

'Yes.'

'And?'

'He whinged a bit.' Sally kissed her. 'Don't be nasty to Richard. I'm sure he feels bad enough already.'

How well she knows me, Helen thought. It was lovely to be with someone totally on her side even when she was wrong. She would have liked to talk to Sally, but Sally had heard it all before and she already looked white with fatigue.

'Let's do the marriage guidance another time,' Helen said, kissing her goodnight, and they both laughed. Sally went up to bed and Helen finished loading the dishwasher. She was about to close the door and set the controls when she changed her mind and carefully removed a plate, which she hurled across the room. It smashed satisfyingly against the wall and she left the pieces where they fell, already feeling much better.

She didn't speak when Richard finally came in, but let him undress in the dark. She half expected him to put on the light: he must have known from her breathing that she was not

41

asleep. She had been thinking how she would feel if he had really been making love to Inge, as Felix had somehow contrived to suggest he might be, and she allowed her resentment at the imaginary offence to spill over into the silence. It was oppressive, like fog; it choked her and made her eyes sting.

He got into bed and lay apart from her. She sensed his exhaustion and longed to comfort him. But the urge to punish was stronger.

'Will she live?'

'Yes.'

'Pity.'

The silence extended. How was it possible to treat someone you loved so badly?

'Did she ask you to stay?'

'Yes.'

'Why didn't you?'

If only he were not so unfailingly patient. If only he would lose his temper with Inge, about Inge. Then she wouldn't have to get so angry with him, for him. She could be reasonable, play the whole thing down, put it in perspective. If only he would get angry with her too, call her a bitch. She was resenting all the things she loved him for. She had married a good, kind man because she was sick of bastards, and now she was blaming him for not being one.

'Sorry, sorry,' she said, turning over abruptly and hugging him. If they quarrelled, then Inge had won.

He put his arm round her. 'It's all right. Sometimes I just want to kill her.'

The words were what she had longed to hear but the tone was too calm. She wasn't sure she believed him. 'Oh please,' she said with feeling, 'let me.' They both laughed and the tension was gone.

Helen was twelve when her father defected. That was how she thought of it, as a political gesture, or a bid for artistic freedom, like one of the Russian ballet dancers in the

42

newspapers. Life with her mother was suffocating him, she could see that. It was having the same effect on her, too, but he didn't offer to take her with him. She thought at first he might send for her later, when he had got himself settled; she told herself it couldn't be easy for him finding somewhere to live with Mrs Watson and her three children. Her Auntie Maureen, she had been, living three doors along, but her mother made it clear she wasn't to be called that any more. In fact she became known as that woman, only Helen felt silly calling her that just to please her mother. She had eaten jam doughnuts too often in her kitchen to be formal now.

Uncle Jim came round a lot at first. He was very tall and thin and had to stand with his neck slightly bent to fit under the ceiling. Her mother didn't ask him to sit down. He wanted to talk about Auntie Maureen and sometimes he cried, which was very embarrassing. He kept saying if only she hadn't taken the children, and Helen could see his point; she wanted to say if only they had taken me instead, but she knew it would upset her mother, who kept telling her they would manage, they had each other, and they didn't need anyone else.

After a while Uncle Jim stopped coming round; even he could tell that he wasn't welcome. Real aunts and cousins fell by the wayside, too, as they implied that some of what had happened might be Mother's fault. Aunt Gloria, Dad's sister, was banned from the house after she told Mother she had always been cold. Aunt Gloria was divorced, but she had remarried and she didn't have children. Helen had always liked her because she looked like Dad and she smelt nice, but Mother said she was fast and it was typical of her to stick up for her brother no matter what he did: she had the morals of an alley cat.

Helen kept waiting, but Dad didn't write or phone and he didn't send for her. Her mother said it was because he was too ashamed. He must have sent money, though, because their standard of living didn't change much. Helen wondered how long she would have to wait. She couldn't believe that she would never see Dad again. She imagined him writing and Mother intercepting the letters. She tried getting up early so this couldn't happen but there was never a letter when she looked and some mornings she overslept, so she couldn't be sure. She wanted to write to him but Mother said she didn't have an address.

She tried to think what it meant. She knew Dad had loved her because he had hugged her a lot, tickling her with his moustache, and told her she was his favourite girl, although she doubted that now that he had gone off with Mrs Watson and her three little girls. Of course they were much younger. Perhaps he didn't like little girls so much once they started to grow up. Or perhaps she had done something to annoy him. It was hard to tell because they had not really spent much time together. He was a commercial traveller and often away. And he didn't really talk, he just made jokes. If he had to run off with someone, Helen would have expected it to be someone he met on his travels: he had scarcely been at home enough to get to know Mrs Watson that well. It just went to show how wrong you could be.

She was so preoccupied with her own feelings that it was a long time before she realised that her mother was very unhappy. She had always been thin but she got thinner; her mouth made a longer, tighter line and she moved slowly, as if everything was a big effort. But she didn't talk, either, except about everyday things like meals and laundry. In the evenings Helen did her homework and Mother sat in the other room, watching television. When she could put it off no longer, if she wasn't going out with her friends, Helen would join her, and they would both sit in silence, side by side in separate chairs, staring at the screen. No one sat on the sofa where Dad used to sprawl with his feet up, ridiculing the TV programmes and drinking beer from a can. When she thought about it, her parents were so different it was extraordinary that they had ever married and she could think of no explanation other than sex, which made it all a great deal worse. They had no interests in common and they didn't talk, so it must have been a grand passion and now it was over. That was what happened to grand passions: they didn't last.

Eventually, with infinite daily pain, Helen admitted to herself the obvious truth that her father was not only not going to come back or send for her, he was not going to write or phone either. It was almost beyond belief but it was a fact. Or if he did get in touch one day, it would be too late to do any good. It took her years to accept this; every birthday and Christmas was a fresh trial of hope. She painted more and more, finding that was the only thing that could take her mind off the pain, the disbelief. She remained astonished that something so important could happen without warning and without aftermath, an event complete in itself, like sudden death in wartime, far away in a foreign land. A part of her had been amputated and there was nothing to be done about it.

Just before she went to art school, her mother showed her a letter from a lawyer saying that her father was actually dead. He had left enough money for her to finish her training, but still no message. She said nothing and it was months before she could cry. At art school she resolved to have lots of affairs but never to fall in love. When she met Carey she forgot her resolve. Her mother said Carey was just like her father and it would never work. When Helen got divorced, her mother said I told you so. They did not talk much after that. When Helen thought of her youth, it was the silence she remembered most.

Felix has invited me to lunch. It's incredible. He says I can just ring him up at the flat where he works and he'll take me out. God, will I ever have the courage?

Tonight was amazing. I heard them arrive and went into Mum's room to borrow her earrings, so I could look out of the window. My heart gave such a thump when I saw him, I thought Mum would notice, but she didn't, just went on about Elizabeth having put on a lot of weight. She's always very intolerant of people who get fat, just because she doesn't, although she doesn't have to make any effort at all to stay thin and maybe they do.

It's funny when you've had a thing about someone for years and they go away – you don't know if you'll still fancy them when they come back. They might have changed or you might have grown out of them. I was almost afraid to look but it was all right, Felix hasn't changed a bit, in fact he looks better than ever, and I still fancy him rotten, I even think I might be in love with him.

The thing about Felix is he really looks at you and pays attention as if you're important and he's really interested in what you're saying. Lots of parents' friends don't do that, they just say polite things but really they're hoping you'll go away soon so they can get on with their conversation, and that's fine because usually you can't wait to go off and do something more interesting and leave them to it. But Felix makes you feel you really matter. He's got a sort of lived-in face that even looks a bit sad, but when he smiles it really lights up and you feel you're the only person in the world. It's a lovely feeling.

He kissed me on the cheek and said well done about Sussex. I know I blushed, I could feel it, I just hope he didn't notice. I couldn't think about anything except him at the disco and I was horrible to Chris but I couldn't help it, he got on my nerves. I wish I hadn't told Jackie and Maria about Felix because they keep teasing me.

Richard had made his usual fuss about fetching me at one o'clock but Felix turned up instead. I got such a shock and Jackie and Maria were really impressed, which was lovely. It was fantastic walking out of there with Felix and getting into his car, as if we were a couple. I was so excited I couldn't think of what to say. Poor old Richard had to go and see Inge because some man beat her up. I felt a bit guilty that I was having such a treat only because they were having a rotten time.

Felix took me to a coffee bar and we talked. He complained about the music being too loud, which was a bit embarrassing but didn't really matter. We talked about college but he kept staring at me as if he fancied me, which was fantastic. I felt he was really seeing me for the first time as somebody grown up. Then he told me he was scared of writing novels again instead of thrillers. Imagine that – Felix being scared. I wanted to touch him but I didn't dare. When we got home I thought he might

46

kiss me, but he didn't. He gave me his phone number instead, which is better really, because it means he wants to see me again and take me out. A kiss might have been just goodnight or goodbye. I do wish he'd kissed me though. When we went in together I felt as if he had, as if we had something to hide. I thought Mum might notice, I was in such a state, but she was in a filthy mood about Inge and Richard and that was all she could think about.

God, I hope Felix meant what he said about lunch. I'll have to ring him up soon before I lose my nerve. It's weird when you dream about something for years and suddenly it may be about to happen.

All week Richard had been looking forward to this evening. Felix was going to come round to the house for drinks and they were going out for dinner, a real chance to catch up after all this time. He was just leaving his office when the phone rang and they were telling him Tracey had taken an overdose and left him a note. He felt weak with shock; he said he'd go to the hospital at once. She was unconscious, so there was still a chance. He rang Felix at the flat, but got the machine. He rang Helen at home, but got Sally: Helen had already left for supper with Elizabeth. He gave Sally the message for Felix and left in a rush for the hospital, feeling a terrible sense of failure, praying that he would not be too late.

When Felix got to the house there was no Richard, only Sally in a pink dress, looking very pretty and very young, wearing hardly any make-up and playing Mozart. He felt as though he had walked on to a stage set, specially primed for his arrival. Suddenly he was very conscious that they were alone in the house and upstairs there were bedrooms full of beds. In an ideal world, he thought, in a fantasy, they would have been able to take full advantage of this, to go upstairs and get into one of the beds and make love instantly, without speaking another word. Instead, of course, he had to go into the living-room and make polite conversation.

'Richard asked me to tell you he can't make it,' Sally said. 'One of his clients has taken an overdose and he's had to go to the hospital. He's very sorry.'

Felix contemplated the chaos of Richard's life and was thankful it did not resemble his own. 'Poor old Richard,' he said inadequately.

'He said he tried to ring you,' Sally went on, 'but he got your machine. Does that mean you didn't get my message either?'

'What message?' He was alarmed how much he wanted her, uncertain how far his desire depended upon her dangerous status as Helen's daughter, Richard's step-daughter. In a lifetime of adventuring, this was the most risky affair he had ever considered, emotional incest, potentially fatal, violating taboos of friendship normally regarded as sacred. It gave him a terrific adrenalin charge just to think about it. Perhaps she felt the same.

'I rang about lunch,' she said, blushing. 'You said I should. I hate those machines.'

'At least you had the guts to speak. You wouldn't believe how many people just hang up. I can't bear it when I get back and there are flashing lights and I get all excited about my messages and then it's a great yawning silence punctuated by bleeps.'

They smiled at each other. He was aware of how childish he had made himself sound, and how much they were both smiling, goodwill overflowing everywhere. He did hope she wasn't a virgin: he wasn't sure he could face such a responsibility. Two or three clumsy lovers ahead of him would be fine.

'This is nice,' he said, indicating Mozart on the stereo.

'I told you I could be civilised.' Now it was like role reversal, with Sally trying hard to be grown up. 'Would you like a drink?'

'No, thanks.' He was going to need to be clearheaded. 'I just had a couple with my agent. Poor woman, she did her best to motivate me, but it's uphill work.' He paused: the

48

pink dress seemed demanding of his attention. 'You look very smart.'

'Do I? I was going out but it's been cancelled.'

He didn't believe a word of it and he was touched. Kids didn't go out with each other dressed like that. She was dressing for him.

'Tell you what,' he said. 'As we've both been stood up, why don't we have dinner together instead of lunch?'

'That would be lovely,' she said, sounding demure.

He took her to one of the clutch of restaurants he had collected over the years, near the flat for instant seduction (though he was not expecting that tonight) and also to minimise drunken driving, absurd expense and detection by Elizabeth or one of her friends. One could never be sure, of course, but by now he had half a dozen of these places that he thought of as safe houses but which were yet glamorous enough to gratify his companion. Sally, in any case, was too young to be fussy, and tonight they were actually innocent enough to afford discovery, though of course it was always better avoided. He found himself still taking refuge behind school and asking her about her set books, which seemed a pure enough topic, but even so there was a strong sexual undercurrent to the conversation, as if they were speaking in code or a foreign language which both could translate at will.

'*Othello*'s a bit weird,' Sally said. 'I don't really understand about jealousy. Why couldn't he talk to her? It somehow spoils it that it was all a misunderstanding – like the letter going astray in *Romeo and Juliet*. I hate things to happen by accident.'

'A lot of things do in real life,' said Felix, thinking that this evening was one of them.

'Yes, but not like that. It's the same in *Tess* and I always feel it's a cheat.'

'You look rather like Tess,' said Felix, still fascinated by her mouth.

'Do I?' She sounded pleased but embarrassed, and there was an awkward pause.

'What about *Vanity Fair*?' He was longing to get off these academic topics yet somehow unable to. He began to

49

understand why he had never bothered with someone so young before: it was simply too much effort.

'Well, it's too long.'

'Most books are. Except mine, of course.'

'And it's sad.'

'Sad?' He was surprised. 'Most people find it amusing. Well – a good read, anyway.'

'Yes, it is, in a way, but . . . oh, it's so sad when Dobbin finally gets Amelia and then he doesn't really appreciate her.'

'He'd waited too long,' said Felix, identifying with the poor sod.

'Yes, but that shouldn't matter – not if he really wanted her.'

God, the idealism of youth. 'Oh, but it does. Timing is very important. It's like catching the tide.'

'If I really loved someone,' Sally said, looking him straight in the eyes, 'it wouldn't matter how long I had to wait.'

'If I really loved someone,' Felix said, looking straight back at her, 'I'd want them right away.'

Suddenly he had the feeling that they were having an important conversation. There was quite a heavy silence while they applied themselves to their food and wine; he could almost feel the weight of their thoughts. When Sally spoke again it was as if they had reached a different level of intimacy.

'Did you mean what you said the other night – about losing your nerve?'

'Yes.' He never bothered to lie if it wasn't essential. 'Not very glamorous, is it? When you're young you've nothing to lose, but later on, there's everything at stake.'

She seemed to identify with that, leaning forward as if to touch him, reminding him with her body that they still hadn't touched. He hoped he wouldn't have to spend so much time getting to know her that by the time they finally did touch all the excitement would be gone.

'But you'll always have what you've done,' she said, sounding envious. 'I haven't done anything yet.'

'You've got it all ahead of you,' he said, thinking how young she was.

'But suppose I never do anything worthwhile.'

'I don't think that's very likely. What d'you want to do?'

'Well, I've always thought . . .' She looked embarrassed. 'Oh, it sounds awful saying this to you – I'd like to write but I'm not very good. I keep a diary but . . .'

'That's a start,' he said encouragingly.

'Now you're being kind. You must be sick of people telling you they want to write. I bet it happens all the time.'

'Now and then.' Millions of would-be writers swarmed before his eyes, accosting him at every turn, everywhere he went, and he saw himself with a machine gun, mowing them down and laughing. 'Most of them don't really mean it.'

'I do, but I'm not sure I'm single-minded enough. There are so many other things I want to do as well.'

He smiled; he knew the feeling well. 'Such as?'

'Oh, just living. But when I say that to Mum, she says, "Well, it's not a career."'

Felix laughed; it sounded so much like Helen. Helen whom he would never have, no matter what he did, no matter how long he waited.

Sally said, 'D'you want to write more than anything else in the world?'

'Not any more.' How long ago it seemed. 'I used to, when I was young. Now I just want to be happy.'

'Before they drop the Bomb,' she said, as if she understood.

'Before I get run over,' said Felix, with deep anxiety at the knowledge of his own mortality. 'In case I die in the night.'

In fact Felix loathed writing. Like acting, he thought, it was not a job for a grown man: pretending to be someone else. Unlike acting, it could only be done alone, in an empty room, so it did not even offer the consolation of sociability, though you did get to play all the parts. It was a sick profession; there was no doubt about that. No wonder they all talked about money: it was comforting to pretend to themselves and to others that was why they wrote. Too alarming to admit that they were addicted to sitting alone in a room facing the blank sheet of paper, making up stories about people who did not exist, people who were their other selves whom even the shrink could not tolerate, spinning a web of words from their own entrails until they went mad with the loneliness of it all and escaped to be interviewed on television.

At the same time it was the ideal life. Your time was your own; you were answerable to no one. You had the satisfaction of creation, and your work, when good (or lucky) enough, could keep you in idleness for years. People confided in you and lusted after you, because you had, it seemed, the combined allure of psychiatrist, magician and priest. It amazed Felix that you were not seen instead as someone who had been granted a licence to remain a child for ever, someone to be pitied as well as envied, because only children were allowed to live in a world of make-believe. Felix felt about his profession as he might about a woman he detested but with whom he was violently in love – alternately sickened and thrilled. He saw all writers, especially himself, as social misfits who could only exist in the world by withdrawing from it, as if into a secular monastery, from which they emerged at intervals to be reassured, flattered and paid.

Tony Blythe had come into Felix's life almost by accident. After his first three novels, a university trilogy entitled *Going Up*, *Up and About*, and *Coming Down*, which were praised by the critics and made no money at all, he had come to an end of all possible postgraduate grants, dabbled in journalism, and married Elizabeth, letting her keep him while he wrote *The Heartbreak Merchant*, in which a lot of women fell in love with a man who treated them badly. This made a great deal of money, thanks to the tough bargaining of Felix's agent, Natasha Blor: paperback, American and foreign rights rolled in, and in due course the film, with a script by Felix rewritten by a well-known playwright and further rewritten by the sister of the producer's mistress. The critics all agreed that the book and the film were rubbish, and Felix was suddenly, by his own rather low standards, rich.

He was bemused by the turn of events. He had in fact thought of his first three novels very much as prentice work, salad days produce; but he had poured his soul into *The*

Heartbreak Merchant, which he truly believed was a work of genius, though he agreed with the critics about the film. It was very pleasant to be rich, and for a year or two, or three, he was able to drift along doing interviews and taking expensive holidays and thinking about his next novel, until he finally had to face the fact that he didn't have an idea in his head. Natasha was nagging him, ever mindful of her ten per cent, but Felix felt frozen in his success, like a fish in a block of ice. Everyone now expected more of the same: because he had done it once, he could do it again, that was how the thinking went, which could hardly be further from the truth. He had no idea how he had done it once and there didn't seem the remotest chance of his doing it again. Besides, that was all there was: he had written about himself at university and about his marriage to Elizabeth and about screwing around and about his mother, and that was it. He had done it. Unless his life changed dramatically, there was nothing more to write about. He was a journalist masquerading as a novelist: his style had carried him through, but he had run out of material.

He was then thirty-two and beginning to panic, because he had grown rapidly used to the fruits of success and saw no way of replacing them when they had rotted away. Accustomed to poverty once, he found the prospect of returning to it, after being comparatively rich, quite intolerable. The terrible spectre of job-hunting danced before him: interviews leading to rejection (a blow to the ego) or to acceptance and regular hours (worse). Besides, what was he equipped to do except write or (God forbid) teach others to write? He was virtually unemployable and becoming more so all the time.

'I did like that detective of yours,' Elizabeth said idly one evening when they were watching a thriller on television. 'Much more fun than this lot.'

'Which detective?' said Felix, who had stopped rereading his own work in case it turned out to be not as good as he thought.

'The one in *Heartbreak Merchant*. When she's on drugs.'

'Oh yes. He was rather good.' Felix glanced at Elizabeth affectionately. She had praised every other aspect of the book

53

in immense detail: she must really think he needed cheering up if she resorted to praising minor characters like Tony Blythe. All the same, the idea took root, and next day he looked at one of his many copies of the book and found the relevant chapter. Elizabeth was quite right: Tony Blythe was a sexy, sardonic cop, destined for a book of his own; he had been carelessly tossed into the already rich brew of *The Heartbreak Merchant* back in the golden days when Felix's imagination was fertile enough to be liberal with all his inventions.

He began writing with something like his original excitement. He wanted, while remaining uniquely himself, to achieve a blend of Simenon and Chandler; he wanted also to have fun. It seemed a chance to deal with sex and violence, death and depravity, without incurring disapproval. Tony Blythe, while basically the guy in the white hat, would have endearing human flaws such as a weakness for women and a tendency to thump people he knew were guilty. Felix swiftly got him out of the police force, after he framed some heroin dealers, and into more profitable pastures as a private investigator. Technically it was just as difficult as writing a straight novel, but it had the attraction of novelty and it also spared him from delving too deeply into himself, from being obliged to mine a seam that he feared was exhausted.

Still smarting from the annihilation of his film script, Felix began by having Tony Blythe investigate the murder of a film producer (the greatest problem being the multiplicity of suspects). *Death on the Set* was a success, and Felix, encouraged, killed off his agent, of whom he was actually quite fond, in *The Ten Per Cent Murder*, and moved on to exterminate his obliging bank manager (*Death in the Red*) and his accountant (*Death Ledger*) before turning his attention to his publisher (*Murder Jacket*). Elizabeth then fancied a holiday in France, so Felix wrote *A Nose for Murder* while they disported themselves in Grasse. It occurred to him that Tony Blythe was his passport to anywhere in the world on tax deductible expenses: drilling for oil (*Death Rig*) or lounging in the Caribbean (*Murder Calypso*).

A television series was under way, with scripts written by

Felix, so he and Elizabeth made the decision to live abroad, wherever the fancy took them, away from British taxes and British weather. One or two Tony Blythe books a year was the plan, to finance the gypsy life. Unspoken but heavily present in the air between them was Felix's dream of writing a worthy successor to *The Heartbreak Merchant*, something moving and significant, witty and incisive, a social commentary, a human document. In short, a masterpiece.

Nothing happened. He wrote less and less. They moved from one haven to another, diverted at first by the scenery, the customs, the language, the climate; buoyed up by the effort involved in setting up and dismantling a new home each time. Then they began to quarrel, because they were thrown back upon themselves, marooned in a foreign country without their familiar support system of theatres, cinemas, galleries and friends. They did not trust the natives, who were always so tiresomely foreign, and they did not trust the expats, who were never the sort of English people they would have chosen to know in England. So they clung together like siblings at an alien boarding-school, and inevitably started to fight. This alarmed them because it was not their way; it was not natural to them. They were used to diplomacy and evasion. Now there was nowhere safe to go to relieve the tensions of their relationship: they had not realised before how much they depended upon frequent retreat to achieve close harmony.

They could not discuss this new problem overtly, for they were not programmed for confrontation, but they made discreet sideways movements, crab-like, which they both understood very well, in the direction of England and home, gradually edging nearer as they had originally edged further away, and inevitably ended up in Ireland. Their letters to Helen and Richard were almost a signal of distress, a flare sent up on a dark night over the sea.

Once again in the car on the way home the atmosphere was as highly charged as it had been on the drive back from the disco. He thought it had something to do with the lack of space, with being together in a small dark place and looking out at the lighted world, as if they were in a tent or on a boat. He wanted to talk about something important, so he asked her if she saw anything of her father these days.

'No, I haven't seen him since I was little.' She sounded sad but resigned, as if she didn't expect to see him ever again. 'I often think about him. Sometimes I hear one of his concerts and I try to pretend I can pick him out — you know, I think, now which viola is he? And I sort of imagine he sounds better than the others. It's silly really.'

'Would you like to see him again?'

'In a way. But Mum might feel I was being disloyal and Richard might be hurt. Anyway, I hardly remember him. We might not get on. And now he's got Marsha and all those children, he probably doesn't think about me much.'

Felix said with feeling, 'I should have thought he'd be haunted by you.' At that moment they were driving past his flat and on a sudden impulse he pointed out the building to her. 'That's where I work. Top floor. Why don't you ring the bell one day? Then you wouldn't get that awful machine. I often leave it on when I'm working.'

'All right,' she said, very small, and he felt as if they were conspirators. There was a scent in the car that he now identified as vanilla; whether it was soap or perfume or simply skin, it was the essence of Sally and made him think that kissing her, making love to her, would be like eating ice-cream, a childish, nourishing, exuberant pleasure.

There were lights on in the house when they got back, so he drove past it and parked round the corner. It seemed very dangerous for Richard and Helen to discover them together unless they had agreed to tell the truth. And if they did, that could mean there was no future for them.

'Thank you for dinner,' Sally said, like a well-brought-up child. 'It's been a lovely evening.' But he thought he heard a wistful note of disappointment or even frustration in her voice, and he was pleased. The more he could make her want him and keep her waiting, the less chance there would be of her rejecting him when he made his move; the less blame would attach to him if, God forbid, they were ever found out. It was vital to avoid a situation where he was pursuing her and she had the power: however flattered she might be, that could turn him simultaneously into victim and dirty old man, both unrewarding roles, to be avoided if at all possible.

'It's funny,' he said. 'I feel as if we've only just met.'

'So do I,' Sally said, sounding relieved.

There was a long, tantalising silence.

Felix said, 'Are we going to tell them about this evening?'

'Why not?'

Could she really be so innocent or was she playing with him?

'Sometimes it's nice to have a secret,' he said carefully.

'All right.'

Now it felt like a bond or a pledge: they must be intending an affair or there would be no need for secrecy. He wanted to kiss her but still felt it was too soon and would make him seem like an eager schoolboy. Yet it was important to touch, to put his mark on her in some way, so he stroked her cheek and went on staring at her mouth as they said goodnight. But she looked at him with such longing that he changed his mind and kissed her lightly after all, abandoning his resolution. Her mouth was warm and uncertain; she was trembling and he felt his cock stir. She didn't taste of the vanilla smell, rather of the wine and garlic they had both been consuming, but she felt so new that he was moved almost to tears.

'See you soon,' he said in his sexiest voice, and watched until she reached the house and turned to wave. She's a child pretending to be a woman, he thought, as he drove away; eighteen is very young. He remembered how grown up he had felt at her age and how wrong he had been. No doubt she felt grown up too, and she would be equally wrong. He smiled tenderly to himself, as he tried to imagine what lie she might be telling. The first kiss, the first lie: all the other firsts stretched ahead of them. In a way it was almost a pity to begin. Though sexually impatient, emotionally he enjoyed anticipation as much as recollection. In a love affair or a new book, it was the same: while it was yet to be achieved there was the potential for perfection. And afterwards, you had to accept what you had made, with all its flaws, until enough time had passed for you to reshape it in your memory.

When he got home Elizabeth was alone, watching television and knitting. He was sorry: it would have been an extra pleasure to see Helen.

'Poor old Richard couldn't make it,' he said. 'One of his clients OD'd so I finally made a start on the new book.'

'That's wonderful,' Elizabeth said without looking up.

'Yes, I do feel rather pleased with myself.'

He poured himself a drink and sat beside her on the sofa. He felt comfortable in the warmth and security of knowing she was always there. Later on he would probably make love to her and think of Sally.

Helen hugged him and he showed her Tracey's note: 'Dear Richard, I'm sorry. I know you tried to help me but I don't want to live. Please forgive me. Tracey.' It had proved impossible to contact her parents and he had sat with her till she died. He blamed himself totally. It was his first death.

'I knew she was depressed, of course, but I never picked up it was that bad.'

'How could you?' Helen said, kissing him.

'If I can't do that, I'm useless.'

'But maybe something happened after you saw her. It's not your fault, darling, believe me.'

They heard the front door slam and Sally came slowly into the room.

'Is she all right?'

Richard shook his head.

'Oh God, I'm sorry.'

'I thought you were doing revision tonight,' Helen said, looking at the pink dress.

Sally hesitated. 'I was,' she said, 'but I went out with Chris instead.'

*

Later that week while she still had courage, she rang the bell of the flat. When Felix opened the door he held out his arms as if he had been expecting her and they kissed. She was shaking; she felt she had been waiting for him all her life. It was like coming home, that feeling of safety, of wanting to disappear into the hug, and yet it was also forbidden and dangerous, as if he were a stranger.

'Oh, Sally,' he said, 'you're so beautiful and so young.'

'Please don't send me away.' She pressed her face against his shirt, breathing in the magical smell of him.

'How can I? You don't think I want to, do you? But you know this is crazy.'

She nodded and they kissed for a long time. She felt him harden and press against her, the way Chris had done.

'If they ever find out,' he said, 'they'll kill us.'

'I know.' She was very excited. 'But you said I could just come round and you'd give me lunch.'

He smiled. 'D'you want to go out or stay in?'

'Stay in,' she said. 'Please.'

He stroked her face. 'What have I done to deserve you? I'll be very careful, I promise. You mustn't worry.'

She shook her head. 'It's all right. I've had one lover already and I'm on the pill.' She was afraid it sounded crude, and describing Chris as a lover seemed like an exaggeration, although it was true. 'But if I'd known you were coming back I'd have waited for you.'

'In that case,' said Felix, understanding perfectly, and starting to undress her, 'he doesn't count.'

SUMMER

Sally wanted to know about Elizabeth. As soon as they had finished making love – well, within half an hour or so of what Felix thought of as recovery time, a time he would have liked to prolong, when they let their breathing return to normal, gazed at each other incredulously, stroked sweaty flesh and smoothed tousled hair – Sally came up with a conscience and was asking, 'What about Elizabeth?'

Felix had been prepared for this, of course, but not so soon. He gave his standard reply. 'As long as she doesn't know, she won't be hurt.'

Sally persisted. 'Don't you make love any more?' She sounded as if she expected the answer no.

Felix had not been prepared for such directness. He would not have lied to an adult woman, but he doubted if an adult woman would have asked the question. He wanted Sally both to believe his answer and to feel comfortable with it. If he said he and Elizabeth were like brother and sister, it might sound so convenient as to be implausible, and might also make Sally feel he only wanted her for sex. If he said they made love about once a week, a fair batting average for a middle-aged married couple (more often on holiday, less often when working hard) Sally might feel superfluous, the cherry on the cake of a greedy man. He had only a few seconds to decide and to make his answer sound as natural as the truth.

'Occasionally,' he said. 'But it's not important any more. We're very close, we get on well, we're very fond of each other.' No point in denying what Sally had seen for herself over the last eight years. 'But all that wild feeling we had at the beginning – that's all gone, long ago.'

As soon as he heard his words, he started to believe them: the instantaneous conversion of fiction into truth began. What was more, the words sounded familiar. In his youth he had had a much older mistress who told him a similar story about her husband (as well as teaching him a lot about sexual technique from which he was still profiting). Now for the first time he wondered if she had been lying to him, and he smiled at the memory of his young naive self.

'Why did you never have children?' Sally asked.

The question startled him and he had to think fast: she was too young to understand the truth.

'We both wanted them but Elizabeth found out she couldn't have any. I think that was when she lost interest in making love, though we went on hoping, right up to the menopause. Now it's too late, of course, but we've learned to live with it.'

Sally kissed him. 'Poor Felix,' she said. 'How sad.'

'Lucky Felix,' said Felix. 'Nothing's sad now I'm here with you.'

Sally looked at him in wonder. 'I never thought we would be,' she said. 'Did you?'

'Only in my late-night fantasies,' said Felix. 'Only in my dreams.'

Sally laughed. 'I wonder what Richard and Mum would say.'

Felix considered this nightmare thought. 'Richard might understand,' he said doubtfully, 'but that wouldn't be very much help since Helen would probably kill me. Nothing elaborate. Hanged, drawn and quartered. Dipped in boiling oil. Barbecued on the patio. Just a simple al fresco execution.'

Sally hugged him. He could tell that she relished these dangers from which they were luckily immune. 'Let's protect you,' she said. 'Let's not tell her.'

They lay quietly for a while, contemplating their good fortune.

Sally asked suddenly, 'Have you had lots of affairs before me?'

It was like being pounced on by a kitten that has been lying in wait for you round a corner. 'A few, I suppose,' Felix answered. 'Over the years.' He wasn't sure to what extent his reputation was part of his charm for Sally.

'Mum thinks you've had lots,' Sally said. 'That's why she doesn't approve of you. It's funny because she's ever so broad-minded about other people.'

'Well, she'd never approve of me for you,' said Felix, 'not if I was a saint. I'm too old and I'm married. And she thinks I'm a bad influence on Richard.'

'Nobody could be a bad influence on Richard,' Sally said. 'He's lovely and tolerant but he only ever does what he thinks is right.'

'It's very easy for Richard,' said Felix in a sudden burst of honesty. 'He's had two wives, two sons and a gorgeous step-daughter. He can afford to be virtuous.'

'You sound as if you envy him,' Sally said. 'Do you?'

Felix sensed that the moment was important. 'I think perhaps I used to, but not any more. Not now. Because I'm sure he fancies you but he can never have you. And here you are with me.'

Sally laughed. 'Oh Felix, you are silly. You're not grown up at all, are you?'

'Certainly not,' said Felix.

Felix was secretive because he had learned that sharing a pleasure often dilutes it. In his youth he had succumbed to the human urge to boast, but each time he did so, some of the essence of his current love affair leaked away. He even fancied it was diminished in exact ratio to the number of people he told. The parallel with his work was very marked: the more he discussed a novel, the less he wanted to write it. And so he told no one about Sally.

He preferred not to dwell upon the more urgent but less metaphysical reasons for secrecy: the fact that anyone he knew well enough to confide in, such as Elizabeth, Richard or Helen, would disapprove violently and interfere. He did not wish to see himself as a creature ruled by caution or prudence or even common sense. Had he possessed friends who were both tolerant and discreet, he would still have chosen to hug his happiness to himself.

Sally seemed to him like a miracle. He awoke every morning and remembered her with joyous anticipation, as a child awakens on its birthday. He left the house with a sensation of thrilling unease and hidden wealth, like a man who has swallowed a diamond. The world of popular songs burst upon him again, as if he had been exhumed from the grave. With you I'm born again, they said; you make me feel brand new.

When he looked at Sally's childish face, when he touched her unlined skin, he could believe himself young again, as if her youth were a reflection of his own. He felt he was a better person when he was with her, putting money in collecting boxes and stopping at pedestrian crossings, not just to impress Sally but to express his new-found benevolence. He would have liked the whole world to be as happy as he was, but since that was clearly impossible, he wanted at least to treat the poor, deprived world as gently as he could.

'Why d'you have such a silly car?' Sally asked him when he picked her up from school. 'I practically have to lie on the pavement to get into it.'

'You never complained before.' He accelerated away from the kerb, trying not to run over any little creatures in uniform. The scent of Sally in the car made him slightly dizzy; her long thick straight golden-brown hair that he called an erotic accessory and she kept threatening to cut because (she said) it was old-fashioned; her freckled creamy milk-maid skin that she hated and he called her Tess of the d'Urbervilles look. 'All those times when I hadn't the guts to put my hand on your knee.'

In fact he hadn't desired her then; she was too young and too near home. But it seemed only polite now to pretend. Collecting Sally after dark had been infrequent but routine, a friendly act, if Richard was working late or visiting Inge, if Helen was teaching or at the studio. After all, no one really thought of Felix as having a proper job.

'I don't believe you,' Sally said, surprising him (impressing him). 'I was fat and spotty. But I wish you had, all the same. I'd have been so pleased.'

'But how was I to know that? Me in my silly sports car,

66

symbol of the male menopause, flaunting my lost youth in built-up area. I thought I'd get my face slapped.'

'I always had a crush on you,' Sally said dreamily. 'You dropped your handkerchief once in our garden and I kept it and wore it to school in my knickers for weeks and weeks.'

Felix smiled. 'Good to know I got that close to you. Have you still got it?'

'No, it fell out when I was playing hockey and someone trod on it. It wasn't the same after that. All the magic had gone once I had to wash it.'

Sometimes they couldn't wait until four o'clock to make love and he had to collect her from the school gate at twelve thirty; fifteen minutes to the flat, forty-five minutes in bed, fifteen minutes back to school, hot, dazed, breathless and usually late. 'We'll never get tired of each other, will we?' Sally said. 'We simply won't have enough time.'

He took to arriving at the flat at ten thirty in time for Sally to telephone him at break to make arrangements for the day. The pile of blank A4 mocked him from his desk. 'Call yourself a writer?' it sneered. He didn't care; he felt pity instead of guilt. He had better things to do than write: he was living.

He made coffee and drank it on the terrace if the weather allowed. Waiting for the phone to ring was a peculiarly acute pleasure, like postponing orgasm. The minutes of attentive concentration and the certainty of ultimate delight combined to make him aware of every sound and every sensation around him. Birdsong; the air on his skin; the texture of the chair. At this moment I am fully alive, he thought; sometimes he doubted his sanity. By the time the phone rang he was often afraid of disappointment: no mortal woman could provide the thrill he was expecting, let alone a girl of eighteen. But she never failed him. 'Hullo,' she would say, sounding uncertain as if expecting a wrong number, 'Felix?' And the magic was always there in her voice, warm and full of a sort of nervous confidence that made him feel ashamed because she was so much better than he deserved.

They talked nonsense, lovingly, until the pips went and then he rang her back. They discussed when to meet:

whether at lunchtime or at four o'clock. Sometimes she had extra coaching and had to stay at school. Felix agreed to anything she suggested. He was used to fitting in with married women who had husbands and children to consider; he was adept at accommodating the school run, the au pair's time off, a drinks party, friends for dinner or someone arriving at Heathrow. He had made love in all extremes of ideal and adverse conditions. Nothing deterred him once his heart or his cock was set on a person, so it was no problem to adapt to a schoolgirl's routine.

'Besides,' Sally would tease him, 'we don't want me to fail my exams, do we?' Indeed they did not, but it was more than that. Felix knew he was living on borrowed time, as the phrase went. It was Sally who was doing him a favour, although of course she did not see it like that.

'I love you, Felix,' she always said before she hung up.

'Love you too, my darling. Take care.'

Then he would go to the mirror to study his face. There was no doubt he looked younger, more alert; the lines were smoothed out. His hair looked darker, or the grey was less noticeable. Even his eyes were less shrewd and watchful, more blurred with emotion. He smiled the smile that appeared on book jackets and melted the judgment of women all over the world: he didn't even hate his crooked teeth any more. He just wanted to remember, for future use, what perfect contentment looked like. Because, of course, he never expected it to last.

Sometimes, satiated with Sally, coming home cock-sore with aching balls, he would want to have Elizabeth too, would be consumed by desire for her, excited by the pain in her eyes, the knowledge she would not admit. She never refused him and she always came several times. Often she cried. He held her very close and kissed her tenderly, but they never spoke on these occasions. Felix would feel as if he could fuck for ever: exhausted but insatiable, Sally and Elizabeth merging in his erotic imagination, jet-lagged with sensation like the only man in the world to know about sex because he had invented it, weary and rejuvenated at the same time. But eventually nature would take over, quite suddenly, and he would sleep very soundly indeed, without dreams.

'Darling, I'm going away.' Felix's mother had held his face between her hands and kissed him. 'You must understand. I love you terribly much but I love Martin too, and Daddy won't let me have you both, so I'm going away.'

Felix understood. She loved Martin better than him and it was all Daddy's fault. If he killed Daddy, then he and Mummy and Martin could all live together and be happy for ever. Only he was too small to kill Daddy, and even if he could think of a way, there wasn't time, because Mummy was leaving tonight.

Then he had a brilliant idea.

'Can't I come with you?' he said. It seemed so wonderfully simple. If they all loved each other and Daddy didn't love any of them, what could be more natural? It was the solution to everything. He waited to see Mummy look pleased and relieved, but she frowned.

'Oh, if only you could. But we're going to be travelling. Martin's got no money and we're going to be roughing it.'

Felix liked the sound of that. It would be like camping. All three of them in a tent cuddled up together to keep warm. Breakfast in a blackened frying-pan over a log fire. Washing in a stream, or with a bit of luck not having to wash at all.

'Please,' he said.

Tears came into his mother's eyes. 'Oh darling,' she said, 'don't break my heart.'

('You poor little sod,' said Elizabeth twenty years later.)

('You made that up,' said Helen.)

('If it's what he remembers,' said Richard, 'it's real for him.')

Felix was no longer sure what was real or imagined or what he had reinvented. His mother had left him, that much could be confirmed by lawyers who arranged the divorce, but he had written about their parting so many times in his novels that he could not disentangle their dialogue from fiction. He had become Seriozha, and it was Anna Karenina who kissed and caressed him, who wept over him, who stole into the house with presents when he was asleep. He first read the novel with a sense of shock, as if Tolstoy had stolen his life; then later he wondered if he had appropriated the plot for himself. It certainly impressed female undergraduates and made them more eager to go to bed with him.

That part of it was all right to tell, an interesting sorrow. He never quite managed to get around to telling the later bit, when he went to live with his mother after Martin had left her. She cried all the time and he just held her, in a chair, at the table, on the bed. She cried like someone trying to wash herself empty, and Felix, who was seventeen, did not know what to do. He tried not to leave her alone too much, but he had his school work to do and his friends to see. It would not help, he told himself, if he failed his exams. His father had already refused to give him any money as long as he stayed with his mother, so he needed a scholarship or he could not go to university at all.

His mother had long hair and it clung to him. In the middle of a lesson he would find a piece of it attached to his jacket or his shirt. Her scent was on his body when he got into the bath. In later years he thought he had not had such a physical relationship with anyone else, no matter how much he had fucked them. When he listened to Sinatra singing 'I've got you under my skin' he felt sick with love and loathing and loss. He could not forgive his mother for the day he had come home to find a note: 'My darling boy, forgive me, I have gone to Italy with Luigi.'

Obviously he had left her alone enough. The raddled woman of forty had become a radiant escapee. The family at the delicatessen were equally mystified. They had no idea that Luigi and the signora . . . and they shrugged to prove it.

Felix was shocked by the anger he felt. He wanted to seek his mother out and injure her, kill her slowly, repossess the body that had haunted him through school. Luigi he saw as a mere shadow, a pleasant enough youth, twenty-five maybe, with an ingratiating smile and looks no better, no worse, than the average Italian. It was melodrama, it was farce, and the worst part of it was that his mother had made a fool of him. For this he had left home and his father's money; for this he had hurried back from school; for this he had hugged the sobbing body night after night.

His father would laugh. His father would say it was all his fault and it served him right. His father would say he had seen through his mother years ago and Felix was a fool not to have done likewise. He could not tell his father.

He went on living in the empty flat, alone. One day he took the few clothes his mother had left in the wardrobe and cut them up. Cutting up her clothes gave him an orgasm. He was very frightened.

He passed his exams and went to university without his father's money. His mother wrote to him and said she was expecting a baby. She was very happy and Felix must be happy for her too. He must forgive her and understand. Felix felt he had been doing that all his life. He found he was behaving very badly to several girls at college, who loved him. He was ashamed of himself but he could not stop. Behaving badly excited him. It gave him a sensation of release. He wrote back to his mother that of course he was happy for her and there was nothing to forgive. Of course he understood. He would come out to Atrani in the long vac before the baby was born and be a help to her. He and Luigi would be like brothers.

In June Luigi wrote to tell him that his mother was dead.

It was cold in the studio though the sun shone outside. Helen was desperate to finish the bit of the painting she was working on before the light went, but Elizabeth showed no sign of being ready to leave. Officially only Richard and Sally were allowed in the studio, apart from Magdalen and potential buyers, but at some point in the past Elizabeth had joined the ranks of the privileged few and now she seemed in

71

the mood to abuse her good fortune. It was hell trying to work with someone in the room and ordinarily Helen would have said so, but then ordinarily Elizabeth would have known. Now depression blinded her to everything and also stopped Helen asking her to leave, though it did not prevent her from becoming extremely bad-tempered.

'He's definitely got someone new,' Elizabeth said. She was sitting in Helen's battered armchair and watching Helen work, though Helen knew she did not really see what was going on. The painting she was staring at might as well have been television or wallpaper. Elizabeth was too far sunk in gloom to see anything but the inside of her own head. 'I think it started soon after we came back,' she added, 'but I can't be sure.'

Helen longed to be brutal and say who cares. It was of no interest to her if Felix was fucking every other woman in London provided she was left alone to get on with a painting called *Lust* for a mad American whose money would pay for a new second-hand van. She hated commissions at the best of times and today was the first day the painting had begun to give her anything back: she had just a glimpse of how it might be if she could keep her concentration and not let it slip. Tolerable was how it might be, no more than that, but after the despair and rage she had felt as she wrestled with it in the early stages, tolerable seemed like miraculous. At this point she would settle gladly for anything that would not cause her actual shame. At the same time she made the mental resolution never to accept another commission in the whole of her life.

'Any idea who it is?' she managed to ask.

'No. Somebody's wife, I expect. He usually goes for married women. They know the rules, I suppose.'

'Then you've nothing to worry about.' She thought misery made Elizabeth appear very heavy and lumpen; it was embarrassing to see her like this, like watching somebody ill without their permission.

'I'm so afraid this one's different.'

'You always say that.' How often she had heard the sad repetitive story; only the names were changed.

'Do I? But this one really feels as if it might be serious. He's so nice to me. He keeps buying me flowers and presents and taking me out to dinner.'

'I hope you choose somewhere expensive.' The painting was fading before Helen's eyes, retreating into itself, shutting up shop for the day, even possibly for ever, it was so precariously balanced. Red and black, not colours she usually worked in, with a hint of jagged shark's teeth about it that she was trying to submerge but not to lose.

'And he won't show me any of the book. Usually he lets me read it, bits of it anyway, just to encourage him; he's so used to my being his editor, it's a sort of habit. But not this time,' she ended in a positive howl, as if parted from the Holy Grail.

'Maybe he doesn't need encouragement this time.' God, this was going beyond all the reasonable bounds of friendship.

'But he does, well, he did, he was really frightened of starting. Now he says it's going well but he won't let me see it.'

'Don't you have enough to do editing other people?'

'Not really, I'm only working part-time since we came back. I've been feeling tired, but Felix says it's the menopause, he puts everything down to that.'

If she'd been working full-time she would have been safely in her office at this hour and not in the studio. Silence. A chance to do some last-minute work perhaps? No, a foolish hope.

'I'm so afraid he's letting *her* read it instead of me. Or maybe he's too busy and happy to work. He works best when he's on an even keel, you see. Not ecstatic and not miserable. That's why I'm so good for him. Well, usually. Until he gets bored.'

Next time, Helen thought, I won't answer the door. I'll pretend I'm not here. I'll disconnect the bell. 'Terrific,' she said.

Elizabeth looked at her for the first time. 'You despise me, don't you?'

'Christ, I just hate you to put yourself down, that's all.' Helen gave up and began to clean her brushes, longing to ram them down Elizabeth's throat and up Felix's arse.

73

'I'm not, I'm only being realistic.' A long silence. 'I'm sorry, I'm interrupting and you're really busy, aren't you? I shouldn't have come but I thought I'd go mad if I didn't talk to someone.' She got up and began to roam about the studio. 'Are those your *Seven Deadly Sins*?'

'Yes. I thought I'd try and do them all together, then if I get stuck on one I can go on to the next. Maybe that's what painting by numbers really means.'

Elizabeth actually studied them quite carefully for several minutes. 'They're so different from your other work.'

'If you say you like them better, I'll kill you.'

'Of course I don't, but they're impressive in their own way.' 'Well done.'

'No, I mean it.' Elizabeth stood in front of the black and green one, the one with the eye at its centre, the one Helen disliked most. It was banal. But then envy was banal. It was not a subject she knew much about and she had thought of Inge while she painted it, assuming that was what Inge felt, or was it jealousy; and perhaps simple loathing had made the painting even worse than it might have been, or perhaps even thinking of Inge had put a jinx on it. 'Envy?' Elizabeth said, on a note of enquiry.

'Spot on. I thought I'd keep it simple for him, he's not very bright.' But she knew she had lost when she had to put down someone else to excuse bad work. She wondered if she would have to scrap *Envy* and start again, or if somehow it could yet be rescued.

Elizabeth moved on to the painting Helen disliked least, the one that reminded her of the desert. She had placed horizontal bands of colour, yellow, orange, pink, blue, purple, but very gently, so that they blurred into each other like sky and sand. It could be sentimental but if she got it right it might just work. It was meant to be very pure, both oasis and mirage.

'Sloth?' Elizabeth said.

'Give the woman a prize.'

'It reminds me of "The Lotus Eaters" – you know, the land where it seemed always afternoon.' She was silent for a while. 'They're smaller than I expected.'

74

'The prices he's paying, he can supply his own magnifying glass.'

The other canvases were empty or nearly empty. On the other side of the studio was her real work, neglected, waiting for her to take it up again. Elizabeth stood in front of the red and black painting, the one she had almost ruined with her distress. Helen had to grant that she was doing her best to make amends. She was a friend and she was in pain and she cared about painting, though not as much as she cared about Felix. Helen could feel compulsory forgiveness beginning to seep out of her in Elizabeth's direction.

'This has to be lust,' Elizabeth said.

'Three out of three.' She managed to smile.

'It helps that I can't remember all seven.'

'Nobody can,' Helen said. 'I had to look them up myself. Lust was easy.'

'Yes,' Elizabeth said. 'It always is.'

Elizabeth, adolescent in the forties, was inclined to believe her father when he said that men would not respect her if she gave in to them. After all, he was a man, so he should know. It was only later, comparing notes with her girlfriends, that it struck her as odd that he and not her mother chose to impart this information. It was not even as if she had asked him for it; she went naturally to her mother for advice on emotions and bodily functions. But her mother seemed able to deal only with menstruation and childbirth, and both in a vague and weary manner, as if the effort of remembering either completely exhausted her. If Elizabeth ventured to ask about anything else, anything less clearly linked to physical discomfort in a good cause, anything redolent of pleasure, then her mother would sigh and look honestly baffled as if these experiences had somehow passed her by, as if she had never been out in the real world at all. 'Oh Elizabeth,' she would say, looking not so much embarrassed as bemused, 'you must ask your father about that.'

Elizabeth, of course, did not; but inevitably, within a few

75

days, when her mother was out or resting, her father would come to her and say, in the manner of someone addressing a board meeting, 'Your mother tells me there is something you want to ask me.' The first couple of times this happened Elizabeth was dumb with embarrassment, but her father, clearly well briefed by her mother on whatever the subject was, would happily lecture her on the perils of masturbation or the mechanics of contraception (both, it seemed, were useful for men but unnecessary for women). In later life she wondered if he could possibly have meant what he said, but at the time he seemed amazingly sincere.

She gave up questioning her mother and approached her father directly; he had a knack of rendering anything to do with sex as remote as a geography lesson. She was astonished that he could hold such strong views on something so obviously distant from both of them that all embarrassment vanished. She gathered that she was expected to remain a virgin until marriage and faithful thereafter; that she would be rewarded with children; that her husband might not be entirely monogamous; that her parents would appreciate it if she looked after them in their old age. None of this was linked to any religious influence, for her father was a scientist who prided himself on his rationality, but it might as well have been: the path of duty was as clearly marked as if by some celestial spotlight. She gave up asking questions altogether, of either parent, because there seemed nothing left to ask. Her life was mapped out for her as if predestined; it appeared to have no connection with the plan to achieve a degree in English and a career in publishing, and yet that too was part of her duty, for her parents believed in education and work as they believed in cleanliness and fresh air, as self-evident benefits.

Elizabeth's parents were old by conventional standards (forty and fifty at the time of her birth) so there was every chance of their declining years requiring her attention in the very near future. A heavy burden to place on any young man, she thought, so she lived chastely at first, thereafter as a mistress of married men, tutors at college or colleagues at work. She felt safe: none of them would be volunteering to share the parental burden, which she was sure anyone would find intolerable, so nothing could go wrong. She also discovered the depths of sexual pleasure from which her parents had tried to protect her. It was an amazing revelation, comparable to a religious experience: she had expected something difficult or dull and instead she found a source of easy transfiguring joy. Buoyed up by her discovery, she lived in one room and spent all her money on a housekeeper/nurse for her parents. It seemed cheap compared to the alternative, which was living at home. She visited her parents every day and maintained a radiant calm while her mother sulked and her father complained. She knew she was doing all she could, and they had taught her to be rational, so she refused to let guilt intrude. In later years, looking back, she was impressed by the strength of her own resolve.

'He won't make you happy, I'm afraid,' her mother said when Elizabeth announced she was going to marry Felix. 'I should so like you to be happy, Elizabeth. Your father and I have had such a happy marriage.'

Elizabeth stared at her mother. Nothing about this pale, exhausted, non-communicative person had ever suggested happiness. She did not remember the word being mentioned even by her voluble, authoritative father. She had in fact received mixed messages from her parents: study literature, where all sorts of emotional risks are taken, but lead a careful, blameless life. Vicarious thrills had been the order of the day. It was the first time she had realised they meant that was the way to achieve happiness; she had assumed it led merely to safety, and happiness was irrelevant. It had never occurred to her that for her parents safety and happiness might be the same thing.

She was then thirty-six. Meeting Felix had been a profound shock. Suddenly there was this attractive young man of twenty-five in her office, author of three well-written novels and requiring an editor's help with his fourth. When he smiled at her, she felt all the feelings she had read about. He was amusing, sexy and frivolous: a character straight out of the fiction she had consumed like a drug all her life. He loved her but he would hurt her because he wanted to be free. Here at last was her chance to be Anna Karenina and Madame Bovary and Camille.

It was the end of the sixties. She had watched mini-skirts and free love, the drug culture and flower children. She had tried to join in as well as she could but always with a slight feeling of incongruity, like a maiden aunt getting drunk at a wedding. She was a veteran of many affairs, mostly with safe married men who would not challenge her life as dutiful daughter and efficient editor, but she had never been in love. Felix gave her feelings a violent jolt, as if she had suddenly been plugged into the mains.

Shortly before the wedding she found out that Felix didn't believe in fidelity. She was still in her euphoric state and had made some idle remark about the magnitude of the marriage vows, expecting him to deny it with a compliment. Felix actually laughed.

'Well, if you're idiot enough to take them seriously,' he said, 'you deserve all you get. Not you, darling, other people, I mean. All that rubbish about having no one else till death. It's enough to make you turn up your toes on the spot.'

Elizabeth stared at him. 'How do you mean exactly?' They were in bed at the time, having made love with particular intensity and consumed a bottle of champagne. She couldn't believe what she was hearing.

'Well, imagine. The average couple could be married fifty or sixty years. God. Just imagine fifty or sixty years with only one person.'

'That's what I was imagining,' Elizabeth said. She could feel the happiness draining out of her.

'Well, don't. Why put yourself in jail?' He wrapped his arms round her; his hair felt silky against her breasts. 'The thing is,' he said, 'I don't intend to feel jealousy ever again. It's simply too painful.'

She imagined a beautiful woman betraying and tormenting him. Surely it was impossible: no one could do that to him. 'What happened?' she asked.

'Let's just say I've been inoculated against it.' His face had an unfamiliar shut-down look about it, denying her information. 'You must never leave me,' he said. 'If you leave me, I'll kill you.'

She quite liked the sound of being killed, knowing it would never happen. No one had ever threatened it before: it suggested a depth of passion that belonged appropriately in fiction.

'But you can have lovers,' he went on, 'all the lovers you want, and I won't be jealous, especially if you don't tell me.'

'But I don't want lovers,' she said. 'Are you saying you do?'

'Not yet,' he said, 'but eventually I will. We both will. Everyone does.' He smiled at her, his melting smile that could make her forgive him anything. 'And I'm only twenty-five.'

She waited for him to remind her that she was thirty-six, but he didn't.

Felix met Sally from school after her last A-level. She ran all the way to the car, despite the summer heat that always seemed to accompany exams, books and cribs spilling out of her rucksack, and they hugged and kissed. She hoped everyone saw them.

'How was it?' he asked.

'Dunno. It's just a blur.'

'I remember it well. The human brain can't play and record at the same time. But Japanese technology is probably working on it.'

He always knew how she felt. He understood. Whatever she said, he had been there first and he remembered. He dressed carefully too, casual but smart, not trying to look young and scruffy to match her, but not too formal either. Just looking at him made her ache with love. And to have done her last exams as well. How could she contain such bliss?

'Well,' he said thoughtfully after a final kiss, 'what are we hanging about here for? Unless you want me to rape you in the car.'

'Probably better not. I wouldn't struggle convincingly enough.'

He roared off, accelerating hard, then had to break sharply at the lights. There was a litter bin right beside them and the temptation was irresistible: she dropped the rucksack into it with all its contents, something she had longed to do all her life.

'Sacrilege,' he said lightly.

'Not really. They weren't proper books. Just the ones that get you through exams, God willing.'

Waiting for the lights to change, Felix reached under the seat and produced a bottle of champagne from an ice bucket. She watched, mesmerised, as he started to open it.

'You think of everything.'

'Glove compartment.'

She opened it and found two glasses.

'They were just notes and cribs and junk like that,' she said, glancing from rucksack to champagne and back again. 'Honest, guv. And I'll never need them again. I'm free.'

The cork popped just as the lights changed. How could it be otherwise when this was her day and they were together? He handed her the lightly foaming bottle and drove off.

Felix was almost asleep. There was something about making love in the afternoon that met all his requirements: he was not stupefied from a night's sleep, with a lively cock but his brain out of gear, nor was he exhausted from a day's eating and drinking and television. Work had been done in the morning and more might be done before dinner. Meanwhile it was perfect stolen time. Outside in the world other less fortunate people were engaged in boring routine tasks and here he was, blissful, off duty, totally relaxed. He never did really sleep at these times, or perhaps he was not sure if he did or not, but it felt like a kind of sublime doze that could refresh him magically without ever quite making him lose consciousness.

Sally said, 'I'd like to stay here for ever.'

He smiled. 'People might talk.' He could feel her studying him through his closed eyes.

'Why does anyone bother with drugs when they can have this?'

'I'd like to think I'm addictive. But not deadly, of course. Quite the reverse.'

She kissed him in various places. That took a long time. 'It just gets better and better,' she said with a deep sigh of satisfaction, as if worn out by so much pleasure. He was indeed impressed by her orgasmic capacity: at the beginning it had taken them a little while to find the right places because she had got into the habit of pretending with that silly young Chris, but once found they could not be lost and seemed inexhaustible. A triumph, he thought happily, for both of them, particularly considering how high their expectations had been. It would have been easy to be subtly disappointed and afraid to say so.

'Let's say you bring out the best in me,' he said, and they laughed. Red afternoon light danced behind his eyelids.

'You won't get bored with me, will you?' she said in an anxious voice. 'Promise you won't?'

'How could I?'

'That's all right then.' Now she sounded like a child, simply reassured that a beloved father would not leave her. And like a child, she was easily distracted. 'Did we finish the champagne?'

'There should be a couple of glasses left.' He opened his eyes, leaning over the edge of the bed to find the bottle on the floor and pour out the remainder, predictably a little less than expected. 'Well, nearly. They seem to be making the bottles smaller these days. It must be something to do with the Common Market.'

She didn't smile; it was not her sort of joke. Elizabeth would have actually laughed. He supported her head with one hand and held the glass to her lips with the other. The gesture, one of his favourites, much appreciated by older, married women and often remarked upon, was simply

81

accepted: she did not know there was any other way to drink champagne in bed. She drank greedily, treating it like lemonade. Later when she got up she would be surprised to find herself thirsty and would drink glass after glass of cold water from the kitchen tap. There was an obscure delight for him in having so many of his courtesies taken for granted. He watched her drink, studying the freckles on her champagne-wet lips, the down on her cheeks still flushed from good sex; he breathed in the vanilla smell of her skin mixed with sweat and semen and some new expensive scent he had bought her recently.

'Have you thought any more about our weekend?' she asked, as he took the empty glass away and drank from his own.

'We might be able to manage it when I go to the crime writers' conference.'

'Oh Felix! Could we really?' She flopped back on the bed, a big childish grin of delight spreading over her face. 'I do so want to spend the night with you. It's too long to wait till I go to college. I hate getting dressed and going home all the time. I want to go to sleep with you there and wake up with you there. I've never spent the night with anyone. Can you imagine?'

'I may snore,' he said reluctantly. 'Elizabeth says I do.' It seemed politic to slip her name into the conversation every now and then.

'I won't notice. I'll be asleep. Can we pretend to be married?'

'Why not?' But a small inner voice whispered it would be unlucky.

'Oh Felix, won't it be fun? Will you get me a ring?'

'Of course.'

'I don't mean an expensive one.'

He kissed her then and that took a while. 'It's all right, my darling. I'd love to buy you something pretty. The hotel won't give a damn if we're married or not, but we'll enjoy pretending.' He stifled the small inner voice. It was just a game. What harm could it possibly do? But it was not something he usually did. It was a concession to her youth, a romantic gesture outside his normal pattern, a daring V sign at fate. 'Have you any idea what a miracle you are?' he asked her. 'No, of course you haven't. Silly question.'

'I just love you,' she said, watching him with large, clear eyes. 'That's all.' Sometimes the sheer simplicity of her took his breath away.

'I must have been very good in a previous incarnation.'

Richard tried to be impartial, but found it impossible not to have favourite clients, and Ben was one of them. His offences were so petty and foolish, and he was full of good will. It was useless trying to get information out of him, though. He operated on charm, and information was incidental. Richard admitted to himself that he was susceptible to Ben's charm but he also knew the court might well not be.

'Why d'you do it?' he asked.

'I needed some money,' Ben said simply, as if he had just cashed a cheque.

'So you grabbed a chain round someone's neck at the unemployment office. Didn't you think you'd get caught?'

'No. I thought I'd get away. But I slipped.' He gave Richard one of his sudden big grins and Richard couldn't help smiling back. The image of Ben, gold chain in hand, running off and skidding on the polished linoleum was too much for him.

'How would you feel if someone did that to your girlfriend?' he asked, trying another approach.

'She doesn't wear gold chains.'

'Or to you?'

'I'd hit back.'

The phone rang. Richard answered it and dealt with arrangements for a client who might or might not be willing to go back into a psychiatric unit.

'Ben, you're not helping yourself much,' he said when he hung up, 'and you're certainly not helping me. I wrote a glowing report for you when you nicked that answering machine from the community relations office, which was a

83

bloody stupid thing to do, and now you go and do this while you're still on probation.'

Ben nodded and looked sheepish, but Richard felt it was just an act, designed to please, one of Ben's games.

'I mean if you go on like this,' he said, trying to toughen up, 'you'll get put away, and how's Lucille going to cope if you're inside when she has the baby?'

'Yeah, I know,' Ben said, looking contrite. 'Only we can't manage on the money, see We only get twenty-one quid each.'

Well, there was no answer to that. It would be simpler really to hand Ben a fiver as soon as he came in and skip the interview.

'I know it's very difficult. But this sort of thing makes it worse, don't you see that?'

No answer. He felt in Ben's silence the knowledge that he had a job and Ben didn't.

'Look, try your best,' he said hopelessly, 'and when you see your brief, tell him I said it would help if he can get your case listed for later, it'll give you time to do more community service. And get a TV licence or they'll do you for that.'

Another big grin. 'Don't need one, my telly got stole. Someone tief my telly.'

The door opened suddenly and Marion put her head round it. Richard felt his customary wave of anger that she should behave as though seniority gave her the right to dispense with knocking. 'Oh sorry, Richard,' she said, seeing Ben and smiling her usual cheerful, resolute smile. 'I'll come back another time.'

'It's all right,' Richard said, 'we're just finishing.'

'Oh, good.' She came in and directed her smile at Ben, who Richard knew was not one of her favourite people. 'Hullo, Ben. And how are you today?'

'OK,' said Ben happily, oblivious of likes and dislikes. 'Cheers, Richard.' He went out and Marion seated herself in his chair.

'Is he in trouble again?' she asked.

'Just a little.'

'Oh dear. They never learn, do they?'

'They?' Richard wondered if Marion was colour prejudiced. Could it be that simple?

'You mustn't let these trivial cases get you down, Richard. Not with the inquest coming up.'

'I don't see Ben as a trivial case. I don't see anyone like that. He can't find work, he can't manage on the dole, so he turns to petty crime. If he gets done for burglary his girlfriend could wind up alone with the baby.'

Marion recrossed her legs, thick in tweed stockings. 'Yes, it's very sad, but they've really no business to be having a baby when they can't support one. It's very careless of them.'

'It's very much a wanted baby. I think it's the one bright spot in their lives.'

Marion smiled her maddening smile, loaded with sweet reasonable logic. If you listen to me with an open mind, you will end up agreeing with me, said the smile. 'Yes, but they can't afford it, can they? Babies are a luxury, as you and I well know. And I wonder how hard they've tried to find work. Some of these people really seem to expect the state to do everything for them. It's so bad for their morale.'

'So is living in a bedsit with water running down the walls.' Uneasily, Richard remembered having heard some of Marion's views expressed by Helen. 'What did you want to see me about, Marion?'

'I was wondering if you've had any more thoughts about the inquest. What you're actually going to say when they ask you why Tracey killed herself. Your professional opinion, I mean.'

Richard was profoundly irritated at the implication that they should cook up some acceptable statement between them. 'Professional, personal, what's the difference? She was bloody depressed about having her baby adopted, so she stole one from a pram, got probation, and I failed to pick up how desperate she felt.'

Marion pursed her lips. 'You're not actually going to say that, are you?'

'Say what?'

'The bit about failure.'

'Why not? It's the truth.'

Marion looked at him indulgently, as if he were a well-meaning child who had got things slightly wrong. 'We're not always objective about ourselves though, are we, Richard? I'm sure you did your best. And the press are so quick to throw stones, we really don't need to help them. How will it look if you rush into court so eager to take the blame? For all we know, poor Tracey may have been very unstable. She might have killed herself anyway, no matter what you said or didn't say.'

'She was eighteen,' Richard said, outraged, thinking of Sally.

'Yes, it's a very unstable age. Didn't we all play with the idea of suicide then? What I'm anxious to avoid, Richard, is the sort of thing the gutter press loves: "Yet Another Social Worker Gets It Wrong." '

In meetings Marion was fond of saying they were a team, that a chain was only as strong as its weakest link. Richard gazed at her without replying.

Eventually, reluctantly, they dragged themselves up and began to turn the bed back into a sofa. It was, Felix thought, the nearest they would ever get to domesticity together and was oddly touching.

'You know, I'm actually going to miss school,' Sally said.

'*What?*'

'Oh, not like that. Just the way it fitted in with us. Sitting there in class and knowing I had a secret. Ringing you up at break and arranging when to meet. Showing off to everyone when you picked me up in the car. It's been such *fun.*'

'Waiting for you to phone was quite amazing too. I actually didn't want you to ring sometimes, so I could go on looking forward to it, and yet I couldn't bear to wait another minute, in case I exploded. A bit like wanting to come and wanting to put it off a bit longer.'

They smiled at each other across the sofa bed, two people secure in the knowledge that they had invented sex. He caught her looking uncannily like Helen, an extra pleasure for him. Helen whom he would never have.

'Sometimes I feel so happy I think I might burst,' she said matter-of-factly. 'Aren't you amazed they haven't noticed?'

'Thank God they haven't.' Surely that wasn't disappointment he heard in her voice.

'But it's so obvious, how can they miss it? I feel I'm all lit up like a Christmas tree when I go in the door. Are they *blind*? But Mum only thinks there's some boy at school and Richard's too busy to notice anything.'

'Hiding something in plain view, that's the secret,' Felix said firmly. 'Put your precious object in an obvious place and nobody spots it. Like concealing the stolen diamonds in the chandelier.'

'I do worry about Elizabeth though.' The name fell between them like a gauntlet. It sounded different when Sally used it. More of a challenge. 'She's so nice and I'd hate her to be hurt.'

'As long as she doesn't know, she can't be hurt,' Felix said, uneasy. 'Don't worry, my love.'

'But she'll have to know some time. Won't she?'

Now what was all this? 'Don't think about it now. You've got three years at college first.'

'You won't find someone else, will you?'

'How could I? You're the one. You'll meet someone your own age and forget about me.'

'Don't say that, you know I won't. They're all so boring compared to you. Please, Felix, don't ever say that again. It really hurts.'

He promised.

She tried to explain to Maria about the holiday, but Maria was angry and didn't understand. 'God, Sally, it's only a month and I was looking forward to it.'

'I know. So was I. I'm sorry.'

'Forget it.'

'You know I'd like to come, I always love it, but –'

'It's all right,' Maria said.

'It's not though, is it?'

They stood with their noses against the wire fence watching Jackie play tennis with two boys and another girl. Wimbledon always inspired her.

'Just don't let him hurt you, that's all,' Maria said angrily.

'He won't,' Sally said, surprised. 'He loves me.'

'Oh, Sal.' A sudden fierce hug. 'Be careful.'

'I am. You know I am.'

'I don't mean that.'

Later in the pub she had to sweet-talk Jackie.

'But you always go to Cyprus.'

'Yes, I know.'

'She must be awfully disappointed.'

'She is and I'm sorry, but I can't help it. Don't you give me a hard time as well.'

'God, he's really turned your head,' Jackie said, looking at her as if she were a freak.

'What d'you mean? I just want to be with him, that's all. What's so terrible about that? You want to be with Pete, don't you?'

'It's a bit different.'

'Why? Just because he's older, is that what you mean?'

'Oh Sal, leave it out.'

'That is what you mean, isn't it?'

Jackie lit a fresh cigarette and blew smoke over Sally. 'I don't know why you need the aggravation, his wife and all that, when you could have a holiday instead. He'll still be here when you get back. Probably do him good if you go off somewhere. Make him keener.'

'I don't want to be apart from him for a single day,' Sally said. She thought the simple truth might reach Jackie somehow. But she only stared.

'Blimey, you've got it bad.'

Well, there was nothing for it but the direct approach. 'Jackie, can I come to Aldeburgh with you?'

Jackie looked thoroughly amazed. 'But I'm going with Pete.'

'I know, I'm sorry, but I've got to have a weekend with Felix and we can't both get back at the same time. If I tell Mum I'm staying with you for a week she won't worry.'

Silence from Jackie. The whole trip hung in the balance.

'I'll go out a lot,' Sally said urgently. 'I'll wear ear plugs. I'll keep my eyes shut.'

Felix had to admit that Richard was the better squash player. He had to use quite a lot of guile to beat him these days. He supposed Richard's lifestyle was healthier, less hedonistic; or else it was sheer adrenalin from the Marion conflict that raised his game. Afterwards they went for a drink in the bar and Richard told him the story again. He half-listened, reflecting that he had had a near perfect day and there was still dinner with Elizabeth to come.

'She's a miserable cow, that Marion,' he said when Richard paused. 'Probably needs servicing.'

Richard smiled. 'She's got a perfectly nice husband, oddly enough.'

'Well, he won't be giving her one, will he? Not if he's got any sense.'

'And two perfectly adjusted children. Not a hint of rebellion there. It's sickening.' They both laughed. 'Oh, she means well, of course. She's one of the old school. The poor should be grateful and deserving. The rich should be kind but firm. And the state shouldn't interfere too much. Country going to the dogs. Bring back national service. All that.'

It didn't sound too unreasonable to Felix. Why else did he pay tax? But it wouldn't be tactful to say so. Not now. 'Maybe they'll promote her out of your area,' he said. 'Too much to hope she might get the sack, I suppose?'

'Oh, she's very efficient. I just wish she didn't make me feel eleven again, waiting to see Matron for castor oil.'

'That bad, eh?'

Richard said with enthusiasm, 'I have fantasies about cutting her up into very small pieces but I think I'm probably over-reacting.'

'Sounds to me as if you need a holiday.' He didn't know how Richard stood it, the case load, the long hours, the problems, endlessly fighting the system for ungrateful moronic clients with a death wish. 'But I like this violent streak smouldering away under your calm exterior. It's good stuff. You're a bit like a dormant volcano, aren't you, Richard? Who knows when you might erupt? Play your cards right and I might slip you into my next Tony Blythe.'

Richard warmed to his attention. 'Surely you've noticed before that I have homicidal tendencies?'

'Now and then. There were a few times I thought Inge mightn't live to reach the divorce courts and you might end up in one of your own jails. Quite a good twist that would have been. Bit rough on Helen though.'

'She'd have masterminded my escape,' said Richard, enjoying the fantasy. 'The file in the cake. The getaway car behind the wall. Hey' – and he paused, the idea clearly visible in his open face – 'I suppose we couldn't get away together – just a short break? I might be able to manage a few days when you go to Cambridge on your crime trip. Be nice to see the old place again.'

Felix felt a beast to refuse, yet he also noted the negative way Richard put the suggestion, as if his whole life was geared to refusals. Really, his expectations must be very low. 'Sorry. It's a great idea but –'

'You have other plans.' He sounded disappointed but not surprised.

'Well, I do have a little friend there and I promised I'd look her up. You know how it is.'

'I do indeed.' Richard looked admiring and stoical. 'Never mind. I can't really spare the time anyway. And I'm probably only chasing my lost youth.'

Felix had always been a magic person for him, arriving at Cambridge with a secret sorrow, something to do with death and divorce and his mother, a story no one ever got quite clear, a tragedy with strong sexual overtones. Felix had drifted around in voluminous Byronic shirts, affecting a Byronic limp, seducing every woman who crossed his path if he considered her beautiful enough, drinking too much, failing to work, sleeping all day and screwing all night, yet still now and then turning out brilliant essays. Felix embodied all the romantic chaos Richard had read about and dreamed about: Felix could break all the rules and get away with it while he, Richard, had to go on being responsible because he was set that way, like cement. He could hardly believe that this careless, glamorous person was to be his friend; he feared that every invitation would be his last, yet knew that too much humility and gratitude would be fatal. Felix needed him: his solid values were like firm earth in which Felix could plant his rockets before lighting the blue touch paper and failing to retire.

Felix's friendship seemed to Richard a vindication of his own character, a sense of self esteem painfully maintained in the face of his mother's clearly expressed preference for his younger brother. Whatever his brother did wrong was excused or transposed into virtue, while Richard's achievements were ignored or taken for granted. It made sense: his brother was better looking and more fun, rather like Felix, in fact, but he did not have a friend like Felix. That privilege belonged to Richard, and it proved that he was not as dull as his mother thought. Or possibly it proved that she was right to prefer her other son. Once Richard had Felix as a friend, he understood his mother's partiality for his brother and ceased to blame her for it. He even became quite fond of his brother.

His mother had hardly appeared to notice the death of his father, which left Richard the unwilling head of the household, but she never recovered when his brother emigrated to New Zealand, unable to bear the burning heat of her affection at first hand any more. She seemed to blame Richard for his departure and she went into the kind of mourning that Richard associated with Queen Victoria when she lost Albert. It made another bond with Felix, the lone mother and the lone father, parents bereaved by death and divorce, parents at odds with their sons, parents who needed comforting, parents who had never grown up. It made Felix more than ever his opposite and his twin, a mirror image of himself. They were light and dark, yin and yang, good and evil: put together, Felix said, laughing, they would make up a whole person.

When Inge came into his life, Richard discovered sexual obsession. Even though it was the sixties, allegedly an ideal time to be young and free, he had never been much good at casual sex because he worried about hurting other people's feelings and, to a lesser extent, his own. All that dangerous activity was better left to Felix, who either managed to stay friends with women whose hearts he had broken or simply didn't care if they were left bitter and wounded. Richard didn't really approve of Felix's behaviour, but he admired the way Felix seemed to raise irresponsibility to the level of an art form. Never having managed to be irresponsible himself, Richard found it a thrilling quality to observe in his friend. He worried sometimes that the vicarious pleasure he took in Felix's affairs was positively unhealthy, but there wasn't much he could do about it: it seemed to be addictive, like a drug. Felix claimed to find the same fascination in Richard's moral rectitude, though Richard privately doubted this. He thought it more likely that Felix enjoyed having an adoring audience and he was content to provide one. He found Felix so attractive and charismatic himself that it seemed only natural that vast numbers of other people should fall in love with him, that he should operate under a special dispensation, that the ordinary rules of conduct should not apply to him.

Richard was engulfed by Inge's passion for him: he was amazed that anyone could feel so strongly about him because it had never happened before. If this was how love affairs felt, no wonder Felix liked having so many of them. The foreignness of Inge was an added attraction, making her mysterious and dark. They would never speak the same language, no matter how fluent they each became in the other's: they would have no common ground. Their child-hoods would forever contain different points of reference and their memories would be alien. It excited him uncontrollably to merge himself with this strange, exotic person and it seemed appropriate that much too soon their half-hearted attempts at contraception resulted in a pregnancy. Such violent feelings were meant to bring forth life. When Felix suggested abortion, Richard quarrelled with him, briefly, for the first time. And yet he knew at some level that he and Inge were much too young to marry, that they were bound to change, that they would wear each other out. He had been deeply flattered that she loved him so much because no one else had done so and it seemed to validate his existence, but gradually he became afraid of the way she sank deeply into him and seemed to suck out his very soul. There was no refuge from her: wherever he went to retreat, she would find him out. She had an inexhaustible appetite for sex, conversation, affection and companionship that left him searching desperately for hidden reserves where he might find something more to give her, yet he knew it would never be enough.

Sally waited until she was helping Helen with supper. It was easier to talk while scraping a carrot, her head bent over the sink. 'I thought I'd go and stay with Jackie when we break up,' she said casually. 'Just for a week.'

'Well, if that's what you want.' Helen sounded surprised. 'Beats me how anyone could prefer a week in Aldeburgh to a month in Cyprus.'

'Oh . . . there's a job going at Tesco. I could do with some money for clothes when I go to college.' She paused, looking for a more clinching argument. 'You should be glad I won't be asking you for the air ticket.'

'You deserve a nice holiday,' Helen said warmly. 'You've worked hard. Much harder than I thought you would.'

'I want to do well. You know. Get the right grades. Make you proud of me and all that.' Was she overdoing it?

'I'd rather you wanted to do it for yourself.'

There was no pleasing her. 'Well, both.'

Silence. Then: 'Sally, I don't want to pry, but if there's some boy you're keen on and he's going to be in Aldeburgh too – you won't forget about contraception, will you?'

Sally felt herself squirming. It was such an intrusion on her time with Felix. She was still wet with him, could still smell him on her skin, feel him touching her, reverberating inside her, and Helen was trespassing on sacred things. 'Oh Mum, you're always going on about that.'

'Not so. I've mentioned it maybe twice a year since you were fifteen. Be criminal not to mention it at all, even if I do embarrass you. I know it's very private but it still has to be said.'

'Well, you've said it. I know all about it, thanks.'

'And there's also VD and –'

'I'm not an idiot.'

'All right, I'll shut up. Just promise me you'll go to the clinic if you haven't already, and I'll never mention it again.'

'It's a deal.' She chopped the carrot savagely, overjoyed to hear the sound of a key in the front door. 'There's Richard.'

'For this relief much thanks,' said Helen drily.

Richard came in. He smiled at Sally and kissed Helen. 'Sorry I'm late. I had a couple of drinks with Felix.'

Sally was careful not to react.

'How was he?' Helen asked without interest.

'Oh, he seemed in pretty good form. How was your day? How are the *Seven Deadly Sins* coming along?'

'Rather slowly. I had Elizabeth crying on my shoulder. She thinks Felix is playing around again. I do feel sorry for her but hell, it's monotonous, she's such a victim, and I really wanted to work.'

Sally didn't want to hear about Elizabeth's pain. Felix would be home with her now, having supper, being nice. Not telling her the truth. How angry Mum and Richard would be if they knew. What a monumental crisis she could make with just one careless word. The knowledge made her feel dizzy, powerful and helpless at the same time. She held the key to all their futures and she dared not use it. Not yet, anyway. Instead she hung on to the thought of Cambridge, like a talisman.

'I'll lay the table,' she said. She was sick of being good and helpful, but that was what they both expected of her, for ever more, it seemed. That was how it had always been.

*

Helen was nearly asleep, but Richard was still talking about Tracey.

'She'd still be alive if she'd been allowed to keep the baby. If we'd all given her more support. We should have helped her keep it, helped her look after it.'

Helen usually listened when he wanted to talk about work, but she also encouraged him to switch off, for his own sake as much as hers, feeling it was not always good for him to bring the problems of the day home with him. Tonight was difficult. *Lust* and *Envy* swam in her head to the sound of Elizabeth's sad voice mixed with Sally's peculiar plans for a summer holiday. It was hard to focus on Richard's words, hard to believe that he was seriously suggesting a girl of eighteen should have been encouraged to have and keep a baby. Eighteen was hardly more than a child.

'Or helped her get an abortion,' she said, yawning.

'No. I don't believe that's the answer.'

Oh well. It was an old familiar argument, a bit of pointless idealism left over from Richard's youth. She attributed it to his Catholic upbringing, although he always insisted he had left all that behind at university. Helen thought it went too deep ever to be totally discarded, but she generally tried to keep off the subject.

'I do. I've been a single parent. I know what it's like.'

Felix and Elizabeth lay back to back. Felix wanted to get to sleep before he had to admit to himself that he had had one brandy too many and might be in for a restless night, but Elizabeth wanted to talk. He could feel her thinking: the tension in her back betrayed her. He braced himself for a conversation. It was essential to maintain a sleepy voice to keep it short.

'Shall I come with you to Cambridge?' she finally said.

'Oh darling . . . I'll be working all the time. You'd be bored. And I want to do some research.'

'Yes, of course,' she said, heavy with disappointment. 'It was just an idea.'

95

'It was a lovely idea. But I've got a better one. Let's go back to Venice in the autumn. Would you like that?'

'I'd love it.'

'Good. That's settled then.'

He always bribed her with Venice when things got sticky. It hardly seemed to matter if they actually went or not. It was just a convenient way of reaffirming love. But tonight it didn't quite work. He could feel the slight tremor in her body that meant she was starting to cry. But since she had chosen to do it silently, he felt entitled to pretend he hadn't noticed.

On the morning of the holiday Richard insisted on taking her to the station. She thought she had talked him out of it the night before, saying she wouldn't be ready in time, but after breakfast he shouted up the stairs to her, 'Come on, Sally, if you want a lift.'

She shouted back, 'It's OK, I'll get the tube.' She felt extremely harassed by his solicitude. Why couldn't he leave her alone? She had finished packing but she was still sorting the contents of her big everyday handbag into a smaller, smarter one and she found it very distracting to be shouted at. Felix was right: it would be a relief to get away from home and all this interference. Now that escape grew closer she could afford to admit how much she longed for it. To be left in peace. Not to be nagged about tidying her room or playing music too loud. Not to be asked where she was going or what time she'd be back.

But he wouldn't give up. 'Don't be daft,' he yelled up the stairs. 'I'm going right past the station.'

She gave up. He was obviously determined to do her a good turn and it wasn't worth making a fuss. She longed to swear at him, to shriek abuse, thinking how surprised he'd be, but instead she grabbed the suitcase and bag and set off obediently down the stairs.

'Have fun, take care,' said Helen, giving her a hug and looking critically at her clothes.

God, why did they all have to treat her like a child? She got in the car beside Richard in a foul temper and sulked determinedly for most of the journey. Fortunately he never talked much in the mornings and she had to admit to herself that a lift was convenient, but it wasn't worth having to leave in a hurry and all the anxiety that somehow he would stop in the wrong place and run straight into Felix and his car. It spoiled the trip before it had even begun, and she wanted everything to be perfect.

By the time they reached the station she was very tense, almost looking over her shoulder, as Richard got her suitcase out of the boot.

'Have a good time,' he said, kissing her goodbye. 'Don't forget to phone.'

'Don't fuss.'

He raised his eyebrows slightly, which meant he was annoyed. 'Thanks a lot. I should have let you get the tube.'

Yes, you bloody should, she thought. 'I'm sorry. Of course I'll phone. I always do.'

She watched him drive off, just to be sure, before she ran through the station and out again into the side street where Felix had said he would park. Her heart was pounding with tension and rage and at first she couldn't see the car. What if something had happened and he couldn't get away? What would she do? Then she saw him waving at her.

'Darling, you're shaking,' he said as she got in and they had a long embrace.

'Richard gave me a lift.'

'What a good thing we arranged to meet here, not closer to home.'

'Yes. And I thought you were crazy suggesting it.'

'The practised criminal always sticks as close to the truth as he can.'

She didn't altogether like his flippant tone but it did calm her down. 'It was awful. I was so afraid he'd see your car. I actually snapped at him and he snapped right back.'

'Richard's a very angry person,' said Felix, sounding pleased.

'But he hardly ever loses his temper.'

'That's what I mean.'

Gradually she began to relax. Once they were out of London the flat open country with its peculiar light soothed her. After a while Felix stopped and took a small box out of his pocket.

'Knew I'd forgotten something.'

She opened it and found a narrow wedding ring of twisted gold. He put it on for her and it fitted perfectly. How did he manage to get these details right? She nearly cried, and they kissed until he said they had better drive on or they'd have to make love in the car. For the rest of the journey she watched the sun glinting on the gold, narrowing her eyes and moving her fingers to make it flash. She'd never had anything gold before. It looked so delicate. It was exactly what she would have chosen. She thought how carefully she would have to hide it until she went away and could wear it all the time.

The beauty of Cambridge startled her as they drove in. She had only seen it in films before. The hotel was breathtaking, too, right on the river. He hadn't prepared her for that, but she could see how her pleasure delighted him. She was never sure if she preferred looking forward to things or being surprised, and somehow he always managed to give her both, as if he understood the dilemma.

She felt conspicuous at the reception desk and hung back rather, admiring the calm way he dealt with everything, though it did make her think briefly of how often he must have done it before. Never here, she hoped, but decided it would be better not to ask, just in case she didn't like what she heard.

Their room was large with a big double bed, TV, *en suite* bathroom and a terrace overlooking the river. She went around opening doors and exclaiming, then they spent some time kissing and hugging and admiring the view. It felt very wicked and grown up.

'Isn't it wonderful?' she said. 'I do love hotels.'

He asked how many she had stayed in, knowing the answer.

'None. We always rented cottages or barges, it was cheaper. So I'm a real expert.'

He said seriously, 'Yes. It's just the way it ought to be,' and she knew they were going to have a wonderful time. They shared a sense of occasion. The place was magic and they both knew it.

Having the whole weekend ahead of them was such an extraordinary treat that it even took away the normal urgency to make love at once. Instead they decided on lunch and sightseeing. Time would stand still until they got to bed. Like the school holidays, the first night of a weekend like this could be postponed or prolonged almost indefinitely. If they didn't begin it, then it couldn't be over. They were waiting to unwrap a parcel and they could put it off as long as they liked.

Somehow over lunch she found herself talking about Helen.

'I know it sounds funny but I always felt sort of responsible for her, as far back as I can remember. As if she couldn't cope and I had to look after her.'

'How very uncomfortable.'

'Yes, it was.'

He poured some more wine. 'I felt a bit like that about my mother too.'

'Oh, Felix.' She was always amazed how he understood everything she said from first-hand experience. It was still a shock that he was every bit as wonderful as she had thought he would be. 'We do have a lot in common, don't we? The mother in *The Heartbreak Merchant* – was it all true?'

He nodded and she saw the pain in his face. She held his hand across the table. 'I thought so. What a shame.'

'Oh, I survived.'

Now he was being brave, pretending it wasn't as bad as it was. She knew that one too. She kissed his hand.

'I felt with Mum that she was trying so hard to be strong, I mustn't add to her troubles. It was odd. As if I had to be good all the time.'

99

'Have you ever told her that?'

'Oh no, I couldn't. It would sound like whingeing. She did her best. It was really hard for her trying to support herself and me by painting and teaching – well, nearly impossible. I don't know how she did it.' She thought back for a moment. 'God, it was cold in the studio. We lived there for years. We had paraffin heaters and we had to wrap blankets round our legs. She actually had to paint in gloves sometimes.'

Felix said, 'You love her very much, don't you?'

'Yes, of course. She's funny, she kind of makes you love her. But I get very angry with her sometimes.'

In the afternoon they roamed round the colleges like tourists.

'It's so beautiful,' she said, marvelling at it all, feeling actual tears in her eyes. 'It's even better than I imagined.'

Felix looked pleased, as if he were personally responsible. 'Yes, it is pretty good. It's nice there are still places that live up to their reputations. Venice is another.'

'I wish we could go there together,' she said quickly, excited by the idea.

'Maybe we will some day.' But he didn't elaborate. 'Byron was an undergraduate here, I think.'

'You're a bit like Byron, aren't you?'

'Minus the limp.' He laughed. 'Maybe I should try it. Might get a bit more attention.'

'You're getting quite enough, I think.'

They strolled on, arms round each other, enjoying the sunshine.

'Oh, this is so lovely,' Sally said rapturously, wondering at the same time if she was being too enthusiastic. Did it make her seem gauche and silly? 'I want to do all the traditional things, like going in a punt and having tea at Grantchester. Can we?'

'Whatever you like, my darling. Provided someone else does the actual punting. I'm a bit out of practice and I don't fancy getting stuck on the end of a pole.'

It was a lovely mental picture. 'If you fell in, I could save you. I'm a good swimmer.'

'Yes, you'd like that, wouldn't you?'

'Or I could hold your head underwater till you promised to love me for ever.'

'You don't need threats to make me do that.'

They kissed and suddenly it was all very serious.

'Felix. What's going to happen if I go to Sussex?'

'Well . . . you're going to have a wonderful time with lots of young men chasing you and I'm going to be very jealous.'

'No, I'm serious.'

'So am I.' He held her face in his hands.

'I mean how often are we going to be able to meet?'

'Well, not as often as now, obviously. But I'll drive down for the day whenever I can, and you'll be coming home for the weekend now and then, won't you?'

It didn't sound anything like enough. It sounded vague and unstructured.

'It's going to be very different,' she said, thinking about it.

'But all that freedom. No more Richard and Helen breathing down your neck.'

She tried to smile, wondering where all her elation had suddenly gone. 'I suppose I'll have to ring them tonight. Pretend I'm in Aldeburgh.'

'Ring from a callbox and tell them the cottage doesn't have a phone.' He kissed her again, but lightly this time, on the forehead. 'Come on, darling, cheer up. We're going to have a lovely time.'

Felix noted with satisfaction that the other hotel was decidedly inferior, the sort given over to conferences or even designed with them in mind. It had that dreadfully functional air about it. Other crime writers were milling around, signing in, greeting each other, having drinks at the bar. He only intended to stay long enough to check the programme for any last-minute alterations and confirm the time of his speech, but someone he remembered slightly came charging up to him looking pleased, rather like an eager Labrador.

'John. Good to see you,' he managed, the first lie of the day.

'Hullo, Felix. How's the world treating you?'

'Not so bad. And you?'

'Mustn't grumble. Things have really looked up since I changed agents.'

God, surely he didn't write as badly as he talked? Who was the poor sod getting ten per cent of all those clichés?

'Who are you with now?'

'Natasha Blor. You put me on to her, don't you remember?'

Oh dear. 'I put so many people on to Natasha, she ought to reduce her commission.'

'Mind you, I need every penny I can get. Running two families comes expensive.'

'Well, if you will make these romantic gestures.' He remembered now. John was one of those who after years of miserable monogamy suddenly ran off with a much younger woman, leaving hordes of screaming children in his wake and embarking on a new breeding programme as if he thought mankind was in danger of extinction. Extraordinary.

'Is Elizabeth with you?'

'No, she couldn't get away.' What the hell was the name of the new young breeder?

'Lorna's here. Why don't you join us for dinner?'

'Actually, I'm staying somewhere else, so I won't be around much. Just dashing in tomorrow to do my spiel and that's about it. Thanks all the same.'

John looked at him admiringly, reading between the lines as Felix had hoped he would. 'Same old Felix. I don't know how you keep it up.'

'I sometimes wonder about that myself.'

By the time he got back to his hotel he was aware of feeling tired. The stress of travel, a heavy lunch, all that unaccustomed fresh air and sightseeing, then inane dialogue with John —

they had all taken their toll. Most of all he was conscious of not having his usual allowance of time alone. His normal day was so differently structured and he was used to it, he needed it. Now yet another elaborate meal awaited him and then a peak performance in bed would be expected. A quickie before lunch would have been much more relaxing. He didn't like all this postponement: it had the heavy aura of a wedding night about it. Had he been foolish to buy Sally a ring? But she had wanted one so much and it had seemed, at the time, like a harmless fantasy.

He mellowed when he saw her. She looked so young, sitting there in her underwear, carefully painting her face as if she could improve on nature. He wanted to laugh and hug her. At the same time he feared her relentless energy. Would she expect him to stay awake half the night? Perform over and over again? Weekends away were something he normally avoided, except with Elizabeth. To be onstage without a break for forty-eight hours with an unfamiliar partner could be overtaxing, and he was too old to see anything intrinsically romantic about sharing a bed or a bath. But she had somehow made him feel he owed it to her before she went away to college, almost as if there were something sacramental about sleep.

He said, 'Did you make your phone call?' remembering she had been worried about it.

'They asked about the weather. I said it was a bit mixed.'

'Well, that should cover everything.'

'I'm so bad at lying. I hate it.'

'Just think of it as a game.'

'Pig. You're so practised.'

He kissed the top of her head. 'Isn't that part of my charm?'

'What charm?'

'Now you sound like your mother.'

'You beast.'

'I'm only teasing.'

They wrestled playfully and ended up embracing.

'God, you're so strong,' he said. 'I'm putty in your hands.'

She laughed and kissed him. The scent of her skin made him want her all over again, as if she were new. He held great

103

handfuls of her hair like heavy silk between his fingers. What it was to be eighteen.

'Did you bring my clothes from the flat?' she asked. 'I love the stuff you buy me and I hardly ever get a chance to wear it.'

'No. I got you something new.'

'Oh, Felix.'

He was warmed by her childish excitement. That was how it should be. Presents were fun. 'Hang on. Just let me out of your vice-like grip and I'll find it for you.'

She let go and he produced a smart carrier bag from his suitcase. She sighed with joy and opened it to find a very slinky black dress in silk jersey, really one of his best choices and in a sale, too; he had been lucky. She said, 'Oh, Felix,' in tones of positively sexual rapture. She said that often but he never tired of it and it always turned him on, making him feel he was magic. 'God, it's wonderful. It's exactly the sort of dress I've always wanted.'

'I was hoping it might be.'

She kissed him several times. 'You're absolutely brilliant.'

He was and he knew it. He had turned buying women's clothes into a fine art and he was justifiably proud of himself.

'I do my best.' He watched appreciatively while she put on the dress, watched with confidence, without anxiety, knowing it would fit and suit her. It was slightly too old for her, of course, but that was part of its charm and what they both wanted. It made her look ever so slightly sluttish.

'God, it's fantastic,' she said, admiring herself in the mirror with just a touch of awe, as if she could not quite believe how beautiful she was. She had great legs. When he could drag his eyes away from her tits, it was her legs he looked at, every time, and he had trained her to wear stockings and suspenders. He wondered if Richard lusted after her. It must be almost impossible not to, but no doubt he would never admit it.

'Now it's got you inside it, yes, it is. And the sooner I get inside you the better.'

They kissed again. The kiss went on and on.

'Come on,' he said, knowing her adolescent appetite. 'Or we won't get any dinner.'

'You're so practical.'

'Got to keep up my strength. Don't want any complaints, do I?'

'Fat chance,' she said lovingly.

They went downstairs. He was proud to be seen with her; he could feel the lust and envy in other men's eyes. At the same time he was careful not to look at other women when they were together, although as luck would have it there was a French woman of about thirty-five in the bar whom in other circumstances . . .

Champagne, he thought. It would have to be champagne tonight.

Like most women he knew, Sally took ages in the bathroom, so Felix put in a quick call to Elizabeth while he was waiting. She sounded resolutely cheerful yet somehow plaintive, her usual tone when he went away without her. They talked about the weather and the hotel and she asked who was at the conference.

'Oh, the usual crowd, you know. It's a bit dull really. No wonder we all turn to crime.'

She laughed obediently. 'Missing you,' she said.

'Are you? Me too. Well, must go, darling, I promised to have a drink with John and Lorna before I turn in.'

'Give them my love,' she said. She probably remembered more about them than he did.

'I will.'

'How are they? Happy?'

'As far as I can tell. They seem OK.'

'All those children,' she said thoughtfully.

Not a subject to get into now. 'Night night, love. See you Sunday.'

He fell back on the bed, inspecting his body for signs of middle age. So far it was holding up pretty well but no doubt he should take more exercise, cut down on booze. The media were always droning on about it. Some day perhaps.

Sally came at last out of the bathroom wearing a négligé he

had given her, her face beautiful but oddly serious, her hair brushed out loose the way he liked it. She walked slowly to the bed and stood looking down at him.

'Hullo, my lovely. You look very solemn.'

'I was thinking how much I love you.'

She got into bed. A faint sense of duty intervened for a moment: now he was obliged to take pleasure in what had been pointlessly postponed all day. Then the smell of her skin and the abundance of her hair worked its usual magic: simple lust took over, fuelled by a curious, slight, almost virginal reluctance about her which he found exciting. Sucking her, fucking her, playing with violence in a sort of rape fantasy game that they both enjoyed sometimes, all gave him a feeling of mastery, as if she were a new conquest. In the end it turned out to be one of their best, and she even cried a little after they had both come. He cuddled her till she fell asleep, then turned over carefully (he could never sleep facing anyone) hoping he would wake with a hard-on, hoping he wouldn't snore.

Sally knew she would remember it for ever. The light on the water, the movement of the punt, the oncoming view perfectly framed in the arch of each bridge. How lucky he was to have spent three years here. She felt she was in a film and she could tell Felix was enjoying it too, despite pretending to be blasé. He was more relaxed after his speech; it had gone well, with a few intelligent questions afterwards, and he had finally admitted when it was over that he had been a bit nervous, or as he preferred to call it, rusty. She had been so proud of him and she had wanted to boast to everyone: he's with me and he's brilliant and beautiful and famous. You can look but you can't touch. She knew it wasn't quite true but for this weekend at least she could pretend.

'What were you like as an undergraduate?' she asked, thinking of him fondly at her own age, the young Felix whom she would never know. Not that he was old now, of course, but before he had grown his protective shell, before he had a public to satisfy.

106

'Extremely poor. I couldn't get my bloody father to cough up any money, he was so pissed off with me for taking my mother's side.'

It was difficult to imagine him being hard up: lavish spending seemed so much part of his style. 'Did you have lots of affairs?'

'One or two, I suppose.'

'That means six or seven.'

'Well, maybe three or four.'

She laughed. There was no point in being jealous of the past, which had made him so glamorous and interesting; enough to worry about the future. 'Did Richard?'

'No, poor sod, he was too busy falling in love with Inge.'

'Really? Here?'

'Yes, didn't you know? That was how they met. She was his tutor's au pair.' He put on a heavy German accent. 'We have ways of making you fall in love. God, poor Richard, he was a lost cause once he met her. She was only nineteen but she was so powerful. He used to go round there all the time, he was really obsessed by her. She was a bit like Lady Caroline Lamb, I always think, you know, mad, bad and dangerous to know.'

'I thought that was Byron.' Too late she wondered if it was tactless to correct him.

'Well spotted. She was like Byron, only minus the limp. And minus the poetry too, of course. Didn't leave a lot. No, that's not fair. She was very beautiful, and she must have been sexy, I suppose.'

How protective he sounded of Richard even now, as if he should have saved him from Inge, all those years ago. Or perhaps she had got in the way, stopped them having fun together. She didn't have any friends she felt that strongly about yet.

'And once she got pregnant,' Felix added, 'he didn't stand a chance.'

Sally trailed her hand in the water, dreaming. Her panic of last night had gone with the morning light and today she was drifting on a wave of pure fatalism. How could she have told him? It would have ruined everything. She thought it was almost sure to be all right and if it wasn't, perhaps it was destiny.

All the same, the image of Inge took hold, Inge as *femme fatale*. It was odd to think of Richard being young and in the grip of an uncontrollable passion for someone else. 'It's funny,' she said when they were having tea. 'I always thought Mum was Richard's great love.'

'Maybe she is.'

'Not the way you tell it.'

'Oh, these wild passionate affairs,' Felix said carelessly, 'they're not the people you stay with.'

'Where does that leave us?'

'Oh darling, we're different. Anyway, Richard and Inge were married a long time.'

'It still sounds like a love affair.'

'That's what I mean. It burnt itself out. When he met Helen, I could almost hear him breathe a sigh of relief.'

'That makes it sound dull.'

'No, not at all. It was like a ship coming into safe harbour. Nothing dull about that. It's essential.'

It was no good, she couldn't make sense of it. It was true what they said about the past being a foreign country. Felix had memories she could never share and they made her uneasy.

Then it was all right again. That evening. Their last evening. It was always all right when they were touching, and there was something about the luxury of making love night and morning that put a magic gloss on everything. She could feel herself permanently wet and aching, a new sensation of being thoroughly used. She was grown up, a woman. She tried to hang on to that feeling, to shut out the terror that time was sliding past and there was nothing she could do to make it slow down.

They had a bottle of champagne on the terrace after Sunday lunch and sat silently for a while holding hands, watching the river. It was very peaceful. She kept telling herself not to waste precious moments, not to hasten the ending by fretting about it, but it was hard to take her own advice.

'It's been the most perfect weekend of my life,' she said finally, aware of sounding solemn but wanting him to know how she felt.

'It's not over yet.'

'Nearly.'

'And it's only the first of many.'

Now did he mean that or was it just something cheering to say? He hadn't said when the next one would be. She had noticed before how he shied away from unpleasant facts. Perhaps he had suffered so much in the past that he had resolved never to be unhappy again. But life wasn't like that. She knew that already. Even the thought of saying goodbye to their room, where they had been so happy, made her want to cry.

In the afternoon he took her to the railway station and bought her a first-class ticket. He settled her into her seat and gave her flowers and magazines. There was an awful feeling of goodbye in the air; they were both so determinedly cheerful.

'I've never travelled first class before,' she said.

'It's always worth it. I learned that when I was quite poor. It really costs very little extra compared with what it does for your morale. In fact it's quite an art, knowing when to be extravagant.'

'I thought you always were,' she said, surprised.

'Oh no, I have my petty economies like everyone else. I turn the thermostat down two degrees and wear an extra pullover. That kind of thing.'

'There's so much I don't know about you.'

'You're better off not knowing boring stuff like that. It ruins my image.'

They both smiled and she shook her head. More minutes ticked by.

'I hate railway stations,' she said suddenly, violently. Part of her wanted to ask why he wasn't driving her back to London and letting her get a train from there, why he didn't want to be with her till the last available moment. But she didn't want to spoil things by complaining and anyway, it was too late now, she was here on the train with her first-class ticket, and she had taken such risks and he didn't even know.

'I always feel they should play Rachmaninov's second piano concerto over the tannoy,' he said.

She had to smile.

'Oh good,' he said. 'I was afraid you were too young to remember.'

'I love old films. I used to watch them all the time on the box when I should have been revising.'

'See? That's something I didn't know about you.'

The train was about to leave.

'Oh, Felix.'

They kissed and it was all right again, just for a moment.

'Take care, my love. See you soon.'

She started to cry as the train started to move. She saw him already disappearing back into his other life. He stood on the platform and they waved until they couldn't see each other any more.

Felix sat in the car for a few moments before starting the engine. He was trying to relax completely. He wished he had studied meditation. He had the slightly sick feeling of a child who has been to a party and had just a little too much of everything. A wonderful weekend. It had all gone perfectly. So why did he feel exhausted?

It was the emotion, he decided. Why did she have to create drama where there was none? They had enjoyed forty-eight hours together and now it was over. But they would be meeting again in a matter of days. No one had died or even gone away. How could she make a tragedy out of that? Tears

110

on a railway station, for God's sake. Or was it his fault for mentioning *Brief Encounter*? It was hard to get everything right, but he had tried his best and it had certainly cost enough.

Gradually he began to calm down, to level out. Time alone, that was what he needed to recharge his batteries; he knew that from experience. The drive home would soothe him. If he left his brain in neutral, it would rearrange the weekend into unalloyed pleasure. By the time he got home he would be himself again. Right now he was suffering from giving out too much; he was emotionally bankrupt. He simply didn't have the energy to respond to another human being twenty-four hours a day without time off for good behaviour. That, apart from his talent, was why he was a writer.

He started the car. Even driving had a calming effect. The simple mechanics of changing gear. He would switch off his mind completely. Stress. It was very stressful to be open to someone else's needs all the time. He had to think of himself again and relax.

After a while he started to feel better, indulging in a little mild speeding on the motorway and slipping a cassette into the car stereo: it was Mozart's *Don Giovanni*, which always lifted his spirits.

He stopped on the way to get flowers for Elizabeth and was home by early evening. She was in the kitchen preparing supper when he arrived and she made more fuss of the flowers than of him. Home seemed particularly attractive, as it always did after an adventure: a refuge, a haven, a safe place where no unreasonable demands would be made. He hoped she was not about to give him a hard time for being away.

'Hullo, darling,' he said, kissing the back of her neck. 'Missed you.'

'How did it go?' she said, arranging the flowers, not looking at him.

'Oh, quite well, I think. Bit exhausting.'

'Didn't you get off on all the adrenalin?'

A shade of sharpness in her tone, or was he imagining it? Best to ignore it, anyway. God, he was tired.

'For a while. Then I wished I was home.' Perhaps a straight appeal to her better nature. 'I think I'm getting too old for these larks.'

Silence. She stopped fiddling with the flowers and placed them on the table. Felix poured himself a large drink.

'Supper's nearly ready,' she said gently.

The coroner wanted to know how often Richard had seen the deceased. He asked him to describe her state of mind.

'She was very depressed,' Richard said. 'She couldn't see the point of the probation order because I couldn't get her baby back for her. She seemed to feel everything was hopeless.'

'In your opinion, was there any indication that she might take her own life?'

'No, but she did, so I must have failed to pick it up.' He paused, feeling Marion's eyes on him. He deeply resented her presence; it proved that she didn't trust him and she ought to have been too busy. And Inge was at the back of the court: he didn't even remember mentioning the case to her. It was as if he himself was on trial. 'I do feel,' he went on, looking at the coroner, 'that her family and social services made an error of judgment in persuading her to have her baby adopted and I blame myself for not realising how desperate she felt.'

Outside the court he brushed off local reporters. Marion shook her head at him. 'I despair of you, Richard,' she said, 'I really do.'

'You were wonderful,' Inge said. 'I was proud of you.'

The two women looked critically at each other.

'You shouldn't be here,' he said to Inge, feeling it applied to them both. Marion drifted away with a look that said he hadn't heard the last of it.

Inge asked, 'Why didn't *she* come?'

'Who?' he said, knowing.

'Your wife.' She made it sound like a dirty word.

'She's working and I didn't want anyone to come. Go away, Inge, please. How did you even know about this?'

'You told me weeks ago, don't you remember? You were dreading it. I wanted to give you moral support. It's important you should have someone on your side.' She put her hand on his arm. 'Let's go for a drink, you look exhausted.'

'I have to get back to the office.'

He walked to his car, hearing one of the reporters say to her, 'Not very grateful, was he?'

'He is living with a bad woman,' she said sorrowfully, in a loud voice.

He saw them go off together. Well, it was not his business.

But the reporter did not ask Inge for a date and she went home feeling lonelier than ever with disappointment at the missed opportunity. It was a relief to find the boys already there. Sometimes she felt she had invaded their youth by making them so aware of her as a heavy responsibility. But they accepted their burden willingly, responding to her need. They were practical, too, not merely self-sacrificial, bringing the motorbike indoors and taking it to bits on the carpet so that they could still talk to her, be with her, while they enjoyed themselves playing with their favourite toy. Or they would arrange their hair in spikes with gel in front of the living-room mirror instead of away upstairs in their own bedrooms. They were generous children. Sometimes she wondered how she had produced them when she herself was so selfish. They took after Richard, she supposed. But Richard had left her. That had not been very generous. Not unselfish at all. So perhaps they were their own people and just naturally good-hearted.

She read aloud to them from a contact magazine, drawing them into her shadowy world to make it safe. 'How about this one? "Sensual man, forties, clean, discreet, well-endowed,

113

seeks mature lady for mutual pleasure." ' She liked the word pleasure very much.

'Sounds like a wally,' said Karl, looking up from the motorbike on the floor.

'Does Dad know you're doing this?' Peter peered at her anxiously in the mirror from behind the spikes.

'He wouldn't care.' It hurt her, it infuriated her, that she could not make Richard show jealousy. 'But I shall tell him.'

'Anyway, you're not mature,' said Karl, 'you're in your prime.'

Inge blew him a kiss. His loyalty brought tears to her eyes. ' "Sexy young man, twenty-five," ' she read, ' "adventurous and virile, seeks older woman for experimental relationship." '

'Mum,' Peter protested. He was only fourteen after all, and easily embarrassed. Too young to understand much about life.

'I'm lonely,' she said, thinking what an understatement it was.

'Why don't you do an ad of your own?' Karl suggested. 'We could help you. Then when the guys show up we can vet them for you.'

'What shall I say?' She was enchanted with the idea, whether she used the ad or not. She scrabbled through a pile of rubbish and newspapers on the coffee table to find the back of an old envelope and dredged up a leaking biro from the chaos of her handbag. The boys took turns like a well-rehearsed double act; she was proud of them.

'Beautiful woman,' Karl began romantically.

'Thirty-eight,' said Peter, facing facts.

'Thirties, you wally. Beautiful woman, thirties, two gorgeous sons . . .'

They all fell about laughing. Inge scribbled.

'Terrific cook, unconventional dress . . .'

'Relaxed attitude to housework . . .'

'Warm, intelligent . . .'

'Lazy, desperate,' said Inge with her passion for the truth.

'Seeks . . .' said Karl firmly, pressing on. 'What are you seeking, Mum?'

'Seeks original husband back again.'

114

'Oh Mum,' said Peter.

'It's true.'

'I know,' said Karl, ever practical, 'but he's not coming back, is he? He's got that woman and her kid, he doesn't care about us.'

'He cares about you two,' Inge said. She thought it was important they should understand that. 'It's just me he wanted to leave. I got on his nerves.'

'Come on, Mum,' said Karl. 'Do your ad. You might meet a millionaire. None of us need ever work again.'

'I haven't noticed you doing much,' Peter said.

'I'm a thinker,' Karl said loftily. 'We thinkers have to rest up a lot. Thinking takes it out of you.'

'Only if it was there in the first place.'

She loved their affectionate bickering: it made her feel warm and cherished. It was like being wrapped in a fur blanket by someone who cared about her.

'Juliet seeks Romeo,' said Karl. 'No. Cleopatra seeks Antony. How about that?'

'Tristan seeks Isolde,' said Peter. 'Has own love potion.'

'Hey, not bad.'

'Well, you're keen on Wagner, aren't you, Mum?'

'Lonely morose frustrated German woman seeks own true love.' She was sorry she couldn't cheer up to please them.

'Come on, Mum.' Karl sounded bracing: perhaps he would become a doctor in later life.

She shook her head. 'It's the truth.'

Sally didn't really believe it and yet in a sense she had known all the time. The weeks dragged by and nothing happened. She told Felix she was worried about her A-level results and he believed her. There was no point in alarming him unnecessarily, but she needed his support so desperately that she was tempted to tell him anyway and the hell with it. But something always stopped her.

She told herself it was normal to miss periods on the pill,

115

although she never had; they were artificial, anyway, and didn't mean anything, she knew all that.

She had brought this on herself.

Perhaps he would be thrilled. Over the moon. So why didn't she tell him?

How could she have been so stupid?

Only of course it wasn't true.

On the way home from Tesco every day she passed a chemist's shop. They had test kits in the window. Predictor, they were called, and Discover 2. Like science fiction. She ought to buy one, put her mind at rest. Only of course it was unnecessary.

She had physical symptoms and she told herself she was imagining them. It was much too soon, everyone knew that. It was psychosomatic. It was ridiculous.

Sometimes it felt wonderful, like a miracle, and she wanted to dance for joy. Sometimes she actually did, secretly, in her room.

Sometimes she knew it was all nonsense.

Always it felt insane that her body knew the truth and she didn't.

One day on her afternoon off she was alone at home and the doorbell rang. It was Elizabeth with a bunch of flowers in her hand. For a mad moment she thought they were for her and Elizabeth knew everything. She was going to be magnanimous in defeat and Sally would always be grateful.

'I brought these for Helen,' Elizabeth said.

'She's not back yet. D'you want to come in and wait for her?'

Elizabeth smiled an ordinary smile, as if she didn't know anything. 'No, thanks, I must dash, we're going to the theatre. Just tell her I said thank you for listening.'

'OK.'

She watched Elizabeth turn away and walk towards her car. She wasn't fat, as Helen said, just normal. And she had a nice kind face and wonderfully shiny dark hair. Sally liked her and hated feeling guilty.

'How's the job?' Elizabeth asked, suddenly turning back.

Sally felt panic, wanting to confess. Please forgive me, only

I love him so much. Elizabeth was like an aunt. You must understand.

'Boring,' she said. 'But the money's useful.'

'I bet. When d'you get your A-level results?'

'Any day now.'

Elizabeth smiled again. 'I'll keep my fingers crossed. I'm sure you've done well.'

'Thank you. I'm not.'

Elizabeth got into her car and drove away. She thinks I'm still a child, Sally thought, closing the door. She doesn't take me seriously. It should have been a relief.

She went back inside and rang Felix in a panic, but got the answering machine and didn't speak.

Each year Richard and Helen celebrated four anniversaries: the day they met, the night they first made love, the day they started living together and their wedding day. They liked the first two best; the others were somehow tainted by Inge's distress. They would go out to dinner and reminisce in almost the same words every time. It became a tradition, like going to a favourite concert over and over again to hear the same music played with slight modifications of tempo and tone. Helen loved ritual, the way it imposed some kind of order on the chaos of everyday life: it was the effect she was trying to achieve in her work. And Richard always sent flowers, which impressed Sally greatly.

'He never forgets, does he?' she said, watching Helen cut the cellophane. 'And your birthday. And Christmas. That's six times a year. And sometimes he does it for no reason at all as well. Aren't you lucky?' She sounded oddly envious, even sour. Not like herself.

'Yes,' said Helen, snipping and arranging. 'But I deserve it as well.'

'I hope I marry someone like Richard,' Sally said. 'Someone romantic.'

'Provided you don't do it for at least ten years,' said Helen, 'then so do I.'

She thought Sally looked pale and tired: her own mother would have called it peaky, a ghastly word for which there was nevertheless no precise equivalent. 'We'll be late back,' she said. 'Why don't you have an early night? You look exhausted.'

'It's the job,' Sally said, flushing. 'It's so boring now they've put me on the till.'

'Well, it's not for much longer. Soon you'll be a carefree student living off the state. You can sleep all day and stay up all night, and who can ask more of life than that?' But as a student herself she had painted all day and made love most of the night and hardly slept at all.

Sally took a letter out of her bag. 'This came today.' She handed it to Helen, who read it and let out a shriek.

'God, you're brilliant. Two Bs and an A. That's fantastic. Why ever didn't you tell me before? God, I'm so proud of you.' She hugged Sally, who felt stiff and awkward in the hug.

'It's good, isn't it?' she said soberly.

'Aren't you thrilled?'

'Yes, of course.'

'You could have fooled me.'

'Oh, I've waited so long for it,' Sally said. 'And I'd have liked two As and a B.'

'Come off it.' It was late in the day to get that ambitious. 'At least you know for sure they'll take you now. That's all that matters. Isn't it?'

'Yes.'

She sounded so unenthusiastic that Helen felt bound to ask, 'Well, you do want to go there, don't you?'

'Yes, of course,' Sally said.

The roses stood up stiff and straight in the vase. Helen hoped they wouldn't droop before they were fully open.

In the restaurant they drank a toast to Sally, but her mood stayed with Helen, in spite of the champagne. 'She was very odd about it,' she said. 'As if it didn't really matter.'

118

'Probably anti-climax.' Richard seemed unperturbed, which made her relax a little.

'Yes, that's what she said, more or less.'

'Well, there you are. Or maybe she's just nervous about leaving home. It's going to be very odd when she's gone.'

'Alone at last,' said Helen, teasing. 'Is there life after Sally?' But she had often thought how strange it would be. They had never been alone together.

'Poor Sally,' Richard said. 'She's not even allowed to be moody like other teenagers. We're so used to her being amenable that we expect it to last for ever. No drugs, no drink, no unsuitable boyfriends. We're spoilt really, aren't we? She's probably working up to a great big rebellion at Sussex.'

'God, I hope not.' The prospect terrified her, although she knew it was inevitable, even natural and right.

'OK then, a little one. She's entitled to that. Oh, darling, we're going to miss her, but think of all that freedom. We can run naked through the house. Scream and shout, have blazing rows, make love in broad daylight on the living-room floor . . .'

'In the bathroom. In the garden. On the roof.' Helen tried to enter into the spirit of the fantasy. Anything to blot out the picture of Sally having a rebellion, great or small, away from home. She knew letting your children go was the essence of parenthood, but as long as she lived she would never think of Sally as grown up.

'I love you.' Richard held her hand.

'I don't know why.' She could never say it back to him when he said it, although she wanted to: it sounded like an echo and insincere. She had told Sally she deserved him, but she did not believe it. Long ago, when he first moved in, her mother had quoted Shakespeare at her, saying she should thank Heaven fasting for a good man's love, and it was one of the few times she thought her mother was right. But it went along with her mother's low opinion of her and that didn't feel so good. 'I think I'm very lucky,' she said, kissing his hand. It was always easier to say it with touch, like painting.

'You know, it's not too late,' he said. 'We could still have one of our own.'

She hadn't expected that, not tonight. They had discussed it several times over the years but never on an anniversary, when it was certain to ruin the atmosphere. It must have something to do with Sally going away.

'Oh, darling,' she said, 'don't spoil everything.'

'No, listen. The boys are growing up and Sally's nearly gone. We'll soon have a bit more spare cash. And if I could persuade Inge to get a job, even part-time, I could pay her less. We'd manage somehow. I'd help you a lot. You know I would.'

She nodded, saddened by the eager, hopeful look on his face. Why did saying no always feel so wrong, when no was the right thing to say? 'I'm sorry it still means so much to you,' she said. 'I was hoping you'd gone off the idea. You haven't mentioned it for a while.'

'It could be wonderful. Just think what we could make between us, you and I.'

Now she could say it. 'But I love you more than that. The people you love most aren't always the ones you have children with. I love feeling we aren't tied together with children, like string. We're just lovers.' She meant it, but some watchful, scrupulous part of her mind pounced on her words and examined them for lies. Was she also finding a nice way of telling him she disliked the mess, the upheaval, the responsibility of children; that her work came first, or Sally came first, or that as long as he put Inge first this would always be his punishment, to do without what he wanted most? She wished she didn't question herself like this when the issue was in fact so clear. They were forty and exhausted and broke. Anyone walking in and looking at them now would say that they needed a holiday or a legacy or even just a good night's sleep. No sane person would prescribe a baby. Yet it still felt insulting to say she didn't want his child, as if it must mean she didn't love him enough. If they had been young and rich and rested, she knew she would still have said no.

'Not lovers very often,' he said.

'We get tired. We work too hard.'

'We could change that.'

'Yes, we could. Why don't we?' She felt the comfortable stirrings of lust, now the dangerous corner was turned. 'D'you remember?'

'Yes.'

'On the floor of the studio, the first time.'

'Yes.'

'When I came, you had to put your hand over my mouth in case I woke Sally.'

He was watching her steadily. 'I remember.'

They smiled tenderly at each other. Talking about it excited them both. Their younger selves could be summoned at any time to evoke desire.

'When Elizabeth took me to your show,' Richard said, starting their litany, 'I felt I recognised you. You were the woman I'd been looking for all my life. The woman who didn't really need me.'

'But I needed you desperately,' Helen said.

'The woman who could manage without me then. I had to have you. I'd have died without you.'

'I never thought you'd leave Inge,' Helen said. 'I thought you were too good and I wanted somebody good. I thought I'd be lonely for ever.'

It had been a shock, breaking up with Carey and finding she wasn't self-sufficient. She had hoped that her work and her child would be enough, that she could live like a man, celibate or having occasional sex with people who were not important, so that no one would have the power to hurt her again. To need love was a human weakness that made you vulnerable for ever. Learning to love someone she could trust had been a revelation, and if she could not offer him the all-consuming passion she had felt for Carey, well, that had been a kind of sickness that passed with youth. Some part of her had been broken in that struggle, but she told herself that what was left was more important and more real. If he loved her the way she had loved Carey, perhaps that was also the way Inge loved him. It was the luck of the draw and there was nothing any of them could do about it.

*

121

They would never have met without Elizabeth. 'Oh, do come with me, Richard,' she had said. 'Or I'll have to go on my own and that's no fun.'

'Why can't you go with Felix?' The pile of mock O-level scripts beside him made it quite clear that he wasn't supposed to go anywhere. From upstairs he could hear squeals and splashes as Inge bathed the children. "When Macbeth first meets the witches," wrote Shirley Baker in 5B, "they put ideas in his head because they say what he has been thinking about already and talking to his wife about."

'He won't come. He says when you've seen one rectangle, you've seen them all. I think she's wonderful but then I'm crazy about Ben Nicholson and she's a bit like him. Come on, Richard, I won't enjoy it half as much by myself. Bring Inge if you like and we'll all have dinner afterwards. Felix says he wants to work late but I'm sure he'll join us for dinner.'

It sounded to Richard as if Felix was having a new affair. He envied Felix and pitied Elizabeth. He said, 'All right. I ought to be marking but I'd love to play truant. I'll talk to Inge and I'll ring you back.'

'Ring me back if you can't,' Elizabeth said. 'I'm sure that's easier. Otherwise I'll pick you up tomorrow about six.'

He had forgotten how bossy she could be and almost rang her back to cancel. But when Inge came downstairs she looked so bedraggled that he thought the prospect of an outing might uplift her.

'Elizabeth wants us to go to a private view tomorrow,' he said. 'And dinner afterwards with Felix. Would you like to? Shall we get a sitter?'

Inge looked sulky. She poured herself the last of the Scotch and sat down heavily in the chair opposite him.

'You know I don't like to leave the boys with a stranger,' she said. 'And it's very expensive.'

He stared at her. Sometimes he tried so hard to see the desperate beauty that had enraptured him when they were both nineteen. He knew it was still there, because other people, including Felix, the connoisseur, admired her extravagantly; but it was a beauty that could no longer reach his eyes, except on rare occasions when he was very tired or very drunk. It had been shrouded by all kinds of domestic emotions such as responsibility, affection, boredom and guilt. He was exhausted. Sometimes just looking at her and knowing how much of him she needed made him feel he was being sucked dry.

'But you're always saying you want to go out more often,' he said. 'How we never go anywhere or do anything.'

'I want to go out with you,' Inge said. 'The two of us alone.'

The word struck his heart like a stone.

'Anyway,' she added, 'if Felix isn't going, then she only wants you as an escort. I'd be in the way. I know she doesn't like me.'

'She does like you, Inge,' he said. 'Whatever makes you think she doesn't?'

'Oh, you English, you're so polite. So hypocritical. Everything has to be so nice. And you don't mean any of it. Of course she doesn't like me. She's a silly fat woman and her husband fucks other women and now she wants my husband to take her out to a gallery because she is afraid to go by herself.'

He got up. 'I'm going to say goodnight to the boys.'

'And there will be silly people there who don't know about painting but they want to drink free wine and pretend to be clever.'

He said, 'Yes, I know. But it's harmless.'

He had reached the top of the stairs when she said, 'And the boys want you to read them a story.'

He said, 'But I always do.' He was suddenly inexpressibly irritated by the reminder. He closed his eyes, but even in the darkness and on another level, he could see her shrug, and the foreignness of her alienated him yet again, and the love he still felt rose up in his throat to choke him. He read to the boys about Pooh, the bear of very little brain who did not have these problems, occasionally getting a word wrong on purpose for the sheer pleasure of having them correct him. The blend of himself and Inge in their faces moved him as it always did, and he knew they were bound together for ever no matter how unhappy it might make them.

In the night she woke him wanting to make love, and when he couldn't or wouldn't, for he was no longer sure which it was, she turned away in anger and then she cried. He tried to hold her, to comfort her, but she swore at him and shook him off. Yet she fell asleep before he did, exhausted by her own emotions, while he lay awake stricken by the amount of energy he consumed in making sure that she did not devour him entirely.

The gallery was already crowded when they arrived because Elizabeth had been slightly late to pick him up and then had had difficulty parking. She was wearing the mink coat that Felix had bought her to celebrate the film rights of *The Heartbreak Merchant*. As an animal lover, Richard resented the coat, and yet he knew that Elizabeth loved animals too. He also thought, on an aesthetic level, that the coat was too heavy for her and made her look older than she was. But he knew she was proud of it and it made her happy, perhaps as a confirmation of Felix's love. He could not say anything to her about it and had to remind himself that he was not as yet a vegetarian. The most selfish part of him hoped that she would not become too hot and expect him to hold the coat.

It was a small gallery, with stark white walls. Elizabeth fussed about getting drinks and he had to fight his way to the bar on her behalf. Then he saw the paintings. There were perhaps a dozen of them, in various sizes: solid delicate rectangles of beige and grey, white and cream, overlapping each other, some flat, some in relief. They had a luminous quality, although the paint did not gleam: it seemed to him that they glowed from within.

He felt instantly at peace, as if all the noise in his head had stopped, as well as the noise in the gallery. There was suddenly no sound at all. Everywhere he looked was cool reflective peace with firm edges.

'She's good, isn't she?' Elizabeth said, whenever he next heard her.

He said yes. His throat felt dry and his voice sounded odd to himself.

Some time later he heard Elizabeth say carelessly, 'That must be her over there.'

He looked and saw a woman with pale hair caught up in a knot behind her head from which it fell heavy and straight. She was dressed all in black. People were talking to her and she smiled at them and shook hands.

A man behind him, looking at the paintings, said to his companion, 'Bit monotonous, aren't they?' and Richard wanted to hit him.

It was then that he realised he had fallen in love.

'Well, I'm glad you're enjoying it,' Elizabeth said eventually.

'I've got to meet her,' Richard said.

He thought later that it was to Elizabeth's eternal credit that she understood so quickly what had happened. But maybe it was easy to read his face. He felt quite lightheaded, as if he were short of oxygen. Perhaps he had been forgetting to breathe.

'Yes, of course,' Elizabeth said. 'We'll just go over and say hullo, tell her how much we like her work.'

Then he was conscious of her staring at him with a curious look of shock and compassion, as though he were ill.

'Oh Richard,' she said. 'I didn't realise.'

He shook his head as if to clear it. They started walking across the room together when Elizabeth stopped. 'I think you'd better go by yourself,' she said. 'I'm going to get another drink. I'll join you later.'

He felt betrayed yet relieved, like a child abandoned by its nurse. He found his way to the small group of people round the painter and hung about behind them, watching her. He sensed she was wary of the occasion, careful to say and do all the right things, but not believing any of it. He waited until there was some sort of a gap and then he went up to her, heart pounding like a schoolboy, and said, 'Can I talk to you for a moment?'

She turned to look at him: her eyes were green and pale, her body angular in the black dress. He felt she could read his thoughts, see into his soul. He shivered in the hot room.

125

'I suppose so,' she said. 'Why ever not?' But she sounded friendly.

'I'm Richard Morgan,' he said. This seemed important information.

'I'm Helen Irving.' She held out her hand and he took it, aware of thinking like a groupie, My God, am I holding the hand that did all these paintings?

'Yes, I know,' he said. 'I love your work.'

She said seriously, 'Thank you. Not many people do.'

They looked at each other for what seemed like a long time.

'Is it going well?' he asked eventually. He still seemed to find difficulty in breathing.

She shrugged. 'People are saying nice things, but nobody's buying.'

'I'd like to buy everything,' he said truthfully. 'But I haven't got any money.'

'Neither have I,' she said. 'It's a common problem.' She smiled at him, as if he wasn't making a total fool of himself. He already had a sense of her as someone quite straight-forward and uncompromising. She wore no make-up and he could see where faint lines were appearing around her eyes and mouth, although he guessed she was about thirty, his own age. She had very white teeth and rather full lips that belied the austerity of the rest of her face. The longing to kiss her was almost unbearable.

He said urgently, 'Look, I don't usually behave like this, but could you possibly have dinner with me?'

She frowned slightly. 'I'm having dinner with Magdalen. You know, my dealer.'

'Could I meet you afterwards?'

She shook her head. 'I have a daughter and a babysitter.'

'Then another time. Any time you say. I absolutely have to see you again. Please don't think I'm some kind of lunatic. I'm a schoolteacher and I have a wife and two sons and I'm a perfectly sober upright citizen and I've never done this in my life before.'

She began to laugh, but very gently, including him in the laughter. She picked up one of the printed invitations and wrote something on it and handed it to him.

126

'Why don't you ring me at the studio?' she said. 'If you still feel the same tomorrow.'

After dinner they walked by the river, holding hands and watching the lights on the water. She felt voluptuously content: it was still, after all these years, a luxury to be securely loved. Presently it began to get cold, and they went and sat in the car and kissed, like a courting couple. It made her feel young again.

'You know,' she said, 'we don't have to go straight home. I told Sally we'd be late.'

Richard smiled and started the car. He drove without speaking, one hand on her knee, and she changed gear for him, an old familiar game. By the time they reached the studio it was lit by bright moonlight.

'Just like old times,' he said, as they started to undress.

'Yes.' But she wished he hadn't spoken: it seemed to break the spell, just a little.

The moonlight touched the half-finished *Seven Deadly Sins*. It was months since she had allowed him in the studio, in fact not since she began work on them. Suddenly, while they were still kissing and undressing, he said, 'Oh, darling, I must talk to Inge. You shouldn't have to do stuff like that for money just because she's so lazy.'

'What?' Desire vanished and a murderous cold rage took its place. She loathed them anyway but she was doing her best and she knew they weren't that bad. From a long way off she heard him desperately trying to wipe out his mistake.

'No, no, I didn't mean it like that, you're doing it brilliantly, it's just I know you hate it and I feel it's all my fault. If I could only get Inge off her backside, you could get on with your real work.'

There was a can of paint beside her ready mixed and thinned. She seized it and hurled it at one of the empty canvases. Thin red colour splashed all over the canvas, the walls, the floor.

'Well, fuck you,' she shouted. 'That's Anger, in case you

127

can't tell, and don't flatter your tiny self anything to do with my work could be your fault. It's my own bloody fault for marrying such an arsehole as you.'

She was shaking with rage. They both stood and looked in amazement at the mess of red paint, then back at each other half naked, and down at their clothes on the floor. It had all happened so quickly, it seemed like a natural disaster, an earthquake, a flood, almost nothing to do with them and therefore beyond their control. Then, by some miracle, at the same moment, the incongruity of it all struck them both and they started to laugh. They hugged each other, still laughing, almost hysterical by now, and collapsed on the floor, pulling off their remaining clothes.

Felix thought at first he could never have enough of Sally. He loved everything about her: the mixture of child and woman in her conversation, her adoring glances, the scent of her skin, the feel of her hair, the warmth of her body against his own, the sound of her cries when she came, the look of pained surprise in her face when he introduced her to some new refinement of pleasure she had never imagined, and above all the intoxication of her youth, making him feel half his age and omnipotent. But in spite of all that, after a few months the day came when he was actually working well, when after all the usual procrastination and displacement activity he had finally got into the wretched thing and got it moving.

He was even tempted not to answer the entry phone, but not tempted enough. It could only be Sally, because only Sally and Richard (apart from past loves) knew this address, and only Sally had permission to drop in without phoning. Of course he wanted to see her, although not at that precise moment, not with Tony Blythe just coming out of the sauna and seeing all that blood on the steps leading down to the pool.

'Hullo, darling,' he said. 'What a lovely surprise.'

'I'm disturbing you, aren't I?' she said. He was annoyed to be so transparent but at the same time he thought it might do her good to know she was not always welcome.

'Not at all, only I've just got a fresh corpse in the jacuzzi and you know how distracting that is.'

'Well, no. But I can imagine.'

He kissed her then and realised he should have kissed her before.

'Darling, you do feel tense. Are you all right?'

Tony Blythe was receding, but Sally was not yet in sharp focus. Felix hated this stage, when he could neither work nor be nice to his guest.

'Yes, of course,' she said.

He could feel the rest of the paragraph slipping away, like Elizabeth's knitting when she wrenched it off the needles. He should have asked Sally to wait till he had finished and trusted her not to feel he was being unromantic.

'I've got my A-level results.'

'Then we're celebrating. Come and have a drink.' He poured two glasses of wine, knowing that really was the end of work for the day.

'You don't know what they are yet. I might have failed.'

She sounded uncharacteristically gloomy. In fact now that he was beginning to be able to give her his full attention, he noticed that she looked gloomy too.

'Don't be absurd,' he said. 'I have the utmost confidence in you.'

'Two Bs and an A.'

'There you are. I'd have got champagne if I'd known. Well done, my love, I'm proud of you.'

She took a large gulp of her drink as if gathering courage for some ordeal and said rapidly, 'Felix, I've got to talk to you. I think – please don't be cross, only my period's late, I mean I haven't had one since we went to Cambridge and I'm a bit worried.'

The worst news in the world. He had heard it several times before but only from married women who said, 'Oh shit, I swore I'd never have another abortion,' and played with the idea of passing it off as their husband's but ended up accepting Felix's cheque. Never anyone so young. She actually bit her lip as she spoke, a gesture he used to love, making her look younger than ever. Now he felt she had

129

kicked him in the balls and he was so angry he wanted to hit her. He simply wasn't equipped for dealing with problems and he had never pretended he was. He was equipped for happiness, for giving pleasure to himself and other people, a rare talent, he thought, and it was unfair of anyone to expect more of him than that.

'Please say something.' She was watching him anxiously.

'I can't believe it.'

'It's probably all right, I mean it's only a slight chance. You can miss them on the pill without being . . .' She paused. 'I'm sorry.'

'Sorry?'

'I know it's an awful shock, it was for me too, only I've had more time to –'

He said, 'Look, right at the beginning, we talked about this. I said were you on the pill or should I use a sheath? We *talked* about it.' God, what more could he have done? It wasn't as if he'd been irresponsible.

'I know.'

'You said it was safe. I trusted you. You weren't a virgin, you knew the score.'

'Felix . . .' She drooped her head, looking miserable, like a beaten dog.

'I can't believe this is happening. What did you do, for God's sake? Throw up? The bloody thing's meant to be 100 per cent, isn't it? Don't tell me you just forgot, I'm not buying that.'

Sally started to cry. He went to her and put his arms round her, realising he should have done it sooner. He had never felt less like doing it. He stroked her hair, noticing it wasn't as clean as usual, and she sobbed.

'Darling, I'm sorry, I'm sorry. It's just the shock. It's all right. Poor little one. Don't worry. We'll think of something.' He thought he sounded like a parody of himself at his most benign.

He poured more drinks and sat with her on the sofa, holding her hand.

'Now then, let's think. Have you seen a doctor?'

'Not yet.' She sniffed most unattractively and he passed her

130

a box of tissues. 'I couldn't face it. But I've done two of those kits you get from the chemist and it was positive both times.'

'Dear God.' It was worse than he thought: it was total nightmare. Absolute panic took over and he wanted to run away.

'I think positive can mean negative though, sometimes, but negative can't mean positive. I think that's right.'

Hopeless. He knew the sound of despair when he heard it. 'Poor darling,' he said absently. 'What rotten luck.' His mind was racing: how soon could he decently mention abortion?

Sally blew her nose and said clearly, even with a touch of bravado, 'It's my fault really. That weekend I left my pills in my other handbag.'

'What?'

'Richard was giving me a lift to the station and I was so rushed.'

He hadn't thought it could get worse but clearly it could. Not only were they in this appalling mess but now she was admitting it could have been avoided. 'Why the hell didn't you tell me?'

'I don't know. I couldn't.' Her head drooped still further. 'I felt so silly and it would have spoilt everything.'

He got up, really fearing he might strike her now. He took deep breaths to calm himself and it didn't work. 'And this? Now? Isn't this spoiling everything?'

'I know.' A small, sad voice. 'I'm sorry.'

'Christ, I'd have gone to the all-night bloody chemist. Or given the whole thing up. We could have wanked, for God's sake. I didn't have to fuck you.' He saw her flinch at the words and he was glad he'd shocked her. They'd always called it making love before. 'Jesus, what goes on in your head?'

'It was our special weekend. It was supposed to be romantic.'

Felix sat down with his face in his hands. Presently she said, sounding older, 'I didn't know you'd be so angry. When you talked about Elizabeth not being able to have children, you sounded sad.'

He sat up with a jerk. 'Now look. You're not saying you

131

did this bloody fucking stupid thing on purpose, are you? Because if you are —'

'No, of course I'm not,' Sally said, looking frightened. 'I didn't.'

Then there was a very long silence that neither of them seemed to know how to break. All Felix could think of was how to plant the idea of abortion without actually using the word. Eventually he said, 'Look, Sally. You know I love you and of course it's like a miracle, *if* you're pregnant, when I always wanted children, but look, you've just got into Sussex, haven't you, and, well, you know Elizabeth's having a rotten time with the menopause.' She didn't answer and he went on, rather more energetically, 'I mean, for God's sake, we just can't do this. Think what it would mean. Richard and Helen would go berserk. We'd ruin everyone's lives.' There was something unnerving about hearing his own voice run on and on, the words dropping away into space, with no response from her. She wouldn't even look at him; she sat staring at the floor, her hands tight together in her lap. 'I mean, you must see that,' he finally said. 'I'm thinking of you. What's best for you.'

Richard tried to be compassionate, practical and detached. Some of his clients needed more than anything to be listened to, often a new experience; others required help to find their way through the maze of benefits they might be entitled to claim, or simply encouragement to stay out of trouble. Those inside needed a link with the outside world. He was no use to any of them if he got too involved: their friends or their families could do that. But sometimes the sense of identification was overpowering, though he kept it to himself.

'It's not as if I meant to hit her,' Fred would say, frowning with effort as he tried to understand his own behaviour. 'I mean I didn't go round there with the deliberate intention of beating her up.' He looked Richard straight in the eye, as if to prove he was telling the truth. 'It was nothing like that. I just wanted to talk to her.'

Richard knew quite well what he meant. Sometimes the

132

longing to hit Inge, to drive into her with violence what could not be driven in with words, was so powerful that he would never understand what made him resist it. 'D'you find her very difficult to talk to?'

'I always seem to end up losing my temper, yeah,' said Fred, quick to take the point. 'I mean I only went round there to try and talk her out of getting a divorce and I end up hitting her. It don't make sense.'

It certainly didn't make sense that you fell in love and had children and time passed, then one day you were apart with bitter memories, pain and rage and never enough money to go round, that this person you had once loved more than life was now someone you wanted to kill, who had the power to torment you for ever, because you had injured them. 'So you weren't really taking the injunction seriously,' he said, feeling obliged to remind Fred of the legal reality.

'I knew I wasn't supposed to go round there and, what do they call it, molest her.' A faint, bitter smile crossed his face. 'That's a laugh. But I thought if I just wanted to talk . . .' He looked honestly baffled now. 'I mean I can't believe they can stop me going round my own house. I'm still paying the mortgage, for God's sake. She's been off on holiday, I haven't seen the kids for a month. I can't afford to run two bleeding homes, can I?'

'Nobody can,' Richard said with feeling. 'Not really.'

'And now I've got to come and see you. Mind you, I don't mind that. I thought I would when they said I had to, but I don't. It's all right. Funny, that.'

Richard savoured the small, puzzled compliment. 'D'you think there's a chance she might drop the divorce? If you play your cards right?' He wanted Fred to look at the possibilities, to see if he had any choice in the matter. If Fred could behave differently, might he be rewarded? And if not, could he accept his loss without further violence?

There was a long silence between them. Phones rang in other rooms. Richard prayed his own phone would not ring. He could feel the painful effort Fred was putting into his thinking, facing what he did not want to face. He could see the effort in the frown, the clenched hands.

'Not really,' Fred said after a very long time, perhaps only a minute. 'Oh, I try and fool myself there is, but she's got this other bloke and . . .' He looked up at Richard, very straight. 'No, she means it all right.'

'Is that why you want to hit her?'

'It's the kids, I think.' Fred sounded surprised, as if he had really thought it was his wife he wanted back. 'I mean, we tried everything, marriage guidance, the lot, you name it. But at the end of the day she's got the kids and she's got the house and that bloke's going to move in with her. I'm paying the mortgage and I'm in a bedsit. She's got it all her own way and there's nothing I can do about it.' He paused for a moment, then added in a very matter-of-fact tone, 'I'd like to kill her.'

Elizabeth had tried to make her office as homelike as possible, with plants and armchairs and a fridge. Often she felt more of a therapist or a nanny than an editor: authors wanted drinks and encouragement and a listening ear. Some, like Suzy, became insecure and aggressive at the very mention of alterations, and had to be pacified.

Suzy's first novel had done pretty well. Respectable hardcover sales, encouraging reviews, a good paperback deal. Her third novel would probably do even better. Meanwhile, they were stuck with her second. Suzy, humble and grateful at first, now had the bit between her teeth: she was flushed with success and had acquired an agent and an inflated sense of her own value. About her potential, Elizabeth thought, she was probably correct, but about this particular novel she was definitely wrong: it was at once too derivative in style and too personal in content and it had been written too fast. It should be put in a drawer for two or three years and then reworked, not thrown away, because there were some good things in it. But if they didn't publish it, Suzy and her agent would take it elsewhere. It would do badly wherever they took it, but Elizabeth would have lost Suzy for ever.

A familiar dilemma, long ago resolved. She had tried suggesting tactfully to Suzy that she might like to publish her third, as yet unfinished, novel before this second one because it would give her more time to make vital cuts and tighten the whole thing up, but Suzy had been outraged and Elizabeth had needed all her diplomacy and several lunches to retrieve the situation. Now she had settled for getting Suzy to make the minimal changes that she would accept as fast as possible.

'I think you've done a fantastic job,' she said.

Suzy stared at her with suspicion. 'You don't like it.'

'Come on, Suzy, you know me better than that. I'm really pleased. You've made it much tighter. All those cuts we discussed have really worked.'

This was true, up to a point. Elizabeth's suggestions, in so far as Suzy would accept them, had improved the novel greatly.

'There's a "but" coming,' said Suzy, who though stubborn was not insensitive.

'Only a tiny one,' said Elizabeth, trying to think how she would proceed if she were dealing with Felix. He was her yardstick, beloved and familiar, the person she knew and loved best in the world, and she was also his editor. She knew it was possible to be involved and detached at the same time.

'You see?' said Suzy with grim satisfaction. 'I knew it.'

'Now don't get excited. It's really very small.' Elizabeth put her finger and thumb almost together. 'Maybe about that big.'

Suzy closed her eyes defensively. Elizabeth seized the moment.

'It's just when she's in hospital having the baby and she finds out her husband's been screwing her best friend. Don't you think maybe – just maybe – she ought to have a scene with him about it?'

Suzy opened her eyes wide. 'But she's so afraid of losing him,' she said very fast, looking at Elizabeth as if she were an idiot.

'Yes, I know. Only –'

'And it was the sixties. You weren't supposed to get jealous in the sixties.'

'Yes, I do remember that,' Elizabeth said. 'But even so, it's such a big thing –' She thought if it were Helen, knowing that

Helen would never do such a thing, knowing that she was safe.

'And she's feeling very vulnerable. Having just given birth and all that.'

'Quite. All the same, we don't want the reader to think she's a wimp.'

Suzy looked shocked. Elizabeth wondered how far the novel was autobiographical. As far as she knew Suzy had a perfectly nice husband and two teenage sons and lived in Woking, but she had been married twenty years and the husband might be finding her sudden success hard to take. When Suzy came up to town to see Elizabeth she wore peculiar make-up and tied her hair on top of her head with what looked like, but could not possibly be, a pair of black fishnet tights.

Elizabeth said, 'Suzy, we did talk about this and you said you'd look at it.'

'I did, but . . .' She paused and Elizabeth could see her thinking so hard she almost put her thumb in her mouth. She suddenly saw Suzy as an endearing child. 'Maybe she could have a scene with her best friend.'

'It's her husband she needs to have a scene with.' Perhaps Helen was not her best friend, but what else could she be? Elizabeth knew many women, but Helen was the one she liked and trusted most. She didn't think she was Helen's best friend, however, and maybe it had to be mutual. She didn't think Helen needed friends at all, never mind best ones.

'You don't think it would make her too assertive?' Suzy said.

'I think it would make her very human.'

Suzy considered. Elizabeth felt like a paediatrician trying to get a mother's consent to a vital operation. 'You're not saying you won't publish it, are you? If I don't change it.' Please don't tell me my child is going to die. Don't make me go to another hospital.

'Heavens no. We all love it. This is a tiny change. I'd just like it to be as good as it possibly can. If she has a scene with her husband, it would make it that much stronger.' And yet why should Suzy's heroine be stronger than she was herself?

136

Was she trying to get things done that she couldn't do? 'Don't you feel she should express some of her anger? Even if it doesn't work.'

'Ah, it doesn't have to work,' said Suzy. 'That's something.'

'Just a short scene,' Elizabeth pleaded. 'Just a little burst of anger to make her human.'

'Maybe she could write him a letter,' said Suzy. 'And then not send it.'

Elizabeth sank back into her chair and lit a cigarette. She was beginning to wonder anxiously how angry she really was with Felix. Perhaps her professional judgment was impaired.

'She's your character, Suzy,' she said.

Suzy's eyes narrowed under the shiny black bow. 'You don't like her, do you?'

At first Elizabeth didn't entirely believe Felix meant what he said, or else she thought he would change his mind. After all, other people did. She had friends who had sworn they would never have children and after a few years had them, some on purpose, some by mistake. Most of them seemed delighted. In the same way she hoped that he might turn out to be faithful, despite his declared intention not to be.

At first, too, she was so enraptured by his physical presence, the luxury of having him all to herself, to fall asleep with and wake up with, to look at and touch at random, to cook for, to chat to, to make love with whenever they felt like it, which was often in those early days, that it was easy to push the longing for children to the back of her mind. But time was against her: if she were to do it at all, it would be wise to start before she was forty.

Casual references did not do the trick, nor did pregnant friends. Hints resolutely dropped were not picked up. She had to raise the subject directly, by which time she was tense and anxious and perhaps did not choose the right moment, or perhaps there could never be a right moment for something he did not want to discuss at all.

137

'But darling,' he said, sounding merely surprised, not annoyed or put out, 'I thought we settled all that.'

'You really meant it?' she said, feeling sad and angry and foolish.

'Yes, of course. I wouldn't have said it otherwise. It was an important conversation.'

He was planning a Tony Blythe novel at the time and she had the feeling that his attention was wandering.

'I suppose I thought you might change your mind,' she said.

'I don't want to share you with anyone,' he said.

She supposed that was meant to be flattering. 'Not even your own child?'

'Certainly not. Just think how jealous I'd be.'

'But I'm not supposed to be jealous if you have other women.'

'When, darling,' he said gently. 'And I said you weren't supposed to know. I'll always be discreet but I can't control what you feel.'

Now she felt like the boy in *Kidnapped*, suddenly seeing the broken staircase lit by jagged lightning. 'You mean it's already happened?'

'Are you really asking me that? Because I'm not going to lie to you.'

She thought about it and went away, screamed and broke things. He waited until she was calm with exhaustion, then he came after her and held her while she cried.

'I don't understand,' she said. 'If you can have other women, why can't I have children?'

'Because that was the deal,' he explained gently. 'And you agreed to it. I don't like children but I do like sex with other women.'

So it was her fault for making a dishonest bargain. 'And you don't care how much you hurt me?'

'Don't be silly. I love you. But I'm a very selfish person and you knew that before you married me. Why d'you expect me to change?'

He kissed her. He seemed excited by her tears and to her own surprise she found that she was too. They made love. Life went on the same.

138

They had been married then about three years. Contraception was left to her and she had tried everything. It would be easy for her to forget the cap, or come off the pill, or have the coil removed. But what if he refused to accept it? What if he made her have an abortion, or if she wouldn't, what if he left her? No more Felix smelling warm and furry in bed. No more Felix making her laugh at breakfast or holding her hand in the street. How could a baby make up for losing Felix? She could see all around her how hard it was for women of her age to find new men. Unthinkable to be a single parent, an object of pity.

Friends said he would probably come round if it happened, get used to the idea, even be pleased, if not with the pregnancy then with the reality of the baby, and if not at first then as it grew up and learned to talk, became interesting. Each time they spoke about it, they made it sound as if Felix would need more and more time to adapt. Perhaps never, said the voice in her head. They didn't know him as she did, however often they had sat at his dining-table. Some of them even said he was a monster, though charming, of course. She stopped talking to those friends.

Once she was over forty she tried to tell herself that a baby now might be deformed. She didn't really believe it but it helped a bit. The longing faded slowly as she grew older, though it also flared up with sudden spurts of panic. Each period became a chance missed, and eventually one would be her last. She found herself looking curiously at the blood that might have been a child. Then she developed fibroids, as if her womb were determined to grow something, and realised the decision had been made for her. She tested the words 'too late' when she was alone and found them bitter.

Felix's women came and went. She never had any actual proof but she felt their stealthy presence on the edges of her life. Occasionally she wondered if they ever got pregnant. It hurt to share him with others, but she told herself they were fewer than she imagined. She tried to think of them as a pastime, a diversion, like a game of bridge or squash, a visit to a health club. Gradually she began to believe he would never leave her, because he never did. When the pain became too great to bear she hit upon the theory that he didn't want her to have a baby in case she died in childbirth, like his mother. Her life was too precious to risk. Felix said he had no idea if there was any truth in this, but it made her feel a little better. Nothing made her love him any less, at all events, and that, she thought, was the main thing, when all was said and done.

Told F. today. It was awful – not a bit the way I'd imagined. He looked really scared and angry and sort of cornered, as if I'd done it on purpose to trap him. I've never seen him look like that before. It changed his face completely. I felt terrible, very cold and sick. It was ages before he hugged me – too late, really. I'm so afraid. I think I'm going to be alone with the whole thing. It's my problem, not ours. God. What am I going to do?

He didn't believe me at first. Went on about the pill being 100 per cent safe and how could I have made a mistake? I explained about switching handbags but he looked at me as if I was stupid and he really despised me. Then he got up and walked round the room a bit, saying Christ and shit and was I sure because those tests could be wrong and I ought to see a doctor. I said of course I would but I knew I was right because I'd missed two periods and done the test twice and anyway I felt peculiar so I just knew.

Then he sat down rather suddenly and put his head in his hands. He looked old and tired – quite different. Haggard almost. It was a shock. I got us both drinks. I felt sorry for him but more sorry for me. I could see him making a big effort. He said of course it would be wonderful, too good to be true after all these years, but had I thought how it would change my life, my whole future was at stake, and besides we couldn't do it in secret, Mum and Richard would have to know, and had I thought about Elizabeth. How could we do a thing like that to her, it would hurt her so much, particularly at her age, menopausal women are so vulnerable.

I just listened. I don't think I'd ever realised before how fond he is of Elizabeth. He hugged me again and said didn't I agree, when we really thought about it, we simply couldn't go ahead, there were too many reasons not to, although of course it was terribly tempting, like a gift from the gods. Only we had to be rational.

I don't want to be rational. I'm not sure I can be. I'm frightened. I want Felix to put his arms round me and say he loves me and I can have the baby and he'll leave Elizabeth and we'll be together. I didn't know I felt like that till this happened. I was just happy and living a day at a time, not really thinking at all, certainly not making plans. And he never talked about the future either. I should have realised that was a bad sign.

Now I think he's saying I ought to have an abortion, though he hasn't used the word yet. I'm not sure I can do that. I want to talk to Mum but I'm scared. She'll be so angry. She'll know what to do all right, but once I tell her she'll take over and whatever she wants will happen and she'll convince me she's right. If Felix was on my side he could stand up to her for me. But all he seems to care about is Elizabeth not finding out. Of course I don't want to hurt her, she's so nice, but I don't see it would be the end of the world.

When he got home Elizabeth was in evening dress – yet another joke that fate had up its sleeve. He said, 'Oh, God, I'm sorry,' as he remembered, and thought for at least a few seconds that life would really be much simpler if he could just drop dead on the spot. Then everyone would be sorry and he wouldn't have to deal with anything.

'Oh, what the hell,' she said, clearly having had more than one drink. 'I don't care if I never see *Traviata* again. You were the one who couldn't live without going to see that fat cow shrieking her head off. I'm only the one who got the tickets and they cost an arm and a leg.'

Felix suddenly understood why children had tantrums. He wanted to scream and cry and stamp his feet. It was all too much: just when he most needed Elizabeth to comfort him in the worst crisis of his life, not only could he not tell her about it, but he would have to comfort her for something as trivial as being late for the opera.

'I'll go and change now,' he said, glancing at his watch. 'I'll be very quick. We can still make it.'

'Christ, what does it matter?' she yelled, as if she knew everything. 'I'll put up with anything, won't I?' And she hurled her empty glass against the wall.

Felix was startled, admiring the extravagance of the gesture and envying her freedom to make it, while he was obliged to behave well. His brain was racing: useless to regret the fact that home could not be a refuge tonight. Perhaps there was yet a way that the situation might be turned to his advantage. At least at Covent Garden he would be able to sit quietly and think and let the music wash over him. It might be easier than an evening at home, being asked if he was all right, being told he was rather quiet. But he still needed an excuse to cover both his lateness and whatever mood he might be in over dinner.

He went over to Elizabeth and put his arm round her; that usually worked. She pushed him away angrily, but he persisted and after a while she gave in: he could feel her body relax into a kind of grateful passivity. It was too soon for a more positive response.

He said, 'Darling, I'm sorry I forgot but I've had a perfectly awful day.'

'Well, so have I.' She sounded sulky. 'You might think about me for a change. It wouldn't kill you.'

Now he had to come up with something good.

'I've been sitting in the office for hours just trying to decide what to do. I lost all sense of time. The fact is . . .' and he paused for a moment. 'I don't know how to tell you this but I think the book is so bad I'll have to scrap it and start again.'

Elizabeth looked suitably shocked at the magnitude of this disaster. Nothing less would have done; he only hoped it would not jinx his work. He kissed her and she kissed him back and hugged him tight. She felt very different from Sally.

'Come on,' he said. 'Let's go and hear that fat cow sing.'

*

142

Sally said finally, 'Look, Mum, you're going to hate this and I'm sorry – only the thing is, I think I'm pregnant.'

Helen couldn't have been more shocked if Sally had suddenly stuck a knife in her. This was the impossible and it was happening. She had taken out elaborate insurance against this moment since the day Sally was born: bringing her up frankly, openly; telling her everything but waiting for her to ask; giving her love and information, security and freedom. She had been the classic liberal enlightened parent and this was her reward. She simply couldn't believe that they had been overtaken by something so carelessly primitive, so curiously old-fashioned, so fatally stupid.

She saw Sally picking this up from her face, tried to alter it, failed. She was aware that anger was paramount, along with terror and disbelief.

Sally said again, 'I *am* sorry.'

'You'd better tell me how it happened.' Helen heard herself sounding calm, almost normal.

'Oh – you know.' Sally shrugged. 'The usual way.'

'Don't be clever.' God, this was awful. Could they start again? She actually wanted to go back to first base, with Sally so far from being pregnant that she was only a few days old in her cot.

'Sorry, I'm feeling a bit tense.' Sally's head drooped, exposing the vulnerable neck that Helen used to kiss when she was a baby.

'So am I,' she said.

'I know. I've let you down, haven't I?'

Helen tried to hug her then, but she could feel the tension for herself. Sally, politely tolerating her embrace, was actually straining away from her mother with all of her body. Helen knew how that felt, she had done it often enough to her own mother, but she hadn't realised before how much it hurt. She wondered what Sally was hiding, why she wanted to be so far away.

'Tell me properly,' she said, letting Sally go and noting her relief. 'You know I'm on your side.'

'I just made a mistake, that's all. I should have known better – I mean, I did.' She looked distressed but sounded

143

angry. 'You don't deserve this, you've always been so modern.'

Helen heard an accusation. 'Tell me what happened.'

Sally looked away. 'Oh – I forgot my pills. It was when I was away and I switched handbags. That's all really. It shouldn't have happened but it has. So there. Rotten luck for all concerned.'

Helen nodded. To her horror, she found she wanted to cry. Now, of all times, when she was meant to be a rock, she was going to let Sally down.

'Who is he?' she asked, blinking away the useless tears.

Sally looked evasive.

'Come on, you'll have to tell me eventually.' Distantly, softly, fear brushed against her, like a tiny curling feather released from a pillow shaken too vigorously.

Sally said again, 'You're going to hate it,' and looked at her with much too honest eyes. The feather-pillow fear crawled up Helen's back, terrifying her.

'Tell me,' she said.

'Can't we just – well, can't we just talk about it without names? I mean, look, it's just someone I met. Can't we leave it like that?'

'You know we can't.'

Sally shrugged again and Helen sensed a feeling of relief, a letting go of responsibility, gladly dropping it on to the parent, where it had belonged since birth or earlier. 'Oh, all right then,' she said. 'It's Felix.'

'Felix?' said Helen. '*Felix?*'

Sally looked defiant, as if pleased to be proved right. 'I said you wouldn't like it.'

It was all so much worse than Helen had expected (a schoolboy, a teacher, a passing rapist) that she could hardly speak. She felt sick. She wanted to kill. Felix.

'I know you don't like him,' said Sally, sounding bad-tempered, 'but he's not –'

'What?' said Helen. 'Dear God, what isn't he? Tell me something good about him and I'll try to believe you.'

Sally started to cry. Helen hugged her. This time she didn't resist. Then they were both crying.

144

'Shit,' said Sally, who didn't swear. 'Oh, shit.'

'We need a drink,' said Helen, kissing her. 'Come on.'

They sat at the kitchen table with a bottle of wine and a box of tissues between them. Helen kept wishing she still smoked.

'How long have we got before Richard comes back?' Sally asked. They were already conspirators.

'Who knows? He's with Inge.'

'Yes, of course. I'm sorry. You've got enough problems already, haven't you, and here I am making more.'

Helen said, hating the sound of the words, 'How far gone d'you think you are?'

'I did a test when I was two weeks late and it was positive. Then I waited two weeks and did another one. That was positive too. Then it took me another week to get up the nerve to tell you.'

Helen thought how reluctant they both were to add up and face facts. 'So you're about seven weeks.'

Sally nodded, looking at the table.

'But you haven't seen a doctor?'

'No. But I feel funny. Sort of different. Not sick exactly but odd. And my breasts itch.'

'Doctor tomorrow.'

'OK.'

'Those tests can be wrong.'

'I know.'

But there was no hope in the room and they both felt it. Helen's mind was racing: seven weeks was early, thank God Sally had told her quickly, vacuum extraction OK up to twelve weeks, get the GP moving fast or go to PAS, even Harley Street if need be, Felix can pay, God this can't be happening to my child and I want to kill Felix, in fact I seriously think I might when this is over.

'Have you told him?' she asked.

Sally, suddenly looking much older, smiled a small, bitter smile. 'Oh yes. He was shocked. He doesn't want to know. He's afraid of upsetting Elizabeth.'

Until that moment Helen had not thought of Elizabeth. Then she was abruptly in the room, standing beside the absent Richard, another person to be protected. It wasn't enough that Sally had to have an abortion and Helen had to arrange it; she must also deceive her husband and her friend. And all because of Felix.

'Oh, I can see his point,' said Sally defensively, hearing the silence. 'She's very nice. It's not fair to hurt her. Only I thought – maybe there's a way we could do it without her finding out – you know?'

For the first time Helen realised they were not both talking about abortion. She was very frightened.

'I mean,' Sally went on, 'from her point of view it could be anyone. Why should it be Felix? If we're careful, if we make up a good story, she'll believe it, won't she?'

Helen said carefully, 'Are you telling me you want to have it?'

Sally looked at her very straight. 'I'm not sure. I want time to think.'

'Right,' said Helen. 'Now listen. You're eighteen, you can do what you like. But I'm telling you it would be a disaster for you to have a baby by anyone right now, especially Felix. You're too young, he's quite unsuitable, it will change your whole life, and Elizabeth is bound to find out.'

'I could go away.'

I don't believe this, Helen thought. Until half an hour ago I had no problems at all. Just shortage of money, a few duff paintings and bloody Inge pulling her usual tricks. Now I have a daughter who wants to go into hiding to have a baby by Felix without upsetting his wife. I don't believe it. And I'm not going to let it happen. At that moment she felt resolve harden within her like clay. Whatever it takes, I am going to stop this happening.

When he arrived Inge was not there, only the boys taking a motorbike to pieces on the carpet. They hardly glanced at him, their curiously shaved and tinted heads bent close together over the machine: they were busy, collusive. When he was away he fantasised about time alone with them,

146

mending fences or building bridges (he noticed that the imagery of conciliation involved shared activity) but now that he was actually here he heard himself saying in a petulant tone of voice, 'Isn't that going to be rather messy?'

'It's all right,' Karl said, without looking up. 'Mum doesn't mind.'

'She said we could,' Peter added.

Richard wondered if this was a normal evening activity for them or whether it had been specially devised to provoke him. He knew himself to be in the right, but he wished he could talk about something more important in the little time they had.

'Well, it's going to ruin the carpet,' he said.

Karl unscrewed a piece of gleaming metal and laid it carefully on a cushion. 'It's all right. It's not your carpet.'

'I'm only the one who has to replace it.' Richard felt as though Karl had actually struck him.

'We can always clean it,' Peter said. 'Anyway, Mum doesn't care about carpet much. She has other priorities.'

They operated as a team. It could hardly be worse if Inge had trained them to do it. He couldn't remember when it had started but he knew it had been going on for years, filling him with impotent rage. He had never found out how to divide and rule, which he felt sure would have been a solution.

'Where is she?' he said, uncomfortable now in their presence. 'I can't hang about all evening.' It was unlike Inge to be out: usually she was watching at the window or waiting behind the door, ready to extract every possible drop of emotion from his visit. Surely he couldn't be disappointed that she was out? The thought shocked him.

'She won't be long,' Karl said. 'She's only gone to the off-licence. She said she couldn't face seeing you without a drink.'

'I think she wants to offer you one,' said Peter, always a little softer. 'You know what she's like.'

That seemed such an understatement that Richard couldn't reply. In the silence he felt them gathering for a concerted attack.

'She drinks too much,' Karl said, 'but we can't stop her. She gets depressed. And those pills she gets from the doctor sort of make her worse. It's like they don't mix with the booze.'

'If you could come round a bit more often she might cut down.'

'I think she's just lonely. We do our best to cheer her up but we can't really manage it.'

'And we're out a lot,' Peter said, as if Richard might otherwise imagine they had no lives of their own apart from Inge.

'It'd be all right if she had another bloke,' Karl said, 'but she hasn't. Not yet, anyway.'

They were only telling him what he already knew, but hearing it from them made it seem more of an accusation, as if he were one of his own clients in the dock.

She had told Sally to get Felix to ring her, since she couldn't ring him at home because of Elizabeth, and Sally wouldn't give her his other number. He rang at ten the next morning and she was startled by his promptness: she had imagined him too cowardly and ashamed to pick up the phone.

'Helen,' he said, sounding subdued.

'That was quick,' she said sharply. 'You got my message then.'

'Yes. I can't begin –'

'I'd like to kill you,' Helen said.

'Yes, I believe you. D'you believe me when I say how sorry –'

'You're a shit, Felix. All you had to do was leave her alone.'

'Yes, I know. But – anyway, let's not go into all that on the phone. Where shall we meet? Just give me a time and place and I'll be there.'

He sounded meek and submissive, yet oddly detached and sure of himself, as if the outcome of their meeting was already decided and all he had to do was go through the motions in a sufficiently cooperative manner to placate her. She was enraged.

'The Old Ship,' she said, choosing a pub midway between their two homes. 'As soon as they open.'

'See you then,' he said. And put the phone down.

Helen cleaned the house from top to bottom with ferocious energy and speed. It didn't need cleaning but she felt better for having done it. She would have liked to dig the garden as well, but there wasn't time. She left the house at eleven fifteen and drove dangerously fast, the old clapped-out van lurching and squealing, until she remembered that if she unluckily got herself killed or incapacitated, Sally might well go ahead with the pregnancy. She slowed down at once.

Felix was waiting for her when she arrived; he looked pensive and contrite. He had a pint of lager in front of him but he had barely touched it. The pub was half empty and smelt of last night's beer.

'Ah, Helen. What'll you have?'

'It hardly matters, does it? The same as you will do.'

'Pint or half?' he asked solicitously.

'Oh, for Christ's sake, Felix.'

'I know,' he said. 'Sorry. Just a habit.' He went to the bar and Helen stared at the back of his head that Sally must have clasped so often, watched the hands she must have held tight. Now they took money out of a wallet, passed it over and received change.

He came back with a half and put it down in front of her. He sat down, sipped his drink, stared at the table, then, as if with a great effort of will, looked at her. She saw him quite differently: the old familiar face of Richard's friend, her enemy, Elizabeth's husband, was now the one that Sally had kissed, the one that had watched her climax, the one that had talked about love.

'She thinks she wants to have it,' she said, and saw alarm on his face. 'Or rather she doesn't know what she wants. But I'm going to make her have an abortion and I think you should pay for it.'

'Yes, of course,' he said easily, as if they were talking about some minor courtesy like picking up theatre tickets. 'That's the least I can do.' He looked relieved, and his relief disgusted her, although it was convenient.

'I imagined we'd be in agreement,' she said. 'You wouldn't want to risk upsetting your cosy little marriage, would you?

149

So I'm going to do all the dirty work and my daughter is going to bleed and risk her life and all you have to do is sign the cheque.'

'Come on, Helen, be fair. You don't want me to upset my cosy little marriage, as you put it, you'd be appalled if I left Elizabeth and ran off with Sally and let her have the baby. And we both know it's not like the bad old days – OK, it's never pleasant, but abortion nowadays is just about as safe and hygienic as they can make it –'

'As far as you know,' she said. 'You don't have to find out, do you?'

'No, but that's not my fault, it's biology. And I don't believe Sally's risking her life. You wouldn't let her, neither would I.'

'Oh really,' she said. 'What would you do instead?'

'It's a safe operation, Helen, you know it is, if they do it early, and this is early, isn't it? I'm sorry about it, of course I am, bloody sorry, but she was on the pill, and if she forgot, that's hardly my fault, is it?'

'I see,' Helen said. 'You get my daughter pregnant and then you tell me it's her fault.'

'That's not what I said.' He was determinedly rational. 'We both wanted to have an affair and she told me it was safe.'

'Of course,' Helen said. 'That makes it all right. She talked you into it.'

'Well, I didn't rape her.' He sipped his beer, looking quite indignant. Helen planned her exit at that moment. It wouldn't be dignified but it would give her some small satisfaction.

'I'm not telling Richard,' she said, 'because he'd probably want her to have it. Then she'd either have to have it adopted, which could be heartbreaking, or she'd want to keep it and I'd have to look after it, which I'm not prepared to do.'

'No,' he said. 'I quite see that.' He spoke absently, as if for him the argument stopped at abortion, and the other possibilities were so theoretical they might as well not be considered. Just like me, Helen thought. Their complicity made her sick.

'I suppose you realise,' she said, 'that if all this came out, it

150

would be the end of your friendship with Richard as well as the end of your marriage. So I'm not just doing the best thing for Sally, I'm protecting you as well.'

'I question that,' he said, looking at her coldly. 'It just so happens that the two things go together. But I don't think you can assume how Richard and Elizabeth would react just because —'

Helen threw the contents of her glass in his face. Beer splashed all over him, soaking his hair, staining his shirt and jacket. The barmaid gazed with open mouth, then giggled, then looked away. Felix, once he got over the shock, took out a handkerchief and mopped his face. He looked ridiculous, dripping. Other drinkers stared or pretended not to notice.

'I hope that made you feel better,' he said with dignity.

'I hope you get cancer, Felix,' Helen said. 'I hope you die very slowly, in great pain, as soon as possible.'

'I'll do my best.' He put the sodden handkerchief back in his pocket.

Helen walked out of the pub, got into the van and drove home shaking. Outside the front door she changed her mind, in case Richard or Sally came home unexpectedly, and drove to the studio instead, where she could be sure of being alone. But she needed to share the problem and there was one person who deserved to know. Perhaps he could even help, she thought: how ironic that would be. She telephoned, feeling there was no time to be lost, but the number was unobtainable, and that too seemed appropriate, after all these years.

The doctor confirmed the pregnancy, then leaned back in his chair and put his fingertips together. 'Well, Sally, how d'you feel about it?'

Sally could feel Helen's eyes boring into her, and the whole force of Helen's personality willing her to say the right thing. She hesitated.

'Take your time,' the doctor said.

The silence stretched. Sally was terrified. She fixed her eyes

151

on a bit of his desk where the leather was peeling away. She hadn't really taken in the fact that she was actually pregnant. Thinking or fearing she was, she still felt different when she heard a doctor say it. Pregnant. A certainty. Felix's child inside her. Her child. No matter how inconvenient, it was still a sort of miracle.

'I don't think we have a lot of time,' Helen said into the extending silence.

The doctor smiled and shook his head. Sally was impressed by his calm. Up to now, everyone had been full of panic and urgency: Felix, Helen, she herself.

'That's the mistake everyone makes,' the doctor said pleasantly. 'This is an important decision. If she's going ahead, we've got all the time in the world. And if she isn't, we can still take a few days, even a few weeks if need be, to make sure we're doing the right thing. It's important that we should.'

It sounded wonderful. Sally imagined going away with the pressure taken off her, getting into bed and hiding under the duvet for days or even weeks. She might wake up and find the problem solved: a miscarriage, or someone saying it was too late for an abortion now. Or even a baby. Could she sleep for seven months? She would certainly like to; she could visualise nothing more enticing.

The doctor smiled at her. 'Sally, why don't you go home and think about it? Come back next week and we'll have another chat.'

'Could I?' She was so grateful. Time to think. Choices. And she loved the way the doctor seemed to find it all routine, something that happened all the time. She wasn't the only idiot around. She wasn't unique. Helen had made her feel that she had been monstrously stupid.

Helen said, 'Look, the father's a married man, a family friend. He's middle-aged. He's got a childless menopausal wife who adores him. She'll have a fit if she finds out. And Sally's going to university in October. This could ruin her life.'

'I know it's very difficult,' the doctor said. 'These things always are. But it's still Sally's decision. You and I might

152

think she'd be crazy to have a baby now, but it's still up to her. And there's always adoption. There's a great shortage of babies, thanks to the 1967 Abortion Act. It would be very easy to arrange.'

'Are you anti-abortion?' Helen asked. 'Because if you are, just tell me and we'll go somewhere else. I have a right to do that.'

'Of course you do. And I'm not anti-abortion at all. I recommend lots of my patients to have terminations. Often it's the best solution. But only if that's what they really want. And I'm not sure Sally's made up her mind yet. Have you, Sally?'

'I think I ought to have an abortion really,' said Sally, just to please Helen, now that she felt sure the doctor would not believe her.

The doctor looked perfectly calm and contented. 'Why?' he said.

Sally didn't know what to say. 'Well, it's the sensible thing. I can't look after a baby and I'm going to college and it'll make all sorts of problems . . .'

The doctor smiled. 'D'you want the baby?'

Helen said, 'For God's sake . . .'

Sally said, 'I don't know.'

The doctor sat back in his chair. 'Come back next week. I've got to be sure you really want a termination, not just to please your mother. As the law stands, in theory we don't have abortion on demand, but in practice we do. Don't quote me on that, I'll deny it. But the situation is this: if you truly want an abortion, I can arrange it. If you want an adoption, I can arrange that too. And if you want to keep your baby, then that's up to you. It really is your decision.'

Helen said, 'I'm sorry, I don't think Sally's old enough to know what this decision means. A baby is a lifetime commitment.'

The doctor said, 'Yes, of course, I appreciate your anxiety. I even happen to agree with you.'

'I wouldn't have guessed,' Helen said.

'I'm sorry. Perhaps I'm going too far the other way. But Sally's got to feel happy about her decision or you and I will have a lot of problems in the future, much worse than this one.'

They sat in the van and didn't speak for a while. Then Helen said, 'Well, that's that.'

'We can go back next week. He said so.'

'Whatever for?'

'To say I want an abortion.'

Helen sighed. 'Don't be ridiculous. He'll never believe you now. He'll just think I'm pushing you into it.'

Sally said, greatly daring, 'Well, aren't you?'

Helen started the van. 'If you want this baby, all you have to do is tell Richard. He'll make sure you have it.'

This was so true that Sally was silent.

'In fact,' Helen said, 'I don't really understand why you didn't tell Richard instead of me.'

'I don't know either,' Sally said. 'Except I didn't want him to be angry with Felix.'

'Or just possibly you don't want to have the baby,' said Helen, 'but you'd rather blame me for making the decision.'

'I just want time to think,' Sally said. 'The doctor said I could have a week.'

'It's no good,' said Helen, parking. 'I'm not fit to drive.'

Sally started to cry. 'I'm sorry,' she said. 'I messed it up, didn't I? I couldn't think fast enough, I didn't know what to say.'

Helen put her arms round her. 'I don't mind if you do blame me,' she said. 'That's what I'm here for.'

Driving into the country reminded Helen how much she would hate to live there. She felt homesick for buildings, threatened by a lack of structure when surrounded by fields and trees. No amount of beauty could make up for feeling unsafe. She still wasn't sure why she had come: whether

154

Carey simply had a right to know that his daughter was pregnant or whether she was actually hoping against the odds that he might even now come up with the help and support he had never been able to give her before. The triumph of hope over experience: she seemed to remember that as a definition of second marriage.

She knew without checking the address that she had found the right house. Discarded furniture lay rusting and rotting in the garden, alongside rabbit hutches and a goat in a pen, morosely cropping grass and staring at her with a challenging look. As she walked up the path she could hear children screaming. God knows how Barbara Hepworth managed with triplets, she thought; she must have been made of sterner stuff than I am.

Marsha opened the door and her face lit up with joyful surprise at the sight of Helen. What a nice person she must be, Helen reflected; no wonder Carey loves her. I can't imagine myself giving Inge such a radiant welcome if she turned up on my doorstep. But her eyes were drawn at once to Marsha's distended belly, and she felt the loss of hope without really knowing what she had been hoping for.

'Yes, now you know what I'm getting for Christmas,' Marsha said cheerfully. 'Oh, Helen, it's lovely to see you after all this time.'

It was hard to remember that Marsha was ten years younger than herself. Her red hair curled wildly and she had put on a lot of weight. But her large freckled face was placid and friendly, rather like a good-natured cow. A child of two clung to her legs, one aged four peered round her and a six-year-old hovered in the background. Yet she seemed remarkably carefree.

'I'm sorry to drop in like this,' Helen said, 'but I need to talk to Carey about Sally and when I tried to ring they said your phone had been disconnected.'

Marsha looked vague. 'Has it? I don't use it much. Well, I don't get the time, not with this lot. I suppose he didn't pay the bill. I do remind him but you know what he's like.'

Helen smiled and nodded. She thought they might have been two mothers discussing a much-loved errant son.

'Oh, do come in, Helen,' Marsha said. 'You're looking ever so well. How's the painting going?'

'I won't, thanks all the same. I'm in a bit of a hurry. Could you just ask Carey to ring me and tell him it's urgent.'

Marsha shook her head. 'I'm sorry, love, he's in Brighton. He's away all week.'

'Could you give me his number?'

'I don't think he has one. Well, he probably has but he hasn't given it to me.' She laughed. 'I expect he's up to his old tricks. Well, you can't blame him really, can you, not with me in this state. I've got his address, if that's any good, only he doesn't answer letters, does he?'

'Not unless he's changed out of all recognition,' said Helen sharply.

'I'll get it for you,' said Marsha, waddling off.

How strange, Helen thought. I actually used to be jealous of her. I used to torture myself imagining her and Carey making love. Now we're like old friends, pleased to see each other and amused by his little weaknesses.

The two-year-old had followed Marsha but the other children remained. The four-year-old put its tongue out at Helen and she returned the gesture. It was a relief to admit to herself that she did not like children. They took up too much time and energy. They tore the guts out of you. She could never have coped with more: she simply didn't have the resources. The depth of her love for Sally told her that, as much as Marsha's cheerful chaos.

Marsha came back and gave her a piece of paper. 'I do wish you'd have a cup of tea. I could do with a chat.'

She sounded lonely, missing adult company. Helen said, 'I'm sorry, I've got so much to do. Maybe another time. Thanks for the address.'

Marsha patted her belly. 'Wish me luck, won't you?'

'Oh, I do,' said Helen sincerely. 'Believe me.'

Marsha laughed. 'This is definitely the last one. Mind you, we said that last time.'

*

Driving to Brighton tested the van to the limit of its powers, but she managed to arrive just as the rehearsal was ending, Sibelius's Fifth wafting out to her as she sat in the lobby. It was her first moment of peace in a day that seemed already long and stressful. She closed her eyes and let it wash over her for a few moments before going to waylay Carey at the exit. Waiting for him made her feel like a wife again and that shocked her, the realisation that she still felt like Richard's mistress. She wondered if he would take that as a compliment. She didn't really believe in marriage any more, but that of course meant she didn't believe in divorce either.

She was unprepared for the rush of feelings that swamped her when she saw him. Like Marsha he looked much older and heavier, and there was far more grey in his hair. She found herself feeling protective towards him, thinking how much he must hate growing old. She remembered the sense of identity they had given each other at the beginning, when one of their favourite fantasies was that they were twins enjoying an incestuous relationship.

He looked startled to see her, too, and then delighted. They stood and smiled at each other while the rest of the orchestra hurried past. Although he looked older, the mere fact of seeing him seemed to put her in touch with her own youth. It was quite a shock to remember how much she had once loved him.

She said, 'Sibelius sounded OK.'

'Yes, it still works, that one.' And after a long silence: 'What are you doing here?'

'I want to talk to you about Sally.'

'Come and have a drink then.'

She sensed him wanting to take her arm and not quite liking to. They walked together towards the nearest pub. Now it felt awkward, like a blind date.

She said, 'Marsha was very cheerful.'

'Yes, she likes being pregnant.'

'Just as well really.'

At the door of the pub he stopped and said to her abruptly, 'You look wonderful.'

*

She told him about Sally and he listened, looking more and more concerned, but not speaking. When she stopped he said, 'God, what a mess. I wish I knew what to say.'

She was conscious of feeling unfairly disappointed and also obscurely blamed. 'Oh, I don't expect an instant solution. I just thought you should know somehow, as you're her father, and I daren't tell Richard. It seems too big a thing to do on my own without talking to anyone.'

'Poor Helen. I'm sorry. I wish I'd been there.'

She said sharply, 'Well, you're here now,' thinking how typical it was that they should meet after all these years at a time of crisis and be almost at once on the verge of a row. It was all so familiar; nothing had changed.

He said, 'Are you blaming me? Is it all my fault for buggering off?'

'Well, I don't think I'd go quite that far. But it did cross my mind that maybe if she'd had her own father around, she might not have found Felix so attractive.'

'I thought Richard was meant to be the perfect step-father.' He sounded bitter and sulky, as if all his life he had been compared and found wanting.

'Yes, he's been wonderful. They get on very well. But it's not the same, is it?' Suddenly she felt quite fragile and reluctant to fight: an alarming sensation when she had trained herself not to be vulnerable. 'Oh, I don't know, Carey. Maybe she needed you, maybe she didn't. I just feel I'm all alone with the problem and I wanted to share it with you.'

Carey put his hand over hers on the table. His touch gave her a shock like electricity. So that too was unchanged. They both looked at their two hands and then back at each other.

'I did mean to keep in touch,' Carey said. 'But it wasn't easy. You were pretty angry with me at first.'

'Yes, I was.'

'I found it very painful, you know. I mean, seeing you both and then just going away afterwards. You made it so clear you didn't need me.'

Helen remembered how much she had needed him and

how hard it had been to pretend otherwise. 'Sally needed you,' she said.

'I didn't have very much to offer her then.'

'What about now? If I can't talk her into having an abortion.' She paused: the alternative was really too dreadful to contemplate. 'I just had this wild idea you might be able to fit one more baby into your household and hardly notice.'

'My God,' Carey said.

'Oh well, it was just an idea. I must say my heart rather sank when I saw Marsha. Four seems a lot more than three.'

'Yes,' Carey said, 'it does to me too.' Their hands were still touching, linked but unmoving, there on the table. 'Can't Sally just have it adopted?'

'Suppose she doesn't want to when it comes to the point and I get stuck with it? I'm not having Felix's child in my house.' When she heard her own words she realised that the decision was made, regardless of Sally's wishes, and she was shocked and relieved.

'Is he as bad as all that?'

'He's a pig. I hope his cock drops off.'

Carey smiled. 'You said that to me once.'

'Did I? I don't remember. Well, it obviously didn't work. I can't be a very efficient witch.'

He looked at their hands, and then at her face. He looked old and grey and tired, a man who had come to terms with his situation. She saw her own lost youth in his face and remembered how they had both intended to be famous and rich and in love for ever.

'Well, what now? I'd like to go back to my hotel for a rest. Will you come with me?'

She heard herself saying, 'I suppose that's why I'm here.'

His skin still smelt the same, but then why should it not? That was normal, although it felt like magic. Their bodies slid together with the same familiar ease and they knew how to excite each other, dissolving the intervening years with laughter and skill. It seemed natural: everything fitted. She

159

felt very healed, letting all her burdens drop along with her clothes, and able to forgive him for long-ago sins that she had carried heavily and angrily for many years. They were at peace.

She said, 'You have a very comforting body.'

'I've missed you.'

They kissed. The kiss went on for a long time, as if they were both afraid of coming out of it and starting to talk again.

'You're better off with Marsha,' she said eventually. 'This is all we ever had.'

'It still feels like quite a lot.'

'But not enough when I started shouting about the unpaid bills, the unanswered letters, the telephone cut off.'

They smiled at each other, because now in bed, all this time later, these were minor crimes and did not matter.

'Not to mention the bits on the side in the afternoons,' she added, thinking that she was now comfortably one of them. 'Maybe it's my fault you didn't keep in touch with Sally. Maybe I made you feel unwelcome because I was afraid I'd do exactly what I'm doing now.' And she remembered how when her father died she had been frantic to go to bed with someone, just for comfort. The warmth of another body as a hedge against death.

Carey said, 'You know . . . we could keep in touch.'

'Oh no,' she said, alarmed at the temptation. 'This is strictly a one-off. A bit of help and comfort in my hour of need. God, you feel wonderful. You feel so solid. I have to keep reminding myself how flimsy you are inside.'

'You don't do a lot for my morale.'

'Yes, I do.'

'Yes, you do.' He smiled. 'I'd really like to see Sally again. Can I?'

'I wish you would. She's going to need someone. I'm afraid she may go off me in a big way when this is over, but that's a chance I'll have to take.'

He said, sounding dubious, 'You're that sure you're right?'

'Yes, I am.'

'I do hate to think of her having an abortion.'

160

As if I don't, Helen thought. Men can afford to have these fine scruples. You won't be the one having to cope with this baby you don't want aborted. Suddenly she was annoyed with herself for involving him in such a female mess.

'So do I,' she said, 'but she'll get over it. She'll grieve for a few months and she'll blame me. That's all right. What she won't get over is a lifetime with Felix's child.'

There was a long silence. Carey said hesitantly, 'When you kicked me out . . .'

'When you left me.'

'When we split up, I thought you might be pregnant.'

She remembered then his old gift for sensing things, for picking up vibrations, without any real evidence. It could be attractive or threatening.

'So did I,' she said smoothly. 'But I wasn't.'

'I'd have come back if you had been.'

'But I didn't want you back. At least, only like this.'

'Just wanted you to know,' he said peaceably.

'Thank you. I think I did know really.'

They cuddled for a while and she thought of the child that might have been with sadness but without regret. It was better as it was.

'Are you happy with him?' he asked.

'Yes. We suit each other. We have a good life. It's warm and friendly and calm. His ex-wife is a pain in the arse, but that's the only snag.'

'You haven't said anything about love.'

Now she felt uncomfortable, pinned under the microscope and dissected. 'And we love each other.'

'So you're not even slightly bored?'

'No.'

'I'm bored with Marsha,' he said, sounding defiant.

'You were bored with me too,' she reminded him.

He turned to her in bed and held her face in his hands. 'Oh Helen. We were too young. It could have worked if we'd been older. And richer.'

She said, 'Perhaps,' and wondered if she meant it.

*

Driving home she thought that now it was really finished in a way it had not been before, although she had not realised. How strange to be carrying all that for so many years without knowing. She was free of him now and she could also forgive Richard for not being accessible in her dilemma. She had balanced her scales.

Sally came to Felix for what he sensed was a last-ditch attempt. He felt pure terror. It was like war-time: he was under fire and he did not know if his nerve would hold. Not that he had ever been in a war but he was sure that was how it would feel. All her guns were blazing at him. He saw her as a woman for the first time, grown-up and alarming, protecting her half-formed child. But he had a marriage to preserve, and he was stronger than she was because he had lived longer and had more practice in self-defence.

He said gently, 'Darling, I'm sorry, but Helen's right.'

'You really don't want it.'

'It's not that, it would have been wonderful, but . . . you're going to college . . . Elizabeth would be terribly hurt . . .'

'I could go away,' Sally said, suddenly young again. 'Nobody would know. My father might help me. Then when I've finished at college I can get a job. You could visit me and . . . the baby.'

What a long view she was taking; how fast she made the years go by.

'My love, it's a fantasy,' he said. 'It's just not practical.'

'You want me to kill it instead,' she said, the angry woman again with her gun.

'That's not the way to think of it.'

'It's practical. And that's how it feels.' Then suddenly she crumpled up. 'I'm frightened.'

He went to her and tried to embrace her, but she pulled away.

'Mum says Elizabeth wanted children but you wouldn't let her have any. Is that true?'

Now it was the really big guns and he felt quite steady.

'No.'

In the silence that followed he could tell that she knew he was lying.

'We're finished, aren't we?' she said. She sounded very sad.

'No. We'll get through this, I'll come down to Sussex. It'll be all right, I promise you.'

But she was too young.

'You really didn't mean any of it, did you? All those things you said. It was just a game.'

It hurt to see her face change, that new look of disillusion and disgust that he had put there. He wasn't proud of that.

He said, knowing she wouldn't believe him, 'Sally, I love you. Nothing has changed. Only we can't have a baby and I never said we could.'

Mum left me alone with Richard tonight. Not that I couldn't manage to be alone with him any time if I wanted to, but she did it very pointedly as if to say there now, there's your chance, don't say I'm forcing you into anything. She went to bed early and there we were, Richard and me.

He was going through a whole pile of probation reports. He looked so nice, so concerned, so remote. I only had to speak. I imagined how it would be if I told him, shock, horror, and a big row with Mum and Felix, and lots of help for me to keep the baby. I nearly did it. I don't know what stopped me. Somehow when it came to the point I was more scared of telling him than not telling him. I felt it would all be out of my hands, although of course it isn't in my hands, it's in Mum's. It seemed such a huge thing to do. It would start such a long chain of events, I'd lose control of the whole thing. Only I don't have control anyway.

I got so close to telling him he actually realised there was something the matter and then I panicked and had to pretend I was nervous about going to Sussex. He was lovely about it and said he'd come and fetch me any time I wanted to come home. I knew more than ever then that I couldn't tell him.

He'd be so disappointed in me. But it wasn't just that. I was disappointed in him too, that he couldn't read my mind. Unfair, I know, but if he'd guessed, then I could have told him. It doesn't make sense. Only I'm so bad at pretending, how can he help me if he can't even see through me? He's just not powerful enough.

Felix is powerful. He doesn't want the baby and that's that. He's not going to give an inch. I tried to talk to him but it wasn't any good. He kept saying he loved me and Mum was lying about him not letting Elizabeth get pregnant, but I know he was lying, I just know it. He's frightened too that I might tell Richard. I hate seeing him frightened. It's awful that he and Mum hate each other and yet they're in total agreement about this. I don't stand a chance. I've lost Felix by getting pregnant and now I've got to lose the baby too. Oh, he says he wants to go on seeing me but I just can't imagine it, not after all this.

Mum is the really powerful one. She's just going to take charge of everything and no one can stop her. I could if I had the guts or someone to help me, but I haven't. Maybe in my heart I think she's right. That's the worst part. Not being sure what I feel.

Next week I'll go back to the doctor and tell him I've made up my mind. And he'll believe me.

Helen thought they had made it as nice as they could. A large anonymous clinic looking out on to flowerbeds and trees, an atmosphere of luxury and comfort, contrasting sharply with the bleak austerity of her own abortion, fifteen years ago. She caught herself feeling terrified that Sally might actually run away at the last moment; she wanted them to sedate her immediately and knew they would not. She couldn't bear the waiting; she wanted the time to pass as quickly as possible and the whole thing to be over. Never mind the guilt and blame, she would cope with that. She could cope with anything once Sally was no longer pregnant by Felix.

Sally's room was small but full of everything she needed: a

bed, chair, phone, television and flowers that Felix, damn his eyes, had sent despite her prohibition. Sally read the card and put it in her handbag. She looked around.

'It's very smart here,' she said. 'It's like a hotel. Did you make him pay for all this?'

'Yes, of course,' Helen said. 'But he offered. Don't you think he should?'

'Why not?' Sally said. 'It's all he can do, isn't it? And we couldn't, could we? But I don't suppose it's a lot of money to him.'

She wandered round the room, fiddling with things and looking out of the window. She opened a door and found a bathroom. She disappeared into it and presently came back. She looked very pale and Helen wondered if she had been sick, although she had heard nothing other than the sound of running water. They had both slept badly and she looked pale herself when she glanced in the mirror. Lying beside Richard at night and blaming him for not divining her secret, yet being grateful he did not, getting Sally ready and bringing her here, all that had exhausted her. She felt close to the end of her resources; she hoped the relief of having it all over soon would give her fresh energy to cope with the aftermath.

'Lovely pink towels,' Sally said. She was talking very fast. 'Only I'll hardly have time to use them. I suppose the next person will. Funny to think of people coming in here all the time to have abortions. Must be quite a rapid turnover if it only takes fifteen minutes. I wonder how long they let you lie down for? Bit like being a blood donor really. D'you remember that Hancock sketch? I wonder if they have a high season and a low season. What d'you think?'

'Oh darling,' Helen said, 'it's going to be all right.' She could see the scare in Sally's face and longed to hug her but sensed this would not be welcome at all.

'They're all being so nice to me,' Sally said. 'I never imagined it would be like this.'

'Of course they are. Why ever not? It's the least they can do.'

'It just seems wrong somehow. But then the whole thing seems wrong.'

'It'll soon be over and you're going to be fine.' She was reminded of taking Sally to the dentist as a child, something else that had to be done, and how hard even that had been, subjecting her to short-term pain for her long-term good. She didn't expect Sally, at this moment, to believe that she would willingly sacrifice her own life to protect her child from suffering of any kind. She would not have believed it of her own mother either. But it was a bitter thing to know it could not be done. 'I'm just so sorry you have to go through this,' she said inadequately.

'I could still change my mind though, couldn't I?' Sally said. 'Right up to the last minute.'

Helen looked at her. It was true and there was nothing she could do about it. She knew there must be a look of dread on her face and wondered if that counted as blackmail. Yet she was still sure she was right or she couldn't have persisted.

'Don't worry,' Sally said. 'I'm not going to. I know when I'm beaten.'

'Don't punish yourself. You don't deserve it.' Helen tried to hug her then, instinct defeating judgment, and Sally predictably pushed her away. Perhaps they both needed that act of rejection, she thought.

'Could you leave me alone please? Only I haven't got much more time.' She tolerated Helen's kiss. 'Please. It's all right. I just want to be alone with it, whatever it is.'

Helen went and waited in the waiting-room but she couldn't settle down with magazines, and other people looking anxious. She went out and walked around; she looked at the flowers and confronted the fear that Sally might actually die and she would have killed her. But it was less likely than death in childbirth and she would not have feared that. Yet even in this extremity she still had no doubts that it was wrong for Sally to have Felix's child, or any child, at eighteen, and she had to save her from it. The decision was entirely hers. She thought of Richard at work, caring for other people and taking on their problems; she thought of Carey, escaping

166

into music and letting Marsha look after him; she thought of Felix, merely writing a cheque and going home to be adored by Elizabeth. She had never felt so alone. When she went back inside, a nurse came up to her and said, 'Oh, Mrs Morgan, I've been looking for you, your daughter's fine.'

Helen resisted the impulse to kiss her, to fling her arms round her and sob with relief. She didn't seem much older than Sally herself. Would she learn anything from her work?

'Can I see her?'

'In a little while. She's only just come round and she's having a little weep.'

The knowledge that Sally was crying seemed impossible to bear.

'Oh, it's all right,' the nurse said. 'They all do that.' And then Helen remembered doing it herself, a buried memory, only she hadn't known it was universal. The nurse put her hand on her arm.

'Why don't you go and have a nice cup of tea?'

She sat with Sally until it was time to go home. She had stopped crying but she looked very white. She didn't speak or look at Helen. When she got up she moved stiffly and she wouldn't let Helen touch her to help her down the stairs or into the car. Helen drove her home and she went straight to bed. The house seemed very quiet. Helen sat alone downstairs for a long time, not moving. If she had been religious she would have given thanks to God.

On the day of the abortion Felix took Richard out to dinner, as he had promised Helen he would. It would help her, she said, to have as much time as possible to get Sally settled after it was all over. Then the next day, if need be, it could all be passed off as a bad period. She was crisp and clinical about the whole thing: he was to pay the money into her bank but he was not to send flowers to the clinic. Above all, he was not to telephone or visit.

He was glad to pay the money, almost wishing it were more, and shocked to find he had no inclination to phone or visit. He resented being cast in the role of villain when he did not see how any of this was his fault, when all he had done was trust Sally to go on taking the pill. He was also terrified that she might be the one in a million or whatever it was who would confound statistics and actually die. He couldn't talk to her any more; they had said everything they could possibly say. But he still feared she might ring him up at the last moment and beg him to save her from the ordeal. This fear made him feel that, far from avoiding such a risk, he actually had to answer the phone all the time in order to give her maximum opportunity to put him on the spot. It was insane generosity, or uncharacteristic masochism, or perhaps he felt more guilty than he knew, because he still had no intention of changing his mind if she did contact him. But of course she didn't phone, and of course he did disobey Helen and send flowers. He couldn't think of an appropriate message when it came to the point, so he just put 'from Felix, with all my love'. Even as he did it, he had the distinct feeling that whatever he said would be wrong.

It was a difficult day to get through: he didn't know what time the abortion was actually being done and he really didn't want to focus on it at all, though he would have liked to know when he could safely relax and think, Thank Christ it's all over, poor little thing, I hope they didn't hurt her. He felt obliged to give himself unpleasant tasks, instead of having a large lunch and several drinks, so he sorted out a lot of papers for his accountant and faced up to a chapter in the book that needed partly rewriting and partly throwing away. By the end of the day he was exhausted and irritable.

At dinner Richard seemed perversely determined to talk about Sally: what a joy she had always been and how much he and Helen were going to miss her once she went to Sussex, although of course they would also enjoy being alone together for the first time. Then he bemoaned the fact that Helen had never been willing to have more children because she was so wrapped up in her work. Felix chafed at the irony of the conversation and tried his best to steer Richard on to safer topics, but only succeeded in talking about Helen's paintings, which he thought were sterile and Richard thought were beautiful.

'Beautiful and sterile perhaps,' said Felix, aware that they were still on aspects of reproduction.

'No, you can't get away with that,' said Richard, smiling tolerantly. 'She's a good painter and it's very unfair she can't give all her time to it. I had another go at Inge the other day about money but it didn't work and the boys gave me a hard time.' He sighed. 'I don't know. Maybe you're better off without kids.'

But Felix knew he didn't mean that. 'Well, you can't get it right, whatever you do,' he said. 'That seems to be the general message. Lizzie's been very moody lately. I think it's her age.'

'How's your little friend in Cambridge?' Richard asked, reminding Felix of the lie he had almost forgotten telling before the fatal weekend. So they were still talking about Sally. The subject seemed inescapable, like chewing gum sticking to your shoes. The more you scraped and struggled, the more it clung to you.

'Oh, that's all over,' he said hurriedly. The last thing he wanted today of all days was to have Richard reminding him of his amorous exploits, though such a conversation would have normally given them both pleasure.

'You'll soon find someone else.'

'I'm not actually looking at the moment. The bloody book seems to take up all my energy.' Perhaps they could talk about work; that would be safe.

'Is Natasha pressing you?'

'Not really. She knows when she's beaten. I've explained to her that I'm almost suicidal and one more nudging phone call could push me over the edge.'

Richard laughed. Felix was glad to be amusing, and relieved to have got off the subject of Sally, babies and sex, but the irony of the situation left him discontented. If it were any other problem, he could have talked to Richard about it. He reflected how curious it was that he had led such a tranquil life, despite being generally regarded as a rogue, while Richard, the good Samaritan, had deserted his wife and abandoned his children. For a wild moment he wanted to throw himself on Richard's mercy, confess and be forgiven. Richard of all people should understand; burdened with his own guilt, he should not condemn others. But he would. He would be outraged and it would be the end of the friendship. Felix knew that: he had finally trespassed too close to home. Suddenly he felt very afraid. He had been so preoccupied all day with the abortion that he had failed to notice that now and in the future lay the greatest danger. For ever more there would be a secret between them, like an unexploded mine.

'I know the feeling,' Richard said. 'That's exactly the effect Inge has on me.'

'You'll get her off your back one day,' Felix said. 'She's bound to remarry eventually.'

Richard sighed. 'The boys say all she needs is a new man. As if they expected me to find one for her.'

'Is she still as beautiful as ever?' Felix had always desired Inge as indeed he desired Helen, though they could hardly be more different.

'I suppose she is. I don't really see her any more, I just see problems.'

'You always marry such beautiful women,' Felix said.

'Both of them, you mean? God, you can't be envious, after all the women you've had.' But he sounded pleased and flattered.

'You really think I lead a charmed life.'

'Maybe I want to,' Richard said fondly. 'Anyway, don't you?'

'Some of the time,' Felix said. 'I've been feeling very old lately.'

It was a long time before Sally slept. She had refused to let Helen sit with her, saying she wanted to be alone, but really it was a comfort to know Helen was only downstairs.

In the clinic she had lain with her hands on her stomach for those final minutes, saying goodbye to the baby, calling it little one, saying she was sorry, asking it to forgive her. Now she wrapped her arms round herself for consolation, feeling hollow and empty, needing Felix to hold her, loving him and hating him, longing to call for Helen but too angry to open her mouth, and confused, most of all confused, that she could feel already, acutely, both a sense of loss and a sense of relief.

AUTUMN

She let them drive her to Sussex when the time came. She had meant to be independent, doing it all by herself on the train, but in the end it was too much effort, she simply had too much stuff. It was a shock to see the place again: she hadn't been down since her interview and now it was going to be her home. So many people, so much to do, to see, to learn, to explore. It was exciting and it scared her. She was afraid she could be very lonely here among all these people; she felt remote inside her head and shut off from everyone, as if behind glass. She couldn't wait for Helen and Richard to go and yet she was scared to be alone.

'Don't worry if I don't write,' she told them. 'I'm going to be very busy. I'll just ring you now and then.'

Inge loved Sunday mornings. In the days of her marriage it had been a particularly good time to make love, with no excuses from Richard about being late for work or having to go shopping, the boys trained to play quietly in a cot full of toys (the bedroom door locked just in case) or, later, visiting their friends and preventing other people's parents from making love. The atmosphere lingered although Richard had gone, and she always woke feeling restless and hopeful. Even without Richard, there were still the delights of the Sunday papers and bacon frying and loud music. Even without a job to relax from or a religion to practise, the morning presented quite a different texture from the rest of the week. It was not until later in the day that alcohol and depression took over.

The boys were more organised than she was, viewing the morning as a time to catch up on chores before they embarked on pleasure. Around noon Karl would appear in the doorway with a black dustbin liner stuffed with dirty clothes. She was pleased her children chose to take on these burdens that she had cast aside.

'Anything for the launderette, Mum? I've got the sheets and towels.'

Inge considered. It was a good opportunity but too much effort to work out what really needed to be washed. 'I don't know. There may be something under my bed.'

'Right. I'll look.' He stomped off, sounding resigned but not resentful as she would have been if her mother behaved like that. But she felt Richard's desertion excused everything. Mere survival took all her energy: it was a daily achievement, she thought, not to kill herself out of sheer despair. She went on reading, turning up Götterdämmerung on her stereo because she could hear Peter's hard rock intruding from upstairs, when a familiar face caught her attention in the paper. She had seen it many times, long ago at her own dinner table, enjoying her food and wine, expressing strong opinions, and favouring her with a particularly suggestive smile. She had always thought they would like to make love to each other, but in those days she was faithful to Richard so it was not possible. She had also thought there was interesting chemistry between Richard and Felix, although neither of them, she knew, would ever do anything about it. And now, the newspaper informed her, Felix Cramer would be signing copies of his new paperback *The Shamrock Murder* at the Penguin Bookshop in Covent Garden on Wednesday between twelve and two.

'Five pairs of knickers and a cheese sandwich,' said Karl, returning. 'And Pete says could you turn down the Wagner a bit.'

Inge went on reading. It was years since she had seen anything about Felix in the papers: perhaps he had been ill or away or not writing much. She had read only one of his books because she didn't like thrillers and it had seemed awkward to have a dinner guest constantly expecting praise. But the face was still attractive and looked as if it had seen many interesting things. She went on staring at the smiling photograph and felt herself responding to it. The house shook as Karl slammed the front door; Peter shouted from upstairs, 'Mum, can you give it a rest?'

Inge smiled at the photograph and turned up the Wagner. It made a triumphant sound.

On Wednesday she dressed carefully, went down to the bookshop and stationed herself at the window. He looked older, she thought. There was definitely more grey in his hair than she remembered, but at least he wasn't losing it. She studied him closely. There was a look of strain that she didn't recognise, exhaustion or anxiety: that was new. As if he had passed through some recent trying experience which had left its mark. Odd, because she had never believed in Felix as a person who was affected by his experiences, except to convert them into copy; she had always seen him, enviously, as someone who could walk through fire unscathed. Perhaps he was having problems with his wife; perhaps he needed a good fuck.

But when he smiled, all the old charm was there and the years fell away. It was an amazing transformation: he looked young, gentle, vulnerable. Everything she knew he was not. Memories flooded back, of all the happy evenings she had spent with him and Richard, talking and laughing and getting drunk. Just looking at Felix made her feel closer to Richard.

She watched the women crowding round him. How happy they looked when he smiled at them, and how lonely he looked when they went away. It was an unfamiliar look: she had never thought of Felix as capable of loneliness. But she was pleased to see that he was; it meant they had more in common than she had realised. The bookseller and the PR person from the publisher fussed round him (at least she assumed that was who they were) but he still looked put out, a mixture of embarrassment and bad temper, like a film star deserted by his fans. She wanted to laugh but she also felt tenderness for him, as if he were one of her children at a party where he was not having a good time.

*

Felix always forgot how dreadful signing sessions could be. He wondered if mothers of large families felt the same about childbirth, memories of the pain blurring with time, or natural optimism making them hope it might all get easier with practice. At all events he felt a perfect fool sitting beside a pile of books that not enough people were buying. When he did get to sign one it meant engaging in idiotic conversation with his public, who all seemed convinced that they too could write books if only they had the time, because they had led very interesting lives and their friends often said they should put it all down on paper. When Felix asked what was stopping them, they didn't seem to know, but some of them were keen to find out if he wrote in longhand or typed or used a word processor, as if therein lay some magical secret. Many more enquired if he had a say in the casting of the television series. Felix would have liked a pound for every time he had been asked this question, as he thought it might well exceed his bi-annual royalty cheque; he also felt close to hysteria as he answered, as if the day were not far off when he might burst out laughing, fall on the floor, chew at the carpet and foam at the mouth. Yet he was profoundly grateful to all these people: without them he would have no career, no money, no freedom, no identity. Why then did their questions make him feel a fraud, as if someone else had written his books? Why did he fear that his physical presence was subtly disappointing to most of them, as if he were an actor who looked smaller in person than on the screen?

'We haven't done at all badly, you know,' said the PR girl, who had glasses and a cleavage. 'It's just slowed down a bit this last half hour.'

'You could say that,' Felix agreed.

The bookshop manager poured him another glass of wine. 'But we've sold quite a few,' he said encouragingly, reminding Felix of a doctor explaining that his illness, though chronic, was not fatal.

'Quite a few isn't enough though, is it?' said Felix, downing the wine in one go. 'What we needed was a stampede. Wild-eyed women fighting each other to reach my side, fivers clutched in their hot sticky hands.'

The manager refilled his glass.

'These things are always difficult to predict,' said the PR girl. 'It could be anything, even the weather. Nothing to do with you or your book.'

Felix was just wondering if it would be worth trying to get the PR girl into bed when he recognised someone standing in a corner of the shop and watching him. As he stared at her she began to advance towards him.

'I'm sorry, I may have to skip lunch,' he said, touching the PR girl's hand. 'I've just seen an old friend.'

She was still beautiful in her own bizarre fashion. Dark brown hair worn long and gleaming with burnished red like henna. Eccentric clothes that might have come from a junk shop but were obviously chosen with care, a bizarre mixture of lace and satin and velvet in shades of brown and rust. Her skin was pale and slightly freckled: without make-up it looked almost damp with pallor, making the red lipstick stand out and the kohl round the eyes. The new soft lines marking eight years of endurance and disappointment were obvious and touching: he remembered her as young.

'Inge,' he said, wondering if they should kiss on the cheek. 'What a lovely surprise.'

She put both hands into his and squeezed hard. 'Hullo, Felix, how are you, how's it going?' She smelt of musk oil.

'Not very well,' he said and they both laughed. 'Would you like to have lunch?'

He took her to a restaurant round the corner because it was already late to go further. They had large gin and tonics to start them off while they ordered their food and they kept laughing a lot at very small jokes, which Felix thought probably meant they were both nervous. He noticed that she still wore her wedding ring.

'I felt such an idiot,' he said, 'sitting around waiting to sign books nobody wanted to buy.'

'But there were quite a lot of people, I think. I was watching.'

'Not enough. Perhaps the gods are trying to tell me something. Perhaps it's a lesson in humility.'

They both laughed at this unlikely idea.

'Is it good, your new book?' she asked, as if he could be quite dispassionate about it.

'As far as I remember. The hardback came out last year so it's not new to me. I suppose it's all right, if you like Tony Blythe. Personally I'm sick to death of him, silly bugger. I can't wait to kill him off.'

'But I thought he was meant to be sexy, like you.' Her light blue eyes held his with a challenging look: there was nothing coy or evasive about her. Felix felt he was being undressed at the table. He wondered if he looked at women in the same way; he hoped he was more subtle.

'Well, that's possible, I suppose.'

When their food and wine arrived she drank quickly and ate as if she were starving. He thought of all the meals they had shared in the past with Richard and Elizabeth, how cosy it had been compared to Helen's cold hostility. He had never felt judged or condemned by Inge; he had always regretted that she was so tantalisingly out of reach. And now they were alone together for the first time. He sensed a tremendous need emanating from her, not just for food and wine, but for sex, conversation, human contact, as if she been let out of solitary confinement.

'You know, Inge,' he said, warmed by his memories, 'it really is extraordinarily nice to see you. I'd forgotten how beautiful you are. Richard must have been crazy to leave you.'

'I think so,' she said matter-of-factly. 'Sometimes I'm so lonely I nearly kill myself.'

'That would be a terrible waste.'

She shrugged. 'Well, I survive so far on hope. Hope and hatred. I believe in a god of vengeance. He'll punish the cow for stealing my husband, but he's very slow.'

'I suppose in eternity these things don't feel very urgent.'

'D'you believe in God, Felix?'

Felix thought about it. 'Not exactly. Sometimes. I think I'd rather steer clear of vengeance, but a god of pleasure, I could believe in that.'

'There's not enough pleasure in the world,' said Inge with

enormous energy. 'This is a puritan country. People are sick, they're afraid of pleasure.'

'I'm not,' said Felix, feeling religious and dedicated like a knight in pursuit of the Holy Grail. 'In fact I've spent my whole life trying to have as much as possible.'

'Yes, that's true. I think you are very healthy, Felix.'

'I think so too,' said Felix.

They stared at each other thoughtfully. Inge was such good value, he felt: there was an earthy intensity about her. He poured two more glasses of wine, and presently suggested he should drive her home. He had been rather depressed since Sally left and felt in need of a treat.

'You have a beautiful cock, Felix,' said Inge reflectively.

Felix, who was still slightly out of breath, felt himself in the presence of a connoisseur. 'D'you mean in action or at rest?' he enquired in the spirit of a genuine seeker after truth.

'Oh, it moves very nicely,' said Inge, 'but it's also good to look at as an object. I mean it's pleasing aesthetically. You know?'

'Yes, I think I know what you mean,' said Felix, gratified.

'The length is average but the width is excellent,' Inge went on. 'Width is more important than length, of course. You fill me up so beautifully, Felix. You give me a great deal of pleasure.'

Felix, who had counted six clitoral orgasms (evenly divided between mouth and fingers) and four vaginal orgasms (unevenly divided between man on top, woman on top, and both on all fours) before he gave up and surrendered himself to his own climax, was bound to agree. He did not subscribe to popular mythology that defined only one type of orgasm. Too many women had shown him otherwise.

'It's good that you're circumcised too,' Inge continued. 'It's more attractive and hygienic, I think. D'you remember how Richard didn't want me to have the boys done, he said it wasn't necessary, but I told him I knew best about such things.'

Yes, Felix thought, I'm sure you did. 'Why don't you like me to kiss you, Inge?' he asked provocatively. 'Is it because you're still in love with Richard?'

Inge looked at him as if surprised. 'Yes, of course,' she said. 'Aren't you? Isn't that why we're both here?'

Felix forced himself to laugh but he felt the chill of the consulting-room settle on his soul. 'Put away that paperback psychology,' he said. 'We're here to have fun, not delve into the subconscious. Don't spoil a good thing.'

Inge sighed. 'Oh, that's what I always do.' She lay back, her brown hair merging with the brown sheets, her breasts sagging, her pubic hair still wet with their mingled juices. The scent of her was everywhere: musk oil and new sweat and something else he feared might be the result of not actually taking a bath every day. He did not want to name this hidden ingredient to himself (she was not visibly dirty at all) but there was something the exact reverse of Sally. With Sally he had felt she had always just had a shower and washed her hair, while with Inge he hoped that both events, with luck, had occurred yesterday or the day before. Sally had smelt of soap and shampoo and vanilla, whereas Inge smelt of Inge, in varying degrees of strength. Was it perverse of him to find this sexually exciting or was he simply in revolt against the twentieth-century Western obsession with cleanliness? Perhaps Napoleon had been right, telling Josephine not to wash for three days because he was coming home.

Sally's hair was always shiny and swinging, gleaming with health and care as if advertising conditioner; Inge's, though equally long and thick, was slightly sticky and smelt like a warm animal which had just crawled out of a nest of straw. Her cunt tasted like smoked salmon. Dark hair flourished on her legs and in her armpits; her teeth were uneven and sharp. Her body, too, was out of proportion. Whereas Sally was straight up and down, a sturdy five foot six and size twelve, Inge, though an inch or two shorter, appeared to be a blend of size ten and fourteen. Her breasts were large and tended to droop, and her hips were wide. But in between there was a ridiculously tiny waist and ribs that actually showed through her skin. Sally's stomach curved, whereas Inge's, though

182

stretch-marked, was almost flat. He had the feeling that Inge, if seized abruptly at each end, might snap in the middle.

How pleasant life would be, he reflected, if he could have all three of them: Sally and Elizabeth and Inge. The virgin and the mother and the whore. The women's liberation people, with whom he agreed intellectually, would probably dismember him for even having such a thought, but it was true. All aspects of himself would be catered for and he would have nothing further to desire. Nor would he fear boredom: in these three he would find the infinite variety of Shakespeare's Cleopatra. But it seemed that only two out of three were allowed at any one time.

'I'm hungry,' said Inge. 'And I want a drink.' Abruptly she got out of bed and pulled on her clothes, a T-shirt and a long full skirt in various shades of mulberry, the same clothes she had been wearing before they went to bed, but without her underwear, which still lay discarded on the floor. Felix got dressed, since she was not offering him a bath or a bathrobe; it was obviously not going to be one of those cosy afternoons.

The bedroom had been a novelty but it was eerie to be back in the kitchen where he had spent so many evenings with Richard during the marriage. Inge poured whisky for them both and started doing something complicated with sausages. He had never been sure whether or not he liked Inge's cooking, but it was certainly distinctive.

'So,' Inge said, licking her fingers. 'Tell me. How is the cow? Does she still paint silly pictures that nobody wants to buy?'

Felix wondered how best to answer that. 'She seems to be very busy,' he said cautiously.

'She's a cold woman,' Inge said, lighting a cigarette. 'No wonder her husband leaves her. So she steals mine. But he can't be happy with her, I don't believe it. You wait and see, Felix, he is going to come back to me one day and the cow will be all alone with her silly pictures and it will serve her right.'

Felix watched ash falling into the frying-pan. 'I could take you out for dinner, Inge,' he offered.

'No, the boys will be home soon and they are always

hungry. Don't you believe me, Felix, don't you think Richard will come back?'

'Well,' Felix said, 'after eight years it's not very likely but I suppose there's always hope.' He was impressed by the way Inge made the whole thing sound so recent.

'If I didn't believe it, I would kill myself,' Inge said matter-of-factly. 'But you can take me out to dinner another time. I love to eat and I never get fat. Will there be another time, Felix? Are we going to have an affair or is this a one-night stand?'

'Oh, I think an affair, don't you?' said Felix, startled.

'Good. It's very important to me to have regular sex. I don't like one-night stands, they're so much effort, but I have them. I see a man I like and I bring him home and we fuck and off he goes and I never see him again. If the sex is bad I don't mind, but usually it's good and still they go away. Isn't it strange? If you have a good dinner in a restaurant, you go back, don't you?'

'I do,' said Felix. 'Very often.'

'Perhaps it's my fault,' said Inge. 'Perhaps I talk to them about Richard and they don't like it. But you don't mind, do you, Felix?'

'No,' Felix said. 'I don't mind.' He was overcome by sudden compassion for Inge; he got up and put his arms around her and she hugged him with a fierce strength that she had not used in bed.

'Oh Felix,' she said, 'life's so sad, isn't it? Sometimes I can't bear it.'

He felt her beginning to cry as he held her. The sausages smouldered in the pan; the cigarette burned on the pine surface. Felix felt sorrow for the whole world.

'I always wanted to have an affair with you, Felix,' said Inge faintly into his shoulder. 'You understand about sex and love and how different they are. And you know about Richard. He doesn't understand, you see. He gets confused. He's like a child really.'

The front door opened and the moment was gone. Inge pulled away, wiping her eyes, rescued the sausages and retrieved the cigarette. The boys that Felix recalled as children of six and eight when Richard, frantic with guilt, had left them, came in as young men with pink hair, shaven hair, leather and studs, and endless height.

'You remember Felix, don't you?' said Inge. 'He was your father's best friend.'

'Oh yeah,' they said. 'Hullo.'

'Hullo,' said Felix, managing not to comment on their growth. 'Nice to see you again.'

'This is Karl and this is Peter,' said Inge, pointing.

'Yes,' said Felix untruthfully, 'I remember.'

'Are you staying for supper?' one of them asked, a polite enquiry, not indicating any preference either way. Felix hesitated.

'No, he isn't,' Inge said. 'We don't have enough sausages.'

Felix left soon afterwards, feeling superfluous. Inge had a decidedly clinical approach to sex, he thought, which was both convenient and disconcerting. On his way home it occurred to him that he had been somewhat impulsive: there was no guarantee that she might not use the incident to make Richard jealous, if such a thing were possible. It might be as well to safeguard himself by discussing the possibility with Richard, as if nothing had happened yet. Then if Richard objected he could retreat and deny everything; while if he agreed he could continue with an easy mind, and hope that no one enquired too closely into actual dates. It was always these tiny details that betrayed even the most practised criminal, as both he and Tony Blythe knew only too well.

'Doesn't he look old?' Karl said, after Felix had gone.

'He looked poofy to me,' said Peter, eating. 'Is he a poof, Mum?'

'No.' Inge looked fondly at them. They cared about her. They asked questions. They ate what she cooked. She loved them so much she sometimes felt quite faint. But it was

185

always easier to love them after someone had made love to her.

'I don't remember him at all,' said Peter.

'He looks ancient.' Karl sounded quite pleased. 'He used to be all right.'

'He's still all right,' said Inge, smiling. At that moment she felt immortal.

'Oh blimey,' said Karl, 'he's not your latest, is he?'

Peter looked confused. 'You said he was Dad's friend.'

'He is,' said Inge. 'But I'm lonely. I need someone.'

'I thought you needed Dad,' Peter said.

'I do,' said Inge. 'But he's not here, is he?'

'Is he famous, this Felix?' Karl asked.

Inge considered. 'He's a writer. He's well known.' She wondered how Felix would like this description.

'Is he married?' Karl wiped a piece of bread round his plate.

'Yes, of course. Don't you remember Elizabeth? She was rather fat.' Like most thin women, Inge regarded anyone less thin than herself as fat. 'And they didn't have any children.'

Richard passed the phone to Helen and went back to his pile of probation reports. Sally's voice was bright and cold. 'Hullo. How's everything?' She sounded like a stranger met once at a party and dimly remembered, the sort of person you gave your number to when you were rather drunk and then when they rang, you didn't recognise the voice, couldn't put a face to it.

Helen said, 'Hullo, love. How are you? How's Sussex?' She was shaking inside. Weeks of silence had demoralised her.

'Oh, great. It's wonderful. I'm having a fantastic time.'

'Good. I'm glad.'

There was a pause and then this brisk social person added, 'I'm going to meet Dad actually.'

'Oh, are you?' It felt like a blow to the stomach.

'Yes. He rang up. You don't mind, do you?'

'No, of course not, I'm pleased. It's about time.'

'Yes, it is, isn't it? He's playing in Brighton. He sent me a ticket and we're going to have a meal afterwards.'

She wanted to scream at Sally, to stop punishing her, to talk to her properly, to say she was angry and hurt and unforgiving, but at least to be real, not this dreadful phony stranger. 'Good.'

'He sounded awfully nice.'

'Yes, he is. I hope it goes well.'

'Oh, I'm sure it will. Look, I better go. I've run out of money.'

'Shall I ring you back?'

But the phone made a pathetic noise and Sally was gone. Helen hung up, conscious of Richard watching her. It was hard to speak normally.

'She's going to meet Carey. Apparently he rang her up. He's sent her a ticket for a concert and they're going to meet afterwards. In Brighton.' She poured herself a drink.

'Bit of a shock.'

'Not really, they had to meet some time.' She heard herself sounding defiant. 'I've been hoping they would.'

'Still. It's a big moment.'

'Yes.' She blinked rapidly and bit her lip.

'She didn't talk for long.'

'No. She ran out of money and she wouldn't let me ring her back.'

He said hesitantly, 'I thought she sounded a bit distant.'

'Yes. That's independence for you. She's trying her wings.' The bloody awful tears managed to escape.

He got up and put his arms round her. 'It hurts, doesn't it?'

She nodded, not able to speak.

'Darling. Don't worry. She'll be all right.'

'Yes, of course.' The hug felt wonderful but dangerous: if she let herself relax into it too much she might cry and cry and end up telling him the whole story. The temptation frightened her. She kissed him and pulled away on the pretext of getting some Kleenex.

He said, sounding tentative, 'I did wonder . . . before she went off, just the last couple of weeks, she seemed very moody, and you and she . . . well, you seemed a bit scratchy with each other.'

'Yes, you mentioned that at the time.' It was a relief to be sharp. Much safer. It was so hard to deceive someone you were close to and it didn't end with the abortion or with Sally leaving home, it went on and on. This awful secret would be between them for ever.

'I just wondered . . . is that why she's being a bit strange on the phone . . .?'

'You mean is it all my fault?'

'No, of course I don't. As if I would.'

'We did have a bit of a thing.' She blew her nose and poured another drink. 'Nothing serious. Just me being overprotective. I told you at the time.'

'Not like you.' She could see him being puzzled and hurt by her sharpness.

'No. Well, there you are. Even I can act out of character. Baby leaving the nest and all that. I overdid the gypsy's warning and she resented it, so now she's sulking.' Then she wanted to make amends so she added, 'Want a drink?'

'No.' He was still watching her compassionately. 'Don't worry about her meeting Carey. It had to happen.'

'I'm not worried.' She heard herself being as bright and cold as Sally. 'He'll charm her. What else can he do?'

Carey told her there'd be a ticket waiting for her at the box office with her name on it. Our name, she thought with satisfaction, for that was one thing Helen had never been able to achieve, a change of name: she was still Sally Hinde, not Sally Morgan or Sally Irving. She had often thought that his name was all she had left of him and she was glad it was a pretty one; in history lessons about the *Golden Hind* she had seen herself streamlined and sinewy, darting about the forest or gliding through the water, animal or ship or a strange amalgam of both, with a glamorous pale gleam, like something she had seen in a commercial for petrol or butter.

She looked up the programme and it was Shostakovich's

Fifth with a Rossini overture and the Sibelius Violin Concerto. A really jammy selection, she thought. Shostakovich was a favourite; she had often played him very loudly in her bedroom to remind Helen and Richard that it wasn't just pop music she liked. Revenge through culture. A Soviet artist's reply to just criticism. She liked to think that Dmitri had been rebellious too.

She had never thought to ask Felix if he liked Shostakovich and now it was too late.

It was hard to believe that she was actually going to meet Carey, that from being someone she didn't remember he had become a voice on the phone and tonight she would see him and touch him. A bit like the Cheshire Cat in reverse, building up from the grin. When she was in her seat she looked at her programme and stroked his name in the list of viola players; when the orchestra filed in she strained to pick him out from among the others but couldn't.

Rossini was nice and cheerful as always and made her want to laugh out loud but she thought people would think she was mad so she made do with smiling. Sibelius was better than she remembered, so good in fact that she wondered why she hadn't bought a cassette of it, except that she wasn't particularly fond of the violin. She must remember not to say that in case he thought it meant she didn't like the viola either and she did. In the interval she had a drink she didn't really want, hoping it would stop her feeling so nervous. She wondered what other people would say if she suddenly accosted a complete stranger and announced she was going to meet her father whom she hadn't seen since she was little. There couldn't be anyone else at the concert for such a bizarre reason, she was sure of that.

Then it was time for Shostakovich and she started to cry. Not hard painful sobbing that could block up your nose but a few luxurious tears spilling over. She felt wonderful. She also didn't want the concert to be over because it was comfortable and exciting to look forward to meeting Carey but the actual meeting would be alarming; and then if they didn't get on, the let-down would be so awful that her heart thumped at the thought and she had to take deep breaths to calm herself.

Eventually, though, she couldn't stop it being over and she had to go and wait at the artists' entrance where he had told her they would meet. As usual she was surprised by the speed with which the players came out but he wasn't among the first. Perhaps he was as nervous as she was, hanging about inside and putting off the moment until he couldn't put it off any more. It was the first time she had considered his apprehension as well as her own.

Then he came out and she knew it was him because he had her own face. She had always thought she looked like Helen; photographs of him had not made the connection for her. But now he was in front of her it was like looking at herself in the mirror. They stared at each other for a long moment and then identical smiles spread over their faces and he held out his arms.

He took her to a Chinese restaurant and she talked about Sussex.

'I keep telling Mum and Richard I like it, it's OK, it's fantastic, whatever I think they want to hear, just to keep them happy, but really I can't believe I'm there. I mean, I keep thinking, is this it? At school they go on and on to you about university and when you finally get there, it just isn't how you imagined it. I don't know what the difference is but it doesn't feel real.' She heard her voice running on but she didn't know how to stop it. 'Maybe it's me. It's like sleepwalking somehow. I feel I'm just drifting through and I needn't bother to make an effort because soon I'll wake up and I won't be there any more. I'm sorry, I'm talking too much.' The effort of stopping was terrifying: it jolted her, as if she had deliberately steered into a tree.

He said, 'Helen did tell me what happened.'

'Oh.' The sound came out very small. She felt relieved but also somehow deflated. She would have liked to tell him herself. And knowing he knew also meant knowing he had not offered to help. She wasn't sure how she felt about that.

190

'I should have written to you but I'm not very good at letters.'

'It doesn't matter. I probably wouldn't have answered anyway.'

Now she sounded angry.

'It must have been awful for you.'

'Oh well, it's all over now.'

He said, 'Are you very angry with me?'

She shrugged, embarrassed by his directness. It was too awful if they were going to quarrel when they had only just met.

'I was afraid you wouldn't want to meet me. After all, I haven't been much of a father, have I?'

'You haven't been a father at all.' It was a shock to hear the words come out. 'I'm sorry. I didn't mean to say that.'

'Why not?' he said mildly. 'It's true.'

Now she had tears in her eyes. 'But I've been longing to meet you, I've been counting the days, and now I'm being rude. I meant to be very nice and careful and make a good impression. I actually wanted you to like me. And now it doesn't seem to matter, I can say whatever I like. It's as if you're a stranger on a train. It's weird. I don't understand it.' Helen and the doctor would probably say it was her hormones, she thought with resentment; they were bracketed together in her mind as powerful people.

'Sounds like a good thing to me. Come on, eat up.'

'I'm not usually like this but I've been feeling funny lately.' She applied herself to the food. 'This is lovely. I didn't realise I was so hungry.'

She ate in silence for a while and he didn't speak either. When she looked up from her plate she found him watching her with a wistful expression that she found puzzling.

'D'you think we can possibly make up for lost time?'

She didn't know what to say. It seemed such a large question.

She had intended to get the train but in the end he insisted on driving her. They discussed the amount of lager he had drunk and decided it wasn't very much. Going from the restaurant to the car broke their concentration and made a

191

different atmosphere. She was conscious of feeling suddenly very tired, thinking how lovely it would be to be back in her room and alone and able to lie down and think and go to sleep and not have to please anyone.

She said, 'It was a lovely concert. I love Russian music, it's so over the top. Was he a good conductor, d'you think? I can never tell.'

'Don't know, didn't look.'

She was so tense now that she laughed much harder than necessary and he seemed pleased.

'The old jokes are the best.'

'But I hadn't heard that one before.'

He said urgently, 'Every year I meant to write to you. For Christmas. For your birthday. And I never did. It was too painful. I kept thinking of you and Helen and Richard all cosy together and I felt it might be better if I kept away. And the longer I left it, the more impossible it got.'

She felt cross. He had behaved like that and now she was expected to forgive him. 'It doesn't matter. Really. We're here now, aren't we?'

'I think I was afraid of seeing Helen again and wanting her back. And frightened you might reject me. And there was Marsha and all the children.'

'It's all right,' she said, raising her voice slightly. 'Honestly it is. I had a very happy childhood. You didn't ruin anything. There's no need to feel guilty about it.'

Then they drove in silence till they were on campus and she had to direct him to East Slope. She wondered if she should ask him in to see her room but it was late and she was tired. Another time, she thought.

She said, 'You're the nicest stranger I've ever met,' to show she had forgiven him but also to remind him there was a lot to forgive.

He kissed her on the cheek. It felt strange. 'Bye, Sally. Keep in touch. I don't want to lose you again.'

She said suddenly, almost with panic, 'I don't know what to call you.'

*

Elizabeth came round to ask how the meeting had gone. She caught Helen in the garden.

'I don't know,' Helen said. 'She hasn't rung.' She wasn't surprised but she was disappointed.

After a while Elizabeth said, 'It must be very difficult being a parent.'

'Yes, it is.'

'Still envy you, though.' She watched Helen's savage pruning. 'My God, you really do cut them back.'

'Yes,' Helen said, 'I believe in drastic measures.'

Elizabeth scrunched through the dead leaves on the grass. 'You know, it's funny,' she said, 'but I feel ever so much lighter these days. Oh, physically I've still got all the same boring symptoms, but in myself, as they say, I feel I'm floating. It's as if Felix and I have passed through some crisis I didn't even know about. I wanted to talk to you about it but you seemed so preoccupied with Sally going away.'

Is she really blind, Helen wondered, or just very stupid, or perhaps absolutely brilliant at protecting herself? 'Yes, it was quite a wrench,' she said.

Elizabeth pulled up a couple of weeds and tossed them on the compost heap. 'I wish I felt you could talk to me if you had a problem. You've been such a help to me and it would make things a bit more equal.'

Helen almost laughed. 'Don't worry about it,' she said. 'I don't really talk to anyone.'

'I suppose it's enough to have Richard,' Elizabeth said comfortably. 'You can always talk to him, can't you?'

Richard never quite got used to prison visits. He tried to think of them as just part of the job, but in many cases the sentence seemed disproportionate to the crime and the loss of liberty such a savage punishment that he had no patience with anyone outside who complained that conditions were too soft. Knowing that he could leave and his client couldn't gave an uncomfortable edge to all his interviews. And yet at the same time he knew he was often a vital bridge between them and the outside world. The smell and the feel of prison stayed with him for hours afterwards, tainting the day.

'I just know there's something wrong,' Bob had said. 'You know how you can tell but you can't put your finger on it.'

Richard did know, all too well. 'Have you asked her?'

'Oh yeah, but she keeps smiling and saying don't be silly. It's that smile really . . . I just know she doesn't mean it.'

Richard knew the smile too because Sandra had used it on him, seeming to agree with him and then ignoring all his suggestions. It was a docile, secretive, subversive smile: he could picture her as a child using it on parents and teachers to get her own way, hoping they wouldn't notice what she was doing.

'Maybe it's something she wants to save up till you get home,' he said without much hope. 'Maybe it would be easier to talk about it then when you have all the time you need.'

'I can't last out till then,' Bob said. 'There's no way.'

'But it's not long now, if you can just hang on.'

'I'm afraid I'll do something stupid. Can't you go and see her for me and ask her? Tell her to give it to me straight. I'd much rather. I can't think about nothing else.'

He thought of Bob now as he sat in the pub hearing Felix talk about Inge. 'I wasn't at all sure how you'd react,' Felix said.

'You shouldn't have worried,' Richard said, 'it's a weight off my mind.'

Felix looked relieved. 'D'you mean that?'

'Yes, I really think it might be good for both of you.'

Felix turned his glass round and round on the table and Richard found the gesture irritating him almost to screaming point. 'Nothing's happened yet. But when she turned up at the shop I thought it was only fair to take her out to lunch and I got the impression she'd quite like to have an affair.'

'I'm sure she would. She's always telling me how frustrated she is. I think she feels it's not such a humiliating word as lonely. It'd be ideal for her – someone like you to keep her happy. And she'd be no threat to Elizabeth.'

'No, of course not,' said Felix, looking surprised. 'Well, we'll see. I just wanted to clear it with you, just in case. It does feel a bit incestuous.'

'It wasn't her fault I left her,' Richard said, trying to be fair. He had never liked the position of dog in the manger. 'She didn't do anything wrong. I just felt I was being eaten alive.'

'She does still adore you,' Felix said thoughtfully, as if meeting her again had given him a fresh perspective on the stale known facts. 'It's very impressive.'

'Yes, I know,' Richard said irritably. He felt Felix was trying to reassure him and he resented it.

Felix went on turning the glass. 'The boys are amazing. So tall. It was all I could do not to comment on their growth.'

'Oh, were they with her?' This was a surprise. It seemed unlikely Inge to take them to a bookshop.

'No, but I drove her home.'

'That was kind of you.' It was odd to think of Felix arriving at the house with Inge, seeing the boys. Odd not to be there with them. The whole thing was odd.

Felix stood up, glass in hand. 'Same again?'

Richard thought of Bob again when he went to see Sandra. Her council flat was cold and cramped and smelt of damp washing. With three children under five Sandra often found it too difficult or expensive to get to the launderette. But her face had a new look of determination and self-satisfaction as she listened to Richard, the look of a woman who has finally got her life in order. She was twenty-seven, though she somehow managed to look both older and younger, like an elderly child. She listened but she did not hear. She was starting a new life. Soon all her washing would be drying in the sun.

'He'll go mad if I tell him now,' she said.

The children played round their feet, demanding attention or stumbling off to hide behind the furniture. 'But he's already going mad worrying about it,' Richard said. 'He knows something's wrong.'

195

Sandra's face set with a stubborn mulish look. She wasn't bothering to smile today. She didn't have to be ingratiating to Richard any more. Or to Bob, come to that.

'I can't help that,' she said. 'We're going. Dave's got the tickets.' She said his name with pride. Another man wanted her. Her and Bob's three children.

'Does it have to be Australia?'

'Yes, it does.' The two-year-old wailed. 'Oh, shut up Darren. I'll be safe there. He can't have another go at me if I'm in Australia, can he?'

'But he'll never see his children.'

'He should have thought of that before.' She sounded almost smug.

Richard tried a different approach. 'Look, I know he gave you a bad time –'

'A bad time? My doctor says I nearly died.'

'I think you're exaggerating a bit. I did see you in hospital and I talked to your doctor . . .'

'Well, Dave says I nearly died.'

'I'm not defending what Bob did, but you did know how violent he can be and you did make him very jealous.'

Sandra looked shocked. 'Are you saying it's all my fault?' The four-year-old started investigating a power point. 'Samantha, come out of there, you'll hurt yourself.'

'No, of course I'm not. Bob has to take responsibility for what he did, just as you have to. But he is very sorry and he does care a lot about you and the children. He knows something's wrong and he's in quite a state about it.' But he could tell he wasn't getting through. Sandra's gaze drifted around the room. She stubbed out her cigarette and lit another. 'Couldn't you tell him the truth and maybe put off going away till he's out, so at least he can have some time with the kids? It's going to be one hell of a shock for him to come out and find he's lost his entire family. It could push him right over the edge.'

'It's funny really,' Sandra said thoughtfully. 'If he'd married me when I wanted I couldn't do this, could I? It's like he's brought it on himself.'

Richard said, 'Look, Sandra, will you think about it? If you can't face him with it, can you write him a letter and I'll support him all I can.'

Now Sandra smiled. 'I want you to tell him for me. After I've gone.'

Helen watched Magdalen walk round the studio, pausing in front of each canvas. It was agony. In the old days she would have lit a cigarette. But in the old days the paintings would have been finished. She had never let Magdalen see unfinished work before. It felt dangerous, unnatural, even slightly obscene.

She tried to think about something else while Magdalen walked and looked. She was reminded of the indignity of lying on the gynaecologist's hard couch for one of what felt like countless internal examinations for pregnancy, contraception, abortion and minor forms of VD. It was the same process of trying to disassociate her mind from her body and remind herself that this was an unpleasant necessity. Somewhere out there Magdalen was examining her intimately and it had to be endured: she had to grit her teeth and relax and soon it would be over.

Time passed. She remembered the cold hard speculum. Magdalen said, 'I don't know what you're worried about. I think they're wonderful.'

Warm relief flooded Helen. She knew Magdalen never pretended. She heard herself talking fast and excitedly, like a child. 'I'm pleased with some of them, but they're not all finished and I can do better, I know I can, and there aren't enough of them . . .'

Magdalen turned her back on the pale oblong shapes. 'What is all this? It's not like you at all.'

'Oh, they're meant to be about serenity and I'm not feeling serene.'

'No, I can see that.' She studied Helen's face. 'Why not do one about how you're actually feeling?'

'It's too soon.'

'We could settle for a smaller show.'

'No, I must get it right. It's important. I want to get it right.'

Magdalen lit one of her small cigars. 'Helen, stop saying yes but. How much more time d'you need?'

'To be realistic, not optimistic . . . about three months, I think.' She had rehearsed this in her head but it was still hard to say.

'OK,' Magdalen said easily. 'It's not the end of the world.'

'Oh Magdalen, I'm sorry. Sackcloth and ashes. I've had one hell of a year.'

Magdalen looked puzzled. 'The last time we talked it was going so well.'

'Yes, it all fell apart in September.' She needed a shield against the facts; she went over to the corner where she kept a bottle of whisky and poured herself and Magdalen two drinks.

'What happened?' Magdalen said.

'Oh – life just got in the way.'

'You're not doing too much teaching?'

'No, that's all fine, the students are lovely. Besides, I need the money.' She watched Magdalen shrug. 'Yes, I know, if I did more work, etc, etc. Anyway, there it is. I can't be ready on time.'

The shame of it. She had never before had to postpone a show. She had never had to ask Magdalen to look at unfinished paintings. She had never been unprofessional and let people down.

'Come and have lunch,' Magdalen said, as if it didn't matter at all.

'I don't deserve lunch.'

'Helen. I've never seen you so punitive.'

'No, neither have I.'

Magdalen sat on the arm of the old brown chair Helen had never replaced. It was hard and prickly, horsehair stuffing bursting from it. Helen sat in it every day to look at her work and think about what to do next. It had been second-hand when she and Carey bought it for the first flat they had ever shared. Magdalen said, 'Are you missing Sally?'

'Yes, I expect that's part of it.'

'How's Richard?'

'He's fine. Busy as ever.' She could feel Magdalen probing for clues and she didn't like it: they had always talked about work or trivia. She didn't feel she owed Magdalen information because she had been understanding about the show.

'Well, I'm not just here to make money out of you,' Magdalen said after a short pause, and they both smiled. 'Not that I object to that. But you know I've got every confidence in your work. If there's anything you'd like to talk about, or anything I can do to help . . .'

'I know. I appreciate that.'

'Thank you but no thank you?'

Helen went on smiling.

'I wish you'd come to the Jerome Ellis party,' Magdalen said, grinding her cigar out on the floor. 'He's so pleased with your *Seven Deadly Sins*, and they really look very good in the oast house.'

'He just thinks of me as an interior decorator. Only cheaper, of course.'

'Look, I know he's a pretentious git on a bad day, and a pain in the arse on a good one, but he *is* rich and he fancies himself as a patron. They're thin on the ground these days.' Magdalen eased herself off the chair and Helen tried once again to work out how she managed to look so elegant when she was considerably overweight. 'You might meet some useful people at the party and if you let him commission you again . . .'

'God, I think he must be the original fate worse than death.' Helen felt safer now they were talking about someone else; she could relax. 'He wouldn't know a real painting if it jumped up and bit him.'

'I know you hate doing commercial work but you do it very well. I don't think you realise how versatile you are. You could have two quite separate careers.'

They faced each other across the ancient chair, Magdalen pulling on her gloves.

'Sorry, Magdalen, I know I'm hard to promote. It must be a nightmare for you.' She wanted to placate Magdalen now the heat was off. She could feel her attention span was coming to

199

an end. In a moment, like the searchlight beam from a lighthouse, it would move past Helen and be focused somewhere else.

'I don't mind. It just seems a pity for you. Such a waste of potential. Still, if that's how you want it.'

Felix was nearly asleep when he heard Inge say, 'Shall I get us a drink?' He had been aware of her moving restlessly beside him and he knew she hated him to doze off after fucking: he had had the same problem with many women, who seemed to take it as a personal affront, but he had kept his eyes shut nevertheless.

'That would be nice,' he said, wishing she had left him in peace for another ten minutes. It didn't seem much to ask after all his exertions. He was beginning to find her heavy going because she always seemed to want more. He understood that he had to make up for years of starvation, and for the fact that he was not Richard, but he still found it a strain.

She got out of bed and he heard her moving around and the clink of glasses, then she said, 'I do hope you're right, Felix, I hope you're sure we're not going to catch any infection.'

The remark irritated him profoundly. She had made it before, but always after the event, which indicated, he thought, that she was not really worried at all but merely did it to annoy, because she knew it teased him.

'We've been into all that,' he said, immediately regretting his choice of words. 'I'm quite sure we're both perfectly healthy.'

'Perhaps. But I can't take any chances. It would be terrible if I give Richard a disease when he comes back.'

'Well, that's an original way of looking at it.' He was now thoroughly awake, noticing her mad certainty that Richard, like Pinkerton, would return. Inge as Madame Butterfly. It was an intriguing thought and one that had never occurred to him before. He wondered if he should share it with her.

'Don't you agree?'

'I don't believe you and I are at risk at all but if we were then I don't think Richard's health would be my first priority.'

'Ah,' she said, with a curious note of triumph mixed with sadness in her voice, 'then you don't love him as much as I do.'

'That's hardly surprising,' said Felix, feeling uncomfortable and forgetting about opera.

'Don't you even worry about Elizabeth?' She came back to the bed with two glasses of wine and stared at him. He always found it disconcerting that her eyes were blue when the rest of her seemed like a sepia print.

He said, 'Inge, in a long career, I'm happy to say that none of these dread diseases has ever materialised.'

'You've been lucky.' She sounded sulky. 'It's very boring at the clinic. You always have to wait a long time and occasionally they are rude to you.'

'I'll take your word for it. Maybe you could get Richard to pay for Bupa.'

'Poor Richard,' she said. 'He can't afford anything now he has to support the cow.'

Felix drank his wine rather fast. Really she was stuck in a time warp, as if desertion and remarriage were recent events. Perhaps she was more like Miss Havisham, with her yellowing wedding dress and cobwebbed cake. 'Actually, I don't think that's quite accurate. I think it's supporting you that he finds a strain.'

'Have I made you angry talking about disease?'

'Well, it's not exactly romantic.'

Her eyes widened and he realised that he had fallen into a trap. 'But I didn't know we were supposed to be romantic. I thought we were two old friends who have sex together. I thought we could speak frankly. Anyway, I like to speak frankly with everyone. Don't you think it's the best way?'

This was so far from being Felix's philosophy that he was amazed she could even ask him such a thing. It must be her foreign sense of humour again. She was playing games and he felt tired at the thought of it. He had played games in the past, but Sally had not played them and he had got out of the habit.

201

'Not always, no,' he said. 'I think it can cause a lot of damage.'

A slight look of worry came into her face, as if he had threatened her. She got up and wandered off in the direction of the wardrobe.

'If you're looking for the bathroom,' he said, as she opened the wardrobe door, 'it's over there ... and that's the wardrobe.'

Inge stared at the clothes he had bought Sally. Felix felt naked, exposed and angry as never before in his life.

'Full of beautiful clothes,' she said. 'Now I know your secret, Felix. You like to dress up.' She laughed. 'Don't worry, I won't tell, so long as you are nice to me.'

It was his own fault, of course. He should never have let her come to the flat. But he was so used to entertaining women on his own territory, safe from the unexpected return of husbands and children and au pairs, that it had become a habit. Besides, it was tiresome to have to keep driving to Camden Town from Putney or Fulham and Inge was eager to get out of the house, so the arrangement suited them both quite well.

He said, 'Inge, I seem to remember you saying when we started this affair that you always spoil a good thing. I'm beginning to see what you meant.'

She reached out a hand and very slightly flicked with one finger a black and silver jacket he had bought Sally just before she had told him she was pregnant. A jacket she had never worn. 'I was only teasing you,' she said. 'Where's your famous British sense of humour? You talk about it all the time, you English, but I don't think you have it really.'

'You do like to push your luck.' The words seemed totally inadequate for the boiling rage he was feeling, but the tone must have reached her, for her expression softened and she turned to face him.

'Don't be cross with me, Felix. They're such beautiful clothes and I'd like to try them on. May I? Did you buy them for a married woman who could never take them home?'

He supposed they had just had their first row and he found it oddly stimulating. They couldn't love each other but at least they could fight. She was still Richard's wife and the smell of her excited him and she had the most responsive body he had ever touched. Now she had blundered across Sally's clothes and he wanted to punish her. He could be violent with her in a way he had never been to Sally and she would understand and they would both enjoy it. Perhaps she had even done it on purpose.

'That's right,' he said. 'Now shut the wardrobe door and come back to bed.'

It was noisy in the coffee shop and Sally didn't know all the people round the table, only the ones in her seminar group. They were discussing a case in the news, about a student who was taking legal action to try to prevent his girlfriend from having an abortion. Sally wished they would talk about anything else. She wanted to run away but she had only just come in and she was hungry; she wanted to finish her pie and chips and her nice fattening cake. She had been eating rather a lot lately but it never seemed to be enough.

'But it's her body,' said Tessa, who was a keen feminist. 'How can he possibly make her have a baby she doesn't want?'

'It's his baby too,' said a bloke with a beard. 'He must have some rights.'

'You'd be the first to shout if he was insisting she had an abortion.'

'I think it's murder,' said someone with a cross round her neck.

'God, you're living in the dark ages,' said Tessa's friend Ann, munching a doughnut. 'It's a woman's right to choose.'

Sally wondered if any of them had any idea what they were talking about, what it felt like to make that decision, to have a child inside you and let someone take it away. How surprised they would all be if she stood up and shouted at them that they just didn't understand.

'What about the man's rights?' said the bearded guy.

'He doesn't have any rights.'

'Why not? Just because he's a man?'

'No, because it's her body. I just said that. You don't listen.'

'Anyway, if he cares so much about babies,' said a girl Sally had seen at the debating society, 'he should have been more careful.'

'She should too. It's not that difficult,' said the beard.

'Anybody can make a mistake,' said Tessa. 'There'll always be abortions because nobody can get it right all the time.'

'It's not about abortion,' said Jamal suddenly. He was in Sally's seminar group and she liked him but he was usually very quiet. 'It's about one person trying to force another to do something against their will. That has to be wrong. What do you think, Sally?'

Sally couldn't speak. She was afraid she might start crying. She could feel Jamal watching her and she shoved more pie and chips in her mouth as an excuse for not answering.

'If you don't want that lasagne,' said Ann to the beard, 'can I have it?'

'God, you're such a pig,' said Tessa fondly.

The next student was a girl. Helen wondered if she had realised yet the particular difficulties that lay ahead of her as a woman painter, or whether she thought the pill and woman's lib. had taken care of all that. She wasn't sure which way up her paintings should be, so they took some time to arrange. There were four of them, all different sizes, in red and orange and yellow, full of lines and holes and cuts.

'They're quite slow,' Mike said after studying them for a while.

Helen said, 'They seem to be about something in decay. Something bruised or damaged in some way.'

'I've been leaving them to dry and then removing bits so I get a mark where they've been,' the student said. 'It's like a sort of controlled accident.'

'It's as much about the edge as what's inside,' Andy said.

The student lit a cigarette. She looked as young as Sally,

although she couldn't be if she was in her final year. 'I see the interior shape as an animal skin,' she said.

'The two middle paintings seem to receive light from outside,' said Mike.

'I'm thinking of making the canvas do the drawing for me,' the student said.

'That's a neat trick if you can manage it,' said Helen.

Andy said, 'D'you see the paintings as concrete memories?'

The student looked surprised. 'No. I feel they're living things.'

Helen said, 'Does anything about them disappoint you?' She liked the students to be self-critical.

'Yes, the scale is wrong. I worked on it too long without stretching it.'

'What did you do in the summer?' Andy asked.

'I've been looking at wall paintings in monasteries in India. And Tantric art. And torn posters and stains and water marks.' She sounded enthusiastic.

While I arranged my daughter's abortion, Helen thought. But no one wanted to hear about that. Or at least there was no one to tell. No one to congratulate or sympathise or absolve. Was Sally punishing her by not writing, not ringing up? Or was theirs a conspiratorial silence to evade detection?

'Have you seen Regent's Canal since they drained it?' Mike asked conversationally. The student looked vague.

'The colour isn't distorted through perspective,' said Andy, still studying the paintings. 'I see it very much as spaces within spaces.'

Helen said, 'The ones that are painted stretched help the decisions you make about the edge.'

'What's your thesis about?' Mike asked.

'Suicide,' said the student. 'In painters and poets.'

'Ah,' said Andy, 'death is a very big subject this year.'

'Have you read Sylvia Plath?' Helen asked, thinking that there was someone who wrote to her mother a lot.

'No, not yet,' said the student, as if there was no urgency with graduation only a few months away.

'There's a very good book about a psychotic girl doing paintings,' said Mike.

Andy nodded. 'And who was that mathematician who killed himself by making cyanide from apple pips, using electrodes?'

It was strange, Helen thought, how they seemed to perk up at the mention of so much death. But that couldn't be why Sally was silent. She couldn't be as unhappy as that. And someone from the university would have got in touch.

'Isn't it interesting,' Andy said, 'how many people commit suicide outside their own country?'

The next student was a tall dark thin young man with glasses. His paintings were busy with vivid splashy colour all over the canvas.

'How d'you know when to stop?' they asked him.

'When I don't know what to do next.' He frowned. 'They're not finished as such, but I don't want to spoil what's there.'

'Well, I feel I'm allowed to sink back into the canvas,' Mike said.

They both lit fresh cigarettes and questioned the student about the scale size. 'How did that come about?'

He didn't answer, although he looked as if he meant to.

'You're controlled by the way you make a gesture,' Helen told him. 'There's a wedge of pictorial information that pushes you through the surface of the painting into another painting.'

The student had brought constructions and collages to be assessed as well as paintings. Helen asked him why he compartmentalised his work, but he didn't seem to know.

'Couldn't you think more in terms of a synthesis?' she persisted.

The student smiled but did not reply.

'We're going to be looking at thousands of these paintings soon,' said Mike. 'That's not to say they're bad.'

'In fact they're close to being very good,' said Andy.

'But they all look the same, or they soon will.' It sounded cruel.

'The nice thing about the collages is, they're a breathing space,' Helen said encouragingly.

The student was doing a thesis on guys who didn't speak in films. There was not much they could say to that. The deadline was the end of March and he hadn't started yet but seemed confident that he would have the first draft done by the New Year. Helen admired his optimism. She tried to imagine Christmas with Sally. Elizabeth asking questions. Felix dropping in.

The last student brought one large blue-grey abstract and a lot of small collages. They had a strong architectural feel.

'These are spaces a human being could inhabit,' Mike said.

'In fact why not have a human presence?' Andy lit a cigarette.

'I want that ambiguity,' said the student. 'I don't want to give those clues.'

'Well, I'm not sure what the hell I'm looking at,' said Mike.

'Well, all right,' said the student, hurt.

'At its worst it's too much about art,' said Andy crushingly.

Helen was looking at the drawings in the notebook. They were quite different from the painting and collages on view.

'These are much your best work,' she said. 'Very stylish, very assured.' She had often found this so: the privacy of the notebook allowed students to relax and work naturally, whereas a large canvas could make them self-conscious and clumsy.

'If you're painting flags,' said Andy, still looking at the picture, 'why not stick on two flags instead?'

The student looked shifty, as if he had been caught like that before. 'I like to hide things with aesthetics,' he said.

'I think you know what the subject-matter is and this is camouflage,' said Mike severely.

The student lit a cigarette. He said he was doing his thesis on the harlequin. He equated the harlequin with art. It was all about frustrated means of expression. Helen sensed an accusation somewhere.

'What next?' she said. 'Are you going to do your MA?'

'Not yet. I thought I might go to Japan for a while.'

'You'll need to speak Japanese, won't you?' said Andy.

'Or Germany perhaps,' said the student quickly.

'Do you speak German?'

'No.'

*

207

Carey came to fetch her and they drove around Sussex, stopping for cream teas or walks on the downs. She found it hard to think of him as her father: it was more like flirting with a stranger, or going out with a new boyfriend or even (if she closed her eyes) being with Felix again. She found she talked all the time about Helen and the abortion, not sure if he wanted to listen but certain she was talking too much, yet unable to stop. Words leaked out of her like tears or menstrual blood, fluid beyond her control, and he answered, but she hardly heard his answers because she was so anxious to talk again.

'I haven't written to her at all and I only ring up when I have to, so Richard won't think it's odd. Then I pretend I've run out of money so I don't have to talk for long. I'm so angry with her, I just want to punish her all the time.' The anger pulsed inside her, alarming waves in which she might drown, yet all mixed up with wanting to see Helen and hug her and be comforted.

'Well, she made you do something very serious,' he said, sounding grown up and reasonable.

'But I let her do it, so it can't be all her fault.' Even now she still wanted to be fair. 'And Felix could have stopped her. It could all have been different.'

'Do you wish it had been?'

'I don't know, that's the worst thing. I don't know what I feel. Sometimes I dream I'm still pregnant and when I wake up I cry because I'm not and yet I'm so relieved I'm not . . . So how can I blame her? It's not fair really, is it?' The dreams were awful and she dreaded them; they made her put off going to bed.

'D'you blame Felix too?'

'Yes, but not so much. I'm very angry with him but I have to keep remembering some of it was my fault. I didn't tell him when I took a risk. I don't know why I did that. I've thought about it a lot.' And right up to the last minute she had thought he might change his mind and turn up to rescue her, but that was hard to say. 'He wrote me a lovely letter all about how sorry he was and how he'd always love me, but I haven't answered it. I want to punish him as well as Mum.

Isn't it pathetic? That's the only way I can punish them, by not writing letters. That makes me look pretty feeble, doesn't it? Maybe they don't care whether I write them letters or not.'

'I'm sure they do,' he said gently, 'especially Helen.'

'Well, I could punish them more. I could tell Richard what happened and I'm sure he'd hit the roof, but I don't want to do that. He'd be furious with them both and he'd be terribly disappointed in me and it still wouldn't make me feel better. Sometimes I just wish I could go to sleep for years until I could be sure of waking up feeling different.'

There was an awkward silence then and she sensed him trying to say something difficult.

'I feel a bit guilty too,' he said at last. 'Helen did ask me if we'd foster the baby if you wouldn't have an abortion, but Marsha wasn't keen. Not now we've nearly got four of our own. She said she would if she had to but she'd much rather not and I couldn't really blame her, as she'd be doing all the work. I mean, I'm away so much.'

Sally felt confused, almost wishing he hadn't said that. 'Mum didn't tell me that. She never made me feel I had any choice.'

'Well, I don't think you did, not really. Not without telling Richard.'

'That's the worst thing. She just made me do what she wanted and I don't know if it was because she thought it was best for me or because she hates Felix so much.'

'Maybe she doesn't know either,' he said, as if that made it all right.

She said, unable to ask directly for what she needed, 'I'm really dreading Christmas.'

Richard was surprised how uncomfortable he felt to know that Felix and Inge were having an affair. He had thought it would be a wonderful relief: a happier Inge, off his hands and off his mind, and a happy friend enjoying harmless pleasure. In prospect, this had seemed an ideal arrangement, beneficial to everyone concerned. But somehow in his mind they had lingered forever on the brink of an affair; he had not thought at all about the reality of them actually having one. When Felix said to him one night in the pub, 'She really does love you very much,' Richard felt a sensation he could not quite identify, a shiver of alarm that Felix was trying to tell him something he did not want to hear.

He said, 'Ah, you've seen her again,' and could not look at Felix although he could feel that Felix was looking at him.

'Yes,' Felix said, very clear and straight, 'we've been seeing quite a lot of each other.'

A strange churning began in Richard's stomach. Images of Felix and Inge naked, in bed, making love, flooded into his mind. It didn't make sense. Surely he couldn't be (it was difficult even to focus on the word, he squirmed at the thought) jealous? He loved Helen. He had been trying to escape from Inge for ten years. He said carefully, 'So it's begun.'

Felix said, 'Well, yes. I didn't know how to tell you. It's a delicate matter.' He sounded pleased with himself, Richard thought. 'I couldn't just ring you up and say "Oh, by the way . . ." now could I?'

'It's all right, Felix,' Richard said, conscious of sounding irritable. 'We discussed it in advance and I gave you my blessing or however you like to put it.'

'Not quite the same as a fait accompli, though, is it?' Felix drained his glass. 'I actually feel quite embarrassed talking to you about it. That's a new sensation.'

Richard said sharply, 'D'you want sympathy?'

'Sorry, sorry.'

'No, I'm being stupid.' Now he felt Felix was trying to humour him. He took a deep breath to steady himself. 'It's all for the best. I'm pleased, really I am. Now maybe she'll cheer up and get a job and Helen won't feel we're being held to ransom all the time.'

Felix said, 'It's no picnic being with someone who's so very much in love with someone else. Never happened to me before. Quite a blow to my ego. All she wants is someone to prop her up till you come back.'

Richard believed him. He knew Felix was telling the truth

210

and yet he felt unbelievably angry, as if Felix was trying to patronise him. He said furiously, 'Tell her not to hold her breath.'

There was a tense silence. Felix said, 'You're not going to let this affect our friendship, are you? Because if you are, I'd rather drop the whole thing. Just think of it as the nearest I'll ever get to social work.'

Richard forced himself to look at Felix and saw the same civilised face that he had known for twenty years. It was odd to see Felix unchanged after what he had just heard him say. He wondered if he was going slightly mad. Felix was very attractive and so was Inge. He didn't desire either of them – how could he? – so why should they not enjoy each other and leave him free to be happy with Helen? It was a perfect arrangement, and he had sanctioned it in advance, so why did he not feel good about it?

'It's all right, Felix,' he said. 'Really it is.'

WINTER

Sally sat in the lecture hall. She had been meaning to write to Felix for ages, ever since she got his letter, but every time she tried to, someone interrupted her or she started to cry. It was a hard thing to do alone: she wanted people around her but she did not want them to interfere. So she hit on the plan of writing to Felix during a lecture. She could not concentrate on the lecture anyway, so she might as well write to Felix, and she would feel safe in a clean, well-lighted place, she thought. She addressed the envelope first and even writing Felix's name and the details of the flat unnerved her, so she was doubly grateful for the people in the lecture hall and the lecturer's voice droning on.

'But no assessment of Donne,' he said, swaying slightly as he spoke, 'would be complete without consideration of Dryden's stricture: "He affects the metaphysics, not only in his satires but in his amorous verses where nature only should reign; and perplexes the minds of the fair sex with nice speculations of philosophy when he should engage their hearts and entertain them with the softnesses of love . . ." '

Dear Felix [she wrote], I've put off writing this letter as long as I could but now it's nearly Christmas and I want to tell you why I won't be coming home. I'm still too angry with Mum and I don't want to see her. I was very angry with you too, but now I just feel sad that you didn't love me enough, and I'm angry with myself for being so stupid as to think you did. I can't blame you for everything because some of it was my fault. I should never have taken a risk without asking you and I should never have imagined you might leave Elizabeth and live with me and our baby. I still have nightmares about the abortion, although at the time it was as all right as they could make it and everyone was very nice to me.

215

She stopped and looked round the room. She didn't believe that anyone else there had such grown-up problems.

Oh Felix, it could all have been so different. I wish I could hate you because then it might not hurt so much, but I don't want to spoil the memory of all the wonderful times we had. It was everything I'd always imagined it would be. I can't wish we'd never begun, I just wish it had ended differently. But I couldn't stand up to Mum without you to help me.

I'm going to spend Christmas with my father and his new family. It may be difficult because his wife is about to have their fourth child, but perhaps that will be good for me. It's wonderful to meet him after all this time and talk to him, when I really need someone to talk to.

I feel because it's Christmas I ought to forgive you but I can't, not yet. I don't know if I ever will. I'm so confused, I can't imagine being able to feel just one feeling at a time ever again.

Don't be sad.
love,
Sally.

She was surprised how quick and easy it had been. She had thought about it so much that it was just there in her head, waiting to be written. She had told him the absolute truth and now she felt much lighter. But she needed to have the last word. If he answered her, it would all get messy. She scribbled at the bottom of the page:

P.S. Please don't write back. I couldn't bear it.

After Magdalen had gone Helen tried to work, but the paintings felt cold and heavy, like leftover porridge. There's no urgency now, they said reproachfully; you've postponed us. Why should we get hot for you? Well, you wouldn't like it if I did you in a hurry or left you unfinished, she argued with them. We might, they said, and were silent. She sat for a while in the worn-out armchair, picking at bits of horsehair and looking at the canvases, but they offered her nothing. She found she was starting to think about Sally and once that happened she knew she might as well go home. As she got in the house the phone was ringing and it was Sally to say she was going to spend Christmas with Carey and did Helen mind?

Helen sat for a long time at the kitchen table after she put down the phone. She held her head in her hands to prop herself up. She thought she was close to despair: if she couldn't work and she had lost Sally, then she might as well be dead, and if she also couldn't talk to Richard about how she felt, she had outmanoeuvred herself totally. She didn't feel suicidal, more that she had already stopped living: the job had been done for her while she had been looking in another direction. Someone had cut off her supply of life.

She wasn't aware of time passing so she didn't know how long she sat there, but eventually she heard Richard come in. She sprang up, poured two glasses of wine.

'Sorry I'm a bit late,' he said, 'I had a drink with Felix.'

'Doesn't matter, it's only macaroni cheese and salad.'

'Wonderful.' He kissed the back of her neck as she stood at the sink. 'I thought it was my turn to cook.' They had always divided household chores scrupulously.

'Oh well, I got home early. I couldn't work properly so I thought I might as well cook. Not that I've actually started, but I meant to.'

She couldn't fool him entirely, of course. He looked at her with sympathy and said, 'Isn't it going any better? I thought maybe once you'd told Magdalen about postponing you'd feel easier about it.'

She shook her head. She was angry to find herself close to tears. 'I'm bloody useless.'

'It'll come right. It always does.'

'You have such faith in me. I wish I did.'

'You're not standing where I am.' He put his arms round her and hugged her very tight. She let herself relax into the hug as far as she could and they kissed. She thought how

217

lucky she was: he had pulled her back from the brink of something dangerous.

'Nice,' she said, thinking how inadequate and yet appropriate the word was. 'Oh, what the hell. Sod the lot of them.'

'That's the spirit.' They laughed. 'Which brings me to Christmas.'

'Oh God, don't ruin everything. You've just got me in a good mood.'

'I only wanted to ask you which day we should ask Felix and Elizabeth round.'

Why now? Why was this suddenly important? 'Do we really have to?'

'Well, we always used to.'

'That's no answer.'

'And it is their first Christmas back.'

Helen extricated herself from the hug and went back to chopping vegetables. She found the feel of the knife in her hand quite comforting. 'Maybe now's the time to break with tradition.'

'But they'll be hurt. And they'll think it's very odd.'

'Let's wait till they ask us round and then I can be ill.'

He looked concerned. 'Oh darling, it's not as bad as that, is it?'

'It's worse. Look, why don't you and Felix go out somewhere and be all macho and festive, and I'll see Elizabeth on her own? It works much better that way. That's what we've been doing lately.'

'Yes, I've noticed.'

Now he had a slight edge to his voice, which made her aggressive. 'Well, it's sensible. We're not Siamese twins, after all. Elizabeth wants to moan about Felix and he wants to boast to you, so really having a foursome is counterproductive. We only have to meet again separately.'

'But it's Christmas.'

'Yes, I do know that. But it's such a waste of time and energy, not to mention the booze. They both drink like fishes, I don't think we can afford them.' Surely this was an argument that would appeal to him.

218

'Well, that's the point really.' He looked embarrassed. 'We can't afford to drop them, even if we want to.'

'What d'you mean?' Helen said, feeling a sudden chill. 'I can afford to drop anyone.'

Richard drank his wine. Without moving he almost seemed to be shuffling his feet on the kitchen floor and she had a sudden vision of him as a schoolboy.

'Well, Felix is doing me a sort of favour with Inge, and if we don't have a normal Christmas with them he'll only think I'm being . . . well, like a dog in the manger.'

'A sort of favour?' Helen repeated.

'Yes, they're having an affair.'

'God, he doesn't waste much time.' The words slipped out before she realised how revealing they were.

'What?'

Now she had to think fast. 'Oh, Elizabeth said she thought he'd broken up with someone back in the summer.'

'Yes, he had. Someone in Cambridge, I think. So he was at a loose end and Inge met him by chance in a bookshop. Well, you know what she's like. I just thought if he could make her happy, I mean a bit less lonely and frustrated, then you and I might actually benefit. She might ease up on all the pressure, maybe even get a job, I could pay her less money. I've never been able to pull my weight here, I'm very conscious of that. If Felix can take care of Inge, then I can do more for you and Sally.'

So many words. He was trying so hard to make it sound all right. She couldn't think what to say.

'He did sort of ask my permission first.'

'How frightfully gallant of him.'

'It's not an easy situation.'

The truth was so awful, it took her a while to face it. 'You're jealous, aren't you?'

'I don't know what I feel. I'm very confused.'

'God, Felix and Inge,' she said, still in shock. She could see the logic behind it but it felt incestuous and disgusting, even dangerous.

He said, 'Yes, but it could work to our advantage,' sounding eager to believe his own words. She thought how quickly the balance could shift: that was the trouble with marriage. Just when you were in need of a bit of help and comfort yourself, you had to dispense it instead.

'It's going to be a funny Christmas,' she said. 'Sally's not coming home. She's going to stay with her lovely new father.'

He could see the distress on her face, hear it in her voice. He put his arms round her again and she let the tears come.

'Have to make the best of each other then, won't we?' he said.

'Tell you what,' Felix said. 'Let's go away for Christmas.'

They were curled up at opposite ends of the sofa watching *La Bohème* on television, within touching distance of each other. It was the sort of evening they both enjoyed: supper on a tray and shoes off and music and closeness. But Felix couldn't relax enough to enjoy it as much as usual. He felt uneasy: Sally's letter had unnerved him, as well as Richard's obvious jealousy about Inge, and Inge's own tiresome habit of prowling around the flat and opening wardrobes and asking tactless questions. None of these factors was in itself a disaster, but taken together they made him feel emotionally over-extended, particularly now that Natasha was chasing him for the book. He was conscious of wanting to run away and hide, like a child before an exam. It was all too much. He couldn't cope; he simply didn't have the resources. He needed help.

'Can we afford it?' Elizabeth said. 'We're living off our hump as it is.'

'I know, but it's so cold, and it's going to be boring, Richard and Helen are bound to want us to go round there and I'd like a change. Let's go away somewhere warm. Just the two of us. I want to be alone with you.'

'I thought that was just what we came home to avoid,' she said rather sharply.

Perhaps she was feeling neglected. He knew he had been rather preoccupied lately. If flattery couldn't divert her, maybe pathos would do the trick.

220

'Darling, don't be grumpy. I've had a very hard day. Natasha's nagging me to get the book finished.'

'Didn't you tell her you'd torn it up?'

'No.' Shit, he had forgotten that stupid lie he had told when he was late for *La Traviata*, the day Sally announced she was pregnant. 'Well, yes, I did, but now I've looked at it again, I think I might be able to salvage some of it.'

On the screen Rodolfo and Mimi were singing some of the most romantic music ever written. Being cold, poor, ill and heartbroken didn't faze them at all; they were coping much better than he was, with all his advantages.

'That's no surprise,' Elizabeth said comfortably. 'It's always better than you think, when you really get down to it.'

'Well, even if it is,' said Felix, hoping to God she was right, 'there's no way I can get it done as fast as she wants it. Oh, come on, Lizzie, let's go off and lie in the sun and make love every night and I'll do a thousand words a day. I want to be a lizard on a rock.'

'Maybe after Christmas. Right now I want to stay at home and see our friends and have a trad English Christmas. I'm tired of travelling.'

'God, you're a hard woman.' He put out his hand to her and when she took it he held on tight. He actually felt panic and he wasn't sure what the panic was about. Just a feeling that the whole complicated edifice of his life could be crumbling, but that seemed excessive. 'You're not cross with me, are you?' he said.

'No more than usual.'

'Don't tease me.' He turned his head to look at her but she was staring at the screen.

'Who's teasing?' she said.

'You know I love you. And all the rest's a fantasy.' Still no answer. 'Lizzie?' Now she turned her face to him but it didn't reveal anything. 'You know I couldn't manage without you. You wouldn't ever leave me, would you?'

'I ought to.'

Perhaps it was all about nothing, just one of their games, shifting the balance of power to and fro. Sally and Inge were much too close to home, he had been reckless there, but she

221

couldn't really know. Could she? 'I'd kill you,' he said, to reassure her, squeezing her hand and banging it on the sofa.

'Oh well, in that case,' she said, smiling for the first time, 'maybe I'll stay.'

At last he felt safe. He allowed himself to relax, sinking back into the music, letting it envelop him like warm treacle.

All the way here in the car I was panicking. I talked non-stop for a while, the way I always do when I'm nervous, then I shut up completely and couldn't say anything. He didn't seem to notice. It was funny being with him in the car on a long journey, so dark outside and the two of us very close but not talking. I thought of all the years we didn't know each other, how he was a stranger till quite recently, still is really, and here we were together in this small space. I got pre-Xmas blues thinking about Mum and how I'm punishing her by not going home, only I'm punishing myself as well, and how awful it would be if Richard gets suspicious because I'm staying away. Then I started worrying about presents, how nobody'd like what I'd bought them and I'd done it in a hurry and done it badly because I didn't have any money. God, I was a real misery. It was a good thing I did stop talking. I got so depressed I actually wanted to jump out of the car. I'm not sure if I wanted to be killed, quickly and painlessly of course, or just slightly injured so I could spend Xmas in hospital. Then I got into a fantasy about a gorgeous doctor falling in love with me and me telling him there was no hope because I'd given up men. That was fun. He was frantic and couldn't do his work properly. The only trouble was, he looked rather like Felix. I bet his life is going on quite unchanged.

I suppose really I was just very very nervous about meeting Marsha.

Then C said it was all going to be a bit chaotic. I said that would be a nice change from home, with Mum keeping everything so orderly so she could get on with her work. Then I thought how silly for me to be telling him what Mum's like at home when he must remember and I bet she hasn't

222

changed very much except get more bossy probably. I got quite a shock when he said, 'You mustn't hate her, you know, she loves you very much.' I was surprised he knew so much, or cared enough to say it, but instead of being grateful I said very rudely, 'Oh God, you're not going to lecture me, are you?' I thought I might have upset him but he just said quite calmly, 'I might. But you can always tell me to shut up.' He was really good about it but I still couldn't thank him, I just sat there thinking about what he'd said and I suddenly felt awfully tired of all of them, Mum and Richard, and Felix, and C, the whole lot. I felt I'd been considering other people's feelings all my life and nobody'd ever considered mine. I was really fed up of fitting in with everybody and being endlessly tactful and cheerful.

I said, 'Are you sure Marsha doesn't mind me coming?'

He said of course she didn't, she was pleased, only a lot of the time she was half asleep, which was hardly surprising, he said. I didn't know if I was meant to laugh or what. Quite suddenly I said, 'I'm so afraid of seeing her,' and it seemed the only really true thing I'd said all day. He didn't answer and I wondered if he understood what I meant, then we were there, drawing up outside the house. It was very dark, that special sort of dark you get in the country and even more so at Christmas, very dense, with only the lighted windows in the distance like beacons, and suddenly the children opened the door and spilled out of the house, running to meet him. He got out of the car and scooped them up in his arms. I just sat there watching, I was sort of frozen. I thought about how he'd never done that for me, or if he had, not for long and I didn't remember anyway – they were already older than I'd been when he left us. And I thought how Felix would never do that for our baby because it was dead. And then Marsha came into the doorway and waved. She was silhouetted against the light, it couldn't have been more perfect if she'd planned it, though of course I know she didn't, but there she was simply hugely, enormously pregnant, just as I got out of the car. And I started to cry.

*

Inge wanted to stay in the dream for ever; she struggled against waking up. In the dream Richard was holding on to her as if he were drowning. She had never been held so close or so tight before. He kept telling her how sorry he was, how it had all been a terrible mistake and he would stay with her always. She wanted to laugh from sheer joy but could not breathe because of the way he was hugging her, and terror of suffocation began to interfere with the joy. She woke with a shock and drew a great sobbing breath that seemed only just in time. Felix was shaking her shoulder.

'Time to get up,' he said gently.

It felt so wrong to see him and not Richard that she started to cry, and said without thinking, 'Oh Felix, I was dreaming about Richard and he was being so nice to me. Then I woke up and saw you.'

His look of mild concern at the tears vanished and he said briskly, 'Yes, I can see that would be disappointing.'

Then she realised she had been tactless and flung her arms round him to prevent him from going away. 'Don't be angry with me, Felix. I'm so unhappy, I want to die.'

He stroked her hair, but more with compassion than affection, she thought. 'It's all right, Inge, calm down. It's only Christmas. It's enough to upset anyone.' He used the sort of reassuring tone she imagined Englishmen found appropriate for startled horses.

She said rapidly, urged on by need and desperation, 'He's got to come back, Felix, I can't live without him.'

'Yes, you've had a very hard time.' His face and voice were both entirely neutral.

'Don't leave me. Can we go on till Richard comes back? I can't be alone again.'

She now saw that he was holding a glass of wine. He took a sip from it before giving it to her.

'Inge, look, we're old friends and we've both been around. These things last as long as they last. You know that as well as I do. And I never make promises I can't keep. We'll go on as long as it suits us both, that's all I can say.'

This sounded so final that she sat up and drank her glass of wine rather fast to give herself courage.

'Come on,' he said gently. 'Time to go home.'

'Christmas Eve was always special, don't you remember?' she said, thinking of her childhood. 'The day itself is nothing. And Richard knows that, but he comes on Boxing Day. The boys go out to parties and I'm all alone. Let me stay here, Felix, just for a little while. I don't want to go back to an empty house. Not yet.' The very thought of it actually made her tremble.

He looked at his watch.

'I've got to get back. Elizabeth's expecting me, we're going out.'

'I'll be good. I'll make the sofa. I'll wash the glasses.' She had generally found that if she went on long enough, people gave in. 'Oh Felix, it means so much to me not to be alone in my empty house on Christmas Eve. If I stay here I can have a fantasy that my life is different.' And the fantasy began to take shape as she spoke.

They argued the point for a while, but she knew from his face he was beaten, long before he said, 'Well, I can't dress you by force and throw you out.'

'You don't understand. It's just so lovely to be somewhere else.'

He smiled; she must have struck a chord. 'Actually, I understand that very well. It's one of the principles on which I run my life.'

She was beginning to feel he owed her this favour, if only to make good the discrepancy between their emotions: his serenity and her agitation. After all, he was going home to someone who loved him.

'Have another drink but don't get smashed.' He kissed her on the forehead. 'I'll ring you as soon as these ghastly festivities are over.'

'Can we meet on New Year's Eve?'

'That might be a little difficult.'

'It's another bad time for me.' He shouldn't need to be told all this, she thought.

'Yes, I know, it's a bad time for everyone. I'll try. That's all I can say. It's not easy to be in two places at once but I'm working on it.' He hesitated and she could see how reluctant

225

he still was to leave her alone in the flat. 'Well, take care. See you soon.'

When he had gone she stretched and closed her eyes, then opened them again, trying to pretend she had just woken up in a place that belonged to her and Richard. But the sofa bed was hard, better suited to making love than lying around, and there were more exciting things for her to do with this stolen time. She got up and poured herself some more wine, then prowled round the room and opened the forbidden wardrobe. The clothes tempted her, like something magical and dangerous in a fairy story. She started to try them on. They fitted, but only just, suggesting in some curious way a both slimmer and sturdier body, and they did not suit her. They were black, or black and silver, not her colours, but they were beautiful and expensive and she loved them. No one had ever bought her clothes like that.

She admired them for a while and herself in them, seduced by the incongruity of her new image. Then she got bored. Perhaps it would be fun to play with the word processor. But she was afraid of causing damage that would make Felix angry. His new novel, then: if she could find that and read a few pages, that would be exciting, and he would never know. It would give her a sense of power, instead of the helplessness she felt, waiting for him to fit her into the corners of his life. She began to open desk drawers at random but found only letters; where did he keep the novel? Still, even the dullest letter could be interesting because it was not meant to be read by anyone else. She found some from his agent and his publisher and even some from fans expressing passionate admiration for his work and even more passionate desire to meet him. When she found Sally's letter, it was a few moments before she realised who it was from, and then her heart beat fast with shock. Felix had made Helen's daughter pregnant and they had arranged an abortion without telling Richard. She sat for a few moments with the letter in her hand, feeling a sense of awe at holding something so valuable.

*

Marsha's nice. She made me feel really welcome when I arrived. She couldn't hug me exactly, being so very pregnant, but she held both my hands and kissed me on both cheeks and said, 'Sally, I'm so glad you've come to us for Christmas. You must have been really sad about having to lose your baby.' It was a shock hearing it put like that and brave of her to say it straight out as soon as we met. I'd been wondering if we'd all have to pretend it never happened. I started to cry, of course, and she said, 'I hope it's not going to upset you, me being like this,' and I said, 'No, I'm glad for you, it's all right, and I'm really pleased to be here.'

You can tell at once she's a good person. There's no malice in her. I think in her place I might be jealous of my husband's long-lost grown-up daughter turning up and I'd be terrified of saying the wrong thing about the abortion and I'd feel almost guilty for being pregnant, like a reproach. But she seems like a very simple person who wants to be kind and just follows her instincts.

I think he was a bit embarrassed actually. He watched us having this great outspoken welcome and then he sort of drifted away and made a big fuss of the children who were climbing all over him. I still don't know what to call him, Dad or Carey, so I don't. I just make sure I'm looking at him when I speak to him.

He was right to warn me it's a bit chaotic. The noise is unbelievable because there's always a child crying or playing or screaming. And he's usually practising the viola in the background. I don't know how Marsha copes. Up to a point she doesn't – the house is really filthy. It must be, for me to notice. Mum would faint. But Marsha's amazingly good-tempered about it all. She's obviously got her priorities all sorted out.

Christmas Eve.
He was right about it being chaotic. Marsha was making chestnut stuffing today and I was peeling a great mountain of potatoes and sprouts for all of us to have tomorrow and C was at the pub. The children kept running in and out. There's

Chloe who's two, and Kim aged four, and Tom, six. There's a goat in a pen in the garden, cropping the grass and staring at you in that slightly insolent way goats have, and chickens running about, and a rabbit in a hutch, and a derelict car rusting to bits with pieces falling off. Kim kept telling Marsha that Chloe was wet and Marsha said, 'I know,' but she didn't do anything about it, just went on making the stuffing. I wondered if I should offer to change Chloe but I was a bit nervous and then Tom brought the rabbit in and let it loose in the kitchen so we all got distracted. Marsha said, 'Oh Tom, not in the house,' but she didn't say it with much conviction so it probably happens a lot. 'But poor Benji's cold, you feel his fur,' Tom said, as if he was used to getting his own way by pretending to be tender-hearted. 'He wants to be with us, he's lonely.' Marsha said, 'He's got a perfectly good hutch,' while the rabbit belted round the kitchen, stopping and starting in that sudden way they do, and Kim kept saying, 'I want to feel your tummy, I want to feel the baby kick,' which made my heart thump a bit, though of course I'd never got to that stage. Marsha said, 'It's not kicking now, lovey, it's asleep, isn't it lucky?' but Kim forced his hand between her stomach and the sink just to make sure. Then she started trying to persuade Tom to change Chloe's nappy, apparently it's his job, but he kept making faces and saying ugh. 'Oh, go on,' Marsha said, wheedling, 'you're ever so good at it.' I asked when C was coming home and she said, 'Soon, I hope,' but she didn't sound cross, in fact she gave me a big smile as she said it. I'd be furious to be left on my own like that with so much to do and a stranger in the house. Then Chloe fell over the rabbit and started howling and had to be kissed better. It's probably all just normal family life, only I've never seen it before so it comes as a bit of a shock.

I don't know what I was expecting. More attention, I suppose. Something momentous. It felt like such a big occasion to me, being there for Xmas. Well, first of all meeting him, and then being brave enough to tell Mum I wasn't coming home for Xmas and actually getting him to invite me to stay with them, and facing Marsha being so very pregnant and meeting all the children. I've done so many enormous things and I suppose I wanted him to take more notice of me.

I'm not disappointed exactly, well I suppose I am in a way. It's just that by the time Marsha and I'd done all the veg for Xmas lunch and left them in big saucepans in cold water and got the children bathed and into bed it was supper time, and while we were getting supper C came back from the pub and went up to read stories to the children. Then w₂ had supper but we didn't talk about anything important, and then Marsha and I washed up and Marsha and C wrapped all the presents for the children. And then we all watched television for a bit, only by then it was after ten and C and Marsha actually fell asleep. I felt really silly sitting there watching TV while they slept, although I didn't blame Marsha for nodding off in her state, but I wasn't even watching a programme I liked, so eventually I switched channels, only then they woke up because the sound was different. C said they still had to do Xmas stockings and we'd better all get an early night because the children would of course be up at dawn. And Marsha said thank God there was only the turkey left to do in the morning.

I feel very funny writing this, complaining about them while I'm in their house and being away from home for Xmas for the first time. I'm cold in here, although it's a nice room, and I miss having a duvet, though they've given me three blankets including a tartan one that looks like a car rug. The country is odd. Everyone says it's wonderful and I know you're supposed to like it, but I'm not sure I do. In London there's either traffic sound or proper silence, but here there's no traffic so the occasional car gives you a shock and there are funny animal sounds going on all the time that you don't understand. I don't feel like that about Sussex, perhaps because there are so many of us there. It's like being in a great room full of people at college, so I've never thought of it as country. And it's so early now. Only half past twelve and I've been in bed for nearly an hour. But if I don't get to sleep soon *and they really do wake up at dawn, I'm going to feel awful tomorrow.*

Dammit, sod it, I think I'm missing my bloody mother.

Richard poured drinks for them all. There was the usual mixture of relief and anti-climax, a sort of forced brightness, that Felix always associated with Boxing Day. Thank God yesterday is over, but we're not out of the wood yet: that was the message.

'It feels very strange without Sally,' Elizabeth said. 'Helen must have been hoping she'd change her mind at the last minute.'

Felix was grateful for small mercies. At least Sally had had the sense not to come home for Christmas. It was going to be difficult enough being ordinarily sociable with Helen.

'Not really,' Richard said. 'She knows Sally wants to spread her wings a bit, get to know her father and his new family. It's quite understandable.'

'How's all that going?' Felix forced himself to ask, conscious of not having spoken. Richard's tone of calm reason enraged him. Such stupidity, though convenient, even essential, was hard to bear.

'Pretty well, I think. She rang up yesterday, of course, and she seemed to be having a great time. A real family Christmas, she said.'

Elizabeth sipped her drink. 'How many of them are there?'

'I think Marsha's about to produce number four.'

Felix flinched.

'My God,' Elizabeth said, 'some people have all the luck.'

'I'd call that going rather over the top myself,' Felix said sharply. So she was in a mood to put the boot in. They had drunk too much last night, which made her randy and him incapable, and so her Christmas was incomplete. Now they were both bad-tempered and hung over.

'Yes,' she said, smiling at him, 'you would.'

'Look,' Richard said into the rather nasty silence, 'I'm sorry Helen's not back yet, she's working. She shouldn't be long, though, she knows I'll have to go and see Inge later on and that cuts into the day.'

'Just like old times,' Elizabeth said.

'Well, not exactly. It may be the last time.'

They were both quite shaken. They looked at him in amazement, forgetting their grievances for the moment. It was like a replay of the original separation and the surprise that went with that.

'It's just got to stop,' Richard said, 'it's not fair to anyone, Helen or Inge or me. I'll simply have to give up going round there. There's really no reason to, now the boys are bigger. I thought I was being kind or doing my duty, but I'm just raising false hopes, I realise that now.' He poured himself another drink. 'I'll have to stop it, no matter what she threatens to do. I can't spend the rest of my life being held to ransom. I've got to break with her.'

And whom would she turn to for comfort? Felix felt a real shiver of fright. 'It sounds to me as if you're trying to convince yourself,' he said to Richard.

'What d'you mean?' Elizabeth said sharply.

'Methinks he doth protest too much.'

'Don't be silly, it's a good idea. Then everyone'll know where they stand.'

'Well, it's a hell of a thing to do at Christmas. Might push her right over the edge.' He could just see her coming round to the flat, distraught, getting drunk, refusing to leave.

'Whose side are you on?'

Richard was looking at them both in astonishment. 'No, no, he's right. I didn't mean I'm going to tell her today. Just some time soon. Before February, anyway. I can't face another birthday visit. So it's like a New Year resolution. A sort of Christmas present for Helen.'

'She'll love it,' Felix said. 'Just what she's always wanted.'

27 December.
I don't know how I've survived the past three days.
I rang Mum on Xmas Day – God it seems a long time ago –

231

and told her and Richard I was having a real family Xmas. I
don't know how I could have said that. In one sense it was true
but in another, the sense I wanted her to believe, it was the
biggest lie I've ever told. Not that I've told many. I know I
was trying to hurt her and I succeeded. I told her originally I
wanted to be here so as not to have to see Felix over Xmas,
but I thought I might also be trying to punish her and now I
know I was.

Well, it's rebounded on me all right. Xmas Day was just
one long round of food and drink and presents and screaming
children and television, normal I suppose, but I got such a
headache. I tried to help but there was never a quiet time just
for me so I didn't feel I got rewarded or even noticed. And
then yesterday.

C went off to his study, which is out of bounds apparently,
and practised the viola. It sounded like Bach. Marsha and I
played with the children and tried to talk. The TV was on in
the background with the sound turned down. I hate that, it's
so irritating. I asked her how she coped and she just said the
secret was to have very low standards and if you didn't have
them to start with, you jolly soon got them. I said I was
surprised how much C practised and she said she thought he
was just trying to get away from this lot, meaning the
children. 'Don't blame him,' she said. 'I would if I could. No,
they're lovely really, it's just when I'm pregnant, I get so
tired.' Then to my amazement when the music stopped she
said she actually wasn't all that fond of the viola, although
she'd never tell him that. In fact, she wasn't very musical at
all, she said, but it didn't seem to matter.

Then C put his head round the door and said he was going
for a walk and would anybody like to come. I said I'd rather
stay with Marsha. I was surprised to hear myself say that.
Marsha made him take Tom and Kim, so that just left us with
Chloe. When they'd gone Marsha giggled and said, 'Ooh,
hasn't it gone quiet?'

I said, 'He doesn't help you much, does he?' and she said,
'He does sometimes. He's a bit lazy. I think he's got more
than he bargained for.' I pointed out all she did yesterday and
the day before and she said, 'Well, you were helping me.' I

asked if she minded and she said, 'Oh, I can't be bothered to make a fuss, I'm lazy too.' I said, 'Mum and Richard share everything,' and then I realised what I'd said, how there's this big secret between them now for ever and it's all my fault. Marsha must have picked it up because there was a very long silence and then she said gently, 'D'you want to talk about it?'

I said, 'I did try but I don't think he wanted to listen.' And then I thought how what she really meant was did I want to talk to her, not C.

She said, 'He gets upset if he can't make things all right. And he feels guilty for losing touch with you.'

I said, 'I've told him it doesn't matter. He hasn't ruined anything.' And as I said it I realised I was very angry with him.

She said, 'I'm sorry I couldn't offer to help if you wanted the baby but you see how things are,' and again I was impressed by how direct she is. And I thought how awful, Mum talking to C and C talking to Marsha and nobody talking to me but it was my baby.

I said, 'No, you couldn't possibly have. The whole thing was crazy. I must have been mad to get into it. Why did I take such a risk? I'm not stupid. I mean my mother's really tolerant and I go and do the one thing that would upset her most. Felix didn't encourage me, not really.'

Marsha said, 'Can't you forgive yourself? You can't change it, so why not just let it go? It's sad but it may be all for the best.'

I couldn't believe what I was hearing. I said, 'You make it sound very simple.' Nobody'd ever put it to me like that before.

She said, 'I'm not trying to put you down. But I used to spend a lot of time fretting about things. Now I don't bother. Either they don't really matter or if they do they're beyond my control or else it's too late. I just let everything wash over me now. It's much more restful.'

I thought about it. I really tried to let her words sink in. 'I'd love to be like that. I suppose I'm used to Mum being in control of everything.'

Marsha said, 'Look, you made a mistake. It happens to lots of people.'

I said, 'But I want to know why. I want to learn from it.'

And then, of course, just as I thought we were getting somewhere, C and the children came back. He just gave us both a big grin and said he was going down the pub to recover. I couldn't believe it. I said to Marsha, 'He did it again.' But she only said, 'Oh well, it gives us more time to talk.'

Then she said she thought I was very brave to be in a house with children and a pregnant woman. I said it was hard to explain but it sort of helped me.

'So long as you're not doing it to punish yourself,' she said.

I said, 'Maybe I am. Would that matter? Anyway it's real life. I can't keep running away. And I wasn't brave enough to face Mum and Felix.' I thought for a bit and she waited and then I said, 'You're so different. It's really hard to imagine he's been married to both of you.' I'd been staring into space and then I heard her breathing and when I looked back at her, oh God I was so frightened, I realised she was having a pain.

She said, 'Sorry. That one took me by surprise.'

I said, 'You're not in labour, are you?' I so much didn't want to believe it.

She said, 'Didn't you notice me puffing and blowing a bit when we were washing up? Don't panic, it'll be ages yet. I ought to know the routine, just think of all the practice I've had.'

I wanted to fetch C immediately but she said later on maybe and why spoil his evening, there was nothing he could do.

So I bathed the children for her and put them to bed. We made out it was a special treat and I tried to make it fun. When I came back downstairs my clothes and my hair were soaking wet and Marsha was lying on the sofa panting.

I was terrified. I just ran out and down the lane all the way to the pub. I didn't even stop to put my coat on and I ran all the way. It was freezing cold and the air made my chest hurt.

When I got to the pub it was very crowded and noisy and hot and at first I couldn't see C anywhere. Then I saw him and he was sitting in a corner tucked away almost out of sight talking to a girl and he was kissing the palm of her hand. I just stared. Then he felt someone watching him and he looked up and saw me.

When we got back to the house Marsha was in bed. C went up to see her and then he came down and rang the midwife. Tom said to me, 'Mummy's trying to push the baby out,' very matter of fact. I put on my coat and went into the garden where I couldn't hear the sounds from upstairs. It was very cold but I quite liked that. I stroked the rabbit for a while and then I went and talked to the goat. I don't know how long I was there but Tom came out and said, 'Mummy's pushing very hard now. Don't you want to come and watch? She has to do funny breathing.' I said, 'No, I don't think so, thanks. I think I'll stay with Benji,' and he ran indoors. Then I went and sat in the rusty old car.

Eventually C came out and found me. He said, 'You must be frozen. Don't you want to come back in the house?' I shook my head and he said, 'It's all right, it's all over. It's a girl and Marsha's fine.'

I couldn't speak.

He said very awkwardly, 'Look, about the pub.'

I said, 'I don't want to talk about it.'

He said, 'Things aren't always what they seem.'

I went back inside with him because I was really cold by now. Marsha was sitting up in bed cuddling the new baby and the children were all round her and the midwife was bringing her a cup of tea. Tom said, 'Look, we've got a sister,' and Kim said, 'That's our new baby.' Marsha looked tired but very well and happy and C put his arm round her and I saw he actually had tears in his eyes. She gave me a great big smile *and I just couldn't take any more, I went to my room and went to bed and cried and cried and cried until I fell asleep.*

The atmosphere grew strained. More drinks were poured. Nuts and raisins were swallowed. Longing eyes were cast at the food ready on the table and jokes made about starting without her, as it was only cold. Still they waited. Felix and Richard went on at length about the horrors of Christmas.

'Well, I think you're a couple of Scrooges, you two,' Elizabeth said. 'I love Christmas. I think it's absolutely wonderful to have tinsel and holly and presents and carols –'

'My God, I can't bear this,' said Felix, groaning theatrically. 'She may be about to sing.'

'– and plum pudding and log fires. I'm sick of spending Christmas in the sun. I like being cold and then getting warm again and doing all the traditional things.'

At last the sound of Helen's van. It was after three.

'Ah, here she is,' said Richard with relief.

'And I think you're both pretending to be above it all. Hating Christmas is just a form of intellectual snobbery.'

Helen came in. Her face was blank behind her social smile. 'Sorry I'm late,' she said. 'I wanted to catch the last of the light. You should have started without me.' She kissed Elizabeth and looked past Felix. Her beauty moved him, an older, tireder version of Sally. He felt a sense of loss that surprised him, an uncomfortable pang that pierced through the layers of hunger, alcohol and boredom, and made him realise how much he had wanted to stay at home.

'How's it going?' Elizabeth asked.

'How would I know? I'm the last person to ask.'

They ate. Elizabeth and Richard did most of the talking. Felix tried to avoid Helen's eyes but the effort was too great to sustain and eventually he stumbled into a direct glance, their first since before Sally's abortion. The strength of pure hatred made all her previous looks of indifference or dislike over the years seem like positive regard. Felix felt quite weak, as if he had swallowed a dose of pale green poison.

236

After lunch they all slumped on the sofas, put on the television, went through all four channels and switched it off. Richard made coffee.

Felix said, 'I wonder why doing nothing is so exhausting.'

'I'm not doing nothing,' Richard said. 'I'm putting off going to see Inge.'

'It's like a conditioned reflex,' Felix said, grateful for the small joke. 'I'm sure the day will come when I won't be physically able to swallow a mince pie unless I'm watching *The Sound of Music* or *The African Queen*.'

Elizabeth said to Helen, 'Will Sally be home for your show?'

Felix wanted to hit her: she seemed to be dragging Sally's name into every conversation and yet he was sure she knew nothing.

'I hope so,' Helen said. 'If it ever happens. Right now I can't believe I'll ever finish.'

'Heavens, you're as bad as Felix. Of course you'll finish. It's going to be wonderful, I'm really looking forward to it. Richard, can't you talk some sense into her?'

'I do, all the time. It's like pouring water into a sieve.'

Felix felt panic rising at the thought of Helen's show with them all there together and Sally arriving.

'I know just what you mean,' Elizabeth said, and turned to him. 'Don't I, darling?'

He said, 'Of course we may be away on holiday.'

'But we can't miss Helen's show.'

God, she could be relentless. 'I need sunshine to finish the book.'

Richard left to see Inge. Helen offered mince pies. But Elizabeth said it was time they were going.

In the car on the way home she said, 'Helen was very quiet.'

Felix said yes.

'I got the feeling she didn't really want us there.'

Felix made a sound of agreement.

'I suppose she's missing Sally. And she does seem awfully worried about work.'

Felix said mm.

Elizabeth said sharply, 'Darling, you've gone awfully monosyllabic.'

'Have I?' He enunciated with savage ironic precision. 'Sor-ry. Is that bet-ter?'

'We can't miss her show,' Elizabeth said after a pause.

'We can if it clashes with our holiday.'

'But we haven't booked it yet.'

'I just have a feeling they're going to clash.' The conversation terrified him, it was much too close to the truth, but if she forced him into a corner he was prepared to fight and she ought to know that and be willing at the last minute to back off.

'Honestly, you and Helen,' she said, after a longer silence. 'You're like a couple of silly children, always trying to score points off each other.'

Felix could feel his breathing just begin to work normally. 'Don't nag. I feel stuffed to the gills with all this ridiculous food and drink, and all I want to do is get home and lie down in a darkened room.'

'Sounds like a fun evening,' Elizabeth said, but in a tone of ordinary annoyance, and he knew the immediate danger had passed.

29 December.
I'll have to go home. Now Marsha's staying in bed (not that I blame her for that) I'm more like an au pair than ever. Meal times are incredible, with C and me and all the children. He keeps telling them old jokes, it's like a quiz show on TV to see who can shout the answer first. For instance: What are the three most useless things? The Pope's sex life, a man's chest and a viola solo. Or: If you were lost in the jungle, who would you ask the way, a pink elephant, a good viola player or a bad viola player? A bad viola player, the others are figments of your imagination. It's meant to be fun, I suppose,

*and the kids certainly enjoy it, but it makes me feel rather
tired.*

*It's strange to hear him calling the viola the box. It makes
me think of coffins.*

*I tried to get him to talk seriously about his work but he
kept making jokes, like how they switch from violin to viola
because they think they'll get better jobs or the school
suggests it, and how they like teasing each other. 'Are you
going to take that up professionally?' or 'I can imagine that
sounding very good.' I can't get him to talk about actual
music. It's almost as if it was an embarrassing question, like
asking about his sex life, and he makes jokes to cover up the
embarrassment. Then I remember how Mum doesn't like
talking about her work and the only time I tried to get her to,
she said if she could do it in words she'd be a writer not a
painter. Only she made it sound as if painting was superior to
writing, because she doesn't like Felix, I suppose. So I gave up
asking. I actually think composing music must be superior to
both because you can reach more people without any
translation and your work can be all over the world
simultaneously and yet it still belongs to you. I tried saying
something about this to C, I thought maybe we could discuss
it, but he was so busy with the children I don't think he was
really listening.*

*He was wearing a jersey without his usual polo neck, so I
could see more of the viola mark on his neck than usual and I
was staring at it and thinking how it looked, like a bruise or a
love bite, or something out of a vampire film. I don't think he
noticed me staring. He kept complaining about backache,
and how he hoped he could fit in a visit to the osteopath
before his next concert, and how Marsha's very good at
massaging his neck and shoulders only of course right now
she doesn't feel much like doing anything. I hope he wasn't
hinting I might do it. I didn't offer, anyway.*

*Perhaps I should have tried to have the sort of musical
conversation I wanted with him before when we were alone
together in Sussex, only then my head was full of other things,
like the past and how I was feeling.*

It's really ironic that all the time he and Mum were married they were so hard up because he was freelance, and then just after he met Marsha he joined the orchestra, so they've always had enough money and been able to afford all these children.

The boys went out after lunch. They shared a joint with Inge to cheer her up and promised to spray the room so Richard wouldn't notice.

'We'll make it smell really disgusting, like pine or lavender.'

'Or lemon verbena. Yuck. Happy Boxing Day, Mum.'

But they wouldn't stay to see Richard with her, even when she started to cry. She wanted to see the whole family together for Christmas but they wouldn't help her. 'Cheer up, it's nearly over,' they said, and went out, whistling, to see their friends.

She poured herself another drink and turned out the lights. Sitting in the darkened room, waiting for Richard, she thought of all the Christmases they had spent apart. She watched the clock on the video, but the prearranged time came and went. He was late. He was always late.

When she heard the car arrive she was in such a trance-like state that it came as quite a shock. She waited behind the front door, noticing how slowly he walked up the path. Was he so reluctant then? He rang the doorbell and she waited another moment: the last few seconds of anticipation were particularly precious. Then she opened the door. As always the sight of him moved her greatly and she flung her arms round him. He tolerated the hug but did not return it, in fact she sensed him slightly straining away.

She took him into the living-room and he immediately put on the lights. She poured whisky for them both.

'I'd like to have seen the boys,' he said.

'They had to go out. You were late. They couldn't wait for you.'

'Seems to happen a lot.' He took two parcels out of a carrier bag and placed them on the coffee table. 'I expect they'll still want their presents though, even if they don't want to see me.'

She couldn't guess from the shapes. He was clever with presents, often concealing small things like cassettes or cameras in shoe boxes. She took her own parcel from behind a cushion and gave it to him. He accepted it reluctantly.

'Thank you, Inge, but I do wish you wouldn't.'

'It gives me pleasure.' In the past she had bought him jerseys and shirts but noticed he never wore them. This year she had chosen a book of cartoons. At least she could make him laugh. 'Aren't you going to open it?'

'Later.' He put it in the carrier bag.

'Did you have a nice Christmas?' It was three years since he had bought her a present.

'It was all right. Very quiet. Felix and Elizabeth came over today.'

'How lovely,' she said. 'So you had your old friends with you. I've been all alone.'

He sat in the big chair opposite her. 'You had the boys. And I'm sure you have friends you could ask if you wanted to. Neighbours even. You must have. You've lived here a long time.'

'I don't want to be with people just because they feel sorry for me.' She was alarmed by the coldness in his voice. 'Oh, that poor lonely woman. We better be nice to her. Since her husband left her she has no one and she's a foreigner too. How awful.'

He said, 'You're not very foreign after twenty years over here.'

'In this country a foreigner is always a foreigner.'

He drained his glass. Surely he couldn't be thinking of leaving already? He seldom had more than one drink but he usually made it last about an hour. 'Well, I'm sure they'd like to be friendly if only you'd let them.'

'If I can't be with you, I'd rather be alone.'

'Well, that's your choice. I'm here now, so can't we be pleasant to each other? Every time I come to see you I hope it's going to be better and it never is.'

'How can it be?' Didn't he understand anything? She had

made it as clear as she could. 'I want you back. I'm in pain.'

He stood up. 'Inge, you just have to let go. I'm sorry but I mean it. You really do.'

'I can't.'

There was a long silence and she saw him actually start to move towards the door.

She said, 'Did your step-daughter come home for Christmas?'

'No, she's staying with her father and his family.'

'Perhaps she has a secret.' Now she was right on the edge, tempted and terrified. 'Not everyone is reliable like me. Some people cheat.'

'What on earth d'you mean?'

But she couldn't do it. 'Oh Richard, I love you so much.'

Helen, left alone, put on the Ravel F major String Quartet. It reminded her of Carey, and for that reason she no longer listened to it often: she had discovered it with him, first on records, then in performance, others' and his own. Its cool intensity and disciplined emotion, the plaintive feeling in the structured framework, seemed to her, then and now, to evoke in music what she was trying to achieve in paint.

It brought him back to her, and that was what she needed today, when he was with Sally and she was not: a moment of fantasy that they were still a couple, still parents together with their daughter. Otherwise she would feel he had stolen Sally from her after all her years of care. Or that Sally had defected, a much more alarming thought.

Remembering the passion she had felt for him was like remembering another lifetime, or an old film in black and white at the NFT, or herself as a mad person. She had imagined killing the women he loved, but never imagined killing him, though after their final parting she had stabbed his shoes with a kitchen knife many times until she was exhausted. When they met, when they married, she would have staked her life that nothing could ever go wrong, though now of course she knew how foolish that was. But there they had been, making love and telling jokes and admiring each other's talent: how could they have known that all that would not be enough?

Her mother had known. Her mother had warned her but Helen would not listen; and after the event her mother had said, 'He was always unstable. Just like your father.'

It seemed late in the day to ask her mother why she had married that unstable person, unless she too had been, like Helen, a prey to the boundless optimism of youth. It made a bond between them, a sudden, unwelcome bond: two abandoned women who should have known better and now had only each other to trust. Helen ran away from this knowledge; she preferred to be alone with Sally, to turn to friends for help, or do without.

When she thought it through, she had to admit the trouble had begun with Sally's birth. They had both wanted Sally and so Sally was conceived, though perhaps, to be scrupulously honest, a little sooner than Carey would have liked. Helen herself had been surprised by the strength of her longing for a child. It was the sixties, a time of equality, and so they had agreed to share everything: they would both cook and clean and work and care for Sally and it would last for ever. That was the deal.

Neither of them had realised how exhausting it would all be: that to be poor and earning a living by painting and playing the viola freelance and also looking after a baby would tax them to the limit of their resources. That Carey would drink too much and forget to pay bills and go to bed with the odd violinist or cellist between rehearsals to remind himself that life could still be fun. That Helen would be at first too tired and later too angry to make love. How obvious it all seemed now and how stupid they must have been not to see it at the time; and yet there they had been, walking around with their eyes shut, blind with hope.

Sometimes she thought that all might have been well if they could just have got enough sleep.

It was inevitable that she would end up with an unfair amount of childcare because she was, quite simply, there. In the flat or in the studio, there she was; and the more she worked, the more she was there. If Carey was working or looking for work, he was out, and he could not take Sally with him. Who had ever seen a viola player with carrycot, interrupting rehearsals for a feed or a nappy change? Even in the sixties equality was not that far advanced. Suppose the whole orchestra had followed suit? He came home drunk or exhausted, full of the excitement or frustration of his exterior day; Helen was still at home where he had left her and very, very angry. Why should he choose to come home to this angry person? He did so less and less. It cost money to hire a child minder and money was what they did not have, whereas Helen's time was free. In theory Sally could sleep while Helen painted, or Helen could paint while Sally slept. Helen even changed back to oil from acrylic to accommodate Sally's schedule with a more flexible medium. But in practice Sally was unpredictable, wanting feeding and changing and cuddling at odd hours, and even when she didn't, just being with her all the time meant that Helen could never give her whole attention to work. She was always trying to do two things at once.

She wanted monogamy, much to her own surprise, as well as equality, but it became clear that neither was going to be possible. They tried to negotiate. He would stop confessing casual flings and she would stop asking about them, but if she asked him he would tell her the truth. This worked for a while in a muddy sort of way, avoiding rows but generating an atmosphere of constant tension, making them both very silent but unsure how to interpret the silence. Was he guilty or innocent? Was she suspicious or trusting? They did not negotiate for serious affairs, because neither wanted to admit that serious affairs were possible. So when a woman rang up claiming to have Carey's child, Helen's shock was total. She listened almost in silence as the woman explained in quite a calm, friendly way that she needed an affiliation order for child support and would go through with a blood test to prove paternity if she had to, but she would much rather keep it all informal if she could for the sake of the child, only now Carey was refusing to return her phone calls. She was divorced with a child of the marriage at school and a part-time job, but she couldn't possibly cope with the new baby without Carey's help. Helen identified with her situation so completely that she found herself almost wanting to suggest reciprocal babysitting. She even admired the woman's reasonable tone, so unlike the shrill hysteria she had often heard coming from herself. In other circumstances she thought they might have been friends. The woman's name was Lola. An unlikely name, but Helen believed her, and she believed the story too. It had the unmistakable ring of truth. She recognised the sound of complete exhaustion in the woman's voice.

It seemed to make the whole thing worse that she actually liked Lola. Another thing that made it worse was fearing she herself might be pregnant. It was a time when doctors were still advising women on the pill to come off it for a rest, and Helen had obediently done this and gone back to a cap for six months. Now her period was nine days late. She was hard put not to mention this to Lola on the phone. They seemed to have so much in common.

Lola rang about ten in the morning. Helen sat at the kitchen table for a long time after the call, letting the facts sink in, like water into dry earth. Some of them bounced off and she had to make space for them with a sharp stick, a common problem with repotting. For a child to be alive and in need of an affiliation order, Carey had to have met Lola at least nine months ago. She had not thought to ask Lola how long the affair had lasted; her shock had been so complete that she had in fact spoken very little. But she knew Lola must be telling the truth because such an accusation could be disproved and there was no point in telling such a tale without evidence to back it up. Yes, it could be revenge, a disappointed mistress, a rejected lover; but it seemed to her that she felt the weight of years had just fallen on her, that Lola and her child summed up the whole unequal struggle of the marriage. A blood test could not prove Carey was the father, but it could prove he wasn't; she had read all about this in *The Guardian* Woman's Page many times before summoning up the energy to take Sally to the studio. Why should Lola be prepared to risk that if she wasn't sure? And even if she was wrong, or malicious, she had not plucked Carey's phone number out of thin air or at random from the directory. They had met, they had spoken, they had certainly made love and they probably now had a little boy who needed Carey as a father.

Sally played around her feet as she thought. Sally now three and more amenable, ready for nursery school if they could find her a place. Sally glad perhaps not to be going to the studio today, imagining that a mother at the kitchen table was an off-duty mother. Helen allowed herself to think of how hard these three years had been for Sally, absorbing all the frustration and anger of her parents: no wonder she had not been an easy child to raise. And how hard it would be for the little boy, whose years were still to come.

Helen knew all the fight had gone out of her. She was defeated; she had given up. A terrible clarity invaded her brain. If it wasn't Lola it would be someone else, and an endless chain of children. All that trying again had failed. All those rows and reconciliations had not worked. She was dealing with something she couldn't change and couldn't accept and it seemed in a way irrelevant that she had to discuss it with Carey. She would accuse him and he would prevaricate and then he would confess and expect her to forgive him, and it was all too late. She was dealing with a corpse. Two corpses, in fact, because she also had to have an abortion.

She wasn't sure how long she sat there but eventually she realised that big tears were falling on the kitchen table and Sally was trying to comfort her.

She must have played the Ravel several times because it was still playing when Richard came back. He actually paused in the doorway and gave her a look of such love that she came out of her reverie with quite a shock. He also looked very tired. He said, 'What a relief to be home.'

Helen said, 'Was it awful?' She felt she had to drag herself back from a great distance.

'I think she's worse than ever. She's relentless. I don't know where she gets the energy to keep going, it's very self-destructive. And she's so bitter and envious – d'you know, she actually tried to make out there was some sinister reason for Sally not coming home for Christmas.'

Helen froze with terror. God, wasn't she even safe in her own home? 'Like what?'

'Oh, God knows what she meant – that she was off with some boyfriend, I suppose. She's just got a wild imagination. She can't bear it that we don't have any problems so she wants to invent some. Drink?'

'Yes, please,' Helen said.

He poured two drinks and pointed at the music centre. 'This is very soothing. Just what I need. You've no idea how nice it is to be back. It's so peaceful here. It's such a haven.'

He went behind the sofa and leaned over her to put the glass in her hand. He kissed the top of her head. 'Well, it's you really. I love you so much.'

She was quite overcome. It was rare for either of them to say it just like that, so suddenly and directly. She said, 'Oh Richard. I thought I was hell to live with at the moment. I'm not really here half the time.'

'You're always like that before a show. Doesn't matter.' He came round the sofa and sat beside her. 'Listen. I'm going to stop seeing her. I couldn't tell her today but next time I will. No more visits. I mean it. A clean break for the New Year.'

She was astonished but she could see from his face that he meant it. She didn't know what to say, so she just kissed him.

They went to bed and made love. He said, 'Even if you aren't really here, you still feel pretty good.'

'Oh, I think you can always get through to me . . . one way or another.'

She came. She always came with Richard and she remembered that she had not always come with Carey. Sometimes the love had been too great and had got in the way.

*

Felix, easing the cork from a bottle of champagne, said, 'Well, how was the dreaded Christmas?' before he remembered that Inge might not be a Goon Show fan.

'Lonely,' she said, sounding heavily German and reproachful. 'And yours?'

'Boring,' said Felix, 'but never mind. It's all over now.' And then as he felt the cork begin its inevitable movement: 'Hey, it's coming. How very erotic champagne is. The point of no return.'

He hoped the reference to sex might cheer her up, but she merely held out her glass and did not smile or speak.

'Happy New Year,' he said, thinking how inappropriate it sounded.

'How can it be?'

'With a little effort,' said Felix, admiring his own determined cheerfulness, which he considered largely responsible for the pleasant life he led. 'I certainly intend to be as happy as possible. I shall have a holiday in the sun and finish my book and make love whenever I can.'

'So nothing has changed,' she said bitterly.

Felix was puzzled by the bitterness: was it because he could only include her in one of the three activities he had mentioned? Or because he could not spend the whole of New Year's Eve with her? He did not care to analyse the shortcomings of any relationship, having found that pretending all was well often made it so, or nearly so, which was good enough for him. In any case it was pointless discussing things you could not alter.

Inge turned her back on him and put the Liebestod from *Tristan and Isolde* on the music centre, much too loud. Gloomy erotic music filled the room.

'D'you have to play that now?' he said irritably.

'Don't you like it?'

'I love it, but it's not exactly festive, is it? Doesn't quite get you in the party mood.'

'I should have thought it was just the thing for you,' she said in a voice loaded with meaning. 'Love and death.'

He stared at her and decided to be flippant: it was all getting much too heavy, time was short and his boredom

248

threshold was low. 'Have you been smoking one of your strange cigarettes?'

'Not yet. Why? D'you want one?'

'Certainly not. But I've noticed before they seem to bring on these Gnomic utterances.'

She laughed, but he thought she seemed close to tears. 'Oh Felix, you don't understand anything, do you?'

But he was too old and wise to be lured into a debate on the meaning of life on New Year's Eve. He glanced at his watch.

'I understand that I have to be out of here by seven thirty at the latest and so do you. Now, d'you want to waste time being miserable or shall we go to bed?'

Helen was checking the progress of a casserole which she hoped would be ready in time for Richard's return from playing squash with Felix. The excesses of Christmas had finally made them have one of their rare evenings actually taking exercise instead of talking about how beneficial it would be. When she heard the front door open she called out, 'You're early. Well done.'

But it was Sally who came into the kitchen. Sally with luggage. Sally slowly returning as if from the dead, from the depths of the underworld, the past. 'I thought I was a bit late,' she said as if unsure of her welcome, and Helen realised she was talking about Christmas. Then they were both crying. They hugged each other and Helen felt the healing power of touch.

'You were right,' Sally said. 'I couldn't have coped.'

'Hush. That's all over now.' Sally's generosity overwhelmed her.

'Oh, it's nice to be home. They were all lovely but it got a bit heavy. She had it on Boxing Day. There wasn't a peaceful minute. It was kids and animals all over the place and the viola going . . .'

Helen realised painfully, again and as if for the first time, that nothing else mattered as much as Sally. Not Richard, not painting, not her own life. Sally was the ultimate reality and

249

she found the knowledge both joyous and oppressive. She said, 'I've missed you so much.'

'She seems very wobbly,' Felix said irritably. 'I really don't think now's the time to pull the rug out from under her.' He was smarting from his unexpected defeat and thinking that he must really play squash more often or else give it up.

'I've put it off too long,' Richard said.

'Yes, well, that's something else. Maybe you should have done it years ago. But if you do it now you're going to land me in the shit for a start.' He was still resentful that Richard had announced his decision at Christmas in front of Elizabeth: he felt Inge was a shared problem that Richard should first have discussed privately with him. 'She's leaning pretty heavily already. If you disappear, I'm not sure I can pick up the pieces.'

'You must be really worried,' Richard said with a smile. 'Your metaphors are all over the place.'

Felix wondered if he was being sarcastic. 'She's a big responsibility,' he said.

'God, d'you think I don't know that?'

'Honestly, Richard, I got into this in a very light-hearted way – well, I always do, you know me – but I'm not sure how much more I can take. There's a lot of pressure. She's so depressed you can feel it weighing on you. And she gets very aggressive. I mean, what if I want to get out? We can't both dump her at the same time. She might crack up. And I can't play Big Daddy indefinitely.'

Richard gazed into his empty glass and did not reply. To Felix it felt like a long moment. Then Richard got up. 'Same again?' he asked.

After the seminar Sally and Jamal strolled back together in the direction of the cafeteria. They had got into the habit of doing this and she felt comfortable with him. 'Why do they call you Jak?' she asked idly.

'I suppose it's easier than Jamal.'

'What's difficult about Jamal?'

They smiled at each other, a smile of complicity.

'Well, I suppose they like to make me sound more English.'

'Yes, maybe that's it. You certainly don't sound very Indian.'

'Wait till you hear my impression of Peter Sellers.'

She laughed. He often made her laugh.

'Why don't you come out with me, Sally?' he asked, as if that had been what they were talking about.

'I'm sorry, Jamal, but I don't want to go out with anyone just now.'

'Usually girls like me. I'm not bad-looking and I'm very polite. Also I make wonderful curry.'

'Yes, I know all that. But I don't want a boyfriend at the moment.'

'We could just be friends. Celibacy is very fashionable. And I haven't even read the *Kama Sutra*. Come out with me, Sally. I really like you.'

An idea was creeping into her head. A lifeline. Salvation. 'D'you mean that?'

'Did something bad happen to you? You haven't been out with anyone since you got here. And last term when we had a discussion you didn't join in.'

'What d'you mean? We've had lots of discussions.'

'I mean the one about abortion.'

She wasn't sure what she felt most, scared or relieved. 'Jamal, if you really like me, there is something you could do for me.'

Helen loathed private views. She felt as if she had taken her clothes off in public in a small room full of greedy sweaty people who were now busy drinking and chatting to each other with their backs to her except when they turned to laugh or stare. It was a crucifixion. Only they didn't know that, so they couldn't even pay her the courtesy of acknowledging her suffering. When they chose to approach her, she had to respond as if she were merely present and important, simply the creator, not the person pinned to the wall. Some of them wanted to touch her, shake her by the hand, and talk to her. Others simply stared.

Occasionally, they looked at the paintings.

'It reads as landscape.'

'Yes, it's full of landscape reference.'

'Frightfully derivative, isn't she?'

'Yes, frightfully.'

'D'you think so? I think she's quite original.'

'I'd call her the foremost urban painter of her generation.'

Richard hovered, trying to give her moral support without intruding, moving out to talk to people and moving back to check she was all right, rather like an anxious dog or a true friend. She appreciated his concern deeply and at the same time felt threatened by it, as if by his behaviour he were telling her she could not manage on her own. It was not his fault: nobody could have got it right. She wanted him to be there and he wanted to be there, and at the same time she wanted to be alone and she wanted to be at home, and the paintings looked different and too naked and the hanging was not the same as the one she had agreed upon, although it was identical, and she was simultaneously proud of herself and afraid.

She saw Felix and Elizabeth arrive and Richard go across to greet them. She was furious that Felix could simply have books published and lunch with the chosen few and go home to wallow in Elizabeth's adoration. He did not have to watch people in the act of reading his books or criticising them or ignoring them. And composers could go to a first performance if they chose and sit there unknown and merely bow to the audience when it was all over.

Suddenly to her horror she saw Jerome Ellis standing in front of a tiny painting she was very proud of and had nearly not put in the show. It was called *Self* and she had thought to keep it. Vanity had made her expose it to public gaze, vanity and Magdalen's admiration. She had meant to make it clear that it was the property of the artist, but she had somehow let herself forget to say this, perhaps because she was afraid to draw attention to it, or perhaps because she was so arrogant and truthful that she believed no one else would recognise its true worth, and so she could have praise without fear of loss. Or perhaps she had simply wanted to take a risk.

'That's the one,' Jerome Ellis said. He was wearing a checked tweed suit that made her feel she was going mad. His greyish-red beard seemed to glow and bristle. It was an insult to Van Gogh, on whom he had no doubt modelled it, with astonishing affrontery. She felt such rage that she wanted to kill him.

'It's too small,' said his companion, who was short and dark, thin and good-looking, and dressed in expensive clothes in extremely good taste.

'No, it's perfect for the john.'

She was in agony. She realised she had positioned herself near the painting to protect it but it was already too late: if she leapt to its defence she would be admitting its value. She could not say it was not for sale. If she did he would know he had reached her, whether he could buy the painting or not. At the same time she was surprised and impressed that he had such good taste; she realised that she had underestimated him.

'Sorry we're late,' Elizabeth said, kissing her on both cheeks. 'Parking's a nightmare round here.'

She always drove to these events, of course, so Felix could get as drunk as he wished. Helen wanted Elizabeth to be there because she truly loved paintings, Helen's in particular, and she very much wanted Felix not to be there. She had always felt this and never more than now, but had not yet worked out a way of communicating it both clearly and tactfully to Elizabeth, perhaps because it wasn't possible.

'How's it going?' Elizabeth asked Richard.

'OK, I think. The usual prats talking rubbish and getting quietly pissed. Most of the big guns came to the press show.'

'I'll see about some drinks.' Felix moved away.

'Isn't she wonderful?' Elizabeth said to Richard, looking at Helen fondly.

'I think so.'

Helen was wearing a beige dress that nearly blended in with some of the paintings. If she couldn't be absent, then she could be almost invisible. She needed protective colouring. And that frightened her even more, the knowledge that she was actually in danger.

I ought to be used to it by now, she thought. There was no one else she would rather be. She tried not to focus on *Self*, thinking of Brer Rabbit and the Briar Patch. It was not enough to look elsewhere, she must think of something else too, empty her mind, meditate. But it was difficult. She was tired and scared and on trial. The room was hot and noisy and the only person she really wanted to see was not in it.

'Hey, aren't you Richard Morgan?' Jerome Ellis said, moving across as if he had a right to join them.

'Yes.'

'Jerome Ellis.' He held out his hand for Richard to shake, smiling with genuine warmth. 'We met once around the time I commissioned your lovely wife to paint the *Seven Deadly Sins* for me.'

'Oh yes, I remember.'

'Great stuff. Great. I think she really enjoyed having a break from her usual line of work.' His companion stood quietly beside him. 'Have you met Mario Caselli?'

'No. Hullo. This is Elizabeth Cramer.'

Mario kissed her hand. 'We have the *Seven Deadly Sins* all round the room. In an oast house it looks very good with the circular wall.'

'It's kind of inspirational at dinner parties. Like there's never a dull moment.'

Felix returned with two glasses of wine and Richard made more introductions. Helen saw Jerome's beard twitch with interest at Felix's name.

'Say, aren't you the guy who writes those thrillers about that detective – what's his name? You know, I'm your biggest fan. I've always got a book of yours on the go. I keep it right by the bed, don't I, Mario? And when I can't sleep, out it comes.'

'Sometimes I am quite jealous,' Mario said.

Helen had not thought to be grateful to Jerome ever in her

life, except financially, but now, at the sight of Felix's discomfiture, she suddenly was. And the knowledge that Jerome was causing discomfort by accident not design, that he could offend Felix while actually trying to compliment him, made her pleasure particularly pure. She could see the totally open look of honesty and admiration on Jerome's large clumsy stupid face alongside the impotent rage behind Felix's set polite smile. Jerome liked both Felix Cramer and Tony Blythe and could not remember either of their names.

More? There was more. Jerome turned to Mario, rather as if he were a secretary with access to the files. 'What's the one I'm on right now? It's got a green jacket.'

Mario shrugged like a secretary who was off duty, out at a party with the boss perhaps, but definitely not available for work after hours. Helen realised she almost loved Jerome. He had not only offended Felix for her by mistake, he had also demonstrated that he cared more about colour, size and shape than words. Then she saw Sally arriving. The words 'My cup runneth over' flooded into her mind and made sense for the first time. If Jerome bought the painting, she would not mind. He deserved it. And after all, she had only called it *Self*, not *Real Self*. That, she now realised, changed all the time and so could not be captured in paint or in life, nor in a book, come to that, and so would always belong to her, its true owner and only begetter, or to no one at all.

She excused herself as Jerome was appealing to Felix to remind him of the title of the green book, and went across to welcome Sally. It was such a big brave thing for Sally to have done, to come to the show where she knew she was bound to see Felix, having gone to such extreme painful punishing lengths to avoid him at Christmas. Helen realised then that Sally must love her very much, though not, she hoped, as much as she loved Sally. After all, it was supposed to be about bringing them up and letting them go. It was both her privilege and her misfortune to love Sally too much and be willing to let her go. That was real love. Unfortunately it did not leave quite enough room for other things, such as sex, work, marriage or friends or making money, although she had tried to fit in as much as she could. Never mind, she

255

thought wearily through the mist of joy, that's the best I can do this time around. It's a tall order. A lot to fit into one lifetime. She remembered the teachers at school telling her she was trying to take too many O-levels but she couldn't bear to give up anything. Her favourite teacher had urged her on, but the headmistress had said she ran the risk of not doing anything properly. At the time she had been angry and scared, not knowing whom to trust, secretly believing both were right because they spoke for opposite sides of herself. Maybe I'll do better next time, she thought now, being older and wiser and more at peace with herself.

Sally was with an Indian boy who had his arm round her. Helen could see how supportive he was as clearly as if Sally had hoisted a flag. She hugged Sally and shook hands with the boy.

'Mum, this is Jamal Mitra,' Sally said. 'He's in one of my seminar groups.'

The boy had an honest, intelligent face that also managed to be quite private. Helen could see him casting about for something to say that was polite, truthful, appropriate and unpretentious, without revealing too much of himself or demanding too much of her. He was obviously a person of integrity.

'I like your work,' he said. 'It's so cool.'

She smiled and said to Sally, 'I'm so happy you came. You've made my day.'

Sally said, 'How could I miss your big night?'

Inge stood outside the gallery gazing in. The posters announcing 'HELEN IRVING RECENT PAINTINGS' seemed like a deliberate insult, although at least she had not dared to change her name to Morgan. Inge felt wounded by Helen's success: everywhere she looked she saw only happy couples. God, was it not enough that the cow had stolen her husband, that she already had the daughter Inge had always wanted? Did she have to be a successful painter as well? Did Felix and Elizabeth have to be on her side too? They were laughing and talking with a red-bearded man and a dark beautiful boy, for

256

all the world as if they were a happy couple. The whole gallery seemed full of pairs and she was excluded; she was almost pressing her nose to the glass, like that wretched child she remembered from her youth when she curled up all alone and read fairy tales to herself, knowing her father was dead, killed on the Russian front, and her mother had to be nice to people so that the two of them could stay together and be safe, because there was no one else to take care of them both.

It was cold here too and she was playing with the idea of going in to get warm and give everyone a nasty surprise, like the wicked fairy at the christening. She knew no one ever checked if you had your invitation to a private view and she couldn't think of anything more fun than making the cow fall asleep for a hundred years, preferably longer, but she was afraid she herself would just end up looking silly and feeling small and Richard would be very angry with her, or, worst of all, he might not even notice. God, it would be humiliating to walk in and not be seen, although why should she mind so much, when he had scarcely seen her for years even when he was looking at her? Still, it would be oceans worse if it happened publicly in front of the cow. That was obvious.

All the same, she felt wretched, shivering with cold and the knowledge that shortly she would either have to go in or go home. She even imagined she could hear someone telling her to move along because she was obstructing the highway, or loitering with intent. Inside the gallery, behind the glass, they were all having fun, talking and laughing and drinking, while she was freezing and dying for a glass of wine. Then she saw Richard moving across the room and going to join the cow, who was making a big fuss of her daughter. This was too painful to watch and so she turned away before anyone could notice her.

'Say, who's the little match girl?' Jerome asked Magdalen.

'I've no idea. Maybe she's a bag lady.'

'She looks kinda interesting. Does Helen do portraits?'

*

Felix had seen Inge. For several very long minutes he had been frozen with horror, but more than that, baffled that she should persecute him like this. What had he ever done but give her harmless pleasure? It was hardly his fault she was obsessed with Richard. It would be quite obscene if she barged her way in and embarrassed them all. Helen would think he had done it on purpose to get his revenge over Sally, and Elizabeth might even suspect there was something going on, while Richard . . . well, that didn't bear thinking about. The whole thing was too ridiculous: Inge had never behaved so stupidly before, or at least he had never noticed her hanging around any of Helen's previous God-awful exhibitions that Elizabeth had always forced him to attend. Elizabeth, with her back to the window, was still being charming to the Italian, and Felix's face muscles ached from smiling at the bloody stupid American who couldn't even remember the name of one of his best detective stories, and Felix was damned if he was going to remind him. It was really too much to see Inge of all people suddenly breathing on the glass in such a menacing way. He was too old for shocks like that. It was unfair. More to the point, it was absurd.

'Come on,' he said to Elizabeth, 'let's have a look at the paintings.'

'You amaze me.' She turned to the Italian, smiling graciously like a society hostess. 'I'm afraid my husband's a bit of a philistine about modern art.'

He was incensed by the injustice of it. He liked plenty of decent painters. He liked Francis Bacon and Lucien Freud and David Hockney. He even liked John Hoyland and John Piper. He was liberated: he had tried his best. He had been dragged round art exhibitions for years. It wasn't his fault that he was better at words and music, and it was bloody ridiculous to be attacked like this in public by his own wife just when he most needed support. He felt betrayed. He had seen the malicious glee on Helen's straight face.

'That's what we came for, isn't it?' he said, aware of sounding like a sulky child and hating it.

Elizabeth excused herself and they moved away, threading their way between the people, who were mostly standing with their backs to the paintings. Felix's main concern was to get Elizabeth away from the window as fast as possible. 'Well, I think they're lovely,' she said predictably.

'You could have stayed at home and thought that.'

'They're full of light and space and they're all about living in the city but still keeping a quiet place in your head where you can examine your emotions at your leisure.'

'God, you're a cross between Pseuds' Corner and the critics.'

She waved her catalogue at him as if she had discovered a great secret. 'No, that's what it says here, but I think it's true anyway.'

They went on walking and looking, Felix still trying to draw her attention away from Inge and Sally.

Elizabeth suddenly announced, 'I think we should buy one.'

'What?'

'I'm serious. I really like them and you know how hard up she is. How about that one?' She peered at the title, *Breathing Space*. 'Yes, I like it, and we should support our friends.'

Felix was shocked beyond measure. All the paintings looked alike to him. It seemed a very easy way of making money, painting overlapping beige rectangles for ever and ever and somehow getting people to take you seriously. It didn't compare with the slog of inventing characters and plot and making it all come alive on the page. Now that really was a conjuring trick and God help him if he forgot how to do it. He wasn't even sure he'd ever known.

'Have you looked at the prices?' he said. 'Maybe you could just buy the title.'

Elizabeth pointed to a red dot on the next painting. 'Look, that one's sold already.'

'That's only that idiot Yank trying to fill up his bathroom. No wonder Yank rhymes with wank.'

'Maybe he's not such an idiot, maybe he's a shrewd investor. You don't get rich by being an idiot and rich people like to hang on to their money. You'll look jolly silly if you stop me buying now and Helen gets to be world famous.'

'Well, if you must do it, for God's sake don't pay gallery

prices. At least you can go round to the studio and get it cheap. Well, comparatively cheap.'

'Yes, I know that's sensible but it's not very stylish.'

He was torn between anger and amazement. It was not like her to be so stubborn. In all their years together they had not had such an argument in public. He was silent, thinking.

'Yessir,' said Jerome Ellis, producing a cheque book not a credit card, and beginning to write his name and the date, 'I really believe in this little lady and I always put my money where my mouth is.'

'You're a very good customer,' said Magdalen, watching him write.

Still writing and now on the name of the gallery, he jerked his thumb over his shoulder. 'There's a poor lost soul over there just crying out to be painted.'

Magdalen turned her head to the window but there was no one there.

Helen was crying with joy. The tears she hadn't shed for Sally tonight were in her eyes now for Sam. How white his hair was but still thick. The aquiline profile was unchanged too: how well she remembered staring at it as she waited for him to pass judgment on her work. Praise or blame, she always remembered what he said. But even at a distance she could see his gnarled hands and the joy turned to sorrow even as she wept. People drifted away, as if he had cleared a path by his arrival, and as they hugged each other she sensed that only Richard, Sally and Jamal were still around her, watching indulgently.

She said, 'Oh Sam, how lovely to see you. I never thought you'd make it.'

He smiled as if she'd been silly to doubt him. 'Helen, my dear, I wouldn't miss one of your shows. Not till I'm in a box. Mind you, that won't be long now the way I'm going.'

She turned to the others. 'You know Sam Frankel. Sam was my first teacher and he's still a better painter than I'll ever be. Sam, you remember Sally and Richard. And this is Jamal.'

'I'm so proud of you.' Sam embraced her in a bear-hug, fanning out to include Richard and Sally with his other arm and vaguely indicating Jamal with an ambiguous wave of his left hand. The sight of his distorted fingers stabbed Helen to the heart. At that moment she would have sacrificed the whole exhibition to give Sam back the proper use of his hands in return for all he had given her. She had never believed in sacrifice before but now she suddenly saw the point of it. Sam was a truly good person as well as being immensely talented, not commercial as it happened, but never envious of her small but evident success. She treasured that quality in him.

'She was always very stubborn,' he said, looking at her with pride. 'Always went her own way.'

'She hasn't changed,' said Richard, looking equally proud and fond.

They all laughed.

'She has,' Sam said. 'She's got even better.'

For a moment they all stood there together and Helen felt that her family was at last complete, that she had passed a dangerous corner, but now all was well in the best of all possible worlds and she could relax. She was safe at last and she felt they all knew it, they must; the feeling was so strong in her that she could not believe that any of them felt otherwise.

Sally was the first to break ranks. She kissed Helen lightly on the left cheek. 'Mum, we must be going, we've got to get back tonight. The paintings are great.'

'Have a safe journey,' Helen said, sad as ever to see her go but more reconciled now that she felt all was well. 'You've made my evening.'

'You keep working now,' Sam said to Helen as Sally left with Jamal, his arm lightly round her. 'Do as much as you can. Don't postpone anything. I often wish I'd taken my own advice.'

*

Elizabeth was in a huddle with Magdalen, writing a cheque. Felix could feel the defiance burning through her back. Perhaps she knew more than he realised. It was an uncomfortable thought and made him feel very tired. Suddenly he saw Sally coming towards him with the Indian boy on her way to the door. There was no escape. His throat was dry with pain.

'Hullo, Felix,' she said in a light social voice. There was no expression in her eyes. He had not known that she could act so well.

'Hullo, Sally.'

Memories of her skin and that vanilla scent. The Indian boy put his arm round her shoulders and they left together.

They had dinner in their favourite restaurant. Helen was past hunger by then but the sense of being cherished with food and wine and candlelight made her feel peaceful and elated. She smiled at Richard, full of goodwill, floating on a great wave of security.

'Happy?' he said, smiling back.

'Very. I never thought Sam would come all the way from Cornwall. I'm going to give him a painting. He can't afford to buy and I'd like him to have one.'

'He means a lot to you, doesn't he?'

'He's like a father figure, I suppose. He always bullied me to go on when I got discouraged. Did you see his poor hands? God, what a terrible fate. Like Beethoven going deaf.'

'And Elizabeth bought,' Richard said. He sounded very pleased.

'She's crazy. Felix will give her hell. He'll probably use it as a dartboard. What did you think of Jerome Ellis's boyfriend?'

'I think they deserve each other. Like Beauty and the Beast.' He paused. 'That boy Sally brought seemed very nice.'

'I liked him. She looked happy, didn't she?' It was something to be vindicated, tonight of all nights, even though he didn't know, thank God.

'Yes. And the paintings are wonderful.' He kissed her hand. 'You're wonderful.'

When they got home after the show Elizabeth felt tired without being ready for sleep. They had had a bad dinner afterwards and the food lay leadenly in her stomach along with Felix's complaints to the waiter. In theory she approved of complaining when things weren't up to standard, but in practice she usually found it made her feel worse, souring the whole experience. She would have preferred to make the best of it, in the British way, but Felix was continental in these matters and liked to stand up for his rights. He was foreign in his driving, too, given to sudden braking and bursts of acceleration, fond of terrorising other road users with his horn, a little light verbal abuse and the occasional obscene gesture. If she was feeling strong and well, all that could be mildly amusing; when she was at all below par it left her with shattered nerves.

She poured herself a brandy, knowing she would regret it later but needing it more than she feared the regrets, and sank down on the sofa, glad of a chance to put her feet up. Felix seemed restless, wandering about the room, fiddling with small objects, looking out of the window. He had hated seeing Helen get so much attention; Elizabeth wondered if Helen felt equally piqued when Felix had a new book published.

'I'm going to have a bath,' he announced.

Elizabeth reflected upon the routine intimacies of marriage: knowing how often another person washed or crapped, smelling their shit in the lavatory or pulling their slimy hair out of the plughole. It was strange that this was where love led you, along with the mortgage and the dinner parties and the conversation at breakfast; stranger yet that you could still feel romantic about the over-familiar body.

'You had one this morning,' she observed.

'So I'm going to have another one. Any objection?'

'There's no need to be so tetchy just because I bought a painting. It was my money.'

'So you keep reminding me.'

'Well, be grateful it wasn't yours.'

Felix went out of the room and upstairs. She was aware of wanting to make love, to put the day to rights, and knowing he was not in the mood. Was that why she had snapped at him? She knew he was only trying to wash away the evening. She could so easily have said, All right, darling, shall I bring you up a drink? and he might have been charmed out of his sulk like a child.

The phone rang and she picked it up but did not speak; she usually let Felix answer it after eleven. A few obscene calls in the past had made her wary. A woman's voice said, 'Felix?'

'He's in the bath. Can I give him a message?'

'No, it's all right.' The voice sounded slurred and sad and unmistakably foreign: it was also familiar.

'Who is this?'

But the person hung up.

Elizabeth felt a great wave of anger breaking over her. She got up off the sofa, refilled her glass and marched upstairs. Felix lay peacefully in the bath, looking dreamy and vulnerable and somehow unfocused, as if he had taken off his brain along with his clothes.

'Phone call for you,' Elizabeth said.

'Who?'

'I'm not sure.' But at that moment she suddenly was. 'She rang off. Somebody with a foreign accent. She sounded a bit drunk.'

'How weird.'

Elizabeth closed the lid of the loo and sat on it. She could see Felix being alarmed and trying to bluff it out; she felt she had him at her mercy but that was not a comfortable place for her to be.

'Yes, it was.'

'Must be a wrong number,' he said without much conviction.

'She knew your name. So it must be someone we know. Or used to know. The weirdest thing is, it sounded like Inge.'

He echoed her feebly. 'Inge?'

'That's what I said.'

'It can't have been. After all these years? Why would she ring us now?'

She was aware of wanting him to confess, or else come up with a convincing lie. Anything rather than this messy no-man's-land in between.

'She wanted to speak to you.'

'Then she'd have hung on. Otherwise what would be the point?'

'Maybe she panicked.'

'What the hell's that supposed to mean?'

She did not like seeing him frightened; she did not like having the upper hand.

'Felix, we both know you're not perfect, but I've never had strange women phoning me at midnight before and I don't like it. I did think you had at least enough elementary common sense to remember what they say about shitting on your own doorstep. If I ever find out you've been messing around with Inge, or Helen come to that, only she wouldn't have you, you're going to wish you'd never been born. Have I made myself clear?'

Even as she spoke she wondered if she meant it.

It was Felix ringing her bell. Her head was pounding so much she could hardly stand up, hardly tie the belt of her bathrobe, and there he was on her doorstep, rested and well-dressed and very very angry.

'Oh, Felix,' she said, conscious of looking her worst but feeling too ill to care. 'You woke me up.'

He pushed past her into the house.

'And what the fuck d'you think you were playing at last night?' he asked with a sort of triumph, as if he had caught her out.

'Oh, God.'

'Is that all you can say?'

Horribly, bits of the evening began seeping through to her brain.

'I rang up, didn't I?'

'And landed me right in it.'

She fought hard against the fear that she might be sick, right there at his feet, perhaps over his shoes.

'I was hoping it was a dream,' she said. 'Come in the kitchen, Felix, I must have some coffee. I have a terrible headache.'

In the kitchen he stood over her while she took aspirin and Alka-Seltzer and made coffee. He was so angry that, ill as she was, she almost wanted to laugh. She was reminded of illustrations in children's books when the boys were young, of dragons breathing fire and smoke.

'Christ, Inge, don't you have any sense at all? First you hang around Helen's show like little orphan Annie, then you ring up my wife at midnight and ask for me.'

It was usually serious when men said my wife instead of using the name. She had noticed that before.

'I wanted Richard,' she said, 'but he was out. I was lonely.'

'Don't you mean drunk?' he said severely, as if he had never been drunk himself.

'Drunk and lonely. You were all having such a good time.' She thought of her last-night self with pity, standing outside the window, gazing in at them enjoying themselves.

'Helen may have been having a good time with everyone slobbering over her, but I had a perfectly dreadful evening if you really want to know and you put the lid on it. Elizabeth knows your voice, for God's sake. You can't just hang up like any old wrong number. If you ring up at all, which is bloody stupid, then you have to speak. "Hullo, Elizabeth, this is Inge. I thought I'd give you a call after eight years, see how you are." Something casual like that. Just the thing at midnight. The way you did it, you might as well send her a telegram: Dear Elizabeth, I am screwing your husband. Just thought you'd like to know. Lots of love, Inge. God Almighty.'

Halfway through, she tuned out and stopped listening. He didn't remind her of a dragon any more. He was just an angry man who enjoyed the sound of his own voice.

'I lost my nerve,' she said when there was silence. 'D'you want some coffee?'

'No. Look, Inge, I'm sorry you're depressed but I can't go

on with this. We're going away on holiday next week and when I get back I don't think we should see each other any more.'

The blow took her by surprise. It was painful. She could feel it in her stomach, churning around with the hot coffee and last night's whisky and wine that she longed to throw up. Perhaps the surprise and the pain showed on her face, because his tone suddenly softened.

'I'm sorry,' he said.

'I told you I always spoil everything.'

Then she saw to her amazement that in spite of her messy woebegone state, or perhaps because of it, he still desired her. There was pure lust in his face; she was never wrong about that. He glanced at his watch.

'How about one more for luck, for auld lang syne? Might be good for your hangover.'

She said with scorn, 'Is that what they call a mercy fuck?' And yet she was seriously tempted. It would be powerful magic and could heal greater wounds than hers.

Sally didn't see much of Jamal for the next few days. Then he got insistent about making her a curry. In the end she went along just to make him stop and also because she was hungry.

'It smells wonderful,' she said. 'How long did it take you?'

'Oh, only two or three days.'

'You're sending me up.'

'Oh, all right. Three or four days.' Then he asked straight out, 'How did I do the other night?'

'You were wonderful,' she said truthfully. 'I couldn't have faced it without you.'

'He was good-looking.'

'Yes.' What else was there to say?

He busied himself with the curry for a moment. 'I think he looked sad and jealous. Is that what you wanted?'

'Yes.' But she hadn't known how painful it would be, like having layers of skin peeled off. She'd thought she was past all that. He had looked just the same. She hadn't been prepared for that either. He should have looked like a stranger after all she'd been through. Or older. Ugly, alien. Something to make it easier. And not sad. It was unbearable that he'd actually looked sad, as if she'd hurt him. She'd never thought she had the power. Had her face betrayed her? She couldn't tell.

'Did you love him very much?' Jamal asked.

'I thought I did at the time.'

SPRING 1986

When Richard got back to his office he found Inge waiting for him. He couldn't blame his secretary for letting her in, although she apologised; if he didn't know how to deal with Inge, why should anyone else? But the sight of her reminded him that months had gone by since he had promised himself to break with her, and promised Helen too, and told Felix and Elizabeth. He had made a vow in front of witnesses, like someone who knew there was no other way he could give up drinks or drugs or go on a diet, who needed to be shamed into it so there was no going back. And still he had been avoiding her so that he wouldn't have to keep his word. He was angry with her for being there, reminding him of his own weakness, and angry with himself for being weak.

'You might pretend to be pleased,' she said, almost in a flirtatious way, as if they were really on good terms. She came over to him and hugged him, and he endured the hug without responding until she let go. He couldn't quite bring himself to push her away. All human affection was valuable when so many went without it; he was reminded of his mother making him eat up his greens because of the starving millions.

'It's so long since I've seen you,' she said. 'I thought we could have a drink together. I've been shopping and I'm so tired.'

But he didn't see any bags. 'Shopping?'

'Oh, I didn't buy anything. I couldn't afford to. But I walked and I looked and now my feet hurt.' She sat down again and smiled at him. She looked somehow young and vulnerable and mischievous. He remembered how much she had enjoyed shopping, even for the smallest thing, when they were together, how it had always been a treat. Her enthusiasm for the trivial things of life had been very attractive, far exceeding his own, and seeming like a source of vitality.

'Maybe if you got a job you could afford to buy things and you wouldn't be so bored and lonely.'

'I think there's something called unemployment. Haven't you heard of it?' She gave a big grin, like a naughty child.

'But you haven't even tried. You speak three languages. You can cook and drive and type and look after children. There must be someone who'd employ you.' He heard his own voice speaking the dreary litany and it gave him a strange, mad feeling in his head that they had had this conversation so many times, always without effect, yet he still felt compelled to try again. It was like endlessly rerunning a cassette that was meant to change your life.

She shrugged. 'I can't leave the boys.'

'The boys are huge. They'll be leaving you pretty soon. And they can certainly manage to make a sandwich and put the kettle on. You'd be happier, Inge, believe me.'

Her eyes narrowed. 'You mean you'd be happier. You'd have more money to spend on the cow.'

'Come on,' he said, forced now to make a stand. 'Time to go home.'

'Will you drive me?'

'No.'

'Then I won't go.'

He tried to stay calm. If she knew how much she was annoying him, she would go on playing. 'Well, you can't stay here.'

'Are you going to throw me out? How exciting. I didn't know you were so violent. Isn't it nice you can still surprise me after all these years?' She leaned back in her chair, smiling again, daring him to do something. 'What will your colleagues think when I start to scream?'

In the car she was silent at first, stretching luxuriously, reminding him of a cat. Then she started to talk.

'Oh, Richard, this is such fun. I can have a fantasy we're still married and we're going home to supper and bed.'

There was something about her strength that frightened him. If she could cling so tenaciously to one idea for eight years, perhaps she had a valid point of view.

'If you know it's a fantasy, why d'you want to have it?'

'Oh, Richard, don't you understand anything?' Now she sounded like an indulgent mother: the little girl was gone.

272

'Sometimes I wonder why I still love you when you have so little imagination.'

He put on the radio to discourage her from talking and she looked out of the window and hummed to herself. Occasionally she stroked his arm. It fascinated him that nothing he said or did over the years had affected her belief that she had the right to touch him whenever she felt like it. He wasn't sure if it showed confidence or desperation, but it earned his grudging respect.

As they drew nearer to their destination, he became convinced that he had to tell her his decision. It was fate: he had tried to postpone it but she had come to his office. It was meant to be done today, a clean break, no matter how shocking, and then they could both begin to heal. By the time they reached the house he was shaking inside. They sat in silence for a moment; then she said, 'Aren't you going to come in for a drink?'

'No, I don't think so.' He felt like a murderer about to strike, while his victim smiled up at him.

'The boys may be there,' she said, trying to tempt him.

It had to be done and he would never be ready to do it. 'Inge, there's no easy way to say this, but I'm not going to see you any more.'

He heard her gasp and then there was a terrible shocked silence. He couldn't look at her. He said gently, 'I'm sorry, love.'

Presently she said, 'You don't mean it. It's a horrible English joke.'

He shook his head. Now all he wanted was for her to get out of the car so he could drive away with his guilt, hoping it might eventually turn into relief.

'I can't believe it,' she said. 'Is she making you do this?'

'No. She doesn't make me do things.' He felt he owed her reasons, and just saying he was too tired to go on, which felt like the truth, didn't seem enough, even seemed insulting. 'I can't take any more. It's no good for either of us. We've tried our best and it doesn't work. I feel guilty and you feel miserable.'

'Richard, please tell me you're joking, oh Richard, please.'

Now she grabbed hold of him, talking very fast. 'Why now? What have I done? I'm sorry, I'll take it back, I'll do anything. I can't live without you, Richard, I mean that. I'll die without you, I really will.'

It was predictable that she would say all these things, yet he still felt shocked to be the object of so much naked emotion. 'No, you won't,' he said, trying to be rational. 'I've spent eight years believing you, but it's simply not true. You'll be depressed for a while but you *will* get over it. I'm sorry to hurt you but I'm making it worse by seeing you. We should have had a clean break years ago. Truly, Inge. It's no good like this. I can't go on being blackmailed.'

Too many words, he thought, even as he said them, remembering Felix teasing him that he protested too much. If he could just tell her he didn't love her any more, he hated her, or better still was indifferent to her, that might finish it. Ten years ago Helen had told him he would find there was no nice way of breaking with Inge and here he was, still trying to find one. He felt sick at the pain he was inflicting from the best of motives.

'I'll kill myself,' she said flatly.

'I hope not,' he said, thinking with terror how appalling it would be if she did just that, how he would never recover, how the boys would be scarred for life. But sooner or later it was a risk he'd have to take. 'That's your choice but it would be an awful waste. Come on. I'll take you into the house.'

Her nails dug into him as he helped her up the path. She moved slowly and awkwardly, like an invalid, and he had a sudden vision of how things would be when they were old.

By the time they got into the house Inge felt quite ill with pain. She couldn't believe what was happening: there must be some way to make sense of it, to make it stop hurting. It was worse than anything she had experienced in childbirth, worse than a dentist drilling on an exposed nerve, worse than torture she had imagined in a dream. She hadn't known such pain existed. It affected her breathing and she thought she might actually die.

Richard helped her into a chair and got her a glass of whisky. She could feel him straining to leave.

'There. You'll be all right, Inge, believe me. I must go now. We can always talk on the phone. And the boys know where to reach me.'

Through the fog of pain, an explanation crept into her mind. 'It's Felix, isn't it?'

'What?'

'Why you're leaving me.'

He said, 'I left you a long time ago, love,' and she thought he sounded compassionate.

'Did he tell you we had an affair?' It would be like Felix to do such a shitty thing. First he deserted her, then he betrayed her to Richard. 'It was only to feel closer to you. I never cared for him, you must understand that. It was only an itch and it's gone.' She wondered if Felix had known that and been upset, or if he was too conceited to believe it.

'I don't mind at all,' Richard said. 'I thought he might cheer you up.'

'You knew?'

'He's a friend. He had to tell me the truth.'

Now she felt like a parcel, passed from man to man by agreement. And the irony of Felix as a truthful person made her angry. Perhaps anger would act as an anaesthetic.

'And you're not even slightly jealous? That's not why you're leaving me?'

He said, 'Inge, I'm leaving you because I can't stand the strain and I owe it to Helen to make a clean break. She's been very patient.'

'You owe it to Helen,' she repeated. All her demons were coming together. She began to see a way out. Then maybe the pain would stop and Richard would understand who really loved him.

'Yes, to Helen and Sally. To put them first for a change.' He was moving to the door, so eager to leave. 'I really am going now. You'll be better off without me. You're always better off without someone who loves someone else.'

275

He had never sounded so determined before. Perhaps he actually meant it this time. And the word love wounded her. 'Before you go, will you just open that drawer?' She didn't want to hurt him, but she wanted to make him stop hurting her.

'No, I'm not playing any more games.'

'Don't you want to know what you really owe Helen?'

'Inge, what *is* all this nonsense?' He looked very tired and she found herself wanting to comfort him, if only he would let her. She had to remind herself that he had pushed her to this point, that this crisis was not of her making. She had kept the letter because it made her feel powerful, but like an ultimate deterrent, she had never intended to use it.

'I want you to know the sort of woman you're leaving me for. Go on, open that drawer. There's a letter from Sally to Felix all about the abortion that Helen arranged.'

She saw him look stricken and disbelieving, like someone in a film, suddenly stabbed to the heart. She said, 'Oh Richard, I'm sorry. I'm so sorry.'

Helen was in the kitchen when Richard came home. His face looked drained, as if he had been dealing with a particularly difficult client. She said, 'Have you had a bad day? You look exhausted.'

'I went to see Inge.' He spoke slowly, as if speech were a great effort.

'Oh well, enough said.' She put down the knife she was using to chop the salad. 'Come and have a drink.'

He followed her into the sitting-room, moving slowly too, so that she began to wonder if he might be ill. She said, 'Darling, are you all right? Was she worse than ever?' She poured him a drink but when she held it out to him he didn't move to take it and she had to put it down on the table beside him.

'I've been saying goodbye to her.'

There was a curious note in his voice: sorrow, anger, shock. Helen wished he hadn't done it if it cost him so much;

276

it was not as if she had insisted on it. She had not in fact ever believed he would do it. Perhaps in a way he still loved Inge and he always would; perhaps she would have to accept that. Inge was family, like one of his children, and he could never be truly divorced from her.

'My God, no wonder you look shattered.' She noticed then that he had picked up the kitchen knife. 'Is that why you've got a knife your hand? Did you want to finish her off?' She hoped he might laugh, relax, have his drink.

He said very calmly, 'No, it's you I'd like to kill, but I don't have the guts.' He picked up the glass and drained it in one go, then with enormous sudden ferocity turned on one of her paintings, an early one that she was particularly fond of, and attacked it with the knife, making a jagged tear. Helen was so shocked she couldn't speak. She felt she was looking at a stranger with Richard's face, a stranger with a knife who had broken into the house and attacked her. At the same time part of her mind was wondering if she could repair the painting. It was one she had done shortly after Sally was born, and had always been special: she wondered if he remembered that.

'Yes,' he said in the same calm voice, 'that's what I'd like to do to you.'

She couldn't believe he had found out; surely Felix had not been so stupid as to tell Inge. And yet what else could it be to make him behave like this? Suddenly she was very afraid.

'She had a parting gift for me,' he said. 'I think that's the German for poison. See what you think. She went through his desk in an idle moment and this is what she found.'

He held out a photocopied letter. Helen barely glanced at it: she could see it was in Sally's handwriting. So it was as bad as she feared.

He said savagely, 'Christ, Helen, why didn't you tell me? I'm only your husband. I'm only her step-father. I've only been around for the last ten years. Don't I count for anything?'

Now that they were actually facing it, the whole thing seemed unreal. It was six months ago. She could see the terrible pain in his face and knew she had caused it, but all she could remember was Sally's pain and her own, and how she had not been able to turn to him for help when she needed it most.

She said, 'I'm sorry,' knowing it was inadequate, feeling an edge of anger underneath the sorrow.

He looked at her incredulously. 'Sorry? *Sorry?*'

'It was a very painful decision.' She found she actually resented having to explain it to him. 'I wanted to talk to you but I couldn't. I knew you wouldn't agree. It was something I had to do on my own. It was very hard, very lonely.' And you should have been on my side, she wanted to shout, no matter what I did.

'You and Sally and Felix,' he said, 'all being lonely together.'

'They didn't want you to know either.'

'How very convenient.'

'Well, you'd have been hurt and angry. As you are now. What was the point?'

'Oh, quite,' he said in a sneering tone, not like himself. 'When you and Felix had already made up your minds what to do. It would have been really awkward if I'd agreed with Sally.'

Helen was almost pleased to be angry: it made her feel less vulnerable. 'I assumed you'd be against abortion, you usually are. And you'd just had that client who killed herself when her baby was adopted. How could I tell you? Sally didn't know what she wanted. You'd have made her more mixed up than ever.'

'You mean I might have stopped you forcing her to have an abortion.'

In a way that was true, but it was only a partial truth. 'If she'd really wanted that baby she could have told you any time. But she didn't. She came to me and I had to do what I thought was best.'

'God, no wonder she didn't come home for Christmas.'

'She was depressed for a while, of course, but she's got over it. She looked happy at the show, didn't she? She's had time to think and she knows I was right.'

He said slowly, 'You're unbelievable. Did you ever think of the alternatives?'

278

'Yes, I did. They were worse.'

'And it didn't matter what I might have felt.'

It was useless: they were ranged on opposite sides, alien and hostile, cancelling out all the years together. There was no sympathy or understanding on his face. He was just as implacable as she had feared he would be, but that only proved she was justified. It felt very lonely.

'She's my daughter. I had to make the final decision.'

'Yes, that says it all.' He turned away. 'God, I don't feel I know you at all.'

She said to his retreating back, 'Aren't you even a tiny bit angry with your precious friend?'

'He's not here, is he? I'll get around to him later. Right now I'm going to pack.'

That sounded so melodramatic she almost laughed. 'Don't be silly.'

He said in the doorway, in quite a reasonable tone, as if she ought to understand, 'I can't live with you after this. If you can do something like this on your own, then we don't have a marriage at all.'

And he went out, leaving her alone in the room. She couldn't believe that this was the price she must pay for rescuing Sally. She had known he would be angry but she had never thought beyond the anger, thought as far as action. Surely in a little while he would come back and say he was sorry and she would say she was sorry too and they could hug each other and start again. It couldn't be the end. People simply didn't end marriages like that.

It began as an ordinary pleasant evening, like any other. They sat on the floor in Sally's room and played draughts and Jamal kept winning. Sally pretended to be cross but really she was enjoying the fact that he cared so much about the outcome. She felt grown up and maternal when she watched his excitement.

'Ugh, you won again,' she said, trying to sound disgusted. 'Why d'you always win?'

279

'I don't.'

'Nearly always then.'

She loved his childish smile of pleasure. 'Well, I'm quite lucky. And also highly skilled, of course.'

'I think you cheat.'

'You can't cheat at draughts.'

'Well, if you could, you would. It's the same thing. It's the spirit of cheating.'

They both laughed and settled themselves more comfortably on the cushions, their knees casually touching.

'D'you want your revenge?' He was resetting the board, eager for more winning, or perhaps more time with her, she wasn't sure which. She loved the seriousness with which he played, his total enthusiasm for whatever he was doing at the time. It made for a feeling of strength, like a current running through him that she could tap into, the fact that he could be so concentrated upon any one thing. She never felt as she had with Helen and Richard and Carey and even Felix that part of his mind was elsewhere.

'Yes, why not? I'm an optimist.' She watched his brown nimble fingers, slim and delicate like a child's hand, and wished they would touch her. 'I love this game,' she said happily, 'it's so utterly pointless.'

'Aren't all games? Isn't that the point of them?'

She giggled and he looked pleased. 'Maybe I could do a thesis on that.'

'God, you're not going to do postgrad, are you?'

'I don't know yet. I might. I rather fancy being a student for as long as possible. What shall I call my thesis?'

She considered. ' "The Utter Pointlessness of Board Games." '

'I'd like something a bit more pretentious. How about "The Intrinsic Lack of Meaning in Board Games as a Therapeutic Activity"?'

'That's perfect. Sounds a bit American though.'

'Maybe I'll do it at Berkeley.'

What fun it all was, how far removed from pain and blood and death. They played again, not talking at all, pretending it was serious, and this time, to her own surprise, she won.

Jamal yawned. 'I must go, I'm falling asleep.'

She felt panic; she didn't want him to leave. She was afraid of sleeping and dreaming again. 'That's no excuse,' she said, doing her impression of a boxer. 'It was a good clean fight and I'm glad to have won.'

He smiled. 'You distracted my attention.'

'I wish I could.' She touched his hand, stroked it, and their fingers interlocked. She looked at their two hands and thought of Othello and Desdemona. The contrasting colours looked good together. It was so long since anyone had touched her. They had all said she would be unchanged, as good as new, but how could she be sure?

'You can. You do.'

'Then why don't you stay?'

He went on holding her hand and said quite calmly, 'I'm not going to make love to you, if that's what you mean.'

She felt disappointed but not rejected. 'Why not? Don't you fancy me?'

'Yes. But I think it's too soon.'

'You don't think I'm still in love with Felix, do you?' She held her breath a bit because she wasn't sure of the answer to that one herself.

'No. But I don't think you're quite over him either. And I don't want to help you prove you are.'

She had been wrong about him: he wasn't young and naive at all. 'That was nasty,' she said.

'No, it wasn't.'

It seemed easy and natural then to kiss. His lips tasted bitter but she liked the taste.

'But I could stay and we could just sleep.'

She was so amazed to hear him say exactly what she had been thinking. 'Could we?'

'I think that's what you really want.'

'I didn't know I could have a cuddle without sex.' Now she felt she was the naive one. Would he think she was silly?

'Why not? Anyway, I'm quite shy.'

'Even with me?'

'Especially with you.'

She took a risk and told him the truth. 'Sometimes I just

281

want someone to hug me so much, I think I'll die if they don't.'

He didn't seem shocked or surprised. He looked at her as if she had said something quite reasonable and held out his arms. She shot into them very fast, like a rabbit into its burrow.

'Oh, that feels lovely. You do realise you're missing a treat though.' She wanted him to know she was sexy and adult, a woman who had suffered, not someone playing childish games.

He held her comfortably tight. 'Won't it still be there another time?'

'Yes, of course it will,' she said, feeling reassured, perhaps even a bit relieved it didn't have to be tonight after all.

The hug went on so long that eventually they were both falling asleep but it still seemed a pity to break it up. They decided he would stay the night after all but they'd keep some clothes on and just cuddle. Once that was settled they both felt very cheerful. Sally stripped down to her knickers and T-shirt and Jamal kept his underpants on. They got into bed like old friends, feeling very comfortable with each other and yet somehow adventurous, and snuggled up together. It took a while to get all their limbs arranged in the right places so they wouldn't get pins and needles later on and have to move away. She was glad he didn't have an erection. At first they kept chatting and telling each other jokes. She felt very safe with him, at ease. She supposed she was trying to exorcise her memories of spending the night with Felix. She thought she might lie awake for hours remembering, but in fact fell asleep much sooner than she had expected.

Richard drove down to Sussex that night, overtaking danger-ously on the motorway, causing other cars to swerve and hoot and flash their lights at him. He knew he was beside himself; the expression suddenly made vivid personal sense.

It was only when he reached the darkened campus that he felt like an intruder, parking his car, finding his way to Sally's building, not knowing what he would do if the front door was locked. But it wasn't and then he was actually walking down Sally's corridor. When he opened the door of her room he might have been quiet and sad if she'd been alone, and merely reproached her, for he was already feeling guilty for coming here at all. But she was in bed with the Indian boy she had brought to Helen's show, and somehow the sight of them curled up together enraged him, as if the abortion had meant so little to her that she could recover from it quickly. He heard himself shouting abuse at her and the boy got out of bed, still wearing his underpants, and put on his clothes as if he needed to be dressed before he could deal with Richard. He was very polite and Richard felt embarrassed. He shouted all the more, or rather he heard someone who must be himself doing a lot of shouting, trying to get the boy to go away so he could talk to Sally alone, but it didn't work. Sally wanted him to stay and he stayed, even though Richard kept saying it was a family matter.

He tried to make Sally understand the enormity of what she had done but she only seemed concerned to know if Helen was all right. He was reminded of her as a child, making sure he wouldn't interrupt Helen's work, and he was enraged by the knowledge that he had always been an outsider, that the mother and daughter alliance was unbreakable. He found himself calling her a tramp and a murderer and trying to get to the bed to drag her out of it, but the boy got in his way and he was tempted to hit him and surprised by the temptation. Sally stayed in bed and put her hands over her ears to shut out his words, so he shoved the boy out of the way and wrenched the quilt off her, as if being uncovered would make her hear him. Then she started sobbing and screaming at him that he was not her father, and he knew he was defeated. He went away.

He sat for a while in the car, which seemed his only refuge, not knowing what to do. He was aware of feeling very tired and rather ridiculous, so he thought he would sleep for an hour or two before driving off, especially as he didn't know where to go. Then it was abruptly morning and Sally was shaking him by the shoulder and asking him if he was all right. He started apologising to her and she kept saying it was OK. She said the Indian boy was just a friend and Richard said it was none of his business. She was very calm and forgiving, and the events of the night receded like a bad dream. 'You look terrible,' she said gently. 'Come and have some breakfast.'

She took him to a cafeteria place but she pushed her plate away half full when he told her about Inge finding the letter. She asked him not to be angry with Felix. He burst out, 'Oh Sally, why didn't you tell me when it happened? We could have worked something out. Didn't you trust me?'

She wouldn't look at him. 'Can't we just forget about it?'

'Did you want to have the baby?'

She said firmly, 'Richard, I really don't want to talk about it any more.'

He knew he should leave it alone but he couldn't. 'God, something this important can happen and you and Helen don't even bother to tell me. Don't I count for anything?'

'Of course you do,' she said, looking at the table.

'Can you imagine what it feels like? You're the two people I love most in the world, more than my own children, God help me, and you can just leave me out.'

'We didn't want to upset you. And we knew you wouldn't agree.'

'It's as if I didn't exist.'

She told him he was over-reacting. 'We didn't have much time and we had to make a decision.'

'Without consulting me.'

'I'm sorry.' She chewed her thumb. 'We thought it was all for the best. We weren't rejecting you. We were just two women sticking together.'

He was struck by her composure, how cool and detached she seemed. He couldn't get her to talk about the baby or admit Helen had pressured her into making the wrong decision. He couldn't find out what her own wishes had been. The child who used to hug him and talk to him and depend on him seemed to have gone for ever. 'I made a stupid mistake but it's all over,' she said. She only became agitated when he told her he had left Helen. She talked about love, as if that

284

made everything simple. He couldn't walk out on Helen if he still loved her, she said. Helen wasn't to blame for anything was the message he got, and he must go back to her. He wondered if she was hiding behind Helen's problems to avoid facing her own, but when he tried to put that to her she got up and walked out.

Richard just burst into my room in the middle of the night. I was so fast asleep, like at the bottom of a well, the first good night's sleep I've had for ages, that it was really hard to haul myself out and there was this mad person, kind of snarling at me and saying I was disgusting. He was like somebody out of a horror film, and it could have been almost funny if it hadn't been so frightening. All I could think of was that something must have happened to Mum.

Jamal was marvellous. He really stood up to Richard and tried to calm him down, but it didn't do any good. Richard just went raving on about how I was a tramp and I'd murdered my baby and why did I choose Felix when I knew what he was like. I sort of cowered under the duvet. I couldn't understand how he'd found out and I kept thinking he ought to feel sorry for me, well a bit anyway, instead of just furious. He didn't sound angry with Felix, either, just me. It didn't seem fair at all. He went on about loving me and taking care of me for ten years, as if I'd done something terrible just to annoy him, he didn't seem to understand I was hurt. In the end he actually pulled the duvet off me and that was it, I went mad and screamed at him, 'Shut up, you're not my father.' It was horrible of me but I was desperate to make him go away and leave me alone.

And he did. His face sort of crumpled up and he just slunk out of the room. It all seemed terribly unreal once he'd gone. We even started giggling about it, we were a bit hysterical. Jamal made some tea and we had that and talked for a while and then we tried to get back to sleep but we couldn't. We kept trying to work out how Richard knew about the abortion when Mum and Felix had been just as keen as I was to keep it secret. I'd never seen Richard in such a rage, it made him seem like a completely different person who might do absolutely anything, and I kept wondering if he'd hit Mum. I felt as if I'd never really known him at all. It made me realise how seldom he must have lost his temper in the past, even slightly.

Eventually Jamal decided to go back to his room and I dozed for a while, then I got up and had a bath because I thought it might make me feel better. I wanted some coffee but we'd used up all the milk, so I went down to the supermarket for some more and there in the car park was Richard's car with Richard in it asleep. He looked so pathetic I stopped being angry with him and felt sorry for him instead. I debated what to do and then I woke him up and took him in the coffee shop for breakfast. He kept apologising in a grovelling way till I was quite embarrassed, so I asked him how he'd found out and he said Inge told him. Apparently she found one of my letters in Felix's flat. I felt so awful then. It must mean they're having an affair. Not that I expected Felix to be heartbroken or never have anyone else, but it does seem awfully soon and it's so much worse that it's Inge. So near home and sort of incestuous. And now there's someone else who knows what happened to me. I'm not even going to think about her and Felix together.

Then Richard started to get all heavy about how could Mum and I not tell him and didn't I trust him and he could have helped me and how left out he felt, as if he didn't exist. It was awful. I began to wish I'd left him asleep in the car. I tried to make him feel better. I told him he was much more of a father to me than Carey'd ever been, but that didn't work because when he realised Mum had told Carey about the abortion he felt even more rejected and furious, which was silly really, because she had to tell him if I was going to spend Xmas with them. I might have been crying all over the place when Marsha had her baby. Well, I was.

I started to feel very tired, what with not sleeping much and then all the drama, but it got worse. Richard told me he'd actually left Mum, walked out, just like that. He doesn't want to live with her any more because she didn't tell him what was

286

happening, she just wanted her own way. I was so shocked. I couldn't believe it. I asked if he still loved her, but he wouldn't answer, he just kept on at me about whether I'd have had the baby if Mum or Felix had offered to help me look after it. I couldn't see the point of asking me that. It's too late. Once I got pregnant there simply wasn't a right thing to do: all the options were horrible. I told him I didn't want to talk about it, I'd made a stupid mistake and it was all over. But he kept on. It was amazing. He simply didn't care if he was upsetting me. In the end I just got up and walked out.

I went to Jamal's room in case Richard came to look for me. Jamal wasn't there, but that was all right, it was just nice to feel safe and alone. I lay down on the bed and it smelt of Jamal, it was very comforting, and I fell asleep. Around lunchtime he came back and gave me a big hug and we went to the pub so I could tell him all about it over a drink. I'm beginning to see why people like drinking so much. It really does make you feel better, for a while anyway.

I can't get over the fact that Richard never said he was sorry I'd had such a rotten time. I said to Jamal, 'Surely it's worse for me than him. I actually had to have the abortion. He just wasn't told about it. Now he wants me to pretend it could all have been different if only he'd known. But he couldn't have made Felix leave Elizabeth and he couldn't have made Mum look after the baby. So what's the point of going on about it?' Jamal asked if I'd said all that to Richard and I realised I hadn't, I'd been too busy trying to make him feel better. God, I'm so tired of trying to make people feel better. How about somebody trying to make me feel better for a change? Well, I suppose that's what Jamal's doing.

Richard told me Felix is away on holiday with Elizabeth and that's why he hasn't had a showdown with him yet. Jamal thought maybe I should write to the flat and warn Felix so when he gets back he'll know what to expect, but I can't be bothered. He's had an affair with Inge and let her read my letters and now he's having a nice time in the sun with his wife. Nothing ever goes wrong for him, at least nothing he can't get out of with money. It's not that I want revenge exactly, although Jamal thinks I do, I just want to let them all get on with it, if they're all meant to be so grown up and clever and such good friends. I've done enough. I don't have any energy left for other people. The thing that worries me most is if Richard doesn't go back to Mum. I hated him trying to get me to gang up with him against her. I said to Jamal, 'We were on our own together a long time before he turned up.' But I remember how pleased I was when Richard came along to look after her. I'm really frightened that if he doesn't go back I'll end up feeling responsible for her all over again.

At home Felix would have given Elizabeth the pages and gone away while she read them, but on holiday the whole exercise felt more light-hearted. It was fun to read aloud to her while they sunbathed and sipped their drinks, fun to send himself up slightly in the way he read. She was a good audience, listening properly and rewarding him with a look or a smile at the right moment without overdoing it. The last bit was the best, and he had stopped as usual, like Hemingway, while he still knew what was coming next.

' "Looking at the young man's sturdy streamlined body, suntanned and covered in curly black hair, his splendid prick, his eyes a curious yellow like an animal, Tony could feel the faint stirrings of something he had denied since his youth.

' " 'I'd like to ask you a few questions about the murder,' he said.

' " 'In that case I'd better get dressed,' the young man said. 'I always think better with my clothes on.'

' "Tony followed him out of the sauna and into the jacuzzi.

' " 'Such a pity about Steven and Bernard,' said the young man, splashing. 'They must have overdone their S-M games. I always thought they would, one of these days.' " '

'Wow,' Elizabeth said. 'Tony Blythe is a closet gay. After all these years.' She sounded impressed.

'Well, why not? It'll give my readers something to think about. With a bit of luck they'll read all the other books again, just looking for clues.'

'Which they won't find.'

'Yes, they will. You can always find something if you look for it hard enough. Especially if it isn't there. That's the basis of most religions.' He must make a note of that, he thought. It had only just struck him and it sounded good.

'It's a great idea,' Elizabeth said.

'I thought so.'

'You haven't forgotten Tony Blythe had a wife and kids at the beginning?'

'So did Oscar Wilde.'

'Right. That was silly of me.'

'Not at all. You're meant to be playing the average reader.'

'And he's always been such a philanderer,' she said hesitantly.

'Well, you know what they say about Casanova and Don Juan.'

She smiled. 'I love it.'

'Ready with the blue pencil?'

'Only a couple of details.'

Felix refilled their glasses. 'Christ, this bit hurts. I never get used to it. That's my baby you're about to mutilate.' Too late he thought it was an unfortunate phrase, but of course she wouldn't notice.

'Not at all. I'm only going to trim its nails. "A curious yellow" reminds me of a film title.'

'Yes, of course.' He should have remembered. 'How about . . . "a curiously light brown, almost yellow"?'

'That's better.'

'I was thinking of a German shepherd dog, actually.'

'Richard's eyes are that colour,' she said.

'So they are. I wondered where I'd got it from.'

'Will he mind?'

'Well, he may think twice before he takes another shower with me at the club.' They laughed comfortably. 'I could always change it. How about . . . "a curiously muddy green, like avocados, somewhere between ripe and rotten"?'

She considered. 'Mm. I like the symbolism. I'm sure the young man's going to be trouble. You'll have to cut "like an animal" though.'

'I'll just make a note of it,' said Felix, scribbling. 'More?'

'Well, I think "faint stirrings" is a bit of a cliché.'

'Would "reawakening" be better?'

'Yes. "Of something he had denied since youth." '

'Cut "his" as well?'

'I thought maybe . . .'

'No, you're going too far. That makes it too impersonal.'

'OK. He's your hero. "Since his youth." '

'Is that all?'

'It's wonderful.'

They always enjoyed these sessions, reminding them of how they had met and what a good team they were, matching their expertise and remembering their youth. 'Just for that, I'll do your back,' he said. 'Turn around.'

She moved languidly: she would probably want to make love again quite soon. Holidays always made her extremely randy. Well, that was all right; there was no one else around. 'How am I doing?' she asked.

'Coming along nicely. A curiously light brown, just like the young man's former eyes.'

She was squirming with pleasure as he rubbed oil into her. She had put on weight on the holiday but it didn't matter so much with a suntan. 'Does the young man have a name?'

'I thought probably Sebastian.'

'Oh, very good. God, your hands are such a turn-on. We may have to have a siesta.'

'Never known to refuse.' And indeed he did very seldom refuse her, which he thought was a point in his favour. One of many, in fact. He was sure if he had been conventionally faithful to her they would be bored shitless with each other by now. The atmosphere of wayward sexuality from his affairs spilt over into the marriage, and the knowledge that he might just leave her or she could just throw him out spiced their deep security with a small thrill of fear.

'I wish all my authors were like you,' she said.

'So you could have an orgy?' He kissed the base of her spine. In the early days of their marriage he had tried to interest her in threesomes, foursomes; it hadn't worked but he still liked to tease her about it. Maybe it was all for the best. Normally greedy for all he could get, he did actually know when he was well off, could recognise that here was the most satisfactory deal he was likely to find.

Elizabeth turned over and removed her bikini. Felix started to suck her warm, familiar cunt, gratified by the whimpering sounds of pleasure that she made. He had rarely met a woman who wasn't turned on by oral sex. His own success (he enjoyed the pun) with women was based, he thought, on three main factors: sucking, fucking and listening. Most men could manage one or two of these, but very few could be bothered with all three. That was his secret, and it was so simple. Oh, and he also made them laugh. Perhaps that gave him an extra edge. The rest of it, the champagne and flowers and presents, those were mere details that anyone could copy.

Inge woke early on Saturday morning. In fact she had hardly slept at all, first from worry at how much she had hurt Richard, then from excitement at wondering what he might say and do to Helen. She imagined a row at least, and hoped for physical violence, or desertion, or best of all murder, although she had to admit that was unlikely. Her fantasies kept her awake most of the night, leaving her exhausted but energised, as if she had jet lag. She knew if she hadn't shown Richard the letter she would merely have been kept awake by her own pain.

When she eventually went downstairs to the kitchen she found the boys already there, Karl tucking in to a large fry-up, and Peter drinking coffee and spooning yoghurt from a carton. She stared at him in amazement. 'Is that all you're having?'

'I'm on a diet.'

'His girlfriend's got anorexia,' Karl said, 'and he's trying to compete.'

Inge was shocked. She had met Rosemary and liked her and assumed she was naturally thin. But she knew the boys enjoyed teasing her because her sense of humour was not like theirs. 'I don't think that's very funny,' she said severely. 'Anorexia is a serious disease.'

'Aren't all diseases serious?' Peter looked at her with an air of innocent enquiry.

'Except piles and chilblains,' Karl said. 'They're pretty comic.'

'Not if you have them,' said Inge, who had suffered from both in her time.

'And gout. And housemaid's knee.' They snorted with laughter.

'So why aren't you eating?' she said to Peter.

'I told you, I'm on this diet. It's for spiritual enlightenment. As you rise above the demands of the body, you gain insight and awareness. It was all in the colour supplement last week. Didn't you see it?'

Karl was shovelling bacon, fried bread and sausage into his mouth. He had always been rather a messy eater and she had given up nagging him about it. 'You save all the labels from the tins you're not eating,' he said, 'and when you've got four million and seventy-two, you trade them in for a ticket to Katmandu. He's on a sixties trip. Peace and love, man.'

She thought he sounded in a good mood. 'Karl . . .'

'No, Mum, sorry.'

'What?'

'I'm not going to do the favour you're about to ask me in that special tone of voice.'

'It's only a little one,' she said. 'Just to ring up your father.'

'But you've been doing that for years.'

'Only this time I can't. Peter?'

'Don't do it, Pete, there's a catch to it, my son.'

'Tell me the catch and I might do it.'

Oh, lovely soft-hearted Peter. That was how it sounded. Only she knew that ultimately Karl was more vulnerable to her. 'Well, yesterday your father was very cruel, he said he wouldn't see me any more, so I told him something bad about the cow, something she'd done, to make him very angry. And now I want to know what's happened.'

Peter said, 'It doesn't sound very spiritual to me.'

'Right on, man.'

'Please. I have to know. It took a lot of courage to do what I did. It was a big risk.'

292

Karl said uncomfortably, 'Oh, Mum, you do keep on, don't you?'

'Yes, I usually find if I keep on long enough, people do what I want.'

'Dad must be the exception,' Peter said. Inge sometimes thought he had a cruel streak.

'There's still hope, until we die,' she said sharply. 'Is that spiritual enough for you?'

'All right, Mum,' said Karl. 'What do I have to say?'

She turned a radiant face towards him. She thought it was lovely the way he responded to her need. He was going to grow up into a wonderful man and some unknown girl would no doubt take advantage of him. 'If your father answers, you have just an ordinary chat. But if the cow answers, you ask for your father. If she says he is out, you ask when he'll be back. Don't let her be vague. Ask for an exact time.'

'OK.' Karl went out of the room, sounding burdened.

Peter screwed up the empty yoghurt carton and aimed it at the bin. 'Mum, don't you think if you let up a bit you'd feel better? All this keeping on at Dad and calling her the cow, it doesn't change anything but it keeps you sort of worked up. I think it's bad for you.'

Inge was annoyed by the critical tone in his voice. Suddenly at fourteen he was trying to sound like an expert on human relationships. She hoped it didn't mean he was going to start siding with Richard. 'Perhaps when you've been on your diet a bit longer,' she said, 'you'll understand more about suffering.'

His mouth tightened, reminding her of Richard in a bad mood, but he didn't answer, merely stared at the table and traced a pattern with some spilt sugar. Presently Karl returned. 'He's not there and she's got no idea when he'll be back.' He hesitated. 'She sounded very odd. Sort of spaced out.'

Inge could hardly contain her excitement. She wanted to clap her hands and jump up and down, like a gleeful child. 'They must have had a big row. Perhaps he has even left her. Oh, it's wonderful.'

'I didn't like doing it,' Karl said, sounding grown up and serious.

She wanted to hug him but sensed he wouldn't welcome a hug at that moment. 'It was important to me and I'm very grateful.'

He wouldn't look at her, but turned to Peter. 'I'm going to clean the bike. Coming?'

'In a minute.'

Karl went out, whistling. He always whistled when he was upset. After a moment Peter picked up one of his discarded sausages and ate it.

'I won't tell,' said Inge softly. She could hardly wait for him to go and join Karl; she didn't want them to know where she was going.

She had to know how Helen was coping without Richard, how her grief looked, had to see her ravaged face. Of course she couldn't be sure Richard had gone for ever, but it was a start, just knowing that he had gone and Helen didn't know when he'd be back. Helen must be in pain and Inge had to see this rare sight, like Halley's Comet. She dressed carefully in her best clothes with plenty of make-up and drove to the house filled with a sense of occasion, as if she were going to the theatre.

Helen came to the door. She looked very tired and red-eyed, as if she hadn't slept and had done a lot of crying. It was so wonderful to see that Inge felt her whole body flooded with triumph, a warm wet sensation similar to orgasm. 'Now you know how it feels,' she said smiling, as Helen just stared at her. 'He's left you, hasn't he? I'm so happy. Even if I never see him again, it's worth it to know you're in pain.'

Helen shook her head. She looked weary and disbelieving, too tired even for anger, Inge noticed. She was impressed.

'Christ, Inge, just piss off, will you?' she said.

She did look her age, Inge thought. 'And even if he comes back, it won't be the same. He'll never trust you again.'

Helen slammed the door in her face, but it seemed to take a big effort. 'You've lost him for ever,' Inge shouted after her, hoping it might be true, or that she could make it true by saying it, like a curse. She felt so elated by her visit that she actually skipped on her way back to the car. The hatred she felt was so pure that it invigorated her whole body like adrenalin. It would take her a while to come down. She thought she would probably go to the wine bar that night and pick someone up for sex.

Sleeping in the car proved so uncomfortable that it made him inefficient and he switched to the office floor, sneaking back in there with a sleeping bag after everyone had gone home. Highly irregular, of course, but it was only for a week, he told himself, ten days at the most. Once Felix was back he could ring up, arrange to see him, and then it would be over. He didn't know quite what he meant by that, only that his plans for living seemed to stop at that point. Confronting Felix was such a milestone that he couldn't see beyond it.

He slept badly, waking early to wash and shave in the lavatory before anyone else arrived, so he thought he was getting away with it, but he was so tired that one morning he overslept and woke to find Marion standing over him. Marion looking sympathetic and tweedy and enormous, viewed from the floor. He was intensely embarrassed. It was like being a little boy again, his first day at primary school.

'I knew you arrived early and worked late, Richard,' she said gently, 'but I didn't realise you actually lived here.'

'I'm sorry, I should have told you.' He scrambled up and out of the sleeping bag, conscious of his grubby tracksuit, thankful he hadn't stripped down to his underpants.

'I was sort of joking, but I see you're not. Whatever's happened, can't you talk to me about it? I've been very worried about you this past week. You seem to be heading for some kind of breakdown.'

'So you've come in early to catch me at it.' Being in the wrong made him sound angry, he noticed.

'I wanted to have a private chat with you. I know we've had our differences in the past but I hope we respect each other as colleagues. You can't work properly if you're having a crisis in your private life.'

'No wonder some of our clients find it so difficult to hold down a job,' Richard said, stuffing the sleeping bag into a cupboard. 'Their lives are one long crisis.'

Marion seemed unperturbed. 'Could we just focus on you for a minute? If you tell me what's happened, I may be able to help you. I used to do marriage guidance and I've been divorced myself.'

'Really? I'd no idea.' In spite of himself, he was interested: it seemed so unlikely.

'Yes, it's a second marriage for both of us, John and me. I know you think I'm a dried-up old stick but I may understand something of what you're going through.'

'You're very sure this is something to do with my marriage.' He resented her confident tone.

'I hardly think you'd be sleeping at the office if things weren't even more uncomfortable at home.'

'Of course.' He almost laughed. 'I'm being very stupid, I haven't had much sleep this week. Yes, I have had a row with Helen, in fact that seems like a vast understatement, I've actually left Helen and I'm here because I've got nowhere else to go. I've also had a row with my step-daughter and now I have to wait till my so-called best friend gets back from holiday so I can have a monumental row with him. And somehow I have to hang on to my sanity while I wait.' He stopped, heart pounding, surprised at how much he had told her. He took his electric razor out of his desk drawer and started to shave rather aggressively.

Marion perched on the edge of his desk. 'Would you like to tell me what all these people have done to make you so angry?'

'Not really, no.'

'If we're talking about adultery, it's not the worst thing that can happen to a marriage —'

'We are not talking about adultery. In fact I rather wish we were. Mere adultery would be much easier to handle. A bit of good honest lust on the one side and hurt pride on the other, my God, I'd almost be grateful for something as simple as that. I'm talking about the kind of deceit and betrayal you can't imagine. Every morning when I wake up on that floor with all my bones aching I have to remember that the three people I loved and trusted most in the world have done this incredibly ugly thing.'

Now he was terrified. One moment he was refusing to talk to her and the next he was telling her almost everything. He couldn't trust his own judgment any more; he had no way of knowing what he might say or do next.

'I've never seen you like this,' Marion said.

'No, well, let me assure you it's even worse from the inside.'

After a moment she said, 'You know, Richard, we do have a spare room and you'd be very welcome to use it.'

He started to laugh and to his horror felt his eyes fill with tears. 'Marion, you're amazing. You really do surprise me . . . You're very kind . . .' He sat down at his desk with his face in his hands and Marion put her arm round his shoulders. It was the first time she had ever touched him and it felt odd.

'That's right, let it out,' she said, sounding pleased at a response she could understand.

'No, that's just what I mustn't do.' He blew his nose on some Kleenex. He always kept a box handy for clients and encouraged them to cry if they needed to, as Marion was encouraging him now. Only now he knew why so many of them resisted. 'It's only anger that's holding me together and I've got to hang on for another week.'

There was a long silence. Marion patted his shoulder and took her arm away.

'I'll make you some coffee,' she said.

Elizabeth was used to authors in general procrastinating, and Felix in particular, but this time he cut it so fine that he was actually reading the last sentence of the book to her while she was packing for their flight home.

'. . . so that when he turned his head just in time to see the blow about to fall, it was already too late.'

He put down the pages and looked at her with an expression of triumph.

'My God,' she said. 'Poor old Tony Blythe.'

'Well.' Felix looked smug. 'It was about time. And I've left it just slightly ambiguous, so if I have to revive him, God forbid, I can.'

'So it was the lovely yellow-eyed Sebastian all the time.'

' 'Fraid so. Or avocado-eyed. I haven't quite decided yet.'

'Poor Tony. I shall miss him.' She thought it was rather like losing an uncle you had always resented having to invite for Christmas. Suddenly there was no one to complain about in a comfortable familiar way. 'I feel quite sad.'

'I don't. I just feel an enormous sense of relief. At last I've got rid of the tiresome little bugger.'

Felix was never sentimental. She always forgot that. Emotional yes, but that was something different. 'Rest in peace, Tony Blythe,' she said seriously, with a feeling of real loss. So many books financing their lifestyle, so many holidays spent on research. Tony Blythe had been family.

'Gone to the great investigation bureau in the sky,' said Felix. 'Good riddance, that's what I say.'

'It's fantastic you've finished on time.' She went on packing: he never helped her with that and on the whole it was simpler that he didn't.

'I told you all I needed was sunshine. And you with your blue pencil. God, I feel wonderful. How long before the euphoria wears off?'

'About two days usually.' She thought it was sweet that he never remembered, that he was always ready to believe it would last for ever. She hated to disillusion him: it was like telling a child Santa Claus didn't exist.

'Yes. But this time . . . it's back to real books.' He was far too high to be reached by mere words. 'I think I've got an idea for the new one actually.'

'Already?' She was pierced by envy, as occasionally happened. She would have liked to be creative.

'It's about a man who's having a midlife crisis and he has an affair with a young girl he meets in a supermarket. He's trying to recapture his lost youth but really he loves his wife.'

'Of course,' she said drily, locking the suitcase and watching him pour champagne. 'So what happens?'

'Oh, the girl leaves him for a younger man, but his wife won't have him back, so he kills himself. It's a cautionary tale, the new grim message for the eighties. You reap what you sow and all that jazz. Why should anyone get away with mere adultery?'

'Except that they do, all the time,' she said, saddened by the flip way he told her the plot, as if it wouldn't hurt at all.

'Well, Anna Karenina didn't, nor Madame Bovary, and that's good enough for me.'

'They were women,' she said. 'They were stupid enough to take it seriously.'

'So does my hero. You can't get much more serious that suicide. He's sensitive. He's the new man, in touch with his feelings.'

'Don't tell me any more.'

'Why not?'

Oh, she must get a grip on herself. 'Or you may not want to write it.'

'You know me so well.' But he saw the tears in her eyes. 'What's the matter?'

She shook her head. 'Nothing. I just . . . don't want to go home. It's been so perfect. I like having you all to myself.'

'Silly old thing.' He held out his arms. 'Come here.'

Felix returning from holiday was like a child on its birthday, excited at first then complaining there wasn't enough post. She thought he was childish too in the way that he always wanted to go away and then always wanted to come back, whereas she, all sober and grown up, usually wanted to do neither, but merely to stay where she was. His exuberance touched her.

'It's almost a reason for going,' he said, 'just to get lots of letters all at once. And one day amongst them there will be –' he made trumpet noises – 'the summons from Hollywood. Come and write scripts for us. Name your price. Sell your soul for a fistful of dollars. What a bargain that would be.'

'And this time . . . ?' she said, playing along.

'Guess they missed the post again. All I've got is a whole stack of bills. Plus an invitation to talk to a Writers' Circle on how to write a thriller – as if I knew, and if I did, why should I tell them? An American student begging for help with her Ph.D. thesis on Crime Writing as a Meaningful Adjunct to Existential Philosophy – well, she may be pretty. And a card from the library that my compact discs are three months overdue.'

'You're in good form this morning.' She served breakfast, waiting on him, thinking what a good bargain it was, that she liked doing it and he liked accepting it.

'Oh Lizzie, I keep forgetting and then I have the pure rapture of remembering, that I've actually finished the book. That bastard Tony Blythe has gone for ever. I'm a free man. It's yo ho ho and eyes down looking for the great novel again. We can make our fortunes or we can grow old together in romantic poverty. What d'you say? Double or quits?'

How could anybody not appreciate someone with such a capacity for happiness? 'I love you,' she said.

'That's just as well because I simply adore you. Or I might be the new Noël Coward. How about that? That's better than the old Felix Cramer any day. Buy a new dressing-gown and knock out half a dozen plays over the weekend.'

She kissed him. 'And I think you have jet lag.'

Marion let her in. Kind, understanding, old-fashioned Marion, whom Helen suddenly found she liked, said of course Helen could talk to Richard and she'd take his calls. Richard himself looked less than delighted when Helen walked into his office unannounced and told him that. He went on ostentatiously pretending to write a probation report as if she wasn't there.

'But what am I supposed to do?' Helen said. 'You hang up when I phone, I don't know where you're living, you look terrible . . . I'm worried about you. I miss you.'

He looked very tired and he had shaved badly. He had a

scruffy, pathetic look, almost like someone sleeping rough. She was annoyed with him for looking like that, for doing that to himself, and she also wanted to take him home and put him to rights.

'I find that hard to believe,' he said without looking up, a coldly controlled voice that didn't match his appearance. 'I'd have thought you were so used to acting independently you'd hardly notice I've gone.'

'God, you can be pompous.' She always forgot that because they quarrelled so seldom. She wanted to kill him when he was pompous.

'Then you're better off without me, aren't you?'

She tried to calm herself with breathing.

'Inge came to see me,' she said, thinking that might arouse a little humanity. 'She wanted to gloat. God, she was weird. High as a kite.'

No reaction.

'All right,' she said, giving in, 'I did something serious without telling you and I'm sorry.' How many more times, for God's sake, did he want her to say it?

'Sorry you did it or sorry I found out?'

'I just can't believe that cancels out the last ten years.'

'Try harder.'

She had come to make peace and instead he was making her angry. Out it all came. 'All right, you wish I'd told you, but what if I had? Abortion's out. Adoption's out. So what do we do? Bring up Felix's child? Have Felix drop in to pat it on the head? Have Elizabeth as a sort of auntie? Have Sally playing at motherhood in the long vac? Make up a tale about some missing boyfriend? You tell me, Richard, what would you have done?'

Now he looked up. 'I wouldn't have forced my daughter to kill her baby.'

Like a politician he still hadn't answered her question. She said, 'If Sally'd really wanted that baby she could've told you she was pregnant.'

'Sally does whatever you tell her, we both know that.'

'She came to me for help and I helped her.'

'You made her have an abortion because you hate Felix,

301

and bringing up a baby might have stopped you doing a few paintings. Sally's baby or my baby. Nothing must be allowed to get in the way of your work.'

So that was it. She should have known, of course; and perhaps on some level she had known. 'Ah, that's what it's about. You've never forgiven me for not getting pregnant by you. This isn't about Sally at all.'

'It's about all of us.' He was looking at her now but not really seeing her, she felt, as if his anger created a fog between them, or as if she had developed a stranger's face. 'Don't you understand anything? How can you and I be married if you go on behaving as if you were still single? No, not even that, still married to Carey. You can tell him what's going on but you can't tell me.'

'Have you been talking to Sally?'

'Yes, of course.'

'You didn't upset her, did you?' She didn't like to think of him going to Sally in this mood.

'Oh, I shouted a bit and made a fool of myself. She was in bed with that Indian boy at the time so maybe she'll get pregnant again. It wouldn't surprise me if she does it just to rebel against you.'

'That's sick.'

'No, it makes perfect sense, you've got her so brainwashed. That's probably why she chose Felix, just to annoy you.'

'I don't want any more of your half-baked psychology.' She found she was actually tempted to hit him. It was all escalating dreadfully, a real slanging match, just what she had meant to avoid.

'Then get out of my office.'

'God, I came here to ask you to come home and all we do is have another row. Why is all this my fault? Isn't Felix to blame for anything?'

'I'm not married to him.'

'You might as well be.' Now it all came spewing out. She was shouting; screaming almost. Everyone in the office would hear but she didn't care. 'As long as I've known you I've heard nothing but how wonderful Felix is, how splendidly romantic, such a free spirit, screwing everything that moves and making his wife put up with it, isn't he clever, isn't he lucky, doing all the things you maybe wish you could but you haven't the guts, and now this happens and it's all my fault. Well, just you try thinking that maybe some of it's *his* fault and maybe some of it's *your* fault, bringing him into my home . . .' She was shaking with rage but she wanted to cry and she wanted him to put his arms round her.

'Yes, it *is* your home, isn't it?' he said. He looked stricken: she had managed to hurt him. 'I left my wife and children for you, I wanted a child with you, I thought of Sally as my own daughter, but really I've just been a lodger all these years. Not even a very good lodger. I couldn't pay enough rent.'

Felix was meeting Natasha for lunch and his mood lasted through the morning spent at the flat putting new pages on disk. When he arrived at the Groucho Club he was still feeling like Tigger, full of bounce. The elation that came from finishing the book and the sense of well-being that a suntan always gave him combined to make the events of last year recede like a distant bad dream. Now all he needed was a new woman and his happiness would be complete.

Natasha was sitting in a deep armchair in a corner near the bar. He embraced her and they kissed the air beside each other's cheeks. She smelt deliciously expensive. 'That's quite a colour,' she said, looking him over appreciatively.

Felix sat down beside her. 'We do our best. Slaving over a hot typewriter in the broiling sun. Is there no limit to the sacrifice this man will make for his art?' A waitress arrived and he ordered a dry Martini because it always felt decadent at lunchtime. Natasha's glass looked disgustingly healthy, full of ice and lemon and fizzy water. 'I see you're still knocking back the Perrier,' he said. 'Can't you do better than that on ten per cent of me?'

'I got kinda used to it on that diet,' she said in her soft mid-Atlantic accent that she had kept or cultivated. He liked the fact that she was steely inside but soft-spoken, like Jackie Kennedy or Nancy Reagan; he trusted her to get her own way and therefore the best for him. In all their years together he had never attempted to make love to her. It would have been trespassing on their professional relationship, like importuning a doctor or a hairdresser or an accountant, all of whom could be difficult to replace. Besides, he had always had the feeling that he might bruise himself on her bones.

'But I don't want the thinnest agent in London.' He knew she liked to be teased about this, seeing it as an achievement. As a little girl (not that he could imagine she had ever been a little girl unless she had run a protection racket in the playground) she had probably idolised Wallis Simpson. 'Give me women about me that are fat. Well, decently voluptuous anyway.'

'No need to ask,' she said, smiling at him and displaying the alarmingly perfect teeth that all Americans seemed to regard as mandatory.

'Finished.'

'Thank God for that.'

'Maybe this time we could have an auction.'

'Why not? Have some fun.'

They talked shop for a while, moving on from the last of Tony Blythe to the new novel.

'I'd like to find out what I'm worth.'

'But you don't really want to move?'

'No, but it wouldn't hurt to frighten them a little. This could be the big one.'

'It might be worth moving in the States,' Natasha said. 'They haven't promoted you too well lately and you could do with a hard sell. If they think they're getting another *Heartbreak Merchant.*'

'Oh, bigger than that.' God, he hoped he was right.

She looked pleased. 'How long will you need?'

'Well, it's been cooking for a while, so I might have a first draft ready in six months, and the final version, well, maybe by Christmas. If I'm lucky. With a following wind.' He even caught himself crossing his fingers like a schoolboy.

'That'd be great. Then it could come out next autumn. Do you have a title or is that still under wraps?'

'I'm not sure. At first I called it *And Then There was Lisa.*

But now that feels a bit soft. Now I'm thinking more of *Anatomy of a Love Affair*.' Elation made him want to be indiscreet but even as he spoke he wondered if it was unlucky to reveal so much.

'I like it,' Natasha said. 'I like it very much.'

Helen looked wary, uneasy, as if now she was here in Elizabeth's office she wished she hadn't come. Elizabeth thought she was thinner than ever, pale and tired; she wondered what was wrong. 'It's lovely to see you,' she said, giving Helen a hug.

'I'm sure I'm interrupting something important,' Helen said, accepting the hug but not returning it.

'Rubbish, I'm just catching up after the holiday.'

'Oh yes, was it wonderful?' She sounded as though her mind were elsewhere, almost as if she had forgotten Elizabeth had been away.

'Yes, it was,' Elizabeth said rather emphatically. 'Felix is always blissful on holiday. Food and wine, sun and sex, work and talk. All the things he likes best. And I have him all to myself. It was a real treat.'

'You're very brown,' Helen said, sounding sour and distracted.

'Yes, I don't believe all this stuff about skin cancer, it's like dieting. Doctors trying to take away our few remaining pleasures.' She smiled at her small joke but Helen didn't respond. 'Are you all right? You sounded very odd on the phone.'

Helen went and stood by the window, looking out for a moment, then turned to face Elizabeth again. 'Richard's left me,' she said almost defiantly.

Elizabeth could feel herself looking shocked and disbelieving. It seemed impossible to accept, like news of sudden death.

'I know,' Helen said ironically. 'We were such a happy couple. Right.'

'God, what a shock,' said Elizabeth, feeling inadequate and foolish.

'Yes.' Helen looked vaguely round the room as if searching for something. 'I do wish I hadn't given up smoking.'

'Have a drink?'

'Yes please.'

'White wine be all right?'

'Anything. Turps. Meths, anything.' She didn't smile.

Elizabeth got a bottle out of her office fridge. Authors always wanted a drink. If there was such a thing as a teetotal author, she had never met one. 'What happened?'

'I'm sorry, I can't really talk about it. We just had an incredible row and he walked out.'

'I can't take it in.'

'Neither can I really, only I've had more time than you.'

Elizabeth could feel her straining to leave. She was drinking fast and watching the door, like an animal that fears it may be trapped if it stays too long. This made her long to keep Helen there, to get her to talk. It was a chance to be helpful, a rare chance, after all the times she had been the one with problems and Helen the sympathetic, faintly impatient listener. She wanted to redress the balance, to make the friendship more equal.

'I must go,' said Helen, putting down her glass.

'But you've only just got here. Look, I have to see an author later on but that won't take long. We could have supper together.'

Helen was shaking her head before Elizabeth had stopped speaking. Elizabeth felt resentful at being dismissed without being heard but she understood Helen's pride and how she must hate being in trouble.

'No, really,' Helen said. 'Thanks all the same. I'm not good company and I'd rather get home. I keep thinking Richard might turn up and I'd like to be there.' But she still hovered, undecided, in the middle of the room. 'He came round one day when I was at the studio and took some clothes. I might as well have been at home, I can't work. I can't do anything.'

'I'm just worried about you. I'd like to help.' Elizabeth tried not to sound too pressing.

'I know, I'm hard to help. That's what Magdalen always says.'

306

'If you'd only tell me what's happened . . .'

'I just did something unforgivable, that's all, and he won't forgive me.' She shrugged as if it wasn't important. 'You've been very good.'

'But I haven't done anything,' Elizabeth said, frustrated. She had felt so well after the holiday, brown and relaxed and filled up with Felix, and now it was as if Helen was draining the well-being out of her.

'It was nice to see you. Nice to talk. I don't know where he's living or anything. I never thought this could happen.' She shook her head distractedly. 'I didn't know I'd miss him so much. I used to be good at living alone. Only I suppose I wasn't alone really, I had Sally.'

Suddenly it came to Elizabeth what must have happened. 'Have you been having an affair?'

Helen looked surprised. 'No. Nothing like that.'

'Then I can only think you've had an abortion or been sterilised or both. Richard's always wanted more children, hasn't he?'

'Please don't keep guessing,' Helen said, sounding cross. 'It's very embarrassing.'

'Sorry. I just can't help being curious. And I thought maybe I could help if I knew a bit more.'

'Nobody can help.' Helen moved nearer the door. 'The details aren't important anyway but they're very personal. I took a decision without consulting Richard. I think I was right and he thinks I was wrong. That's all there is to it.'

Elizabeth felt excluded. How could she help if Helen wouldn't tell her any more, and why was Helen here in her office if she didn't want to talk? 'But he'll come round,' she said. 'He must. He'll have to forgive you eventually.'

'Will he? That's what I keep telling myself but I wonder. I'm seeing another side of him now. Or maybe I always knew it was there and that's why I didn't tell him the truth. It's not easy living with a good person. They're implacable.'

Elizabeth had never thought of Richard like that. She wondered how far Helen's troubles were of her own making. What could possibly be serious enough to make Richard leave her and why didn't she want to talk about it?

'I wouldn't know,' she said. 'Felix is pretty easy going. So long as he gets his own way, I mean. He's self-indulgent but he indulges me too.'

'I never thought I'd envy you but right now I do.'

'Oh?' Elizabeth wasn't sure how to take that.

'Yes. Going home to someone who'll never leave you, never condemn you, no matter what you do, because they haven't a leg to stand on. That must be very nice. Very comfortable.'

'Well, I wouldn't put it quite like that,' Elizabeth said, offended, suddenly wishing she hadn't told Helen quite so much about Felix. 'We do love each other.'

'Sorry. I haven't had much sleep and things just come out. I'm not thinking straight. Don't hold it against me.'

She did look very tired and it was a crisis; Elizabeth had to forgive her. But the words rankled.

'I wish you'd come to supper,' she said, more out of duty now. 'I bet you're not eating properly.'

'I'd rather be alone, honestly,' Helen said, her hand on the door knob.

Elizabeth had one last try. 'Does Sally know about this?'

'I haven't told her anything, but Richard did. She rang up to say she was sorry. What more can she do?'

'I thought maybe she might . . . come home for weekends. Just be with you.' She remembered all she had done, resentfully, for her own parents.

'I wouldn't expect that. She's got her own life. Anyway, she'll be home for the vac and that's not far away.'

'Maybe Richard'll be back by then.' Elizabeth felt Helen was pulling rank on her, telling her she didn't understand what could be reasonably expected of children these days.

'Yes, that's what Sally said. She's like you, she's sure he'll come back.'

'But you're not.'

'No, I'm not. I just have a feeling of doom. But I'd love to be wrong. Well, I'm really going this time.'

How beautiful she was still, Elizabeth thought, even looking old and tired, thin and miserable. Pale and angular and beautiful like one of her paintings. Inaccessible. And yet she must have come with some purpose. Elizabeth felt she was trying to decode something dangerous. She even wondered if they had ever really been friends. Had she ever known Helen at all? She knew Felix desired her and would never have her, and she could see why, and that knowledge would always be between them although it was not Helen's fault.

Helen turned in the doorway, on her way out. She was very casual. 'Oh, Elizabeth, do me a favour. Don't mention any of this to Felix. I'd rather he heard it from Richard. It seems only fair.'

When Richard had finally got rid of Helen he went into Marion's office and told her at some length how angry he was. Even as he spoke he thought he sounded hysterical and he marvelled that Marion could listen so calmly.

Eventually she said, 'I'm sorry you're annoyed with me for letting her in but I did it from the best of motives. She was very upset. She needed to see you.'

'And I call it interference. If I wanted to talk to Helen, I do know where she lives.' He started to laugh. 'God, this must be how our clients feel when we keep interfering in their lives from the best of motives.'

'Richard, I do wish you'd tell me what this is all about.'

'It's an education.' Why couldn't he stop? He knew he had made his point. It was frightening to go on and on, like the runaway train. 'I feel like a client. Or a child. That's how we treat them, isn't it? Like moronic or delinquent children. We patronise them.'

Marion appeared to be giving this serious consideration. 'I don't think so. It's quite possible to respect someone as an adult even though they need help with their problems. Why not? It happens all the time in everyday life. If I call in a plumber, for instance, or go to the dentist or the hairdresser. I need help from an expert. But I don't feel they're patronising me.'

He said, 'Oh, Marion, you're wonderful. You're so rational.'

After a moment she said, 'Richard, d'you have a good GP?'

309

'Why?'

'I really think you need to talk to someone you trust and it obviously isn't me.'

It was difficult to ring Felix when the time came. He woke knowing it was the right day but thinking with relief, It's too early to ring him, he won't be there yet. Then he got caught up in work and suddenly it was lunchtime, so Felix would surely be out. By mid afternoon he was promising himself he would do it after his next cup of coffee.

He had carried his anger for so long, nurtured it until it had become a part of him. It felt unreal that today he was obliged to express it; he couldn't imagine what he would do afterwards.

Felix took a long time to answer and Richard almost hoped he might get the machine instead. Then there was a sleepy hullo. Richard felt a painful sensation of loss when he heard the familiar voice: it was as if he had not fully realised how much he loved Felix until he learned to hate him. He was conscious that the friendship hung suspended: until he broke it, it would still exist in Felix's mind.

'How was the holiday?' He heard himself trying to sound normal and failing. Surely Felix would pick up that something was terribly wrong? But the drowsy voice sounded unafraid.

'Oh – hullo, Richard. Terrific. I finished the book.'

'Congratulations.' His heart thumped and his mouth was dry. Felix knew him so well; why didn't he notice the tension, the rage?

'Thanks. I feel great. At least I will when I wake up. I had my snout in the trough with Natasha at lunchtime and what with that and the jet lag . . .' His voice petered out, sounding sunny and genial.

Richard said, 'I thought I might call in for a drink on my way home.'

'Why not? We could celebrate. What sort of time?'

'I'm not sure when I'll be finished here.'

'No matter. Turn up when you like.'

Richard put down the phone. He was shaking: Felix sounded so innocent, so accommodating, so normal. He opened his desk drawer and took out a half bottle of whisky. He wanted to deal out justice with a cool head but he knew he needed some artificial courage first, though he must be careful not to have too much. The familiar voice had unnerved him, bringing back twenty years of friendship. He took a long swig from the bottle and put it back in his desk. Then he began to focus very deliberately on what Felix had done. Presently he realised that he wanted to kill Felix but that it would also be like killing a part of himself.

As he opened the door, Richard struck him, a heavy blow, catching him full in the face. Off balance, Felix staggered backwards, nearly falling over, catching at furniture to save himself, feeling a mixture of pain and surprise. In all his fantasies of being found out, he had never thought of violence.

'And don't bother pretending you don't know what this is about,' Richard said, coming in and closing the door behind him.

Felix clutched his jaw, tasting blood from a cut lip, hoping Richard hadn't loosened any teeth. 'Jesus. That really hurt.'

'I'd like to kill you,' Richard said, with a kind of grim resolve in his voice, suggesting more of an intention than a wish, as if he might actually do it.

'I do hope you won't,' said Felix, trying to introduce a half-joking tone that he felt might have a calming effect.

'God, I thought we were friends, I trusted you.'

Of course he couldn't be sure how much Richard had found out. It might be just the affair and not the abortion. He would have to be careful.

'Hang on a minute,' he said. 'I'd like to be sure I know what we're talking about.'

But this only seemed to enrage Richard further. 'You're unbelievable. Even now you're trying to wriggle out of it. Look, I know everything. Inge told me.'

'Inge?'

'She found a letter from Sally. *Christ.* You're still doing it. That bloody shifty look. Now you're wondering which letter. God, even now you'd lie to me if you thought you could get away with it. I can see it in your face.'

'No point in asking for trouble,' said Felix reasonably.

'Look, I know about the abortion.'

Well, that made it simpler. Worse but simpler. 'I really am very sorry,' he said, the straightforward approach, man to man. 'About the whole affair, I mean. It should never have happened. I take full responsibility. What more can I say?' He tried to gauge Richard's reaction from his face but it was blank with rage, the eyes wild. 'Let's have a drink and talk it over.'

'You can't imagine I'll drink with you.'

'Well, I need one.'

He poured himself some whisky and drank it quickly. It stung his mouth. He poured some more.

'God, you're a shit,' Richard said.

Felix was irritated: he thought Richard sounded contemptuous and smug. 'Look, Richard, we've been friends a long time. You know I like having affairs. OK, Sally was out of bounds, but she had a sort of crush on me and it was very tempting. I mean she made it easy for me. Well, irresistible really,' he said, remembering.

'Christ, you're even trying to blame her.'

He hardly recognised this Richard: the anger transformed him, like a dormant volcano suddenly erupting. Felix even felt a prickle of fear. He could no longer predict how this person might behave.

'No, of course I'm not. I'm just explaining how it happened. She'd made a start with some boy at school, well, you know I don't go chasing after virgins, and she was disappointed, and there I was. Look, I know I shouldn't have done it, but I'm easily tempted and I was flattered. She's very beautiful.' He was distressed to find that talking about it actually made him yearn for Sally again.

'She was eighteen years old, for God's sake.'

'She made me feel young again,' said Felix, remembering more.

312

'Jesus, she paid a high price.'

'Yes, I know, I know, that was rotten luck. But she said she was on the pill.' He was starting to feel he had grovelled enough and perhaps it was time to stand up for himself a little. 'It's not as if I took a chance on purpose, I'm not that irresponsible. But OK, it should have been belt and braces. People do make mistakes or forget or whatever. I know that.'

'She could have died,' Richard said.

'Oh, come on.' This was going too far. 'Abortion's actually safer than having a baby, for obvious reasons. Done properly, I mean.'

'Did you ever think of letting her have it?'

This seemed an extraordinary question. How could Richard possibly have wanted that? 'I never thought of leaving Elizabeth, if that's what you mean.'

'I mean did you ever make Sally feel she had a choice?'

Felix found this hard to answer. All he could remember was panic. 'I think I felt it was very much her decision. Hers and Helen's.'

'Not mine. None of you thought I had a right to know.'

Now they were getting to the real issue: Richard's pride was hurt. Perhaps that was more important than the affair, more important than the abortion. 'Well, it was up to them if they wanted to tell you or not.'

'Did you offer to help financially?' Richard was moving around the room, small, restless movements that Felix found quite threatening.

'I paid for the abortion, of course.'

'I meant child support.'

'I really can't remember.' What was the point of discussing maintenance for a child he had never intended to be born? 'I don't think I did. But I would have done, of course, if she'd decided to have it. Only I was rather hoping she wouldn't, because of upsetting Elizabeth.'

Richard stopped moving around and stood in front of Felix, close to him. 'I hope you rot in hell.' It sounded like a serious curse, not mere words, and Felix felt uneasy. He had seen too many operas where curses were effective.

'I expect I will,' he said lightly. 'If there is a hell.'

313

'Oh, there is for people like you,' said Richard, staring at him. 'There just aren't any words for what I think of you.'

'I'm getting the message.' Felix moved away. 'You don't think you might be over-reacting, just a touch? It wasn't all gloom and doom, you know. We fell in love. We had a nice time. It wasn't just mindless screwing.' He was edging towards the drinks tray, wondering if a third whisky would be a good idea or whether he needed a clear head. 'When I say I like having affairs, I mean just that. Not only the sex but the chat, the presents, the secrecy. The whole package. It was a magic time for both of us. We were happy.' The more he spoke, the more he believed his own words.

'And that's all that matters.'

'Well, I think it's important.' He tried a small joke. 'My parents named me well.'

'Would you ever have told me if I hadn't found out?'

'No, of course not. Whatever for? I told you about Inge and you had mixed feelings about that. I'm just sorry this one ended in tears.' He could see from Richard's face that he was making it worse, but he was running out of patience. Richard had hit him and abused him and he had apologised: what more was there to say? He poured himself another drink and swallowed it quickly. 'Oh, come on, Richard, relax. You've been getting off on my adventures for years, only you don't like them too close to home. OK, point taken. I'm very sorry. It won't happen again.'

But Richard was staring at him as if he were some strange, alien, deeply disgusting creature. 'You don't understand. This so-called friendship is over. You've ruined my marriage and you may have ruined Sally's life.'

'Now you're being absurd.' Felix had had enough: he couldn't resist the obvious final taunt. 'Maybe you're jealous. You probably fancy her yourself. I've only done what you'd like –'

The second blow was much heavier. He reeled backwards, cracking his head on the edge of the fireplace, and fell into darkness.

*

314

Felix's head hit the edge of the marble fireplace with a sharp crack, like the sound of an egg-shell breaking against a cup, only much amplified. He slumped to the floor with a thud and lay there quite peacefully, looking surprised. Presently blood trickled from the back of his head.

Richard gazed at him intently. He was astonished how calm he felt, quite removed from the event: all his violent feelings had gone into the blow. He was cold now, even to the point of discomfort; he almost shivered. Watching the blood ooze out of Felix, he wondered what it meant. Was Felix dying? Clearly he was not conscious: he did not move or make any sound. But he was not dead. Richard could see that he was still breathing.

It was while he was noticing that Felix was still alive that he first realised he wished Felix to die. Hitting him, he had wished only to hurt him, as Sally had been hurt; but looking at him now sprawled on the carpet, he found himself sincerely hoping Felix would never get up. He was disappointed to see signs of life: it would have been a cleaner ending if Felix had been dead there and then. But evidently it was not so easy.

He sat down for a moment to think. The obvious thing now was to call an ambulance. If Felix came round he would have to help him and he would not know what to do. Unless, of course, he hit him again. Unless he finished him off, now, without waiting for him to come round.

He was surprised how strong this temptation was. There were several heavy objects in the room: lamps, ashtrays, even Felix's typewriter would do. He could easily visualise smashing Felix's skull with any of these items. He could already feel the satisfaction it would give him. That was when he began to be afraid. It was one thing to strike Felix in anger; another to regret he was not dead. But it was something else to contemplate quite seriously committing murder in cold blood.

He had never hated anyone before, though he had listened for hours to many of his clients talking about hatred and violence and sudden death. He had listened compassionately and tried to feel into their circumstances, which had seemed so comfortably remote from his own. Most of them appeared to feel remorse, which was a greater punishment than anything the law could devise.

Richard did not feel any remorse. He looked for a long time at the man who had been his friend and felt nothing but hatred. He knew he was not going to call an ambulance but he was not sure that he would not strike another blow. When he got up, switched off the lights and left the flat, leaving Felix alone in darkness, he still hoped that Felix would die, but at least (with considerable reluctant effort) he was giving him a chance. It was as if instead of going ahead with a hanging on board ship, he had cast the condemned man adrift in a small boat. Without water and without a compass, it was true, so his chance was remote (at least he hoped so) but nevertheless it was a chance. Felix was now on the open sea.

It was only when he got out into the street that he began to shake. He found his way to the car and sat in it, trembling, unable to put the key in the ignition. He did not know where to go, what to do. But he knew it was important not to draw attention to himself, not to be questioned by any passing policeman. So this was how it felt, like a hunted animal, on the wrong side of the law.

He started the car. There was only one place he could go, after all. They were equal now: she had killed Sally's baby and he had murdered Felix, at least in his heart, which was where it mattered. What could be more natural than for one murderer to seek out another?

Helen woke without knowing what had woken her, then very quickly became frightened. She could hear footsteps downstairs. Careful, stealthy footsteps. Burglar footsteps. For a moment she was tempted to pretend she had heard nothing, to lie there with a wildly beating heart and will herself back to sleep. Then she got up, knowing something must be done. She put on her bathrobe and felt around on her dressing-table for her nail scissors – pathetic, she thought, and predicting an alarming degree of physical closeness, but the only defensive weapon she remembered having in her bedroom, or at least could find in the dark. She inched her way out of the door and along the landing, impressed by her own courage and at the same time thinking how ridiculous her behaviour was. She would not deter a burglar in the least and would be quite likely to get herself injured. But she didn't seem able to retreat.

Then the light in the hall went suddenly on and she was looking down into Richard's startled face.

She ran down the stairs, filled with joy and at the same time angry, as she might be with Sally for coming home late and worrying her.

'Oh darling,' she said, hugging him furiously, 'I knew you'd come back – only I wasn't sure.'

Then she noticed he wasn't returning the hug but standing there unmoving in her embrace. 'I think I've killed him,' he said in a conversational tone.

'What?'

'That's why I came to you. I couldn't think where else to go. Now we're both murderers.'

He sounded quite pleased with himself. He walked ahead of her into the living-room and poured himself whisky. She followed him.

'What are you talking about?'

'Felix, I've killed him. At least I hope I have.'

Helen considered this. It was what she thought she had heard. 'Good,' she said after a moment.

Richard finished his drink and refilled his glass. She watched him.

'What did you do?' she asked, trying to sound calm.

'I've been wandering around, then driving a bit, then just sitting in the car. I saw a copper watching me, so I had to move. I didn't know what to do. If I'd stayed I might have hit him again. Or I might have had to help him and that would have been worse. Much worse.' He sat down with an air of relief and sipped his drink, even smiled at her. 'I knew you'd understand.'

Helen felt panic. He sounded so matter of fact. She said carefully, 'Darling, could you tell me exactly what you did?'

He lay spreadeagled in the chair like someone at last

relaxing after a long journey. 'I turned out all the lights before I left. I thought that way there was less chance of anyone finding him too soon. I thought the longer he just lay there, the more likely he'd be dead. And I really want him to be dead.'

'Could you go right back to the beginning?' Helen said. She wanted a drink herself but dared not have one. She needed a clear head more. 'Just tell me what happened.'

Richard frowned. 'I think he deserves to die, don't you? After what he did.' His eyes closed and he looked as if, having shed all his responsibilities, he might be about to fall asleep. Helen wondered if he had actually gone mad. She was still thinking how wonderful it would be if Felix was actually dead, only not if Richard had killed him.

'I'm going to have to call an ambulance,' she said angrily. All her instincts cried out that this was unfair.

'Don't,' Richard said without opening his eyes. 'They might save him.'

'Look, I'd love him to be dead, but not if it means you being arrested for murder. Come on, be sensible. We've got to do something. Anyway, what about Elizabeth, won't she be worried? He doesn't usually stay out all night, does he?' Still no response. 'Come on, Richard, you'll have to give me his address. I won't mention any names, just tell them there's been an accident and ring off, OK?'

'He's such a bastard,' Richard suddenly said in a different voice, a faint voice full of pain.

'I know. Where's the flat?'

Elizabeth woke when the television went off and Felix still wasn't home. She was very alarmed. He never stayed out late without letting her know; it was one of the basic courtesies underpinning their marriage. Then she heard a car drawing up outside. She knew it wasn't his car but she rushed to the door all the same. Perhaps he had drunk too much and Richard had given him a lift. She saw Helen getting out of her van.

'I didn't like to ring you this late in case you were asleep,' Helen said, but in a casual way, as if it were the middle of the afternoon, 'so I thought I'd come and see if the lights were on.'

Elizabeth was very frightened.

'Felix hasn't come home. Oh God, it's bad news, isn't it? Something's happened to him.'

Helen came up to her with a reassuring smile that terrified her still more. 'Don't panic, it's all right.'

'What is it? Tell me.'

'He and Richard had a bit of a row and Richard hit him. But don't worry, I've called an ambulance.'

'Ambulance?' She felt stupid repeating Helen's words.

'Can I come in?'

'Is he badly hurt? What d'you mean Richard hit him?'

'Just keep calm,' Helen said with her hand on Elizabeth's arm, guiding her back into the house.

'I don't understand,' Elizabeth said, feeling like a guest in her own hall. 'What happened? Where is he? I've got to be with him.'

'Don't worry, it's not serious,' said Helen with maddening calm.

'You said ambulance.'

'Just to be on the safe side. He bashed his head on the edge of the fireplace.'

'But that's serious. When did all this happen? Where were they?'

'Where Felix works.'

'I don't know where that is.' She started to cry, thinking how little she knew about his life. 'I've never known.'

'Come and sit down,' said Helen like a nurse, leading her into her own living-room. 'It's all right, he'll be fine. Just a little bump on the head, that's all.'

'Have you seen him?'

'No.'

'Then how can you tell?' She was suddenly frantic. What if Felix died? She couldn't live without Felix. 'Oh God, I want to be with him.'

'I'll ring up and find out where he is,' said Helen, soothing, 'and I'll drive you there, OK?'

Elizabeth watched her, busy with the directory, taking charge. Terrible suspicions began to stir in her mind. 'Why did Richard hit him? I knew they were having dinner together, Felix rang me earlier. I didn't worry, I've been asleep. You know something, don't you?'

Helen didn't answer. She was talking to someone else on the phone. She sounded very bossy, Elizabeth thought. 'Have you got Felix Cramer in Casualty? He should have come in just now by ambulance and his wife would like to visit him. Could you check for me? I'll hold.'

Elizabeth said, 'What's all this about? There's something you're not telling me. First Richard leaves you and now he hurts Felix . . . what's going on? You're not telling me the truth.'

'I see. Thank you very much.' Helen put down the phone. 'He's just been admitted. Come on, I'll drive you.'

'You should have let me speak to them.'

'But they don't know anything yet.'

Sudden icy certainty. 'Have you been having an affair with Felix?'

'No, I certainly haven't.'

They stood looking at each other, not moving.

'I don't want you to drive me,' Elizabeth said. 'I'll drive myself.'

When Helen got home she found Richard had gone. She was disappointed rather than surprised, and almost too tired to care. She poured herself the drink she had wanted earlier and took it upstairs, faintly hoping Richard might have gone peacefully to bed, but knowing really that he hadn't. Well, she had done her best. If he preferred to roam the streets or drive around all night, that was his choice. She ran herself a bath, thinking it might relax her and help her sleep. She felt slimy all over from Elizabeth's accusation. An affair with Felix was the most disgusting thing she could imagine, though it was easy to see why Elizabeth should jump to that conclusion. In fact it seemed almost wilfully perverse of her

320

not to suspect Sally by now: it could only be a matter of time. Perhaps tonight's accusation had been the last bit of self-protective fantasy.

In the bath she managed to make her mind a blank for a while, then the nightmare returned. She longed for Felix to die but she had to erase that longing, since it meant Richard going to jail. Even an injury could have serious consequences and her own discretion was irrelevant: if Richard didn't go to the police, Elizabeth would almost certainly report him.

Much to her surprise she fell asleep, the ultimate cop-out, she thought, and woke half an hour later in lukewarm water. She got out of the bath in a rage, feeling disorientated, and went to bed wrapped in a damp bathrobe. She punched the pillow several times before she fell asleep and wasn't sure if the blows were intended for Felix or Richard.

Elizabeth stared at the doctor, willing him to give her good news.

'I'm very sorry,' he said.

'There must be something you can do.'

'We're doing everything we can, but it's early days yet. Look, I realise you've had a terrible shock, but I won't be helping you if I pretend it's not serious. He's got a very nasty head injury and he could be unconscious for quite some time.'

'How long?'

'It's hard to say. Could be hours, could be days.'

'Days . . .'

He looked too young for such a responsible job, and he also looked very tired, as if he should be tucked up in bed instead of answering her questions. How could Felix's life depend on this exhausted well-meaning young man?

'On the other hand,' he added with an encouraging smile, 'he might come round any minute. Is he a heavy drinker?'

She was shocked at the sudden question. It sounded more like an accusation, as if Felix had deliberately made things worse for himself.

'No. Well, it depends.' She thought how insulted Felix

would have been. 'I suppose we both drink a lot of wine, yes. I never really thought of it like that.' To be honest, she couldn't imagine how she and Felix would get through life without alcohol, whether to dull the pain or lift the spirits or simply as a pleasant diversion, but she was aware this wasn't a fashionable view nowadays. It seemed very unfair. Your best friend deals you a heavy blow on the head and you are accused of heavy drinking, like a victim of theft being blamed for carrying money. Doctors had done their best to eliminate smoking, encourage exercise and dieting, and now they were trying to ban alcohol. What did this young man do in his spare time? Why was she suddenly dependent on a naive child for news of her husband? She lit a cigarette rather aggressively, thinking how tolerant Felix was, how he had never tried to cure her of her bad habits. Tears came in her eyes. She really didn't want to live without Felix.

'He seems to have had quite a bit tonight, which doesn't help. We'll know more when we've done a scan. Why don't you come back in the morning? Have a quick look at him now and then go home and get some rest.'

'He's not . . . in any real danger, is he?'

'Frankly, it could go either way. But at the moment he's stable and we've got him on half-hourly observation. If there was any immediate danger I'd tell you, of course, and you could stay. We'll phone you at once if there's any change.'

It was no good. He meant well but he couldn't or wouldn't be reassuring. She was terrified.

'Can I see him now?'

'Yes, of course.' He summoned a nurse. She thought she detected relief that the interview was over. 'Mrs Cramer would like to see her husband now.'

'Would you come this way, Mrs Cramer.' The nurse was another child, of course. The entire health service was in the hands of exhausted children. Felix would be furious to wake up and find himself here; she should have arranged at once for a private clinic. Why else did he pay so much insurance? But it had all happened too fast.

She followed the nurse down the corridor.

*

When Richard left the house he went straight to the police. He felt quite peaceful about giving himself up; in fact the whole experience was remote, as if it were happening to someone else. He thought he might have slept for a while after Helen went out, because he seemed to be in a different frame of mind on his way to the station and he was not sure when the change had occurred. He remembered desperately wanting Felix to be dead, remembered experiencing hatred so violent that it seemed to burn his skin from the inside, but now that was all gone and a feeling of shame and disbelief had taken its place. He had done wrong and he must be punished: that was the only way to restore sanity to his world.

He had trouble making the duty officer take him seriously at first. They knew each other and perhaps he thought Richard was joking, or too calm to have done what he said. But Richard persevered and was allowed to make a statement. Other officers took charge of him and seemed to go out of their way to do everything correctly, by the book.

'Will you read over these notes, Mr Morgan, and sign them as a true record of this interview?'

He tried his best, but his brain roamed round the letters like snakes and ladders without seeing them as words. 'I'm sorry, I can't seem to take it all in.'

'Just initial your replies if they're correct and sign at the bottom of each page.'

That was a relief. He could manage that, although he had to think a moment to remember what his initials were. At least it was easier than reading. 'Oh yes, of course. I ought to know the routine by heart. Funny. I never thought this could happen to me.'

One of the officers peered at him with a worried expression on his face. 'Are you sure you don't want to see a solicitor, sir? You know you have the right to do that.'

'I just want to go to sleep.' Now that the statement was made he was aware of feeling immense exhaustion that was almost a luxury, like putting down a heavy suitcase or reaching the end of a long overnight journey in some foreign country. He was entitled to sleep now: he had earned it. A solicitor would want him to talk, because they always did.

But the officer persisted. 'D'you want anyone informed of your whereabouts?'

'No, I don't think so.'

'Not even your wife?'

He thought about it, but it seemed complicated. Why did they have to ask him such difficult questions when he was so tired?

'I don't think I've got a wife. Or maybe I've got two. Only they're both ex. In a way. I'm not really sure.'

'Then how about letting somebody know at the office?'

Now they were being absurd. 'I'd like to vanish off the face of the earth, if you really want to know.' He looked at his neat initialling: RM over and over again. It looked much more solid than he felt. He handed back the statement. 'There. I'm sure that's all in order.'

She stayed with Felix as long as they would let her. He looked very ill, his skin drained of colour. There was a dressing on his head and he was attached to a drip. She was very frightened, but the sight of him made her instantly calm, so that she could be useful. She held his hand and kissed it and talked to him in a low voice so as not to disturb others in the ward. She remembered reading that unconscious people could hear what was said to them even though they couldn't respond, and hearing it could help them get better. She told him she was there and she loved him and she would stay as long as she could and come back the next day. She told him this over and over again like a litany. At the same time she was aware of thinking that if there was any question of brain damage Felix would not actually want to live and in that case she should not will him to survive. She would have to let him go, no matter what it cost her. She wondered if this thought, too, could reach him, if he could read her mind.

A nurse brought her a cup of tea and this simple act of kindness brought tears to her eyes.

'Better not stay too long,' the nurse said. 'There's nothing you can do and you'll need your sleep.' She took Felix's pulse.

'How is he?'

'There's no change.'

'Just a little bit longer,' Elizabeth begged.

The nurse went away. Elizabeth drank her tea, holding the cup in one hand and Felix's hand in the other. It seemed important not to let go of him. She didn't feel tired at all; she could have sat there all night pouring her strength into him, telling him she loved him. It seemed the only fact of importance left in the world.

Richard was surprised and annoyed the next day to be summoned to see John Hartley. Apparently Helen had rung Marion, and asked her to check with the police. Now Marion had called in her husband to assist. It seemed an amazing impertinence to Richard: a whole chain of interference down the line, spoiling his day. He had slept wonderfully well. He deserved the simplicity and discomfort of his cell. He felt safe having decisions made for him and it seemed appropriate that he should know at first hand how his clients must feel. Above all, he did not want to be disturbed.

'Come on, Richard,' John Hartley said, 'why don't you tell me what this is all about?' He smiled at Richard in a confident way, as if they were friends or colleagues. Richard felt doubly offended.

'I told them I don't want a solicitor.'

'Well, tough. You've got to have someone to represent you in court. They'll have to charge you in thirty-six hours or let you go, and they're not going to let you go while your chum is still unconscious.'

'Is he going to die?' Perhaps John had information. It would be worth seeing him if he had.

'Who knows? If he does, they can do you for manslaughter.'

'Why not? I wanted to kill him.' In his heart he would always be a murderer, whether Felix recovered or not. It was terrible to live with that knowledge. He was no longer the person he had always imagined he was.

'I hope you haven't said that to them. Have you? Look, this is serious. At the very least they've got you for assault with intent.'

'It was very kind of Marion to send you along.' How strange lawyers were, growing fat and prosperous on other people's pain. John looked fairly typical, Richard thought, grey and heavy and pleased with himself. They had met a few times in the past; he was dimly familiar.

'She didn't send me, she asked me to come, and I had to rearrange my day and put off several other clients to fit you in. It's extremely inconvenient, so I hope you're going to be cooperative.'

'You shouldn't have bothered,' Richard said. 'I'm guilty. Whatever they charge me with.' How angry John sounded; how eager he was to hear gratitude.

'If you go on like this, they'll probably make you see a shrink. I hope he gets more out of you than I have. Look, let's start again. Just tell me exactly what happened.'

Days went by and Inge did not hear from Richard. Was he back with the cow or was he alone? The suspense gnawed at her, affecting her sleep, her appetite. After so much excitement she could not bear the flatness of hearing nothing.

'I have to know,' she said. 'Where is he? A lot can happen in a week. I can't just sit here, I must find out.'

The boys were eating. She looked at them in amazement. How could they eat at such a time, when her whole future, and therefore their future, hung in the balance? She didn't remember ever being so detached when she was an adolescent.

'Absolutely not, Mum,' Karl said. 'I'm not ringing up that wretched woman again.'

Peter didn't even glance up from his plate. 'Don't look at me, I'm too young.'

She was very angry. 'Don't call her a woman, she's a cow. And I think you are both very hard-hearted. Don't you care that I'm suffering?'

'Of course we care, but you do it so often. We run out of steam.'

She picked up the phone, enjoying their looks of horror.

'Oh, honestly, you're not —'

'No, of course I'm not. I have other ways to find out, I'm not as stupid as you think. Hullo, can I speak to Richard Morgan? It's his wife.'

'Oh, Mum . . .' It was almost a wail, a pathetic chorus in unison. She was disgusted at their lack of support for her, now when she needed them most.

'Then can I speak to Marion Hartley? Hullo, Marion? It's Inge. I need to speak to Richard. It's very urgent, it's about his children.' She turned her back on their outraged faces. Then Marion told her something incredible. She listened, trying to make sense of the words. 'What? But why, what did he do?' Marion told her more. It couldn't be a joke, could it? Richard had always insisted Marion had no sense of humour. But if it wasn't a joke then it was very serious. 'Really? I must visit him, where is he?'

She had the boys' attention anyway.

'Has something happened to Dad?'

'Is he all right?'

'Ssh, I can't hear. No, Marion, not you. Please tell me everything. I can't believe it. I want to be with him.'

But Marion said that was all she knew. Inge put down the phone and turned to the boys. 'It's impossible but your poor father is in prison.'

They looked at her with awe. 'Blimey,' Karl said.

'They have locked him up because he hit someone on the head.'

'Dad?' said Peter, in a small incredulous voice, almost as if she had suddenly told him his father was someone else.

'You remember the man who came here, the one who had a fat wife, only she didn't come with him?'

'The writer?'

'The old poof?'

Oh yes, they were listening to her now all right.

'He did something very bad and your father beat him up. Maybe he dies, they don't know yet.'

'But you said they were friends.'

'Dad couldn't murder anyone.'

She said with satisfaction, 'You see how quickly things can change.' She was gratified to see they were impressed as well as worried, seeing Richard in a new adventurous light.

Peter said anxiously, 'What will they do to him?'

Inge shrugged. She didn't want to think about that yet.

Karl said with an edge to his voice that meant he was really nervous, 'Mum, are you sure you're not exaggerating just a bit?'

Inge could feel her appetite returning. She stubbed out her cigarette and began to eat. The situation was so exciting. It opened up a whole new range of possibilities. And it served Felix right for abandoning her. It would show him, if he lived, that drama existed in the everyday world, drama could affect him, drama was not safely contained in the newspapers, happening to other people, or under his control in the pages of his silly artificial books. And if he didn't live, well, it would teach him that he was mortal, which no one ever believed. It was only a pity his cock could not be grafted on to someone else.

'You see, underneath, your father is really quite a violent person,' she said, smiling and proud. 'Perhaps he was jealous all the time.'

But later, when she was alone, the excitement ebbed away and she felt cold with fear. It was wonderful that Richard had done such a dramatic thing but Felix would have to live, or they might lock Richard up for years, and she couldn't bear that. She began at once to pray to her god of vengeance for Felix's survival.

By the time they arrived at Victoria, Sally had really had enough. Jamal seemed to have spent the entire journey staring at her, holding her hand, or trying to make conversation,

328

when all she could think about was Helen. There was some dreadful nightmare going on at home, some awful piece of news that Helen was keeping from her; she could tell from her voice. Perhaps Helen was ill. Perhaps she had just found out she had some dreadful disease with only months to live and she was trying to break it gently. God, she couldn't bear it if Helen died. Or perhaps they were getting divorced. That would be bad enough. How would she ever find the strength to see Helen through another divorce? It simply wasn't fair to expect that of her. She had been through enough already.

Jamal said, 'Don't you have time for a coffee?' and he sounded plaintive, which enraged her still further.

'I'd rather get straight home. Mum sounded really odd on the phone. I'm sure there's something wrong.'

'Well, if your step-father still hasn't come home, of course there is.'

Why did he have to say banal obvious things like that when he was really intelligent? Was it something to do with being foreign? 'No, it was more than that. There's something she isn't telling me.'

'Did you ask her what it is?'

'No, I ran out of money.' As if she could ask a question like that on the phone.

He laughed. 'You always do that with your mother.'

'So what? Why is that funny?'

'I thought maybe you didn't really want to talk to her.'

'And that's a joke, is it?' It was amazing how insensitive he could be. Couldn't he see how worried she was?

'No. I'm sorry. I didn't mean to upset you.'

They marched on. The station was crowded, noisy and dirty after Sussex. She was suddenly very tired and her head ached with anxiety. She wanted to be home, to know what was going on. And she was afraid to find out. She could feel more demands would be made on her. She would be expected to be grown up all over again and she still wasn't ready.

'Shall we go out somewhere next week?' Jamal asked in quite a normal voice, as if nothing at all was wrong.

'I don't know, till I find out what's going on at home.'

'Shall I ring you tomorrow? Oh, you still haven't given me your number.'

It was all too much. She stood still, and put down her suitcase and rucksack. Travellers rushed past them in all directions. He turned back to see why she had stopped.

'I'm going to be awfully busy,' she said. 'What with Mum and that reading list we got and . . .' How dreadfully his face changed: all the light went out of it. 'Jamal, I'm sorry. I like you very much but I think we should sort of give it a rest for a bit.'

'You don't want to see me any more?'

Oh God, this was awful. It was like Chris all over again and she still didn't know how to do it. She tried to be gentle and ended up with a worse mess. 'It's not that. I just want a break.'

'Is it because I said I was falling in love with you?'

'I just think we should see a bit less of each other, that's all. I mean next term as well. I think we should just be friends and see other people.' She knew she was saying too much but it seemed impossible now to stop. She wasn't even sure how much she had planned and how much he had provoked in the last hour. 'I mean it's sort of too soon to get tied down, and if you're going to have an arranged marriage eventually you ought to be making the most of your freedom.' It sounded terrible. She hadn't meant to say all that. She hadn't even known she was thinking it. But there was an element of relief as well, of a problem solved, a burden put down. She hated giving pain but even more she hated people clinging on to her.

Silence. She couldn't look at him. She wanted to run away.

'Don't you dare tell me what to do,' he suddenly shouted in an embarrassingly loud voice. 'I've been useful and now it's over. I've served my purpose. That's it, isn't it?' People were staring at them and still he went on. 'I've been an escort at your mother's show, so you didn't have to go alone, and you could make your old lover jealous, and I've let you show me how clever you are in bed, so you could prove everything was still working properly, and now you want to get rid of me, you've had enough.'

'Jamal, please. Don't shout.' She felt herself blushing. It

seemed quite out of character for him to make such a scene in public. He had turned into someone she didn't know.

'Why not? I can shout all I want. I'm not English. I'm not a hypocrite.'

'I'm sorry. I didn't mean to hurt you.'

She was shocked to see he had tears in his eyes.

'Don't you think I have feelings too?'

She couldn't make it all right. She picked up her suitcase and rucksack and walked as fast as she could towards the tube, fearing he would run after her. But he didn't.

Richard liked the court. He liked the familiar look and smell of it, the way that everyone had a job to do. Only his position in it was different this time, but it was still like coming home. The formality of it comforted him. His mother's curtains or three-piece suite, always slightly too big for the room, might have had the same effect.

It didn't take long. He listened to what was said and he agreed with it. He looked at all the people doing their duty and he admired them, he thought they were right. He felt safe. In a little while it would be over.

Helen broke the news as gently as she could but really she was waiting for Sally to hug her, to rush across the room and tell her it would be all right. She wanted Sally to behave like a mother, although her own mother would never have behaved like that. Instead she saw Sally's attention fixed on Felix, hardly hearing what had happened to Richard. There was no hug. 'Why ever didn't you tell me?' Sally said.

'I'm telling you now.'

'I knew something was wrong on the phone. Is Felix going to be all right?'

God, it was hard to take after all the waiting. 'Is that all you can say? You might spare a thought for Richard.' And me, she thought, like a child. What about *me*?

331

Sally was looking very angry, as if Helen had done her some harm. 'Well, both of them, of course, only he's not hurt, is he? Can I see Felix?'

'Don't be bloody stupid. You and Elizabeth, one each side of the bed? Terrific.'

'But he might die.'

Helen abandoned what was left of her self control. 'I'd love him to die, only that wouldn't help Richard. Can you imagine what it's been like for me, trying to pretend to Elizabeth I don't know why all this happened?'

Sally's expression hardened. 'Oh, I see. It's all my fault, is it?'

'Well, you did have something to do with it.'

'I got rid of my baby, isn't that enough for you?' Sally suddenly shouted. And burst into tears.

Helen watched, not going to comfort her. She felt envy and irritation. She felt isolated. 'You're lucky to be able to cry so easily,' she said after a while. 'I wish I could. If you'd only left Felix alone, I'd still have a marriage.'

Sally stopped crying, almost, it seemed, out of shock. 'Is that really how you see it?'

'Tell me another way,' Helen said wearily.

Much to her relief the phone rang, before they could say any worse things to each other. It was John Hartley, and she listened to more bad news, letting it wash over her, watching Sally wipe her eyes and blow her nose. How lovely it must be to let all your feelings out like that. She was strung so tightly she might snap. She had waited all this time for Sally to come home and now she was no help at all. Too much to expect.

'Who was that?' Sally said, looking anxious, when she put down the phone.

'Richard's lawyer. Oh, don't worry, nobody's dead.' She could hardly breathe. 'Just no bail for Richard. They won't let him out. Remanded in custody for another week.'

'Why?'

'They want him to see a psychiatrist. They think he's mad or dangerous or suicidal. God knows what they think. Oh, what does it matter? They won't let him out, that's all.' She

332

was very tired. On it went. On and on. At some level she had imagined him home tonight.

Sally said, 'I'm sorry.'

Helen sat down and put her head in her hands. She said, 'Can we start again? I didn't like all that very much.'

After a moment, not quite soon enough, Sally came across the room and hugged her. She felt very solid. Helen hung on to her tightly and let the tears come.

Elizabeth saw the consultant next day. An older man with a bedside manner, gained no doubt from familiarity with his own bedside, a man exalted enough not to be woken any more in the middle of the night. She gazed at him, imploring him with her eyes to tell her good news.

'Well, your husband's still unconscious,' he said, smiling encouragingly, 'but we've got the results of the scan so you can relax a bit.'

She felt herself daring to breathe.

'No blood clot. No brain damage. Nothing nasty like that.' He looked at her kindly, as if she were a child waking from a nightmare. 'Of course he's not out of the wood yet but it looks hopeful. As far as we can tell.'

She couldn't say anything. She just smiled.

'Best to err on the side of caution, of course,' he said. 'Then, God willing, you get a nice surprise.'

'Oh yes,' she said. 'Yes.'

A nurse was taking Felix's pulse. 'Can you open your eyes for me, Felix?' she kept saying in an encouraging yet oddly detached voice. 'Mm? Can you try?' She was young and pretty. Elizabeth wondered if Felix could tell. Would he wake up faster for a pretty young nurse? Could his unconscious subconscious register that much? Were his instincts still alive and well? She would gladly grant him access to every woman in the world if he would just wake up and be all right.

'Has he woken up at all?' she asked in an ordinary voice, as if it were trivial.

'Not yet, but we like to keep trying.' The nurse bent over him again but in such a practical way that it occurred to Elizabeth she perhaps didn't realise how beautiful he was.

'Are you going to wake up for me, Felix?' she said again, as if he were just any old patient. 'Can you squeeze my hand?'

There was no response.

'Oh well,' she said cheerfully. 'Maybe next time.'

Elizabeth sat down beside the bed and held his hand. He had particularly nice hands; they had both often admired them and agreed it was appropriate for a writer. Her own hands were broad and ugly. Working hands she called them. Helen's hands were different again, the squat, practical hands of the painter or sculptor. She had seen them on plumbers too, with a sort of utilitarian beauty about them. No. What had happened there? She mustn't think about Helen. Not now.

A sound, a movement. It was too wonderful to believe but it was true. It was Felix waking up.

The nurse said brightly, 'Oh, isn't that nice? He did it for you.'

Elizabeth started to cry. 'Oh, Felix,' she said. 'Your timing's wonderful.'

She had to do something when visiting time ended. Not that he had spoken or sat up or anything miraculous like that, but there had been that sound. a murmur. meaningless, of course, and he had moved, it showed there was hope, he was coming back to her and she wanted to give thanks. She bought flowers. She drove around. She found herself outside Helen's house. Forgiveness, she thought. If I can be generous then God will be too. I can't live without Felix. I love him so much. Do other people feel like this?

Helen came to the door. She looked surprised. She smiled but she looked wary, even reluctant.

334

'He's woken up,' Elizabeth said.

'Oh good,' said Helen, with a tight smile. 'I'm glad for you.'

She really does hate him seriously, Elizabeth registered. It wasn't a joke or a tease. There is something enormous here.

'So I brought you these.' She gave Helen the flowers.

'Thank you. They're lovely.'

'I felt so high. I had to do something to celebrate. I mean, I could have just rung you up but . . . After all, it's good for Richard too, isn't it?' Perhaps Helen had had bad news. She must ask. 'How is he? Have you heard anything?'

Helen's face closed down. 'Remanded in custody for a week. And he doesn't want to see me.'

'Oh, I'm sorry.' A greater effort was called for. 'Look, Helen, about the other night. I said something I shouldn't have said and I'd like to take it back. Can you just put it down to the stress of the moment?'

'Of course,' Helen said. 'It's all forgotten.'

It was odd to be still on the doorstep. Normally she would have been asked in at once. There was music from upstairs, too, well, not really music, odd sounds, a beat.

She said bravely, 'I still think there's something you're not telling me but it's not what I said.'

Helen looked cornered, angry. 'Honestly, I don't know any more than you do. It's something between the two of them. Men can have secrets too, you know, just like us.'

It didn't feel right at all. 'I expect you're trying to protect me,' she said, 'but I'm a bit old for that.'

'Would you like to come in?' Helen said then.

There was a movement on the stairs. Elizabeth, hesitating, saw Sally about to come down.

'No, thanks,' she said. 'I'd rather get home.'

'She knows,' Helen said, closing the door. 'She must.'

'How's Felix?' Sally said.

'Recovering, apparently. Is that all you care about?'

Sally shrugged. 'Then they'll let Richard out, won't they?

335

And that's all *you* care about. Shall I make scrambled eggs? You should eat something.'

Elizabeth, driving home, pushed the thoughts away. Be like Scarlett O'Hara. Think about that tomorrow. Be grateful. Take it a day at a time. If God lets Felix get better, then I won't question anything.

She drove carefully. Not the moment to have an accident. It was a demanding job, life-saving, and she needed all her wits about her.

Richard resented any interruption in his routine. As long as they left him alone he was safe. He didn't want news from the outside world. When John Hartley told him Felix was recovering he couldn't even feel relief, in fact it seemed almost irrelevant. The image of the new recovering Felix simply lined up beside the older one he had killed.

He needed to make sense of himself and his guilt, and to do that he had to see Sally. Felix's words haunted him. He asked John Hartley to arrange a visit.

'They want you to see a shrink,' John Hartley said. 'That's more to the point. Now don't look like that. Her name's Jennifer Daley. You'll like her.'

Jennifer Daley was small and dark with hair that fell over her face. She kept pushing it back like someone modelling sixties clothes. Inge had worn her hair like that once but it had not been straight enough and drove her mad because it wouldn't flop correctly. He remembered her rages well.

He could see that Jennifer Daley was a good, well-intentioned person, but for some reason she brought out the anger in him. She looked too young for her job. She looked like an actress pretending to be a psychiatrist, as if she had been brought in to tease him with her sexuality. And yet he had to be careful, in case she could make things worse for him. He found himself wanting to hit her, and his anger frightened him; he did not know whom it was meant for.

'You know this can't work if I don't cooperate,' he said to her. 'And I'm not going to.'

'Why's that?' she said.

He laughed. 'Come on, spare me all that. I cut my teeth on it.'

'Don't you want to get bail?'

'I've nowhere to go.' What stupid questions they asked. 'I'm better off here.'

'You've left your wife, is that right?'

'You know all this, why ask me?'

'When did you leave her?'

'I don't remember.' It seemed a very long time ago but he knew it couldn't be. 'Last week or the week before. Maybe ten days ago. Ask her. She's sure to remember. She's extremely efficient. She probably made a note in her diary.'

All the months that Helen had lived with him since Sally's abortion. All the normal life they had had, eating and sleeping, talking and making love, all the ordinary things they had done together, and she had known all the time. She had betrayed him and kept her secret and behaved as if nothing had happened. She had behaved as if he didn't exist and she had gone on living with him.

'You sound very angry with her,' Jennifer Daley said.

'Yes, I do have to get pretty angry with someone before I walk out on them. Especially if I'm married to them.'

'And even angrier before you hit them?'

He laughed again. They were so predictable, these people. 'My God, you're brighter than I thought. You're really getting there.'

'Did you want to kill your friend when you hit him?'

'No, but I hoped he was dead the moment after.'

'And now?'

'And now what?'

She fiddled with her hair. 'What are you feeling now?'

337

'Pretty angry with you for asking all these bloody stupid questions.'

To be locked up for ever, that would be peaceful.

'Go on.'

'Isn't that enough for you?'

Jennifer Daley said, 'I'm sorry, I'm not very experienced yet.'

This threw him. 'Oh God, am I supposed to feel sorry for you?'

'No, we all have to start somewhere,' she said, sounding composed. 'But I thought it was only fair to warn you.'

Silence. He longed to be alone. He'd had enough.

'D'you feel sorry for lots of people?'

That was a joke. 'In my line of work, yes I do.'

'As well as feeling angry with them?'

'Sometimes.' And wanting to be dead, there was that feeling too, but she was too young to understand about that.

'And how d'you feel about yourself?'

He wanted to explode. 'Yes, that's the big one, isn't it? Sad. Angry. Is that what you want to hear? I hate myself, will that do nicely? Is that *appropriate*, as you people say? My life's an absolute shambles. I deserted my first wife and kids, now I've lost my second wife and my best friend. I think if you'd done all that, you might feel quite pissed off with yourself too.'

Her hair fell forward again and she pushed it back. He wanted to kill her for being young and stupid and innocent. Life hadn't tarnished her yet. Sally had been like that once.

'I think you're in a lot of pain,' she said, 'and I'd like to help you work through it.'

'Well, don't. That's how I got into this mess, trying to help people.' He saw her eyes look startled. 'Go and take up a nice clean trade. Go and work in a slaughterhouse. Something like that. Where you can really see results at the end of the day.'

He wondered afterwards if he was going mad. But that was for her to find out. It hardly mattered.

*

338

Felix was profoundly impressed that he might have died: it was a solemn fact. He thought it would give greater meaning to the rest of his life and oblige people to behave better towards him. He was also aware that sooner or later he would have some explaining to do. And he had a very sore head.

The ward was grotesque, full of extremely sick people, some of whom were repulsive or made strange sounds. The hours kept were not to his taste, the food and drink on offer were quite extraordinary, and the discomfort of his bed made him very thoughtful. On the whole he found the entire experience rather surreal. He wondered if he had forgotten anything of importance; and he wondered how soon he could escape.

There was a bedside table crowded with flowers and fruit. Elizabeth sat beside it, looking at him with a sort of honeymoon expression, as if he had risen from the dead, which in a sense he supposed he had. She was smiling a lot and at the same time looking as if she might burst into tears at any moment.

'Oh darling,' she said, 'you gave me such a fright.'

He kept thinking of Richard and the attack, and then waking up here. There didn't seem much in between, and yet there was, known only to others. He didn't like thinking he'd been absent that long; it was reminiscent of *Lost Weekend* without the fun and gave other people an unfair advantage over him. He thought he looked older, too, and he could do without that. He had asked for a mirror and had a careful look. Perhaps it was just shock and would wear off.

'Yes,' he said, 'I scared myself a bit too.'

Amazing to think old Richard had all that violence in him. He'd never have been so provocative if he'd known. But locking him up was absurd.

'How are you feeling now?'

Elizabeth was like a sort of auxiliary nurse, he thought. Eager for good news. Any moment now she might pop a thermometer or a grape in his mouth, plump up his pillows. It was appalling to think that some people spent years like this. It was like being an overgrown baby in some science fiction tale.

'Pretty weird,' he said. 'D'you know what I said when I first came round?'

'No. I wasn't here, damn it.'

'I said, "Where am I?" Isn't that humiliating? You'd think I could have come up with something a bit more original.'

She laughed weakly. It was always good if he could make her laugh, but he was seriously shocked by his own dialogue. A blow on the head was no excuse for banality.

'What are you going to tell the police?'

'The truth, of course.' But he was alarmed; it seemed a bit soon for such a question. 'The whole truth and nothing but the truth. Or at least as much as it takes to make them go away and leave me alone.'

'And what are you going to tell me?'

Really she was pushing hard. Surely the jaws of death and all that could not be discounted so swiftly?

'Oh, darling,' he said. 'Not now. I'm very tired and I've had one hell of a crack on the head.'

'Your best friend tries to kill you and that's all you can say?'

'We were larking about. It was all a silly accident.' He had made up his mind about that, whatever Richard might say, and her disbelieving look annoyed him. 'Oh, come on, darling. I'm saving my energies for the old bill.' He closed his eyes for a moment to make her feel guilty, but he was genuinely tired and then there were manipulative layers of tiredness as well, a protective screen. 'There is something you can do for me though. Get me moved to a private room. Put the whole thing on Bupa. It didn't matter while I was out for the count, but now – dear God, there are people coughing and spitting day and night, I don't know how I'm going to sleep now I've woken up, and it's impossible to get a drink round here.' He held her hand and kissed it. 'Really, hospitals are pretty barbaric places once they've saved your life.'

John Hartley asked, 'How did you get on with Jennifer Daley?' He seemed excited by her visit.

'Who?' said Richard, just to annoy him.

'Your shrink.'

'Oh, she tried hard.'

'Don't be fooled by that little girl approach, she's actually quite astute. Mind you, between ourselves, I have trouble hearing what she says because I can't take my eyes off her legs.'

He grinned at Richard as if demanding some sort of complicity and Richard stared back astonished. It threw fresh light on Marion's marriage. John seemed to him like a sniggering small boy in the playground. Was he supposed to laugh?

'Now, with a bit of luck we should get bail this time,' John said, professional again. 'Your chum's going to live and a lot depends on what he says to the police. Is he a forgiving sort of chap, d'you think? Willing to let bygones be bygones and all that?'

Chum. It seemed an odd word for Felix, for someone you'd tried to kill. It had a *Boy's Own* and *Beano* ring to it. 'I don't want to be forgiven,' Richard said. 'I'm guilty and I want to be punished.'

'Oh, come on, Richard,' John said as if he had caught him cheating at cards, 'that's not the right approach at all. Where would we all be if everyone took that attitude? I'd be out of a job for a start.'

'What's the worst that can happen?' Richard was suddenly frightened, a new strange feeling coming at him out of nowhere. He wondered how John would react if he panicked, begged for help, cried? He felt he could no longer predict or control his own behaviour.

'Well, if they decide to go ahead but they stick to assault with intent, you could wind up on probation.'

Richard laughed.

'Yes. Sorry about that. On the other hand if your chum gets a bit heavy, they might go for attempted murder. You didn't help yourself much with that statement you made. Just begging to be locked up, that's the way it reads. Of course that could make them decide you're a genuine nutter and they'll let you out, just to be awkward.'

And where do I go then? Richard thought. John made it all sound quite jolly. He didn't see the abyss.

'I often wish I was dead,' Richard said. 'Oh, not in a suicidal way, I'm much too limp to do anything about it, but I do keep thinking how peaceful it would be.'

'Try telling Jennifer that,' John said eagerly. 'She's very good on depression.'

But Sally was the only person he wanted to see.

Felix had just about settled into his private room by the time the police arrived to interview him. He thought the whole thing was very theatrical and he wondered if he was up to it, if he had sufficient reserves of energy. He hoped they wouldn't stay long; he was rather looking forward to watching television, enjoying the privacy of his own bathroom, playing some music on his cassette machine and generally pretending he was in a hotel. Later he would have to persuade his consultant to allow him some wine with his meals. He really didn't have much time to spare for the fuzz.

'But surely,' he said, 'if I don't press charges, you haven't got a case.'

'I'm afraid it's not as simple as that, sir. The court doesn't have to proceed but Mr Morgan can be charged on his own confession.'

'But that's ridiculous,' Felix said. 'I'm the one in hospital and if I don't want to make a fuss why the hell should anyone else?' It had never occurred to him that Richard could be charged against his wishes; he had been looking forward to being magnanimous, heaping coals of fire and all that. Love your enemy. Do good to those that hurt you. Forgiveness felt like a powerful weapon. It was annoying to be told that the pathetic wheels of the law could grind away without his consent.

'If you could just tell us what happened.'

One of them asked questions and the other took down the answers. Behind the politeness he felt suspicion, as if he might be a criminal instead of a victim, and he found it irksome.

'It was an accident,' he said firmly. He had given a lot of thought to this and had come up with a scenario he found so convincing he was almost beginning to believe it himself. 'We'd had a few drinks and we were acting out a scene from my new book. I've only just finished it and I wanted to make sure I'd got it right, so I said come on, hit me, see how far I can roll. I'm very keen on getting details absolutely correct.'

He wasn't sure if they were impressed by his fame or whether he should play it down.

'Go on, sir.' Their faces gave nothing away but he had the same feeling of unease as going through customs at the airport.

'Well, he couldn't do it. I mean he's a really nice bloke and thumping people just isn't his style.' Unlike Tony Blythe, he thought. 'So just to get him going I said something about fancying his wife or maybe it was his ex-wife or both, I really can't remember, but anyway I made some stupid joke that obviously got him on the raw and he hit me. If I hadn't bashed my head on the edge of the mantelpiece I'd have been perfectly all right.'

'What time did all this take place?'

Oh dear, it was hard work. He could feel his energy flagging and he had a long way to go yet. 'I'm not sure. It was early evening because Richard came straight from work. Seven or eight maybe. I was a bit jet-lagged from holiday and I'd had lunch with my agent, so I had a bit of a kip before he arrived. That's why I'm not too sure of the time.'

'Was it dark?'

'I really can't remember. I didn't know I'd have to describe the evening in such detail or I'd have paid more attention. Does it matter?'

'It was after midnight when your friend's wife called an ambulance.'

Felix could feel irritation swamping his desire to be charming. 'Was it really?'

'So you'd been lying on the floor of your flat for several hours.'

'I'll have to take your word for it. I was unconscious so I really didn't notice time dragging.'

343

Not a flicker of amusement. 'If you could just bear with me, sir. I'm trying to establish what your friend did during those hours.'

'Perhaps you could try asking him.'

'Yes, we did think of that, but he seemed rather vague on the subject. Just wandered about, he said.'

'Then that's what he did. He's extremely truthful.'

'So if he says he was hoping you'd die, we can believe him.'

God, how they twisted everything. 'Certainly not. He's truthful but he's also very confused. He's been under a lot of strain at work and at home and obviously something snapped. He probably lost his memory, poor chap.'

They both looked at him thoughtfully.

'You do realise the longer the interval between knocking you down and calling an ambulance, the more it looks as if he wished you to come to some harm?'

Well, of course he realised that. No one had ever tried to kill him before. Ironic it should be Richard. What deep feelings must be there. It was almost a tribute.

'I can assure you he didn't. He's been having marriage problems and he must have flipped.'

'So your vagueness about the time wouldn't have anything to do with trying to protect him?'

'Rather more to do with a bump on the head, I'd have thought.' He was getting tired: they had a heavy presence. 'But you're quite right, I am trying to protect him, not just because he's my friend but also because he's innocent. I think it's quite absurd you've got him locked up. I'd be happy to stand bail for him if necessary.'

They didn't look as if they believed a word he was saying.

'You're an extremely forgiving man, Mr Cramer.'

'Well, I've known Richard for twenty years and I value his friendship. I'm not going to let a silly accident change that. And I'm certainly not going to testify against him in court.'

'You can be subpoenaed to give evidence, you know, sir.'

How eager they seemed to make trouble. Perhaps promotion depended on it.

'Well, let's hope it doesn't come to that. It would be a terrible waste of public money.' He tried his charming smile on them. 'Can I have a rest now?'

'We've nearly finished, sir. Mr Morgan says you had a quarrel about a woman.'

'Wasn't that what I just said? Look, I'm very tired and I think I've answered enough questions for one day.'

'But he didn't say she was his wife or even his ex-wife. In fact he refused to name her.'

It was all getting much too close to home. 'Well, there you are. He's a perfect gentleman.'

'And he didn't mention acting out a scene from your new book.'

'I told you, his memory's probably not so hot. He's got a lot of problems at the moment.'

Surely that was enough? He was exhausted.

'Mr Cramer, what's your latest book about?'

Suddenly this seemed like a very sinister question. But it was absurd. Why should he let them disturb him?

'A homosexual murder.'

Sally didn't want to be there. 'He'll be out in a few days, what's the point?' she kept saying, but Helen had bullied her into it, making her feel guilty if she refused, implying that it was a matter of life and death, as if Richard were being hung up by his thumbs and Sally could save him. In the end Sally agreed furiously: she knew she was going as Helen's deputy and she resented it. She couldn't feel the same about Richard any more, knowing what he had done to Felix: it altered her whole perception of him and made him seem like a stranger, hostile and slightly crazed. Most of all she didn't want to go inside a prison but she couldn't say that to Helen, who was longing to go and be reconciled.

Everything about it dismayed her: the formality, the smell, the other people. It made her feel like a criminal herself. She thought it was unfair that she was expected to visit him under such conditions when he had got himself into this mess. He looked suitably grateful, though, somehow cowed and subdued.

'It was good of you to come,' he said.

She had meant to say she wanted to see him, one good honest lie to cheer him up, but when it came to it, she couldn't get the words out.

'I know,' he said, reminding her against her will of the old Richard who had understood things, 'it's awful, isn't it?'

She attacked at once on sure ground, before she could get snarled up in feeling sorry for him. 'Richard, what about Mum? She's so upset. Why won't you see her?'

All the warmth went out of his face: he must have put it on just for her. 'I've nothing to say to her. We've said it all.'

'But she's in a terrible state and I have to cope with it.'

'I'm sorry. You're having a rotten time, aren't you?'

But what use was that, sounding compassionate if he wasn't prepared to do anything? What did she say when she went home to Helen?

'How could you hurt Felix?' she said. 'How could you? It was between me and him. It was nothing to do with you.'

He looked at her as if seeing the child she used to be. 'Oh, Sally. Don't you understand anything?'

'But it was none of your business. It was all over. God, it was six months ago.' She wished she could stop thinking about dates. 'It was private. How could you go round there and hit him? How could you leave him like that? He might have died.' And next month it would have been born, she thought. Would anyone else remember that?

Richard didn't appear to be listening. He said, 'Sally, I want to ask you something very important. Will you tell me the truth? It's not easy to ask, but I've done a lot of thinking in here and . . . I'm very embarrassed, so please bear with me.'

God, this was awful. He was going to ask her something terribly intimate about Felix, about sex, something he had no right to ask. She couldn't imagine what it was but she wanted to run away.

'I don't know what you're talking about,' she said.

He clasped his hands together as if he were praying. 'I

know you're very angry with me and you've every right, but will you please think back and give me an honest answer. Have you ever felt I wasn't like a proper father to you? I mean, have I ever made you feel uncomfortable or . . . well, have you ever felt I was, what can I say, lusting after you?'

She was appalled. It was such a horrible idea. It had never entered her head and now it was fixed there for ever. Was he telling her that was how he had felt?

'I'm sorry,' he said, 'but I really need to know. I've never been aware of it but maybe I've suppressed it.'

She said violently, 'God, I never thought about it.'

'Then he was wrong.' He looked extraordinarily relieved. 'Only that's why I hit him. That's what Felix said, that I was jealous.'

Sally got up. All she could think was that she didn't want to hear all this.

'Don't go yet,' he said. 'I had to ask you.'

'You're just trying to put me off Felix, aren't you?'

He looked very serious and yet as if he thought he was entitled to behave like this. 'I need to feel I've got something right and I'd like it to be our relationship.'

She couldn't stand the weight of it. It was bad enough having to cope with Helen, who at least was her mother. And she had problems of her own. Nobody was helping her.

'I don't want to listen to this,' she said. 'You're trying to make out it was my fault you hurt Felix and it isn't.'

She cried tears of anger on the way home and felt better. Helen wasn't there, so she went to the studio and found her sitting on the floor, hugging her knees, head bent. A dramatic attitude but she knew it wasn't a pose and all her anger melted. Perhaps she had used it up on Richard. The smell of the studio reassured her too. She hadn't realised how much she'd missed it since she'd been away. Helen had had the studio longer than the house. It had been their earliest home alone together; she didn't remember the flat. The studio had a reality like nowhere else. The smell of paint and turps was the

347

smell of creativity that went on no matter what else happened. Helen had survived Carey. She could survive Richard. She would go on painting. Sally just had to be patient and loving. It would be an effort but it was worth it. Helen was solid and real.

'I knew you'd be here,' she said, thinking poor Mum, loving Richard more than I knew and he's let her down, what a mess.

'I can't work,' Helen said. 'Can't do anything.'

'You will. Give yourself a chance. It's a bit soon.' She sat down on the dusty floor beside her.

'How was Richard?'

What to say? 'A bit weird. Very wrapped up in himself.'

'Any message?'

'No. Sorry.'

Helen rested her head on her knees, put her hands round her face. Sally thought she looked very beautiful, not old at all. Just tired and sad.

'Come on, Mum. You've still got me. And all this. Remember there was only the two of us for years and years and we managed.'

Helen produced a sort of smile. 'I wish I could cry a bit more.'

'Keep trying.'

Silence. She held one of Helen's hands. She liked the feel of it, the knobbly knuckles, knowing what it could do.

'Magdalen wants me to go to the oast house tomorrow,' Helen said presently. 'See Jerome Ellis and those ghastly paintings I did for him.'

'They weren't ghastly. They were OK.'

'If you like that kind of thing.'

They both managed a small giggle. Helen put her arm round Sally.

'You should go,' Sally said. 'Do you good. Take your mind off things.'

'Come with me?'

But that was going too far. 'No. I want to see Jackie and Maria.'

*

348

What she in fact did was get her hair cut. She had been thinking about it for a while and now was a good time. But she didn't want to tell anyone. It seemed such a large gesture. She remembered Felix telling her never to do it and she felt rebellious. Maria was a hairdresser now and Jackie worked in a bank, so she could have a chat, cash a cheque and get her hair cut all in one afternoon.

She wanted it very short but Maria wouldn't do it. 'It's too much all at once. It's halfway down your back. You can't have it up round your ears all at once, you'll hate it and you'll blame me.'

'It'll be like culture shock,' said Jackie and they both laughed.

'It's my hair,' Sally said, 'and I want to look different. Really different.'

'You could always have it permed. Have an afro.'

'Or dye it red or something.'

'Or both.'

'No, that'll make it fall out.'

'Well, bald would be different.'

They stood round peering at her and she felt the centre of attention. It was strange to be back with them, like a time warp, before anything had happened to her. Like a space capsule re-entering her childhood. They didn't envy her Sussex, or if they did, one look at her reading list cured them. She was really pleased to see them again and yet she felt they had nothing to say to each other, she felt a million years old.

In the end Maria cut it so it rested on her shoulders, and she was quite right, it was enough of a shock.

'You should keep the piece, you could wear it as a plait.'

But Sally said no, she wanted it thrown away.

Once the euphoria of not being dead wore off, and the relief of getting a private room, Felix began to feel rather bad-tempered. His back ached and he wanted to go home. He imagined Richard might well feel the same about jail, in fact it was quite amusing that they should both be incarcerated at the same time. It would give them a lot to talk about when they eventually met again.

He wondered what would happen to the friendship. Did an attempted murder make for greater or lesser intimacy? Was forgiveness a bond or a deterrent? He liked to imagine a sort of camaraderie of the trenches in World War One would result, a blend of Owen and Sassoon, but he might be entirely wrong.

Elizabeth seemed unduly interested in his visit from the police. He told her what he had told them but she didn't look any more convinced than they had.

'Dirty little minds they've got, the fuzz,' he said, trying to make light of it. 'I wonder if the job attracts people like that or if they develop these tendencies on the job, as it were. Gives a whole new meaning to the boys in blue.'

She wanted to know what they had said to him.

'D'you know, I could have sworn they didn't believe my story. They more or less implied old Richard and I had a lovers' quarrel. Imagine that.'

'What d'you mean, story?' she said.

'My statement. About the accident.'

'Story sounds like fiction.'

'Well, I may have tarted it up a bit to put poor old Richard in a better light.' He liked his new big-hearted image.

'Helen once said you were like David and Jonathan.'

'What's that supposed to mean?'

' "And David and Jonathan made a covenant, for he loved him as his own soul." '

'Fancy you knowing that. I really like being married to a dictionary of quotations. Saves me looking them up.'

'Would it be dirty if it was a lovers' quarrel?'

'No, of course not, just inaccurate.' Was she also accusing him of being gay? What a joke. 'Mind you, there is a pleasing symmetry about it. Tony Blythe gets murdered by golden-eyed Sebastian, and I get punched on the jaw by Richard. Serves me right for borrowing his eyes.'

'Yes, that's curious,' she said.

'Only life imitating art. Happens all the time.'

*

Helen enjoyed the drive into Kent. Magdalen drove fast and well and entertained her with scandal about people in the art world whom they both knew. Although she hadn't wanted to go and had ridiculed the idea, she had to admit now that Sally and Magdalen were right: she did feel taken out of herself and it was doing her good. Even the scenery was reassuring: there really was a world out there with trees and fields, houses and other people. Her world had narrowed down recently to home, studio and prison. It was good to know not everyone was locked up.

The oast house was beautiful, set in lovely countryside, and Jerome had obviously spent a great deal of money doing it up. He was touchingly pleased to see her and she felt humbled that the time had come when she was actually pleased to see him.

'You see, Helen,' he said, waving his arm round the circular room. 'What did I tell you? Don't they look great?'

It was a shock to see the paintings again. She could feel Magdalen willing her to be tactful. Actually they did not look as bad as she had feared. She thought now she saw them together *in situ* that they were too small for the space, but away from the studio they had a surprising cohesion that they had lacked while competing with her other work. And they looked so unlike anything else she had ever done that she could almost dissociate herself from them. She could hardly believe these colours, these shapes were hers. She had signed them on the back. Perhaps in a little while she could forget she had ever done them. And perhaps also they were not altogether shaming.

'I'm glad you're pleased with them,' she said.

'Wait till you see your painting in the john.' He was wearing another brilliant jacket that hurt her eyes. 'Reckon that makes it the classiest john in the whole of Kent.'

She had to get used to the fact that a serious painting of hers called *Self* now hung in Jerome's lavatory and he was proud of it. She had to remember that he had embarrassed Felix for her at her show and therefore he was a person who deserved gratitude and respect. Perhaps he really didn't see any difference in quality between the different paintings. It was a curious thought.

'If we don't eat soon,' Mario said, 'everything will be spoilt.' He was in charge of the cooking and kept darting out to the kitchen and coming back with an anxious expression.

'OK, Mario, don't panic,' Jerome said. He seemed unconcerned about food. Helen thought how much she would hate to cook for him. 'Have another dry Martini and relax. You know I want to sell Helen on the idea of doing a gigantic mural in the bedroom. A complete bacchanalia. Helen, how about that? Pan, Dionysus, the whole shebang. How does that grab you?'

Helen smiled. She thought the idea, though unsuitable for her, had a certain lurid charm, and she could think of several painters who might take to it very well. 'I think you need a representational painter for that.'

'Sounds like a big job,' Magdalen said. 'Maybe Helen needs time to think about it.'

Jerome lit a cigar. 'Nonsense, it's more subtle if it's abstract. Half the people who come in here can't tell which deadly sin is which, and I like that, it makes a good talking point.'

'Don't listen to him, Helen,' Mario said. 'He just likes making people do things they don't want to do.'

'Mario, don't you have something to do in the kitchen right now?'

Mario refilled his glass and went out.

'I think it's a very challenging idea,' Magdalen said.

'Take your time, Helen,' said Jerome. 'There's no one else I'm gonna ask. I want a total look for this place.'

A yell from Mario. 'We have a soufflé and we eat it now.'

'That sounds urgent,' Magdalen said. 'I'll go and give him a hand.'

As soon as they were alone Jerome leaned forward and touched Helen's arm. 'Helen, I'm really sorry to hear about your family trouble.'

Helen was startled. How much had Magdalen told him? She felt betrayed but she was also touched by his genuine concern. And the Martinis were strong. She could feel a sensation like mist gathering inside her head, a fear that after struggling to cry safely with Sally she might burst into easy tears in front of Jerome. She felt tired and hungry and drunk, unfit to be out, yet glad to be away from home. It was very confusing.

'Thank you,' she said.

'Yeah, I can really empathise with you. Mario got himself locked up once and I had one hell of a job getting him out.'

He knew too much and yet she was relieved. It made her troubles seem more ordinary, something that could happen to anyone, inconvenient but normal, like needing a plumber in the middle of the night, and therefore more capable of solution. She began to feel hope again.

Mario yelled from the kitchen, 'Don't bother, it's ruined,' and Magdalen returned, smiling like a hostess determined to save the day. 'Don't believe him, it looks wonderful.'

'And I'm not sure it was worth it,' Jerome said.

Suddenly she envied them just for being a couple, able to have fights because they were still together.

Felix, resting with closed eyes, let his thoughts drift. The new book, how to deal with Richard when they both got out, whether Elizabeth really suspected the truth, all these fragments whirled about in his head like snowflakes in a paperweight, important and decorative but insubstantial. Until he was home, he felt, none of these issues would have much reality. Hospital was time out, like floating on his back in a hotel pool. There was not much he could do about anything while he was here.

He heard someone knock and come in, felt them stand there watching him. Not a nurse; it was a different quality of watching. He opened his eyes and saw Sally, a new Sally with shoulder-length hair. He was instantly very alert, aware of the dramatic possibilities of the situation. At last something was actually happening in this place.

'Hullo,' he said. 'My God, you've cut your hair.' It made her look older and smarter; he remembered telling her not to do it. And yet it had a certain streetwise charm. The untidy romantic child had gone. No more Tess of the d'Urbervilles.

Well, at least no one else would have her hair cascading over them, stroking their body, playing Mary Magdalen, the way he had.

'Surprise,' she said. 'D'you like it?'

'It's wonderful. But you look like someone else.'

'That was the idea.'

They stared at each other, smiling slow, delighted smiles.

'And you've just missed Elizabeth.'

'I know. I rang up and checked with the nurse. I think she enjoyed feeling she was involved in a plot. It probably helps that you're famous.' She paused. 'I always talk too much when I'm nervous.'

How strange it was, after six months without contact, that they were instantly conspirators again. 'My God, how devious you've become.'

'That's what two terms at Sussex does for you. I didn't know you wear pyjamas.'

'Isn't it shaming? Elizabeth had to buy them specially. Oh Sally, it's so lovely to see you. Come a bit nearer.'

She walked towards the bed but stopped out of touching distance.

He said, 'Darling, I'm so sorry about what happened. I've never had the chance to say it before. But I've thought so much about you. I kept wondering how you were. Only when you didn't write again I thought maybe you wanted to be left alone.'

'Don't, you'll set me off.'

But she moved closer to him and they held hands. He thought what power there was in touch. She looked so fresh and new, and yet he knew what she'd been through and it altered his whole perspective of her. He hadn't felt so turned on in months. God, he'd like to make love to her again. Wipe out the bad memories.

'Are you really all right now?' she said.

'Right as rain. Christ, what a cliché. You can see my brain's got scrambled in here. Wearing pyjamas can seriously damage your health. What's right about rain, for God's sake?'

They laughed. They were still holding hands loosely, without pressure. Innocently, avoiding significance.

'I was so frightened,' she said.

'So was I.'

'And angry with Richard.'

Her hair swung back and forth as she moved her head.

'Oh, poor old Richard. He was only thinking of you. Doing his good step-father bit. If I hadn't collided with the fireplace I'd have been fine.'

'Right as rain.'

'Yes.'

'A bit over the top though, wasn't it?'

'Straight out of Tony Blythe.'

'But it could have been fatal.'

'Well, I suppose so.'

They were both silent, impressed by the drama they had caused.

She said, 'Felix . . .' and it moved him, just hearing his name like that. 'Can I tell you something? I'll never be sorry about us. It was worth it. When I wrote you that awful letter I was bitter and miserable but I feel different now. I've grown up a bit.'

He was touched by her generosity. 'I don't deserve that.'

'Yes, you do. It wasn't your fault, what happened. And I feel a bit guilty. If I hadn't written that letter, Richard would never have found out and you wouldn't be in here.'

'Oh well. It's all useful experience. I wouldn't have chosen it but I can always write about it.'

'Yes, I suppose so.'

He felt her hand waver in his grasp, so he kissed it and let it go. Watching her, he saw her eyes widen on the kiss.

'Have some grapes,' he said. 'Have a drink. They don't really approve but I've finally got some alcohol in here and it's a great relief, I can tell you. The first few days, it was like being in Saudi Arabia.'

They smiled again. There was immense unformulated goodwill in the room with nowhere to go. He poured two glasses of wine. He hated her seeing him in pyjamas.

'You'll always be special,' she said. 'Whoever I meet later on. I won't ever forget you.'

'Well, here's looking at you, kid.'

'Yes.'

They drank their drinks. He thought it was time to be brave.

'How's that handsome boyfriend of yours?'

'Oh, that's all over.'

Well, that was worth knowing. 'Poor chap. I thought he looked very taken with you.'

'Yes, he was, he was sweet. But I don't want to get tied down.'

Now what exactly did that mean? Was she playing the field or playing hard to get? It felt like a challenge but he wasn't sure of his ground.

'If I'm ever passing through Sussex, shall I look you up?'

'Why not? I'm not on the phone. But you could always take pot luck.'

Elizabeth tired of waiting for the lift and decided to climb the stairs. She was pleased with her purchases and eager to make amends for asking Felix too many awkward questions. She felt she had broken her promise to herself, the bargain she had made with God, that if Felix recovered then nothing else mattered. She must remember how terrified she had been at the thought he might die: it was amazing how quickly the memory faded. Perhaps she was not meant to know too much about his friendship with Richard.

She was walking down the corridor, slightly out of breath, when she saw Sally coming out of Felix's room, and Sally saw her. They were only yards apart.

She said, 'Hullo, Sally.'

Sally blushed deeply. 'Hullo. I've just been to see Felix.'

'Yes, so I see.'

She didn't want to believe what this meant.

'Richard asked me to come and see how he was,' Sally said.

'Oh, that was nice of him.'

'Yes, he's feeling awfully guilty about what happened.'

It was too painful. She would rather believe anything else.

They seemed locked in the corridor together, unable to move apart, she and this child she had been fond of, had envied Helen for having, had watched grow up, who wasn't a child after all.

'How's Sussex?' she asked.

'Oh, fine. I'm enjoying it. Lots of new people. I'm having a great time.'

'Good.'

Perhaps it could yet be innocent. Richard must feel guilty, he would send Sally. She was the only possible intermediary. He had quarrelled with Helen, who wouldn't want to come anyway. Yes.

'But they work us quite hard. Great long reading lists, too many essays.'

'Oh dear.'

She looked older with short hair. She had a knowing look. And they were still stuck there, facing each other, being polite.

'Well, I better get home,' Sally said. 'Mum's a bit low.'

'Yes.'

Elizabeth watched till Sally turned the corner at the end of the corridor. She had a pain in her chest and it was difficult to breathe. She waited a few moments before going into Felix's room.

He looked surprised to see her, and slightly uncomfortable. Or was she imagining that? He said, 'Oh, hullo, darling.'

She put down the book and the bottle, feeling angry and stupid and hurt, longing to be saved. 'I got you the Simenon and the champagne and I thought you might like to have them both for this evening. So I came back.'

'That was sweet of you. How lovely. What a lot of trouble to go to. Thank you, darling.'

It was too much. It didn't feel right.

'And I ran into Sally.'

Watching him closely, too closely for her own comfort, she saw a sort of shift of focus behind his eyes.

'Yes, she came to see how I was. I think Helen made her feel she ought to. She's a sweet child.'

No.

'Well, that's it really.'

She turned her back on him. She wanted to be home but she didn't know how to get out of this horrible place without breaking down.

'Oh darling,' he said, 'stay and have a drink.' He sounded quite normal.

She said, 'No, I think I've had all I can take for one day.'

There was a long silence. She felt he ought to be able to hear all her nerve endings screaming. Something like that. A kind of torture she hadn't known before and couldn't really describe.

'You know,' he said in a very gentle voice, 'things aren't always what they seem.'

She said, 'And sometimes they are. Exactly that.'

She managed to walk to the door but she still couldn't look at him. How was it possible to feel such pain and be alive? All these years, all the love and forbearance, all the pretence, the bargaining, the forgiveness, the compromise. Were there no limits to what she was asked to endure or had she just reached the end?

'What time will you be in tomorrow?'

He sounded casual, but carefully casual. Could she face a showdown now? Could she ever face one? She couldn't imagine life without him, but she also couldn't imagine that life with him would ever be the same again.

If she tried very hard, if enough time passed, could she believe she'd been wrong, made a simple mistake?

She took a deep breath and it hurt her chest. 'Oh – the usual time, I expect.'

Inge stayed in all day but the phone never rang. She left messages for Richard's lawyer but he didn't ring her back. When the boys came home they were eager for news.

'What happened?'

'Did Dad get out?'

She told them she didn't know, she had heard nothing.

'Didn't you go to court?'

'I promised not to. The lawyer said he didn't want me there.'

'We thought you'd go anyway.'

'No,' she said, 'I gave him my word.'

She sat at the kitchen table, despondent, smoking, pouring red wine from a litre bottle. The boys hugged her.

'They'll have to let him out, won't they?' Peter said. 'He didn't kill anyone, did he? That bloke's getting better.'

'Perhaps he's gone back to the cow,' Inge said. The longer she waited, the more likely it seemed.

'Cheer up, Mum,' Karl said. 'You've still got us.'

'And we're quite hungry,' Peter said. 'We need to build up our strength.'

She made them supper. Evening sunshine poured through the kitchen window and lit up the dust and the grime. Well, it was clean dirt, she thought, and did not matter; it bothered nobody. She looked at her children fondly, thinking what good boys they were but they wouldn't always be here. One day they would leave her, it was only natural, and then she would be alone for ever. Perhaps she would kill herself then. She pictured Richard alone in a bedsitter, killing himself. She pictured him going back to the cow. She wasn't sure which was the more painful.

While they were eating, the doorbell rang. Peter went to answer it. Inge called after him, 'Whoever it is, if they want money we don't have any.'

After a few moments Peter came back but there were other footsteps with him. She had her back to the door and saw only Karl's delighted, incredulous face. Then she turned her head and saw Richard. She jumped up, spilling her bowl of soup, and flung her arms round him, saying his name over and over again.

'Don't get excited,' he said. 'I just want to stay for a bit. Is that all right?'

He looked terrible, grey-faced and exhausted. She wanted to kiss him all over but she thought maybe he wouldn't like it.

She hugged him and sobbed and hugged him again.

He said, 'Look, I don't know if this is going to work.'

She took her arms away. 'I'll be very good. I won't annoy you.'

He said, 'D'you mind if I just go and sleep for a while? I'm very tired.'

He went out of the room and upstairs. Presently she heard his footsteps above her head. She sat down again at the kitchen table, thinking that a miracle had happened and she did not know how to behave. When you get your heart's desire, what do you do to celebrate?

The boys hugged her. They looked so happy that just seeing them made her want to cry. All this time they had been suffering too, but she had been too busy with her own pain to pay them much attention.

The footsteps upstairs had stopped. They all had some red wine. They tried to finish their supper.

'We must make it easy for him,' she said. She was laughing and crying. 'We mustn't play loud music or talk too much. Will you help me?'

Helen and Sally waited all day for news, tense with hope, mostly silent but occasionally snapping at each other. Finally, when she could bear it no longer, Helen rang John Hartley.

'He got bail,' she said, putting down the phone.

Sally said, 'That's wonderful.'

'So where is he? Why isn't he here?'

'Give him time,' Sally said. 'Maybe he only just got out.'

'No, it was this morning, John said.'

'He might have let you know.'

'He thought Richard would be here by now.' She paused. 'He said he was going straight home.'

Silence while they both considered what this could mean.

'He can't afford to live alone,' Helen said. 'They offered to put him up but he said no.' She was very frightened.

'He won't be dead,' Sally said, 'if that's what you're thinking. He's not that sort.'

'He wasn't the violent sort either.'

'Come on. He's just sulking. He's had a big shock. It'll take him a while to get over it, that's all.'

They looked at each other, unconvinced. Sally made tea and put whisky in it. They sat at the kitchen table and drank it together.

Helen said, 'Sally, what if he's not coming back? Not ever.'

'We managed without him before,' Sally said firmly. 'We can do it again.'

'I can't believe it. I make one mistake and that wipes out everything.'

'And it's all my fault.'

'I didn't mean that.'

'Well, it is, in a way. You were protecting me and now he's punishing you.'

Helen said, 'I thought I was more independent than this. I didn't realise I'd miss him so much.'

'He'll be back,' Sally said. 'You just wait and see. He's angry with you now but he loves you really. And he's got nowhere else to go.'

But Helen didn't believe her. And she didn't think Sally believed it either. Had she taken Richard for granted all these years? She hadn't been aware of it and yet now he had gone the pain was so sharp that she didn't know how to bear it.

The bed smelt of Inge. Richard burrowed down into it. It was warm and dark and safe. It didn't matter that he had to keep appearing in court, that it would be months before the case was heard, that he might lose his job, that he might go to jail. Just for now he could rest. He could forget everything.

Downstairs were the only three people left in the world whom he could trust. If he listened hard he could hear their voices; if he took his head out from under the duvet he could smell their supper. He had deserted them once and he had been terribly punished. Now he was back, not because he wanted to be but because he did not know where else to go.

He was taking the coward's way out and he was too tired even to be ashamed.

He hoped Inge would not expect him to make love to her tonight; he knew he couldn't manage that yet. The way he felt now, he couldn't imagine making love to anyone ever again. But then he equally couldn't imagine driving a car or cooking a meal: anything requiring the least flicker of energy seemed beyond him. It had taken all he had left to get himself here. It was the last refuge he knew.

In his heart he felt the venture was doomed and yet he had hope, he wanted to make the attempt. He didn't need a court to judge him: he had passed sentence on himself. He couldn't bear to be alone and so he would try to atone for the last ten years.

When she came to bed she would hold him and he wanted to be held; she would love him and he wanted to be loved.

Felix felt quite tired after Elizabeth had gone. A dangerous crisis, narrowly averted, he thought, and containing more drama than he could comfortably handle in his convalescent state. Coming on top of Sally's visit, it was very nearly too much for him.

But he forced himself to be positive. Elizabeth could only suspect now that he'd been involved with Sally; she hadn't actually accused him and he had admitted nothing. She had no proof of an affair and she certainly had no reason to suspect an abortion. If he played his cards right it would all blow over. After all, they both had a vested interest in preserving the status quo. But it had been a close call: perhaps he should be a little more careful in future.

Still, it could all have been a great deal worse, he had to remember that. He could have been dead. That concentrated his mind wonderfully. Or reduced to some kind of slobbering vegetable. Richard could have been put away for manslaughter or GBH. It was very bad luck that Sally had got pregnant but it was her own fault and she seemed to have recovered remarkably well from an unpleasant ordeal. Helen and

Richard had over-reacted but they would eventually calm down, he thought, and life would go on much as before. In his experience, that was what usually happened.

He wasn't sure what to do about Sally: he wanted her, certainly, but she might be just teasing him and perhaps it would be foolish to go back to such a dangerous place. Still, there was no hurry to decide about that: it could be left to time and chance. Even the remote possibility could be a lurking delicious pleasure.

And in the meantime, he was going to be very busy with his new book. He had to get his mind into gear for that; he couldn't afford too many distractions. It was a challenge, certainly, to take such a well-worn theme and make it new, but he welcomed that. The young girl, the middle-aged man, the jealous wife. This time the man would die heartbroken, deserted by them both, and the feminists could make what they liked of it. But *en route* for death there was much to be said about the pleasures of the flesh and the pangs of guilt. And he was scared, as he always was, that he couldn't write it well enough, could never do justice to the vision in his mind. That fear was agony and would never go away. He just had to live with it.

He poured a little champagne to give himself courage, and put on some Mozart. Then he started to explore his memories.